Homicide Chart

a Dana Hargrove legal mystery

V.S. KEMANIS

ISBN-13: 978-0-9997850-7-2
ISBN-10: 0-9997850-7-9

℞ Opus Nine Books
• New York •

Acclaim for the Dana Hargrove novels

"Forsaken Oath…is informed, thrilling action in and out of the courtroom, and few can portray it better than V.S. Kemanis. Highly recommended." — *San Francisco Review of Books*

"Besides being a well-written novel with interesting characters and strong narrative impetus, [*Homicide Chart*] is a law buff's delight, with intelligent discussions of unusual legal situations and excellent courtroom combat. Kemanis is an excellent writer." — *Mystery Scene Magazine*

"Riveting reading… V.S. Kemanis's compelling legal thriller *Deep Zero* distinguishes itself with its powerful blend of vivid writing, legal expertise and insight, and finely and compassionately drawn characters." — *Foreword Reviews*

Thursday's List is "engaging and thought-provoking… Well written, with a plot that…will keep you captivated…" — *The Kindle Book Review*

"Kemanis writes in a precise prose that elucidates the stakes of the cases while delving into the interior lives of her characters… [*Seven Shadows* is] a finely crafted legal thriller." — *Kirkus Reviews*

"*Power Blind* has everything a legal mystery should have: characters you care about, ethical conundrums, ripped-from-the-headlines legal issues, a compelling subplot, page-turning excitement, and an author who clearly knows her way around a courtroom… [A] well-crafted and timely novel." — *USA Today* and *WSJ* bestselling author Amy M. Reade

Homicide Chart is "a page-turner, expertly written and well crafted, deftly plotted with characters that portray real, human emotions… Kemanis is a writer of high caliber worth noting, and this is a novel well worth reading." — *The U.S. Review of Books*

Forsaken Oath "really shines. A powerful book…" — *Mystery Sequels*

Power Blind is "an engaging read, with plot twist after plot twist that will keep readers guessing… Cinematic in nature, the novel's complex plot lines will remind readers of some of television's greatest legal dramas." — *The U.S. Review of Books*

In *Thursday's List*, "Kemanis draws on her experience as a prosecutor at the county and state levels and brings her personal knowledge of the investigation process into the story. Her overall attention to detail makes the work a true page-turner." — *Kirkus Reviews*

In *Seven Shadows*, "tension mounts and leads to a climactic confrontation that is surprisingly different from what one might expect. Kemanis has created an engaging plot on which to build her narrative—one chock full of technical legal expertise. Yet it is the emotional tributaries that flow from that plot that give this story a greater sense of literary weight." — *The U.S. Review of Books*

"In *Homicide Chart*, V.S. Kemanis weaves three separate plot lines into a compelling tale. Her characters are well defined, very authentic, painted with a deft hand. This is Ms. Kemanis' real talent. She makes us care for the characters." — *Online Book Club*

Forsaken Oath is "clever, immersive... Kemanis, a talented weaver of scene and exposition, keeps the reader engaged with each new twist and bit of evidence." — *Kirkus Reviews*

Power Blind "is a family saga, mystery, and legal tale all rolled into one... The author did a fantastic job drawing me into the story through compelling observations, descriptions, and dialogue... Frankly, there is a lot to like in this one." — *San Francisco Book Review*

"Kemanis writes in a style that adeptly dramatizes legal arguments while also finding moments of stark lyricism... [*Deep Zero*] is a well-drawn legal thriller." — *Kirkus Reviews*

In *Deep Zero*, Kemanis "vividly portrays the difficulties of balancing the intricacies of the practice of law with the intimacies of the practice of parenthood. Her principal players seem particularly real... This is a confident author as at home with courtrooms, legal briefs, and summary judgments as she is with bedrooms, term papers, and adolescent anxiety." — *The U.S. Review of Books*

"*Forsaken Oath* is a terrific legal thriller, written by a prosecutor who knows her way around the legal trenches. Kemanis's expertise brings wonderful authenticity to a twisting plot." — Allison Leotta, author of *The Last Good Girl*

Also by V.S. Kemanis

Dana Hargrove Legal Mysteries

Thursday's List
Forsaken Oath
Deep Zero
Seven Shadows
Power Blind

Story Collections

Dust of the Universe, tales of family
Everyone But Us, tales of women
Malocclusion, tales of misdemeanor
Love and Crime: Stories
Your Pick: Selected Stories

Anthology Contributor

The Crooked Road, Volume 3
The Best Laid Plans
Me Too Short Stories
Autumn Noir

Visit
www.vskemanis.com

For friends and faculty at Dance Space, Dance New Amsterdam, Gibney Dance and beyond—let's keep dancing

CONTENTS

RUN

Thursday, November 17, 1994

EVAN FELL INTO an easy rhythm, marked by his favorite internal mantra, the two syllables of his wife's name. *Da – na.* Repeated every two steps, the refrain drove him forward with the climbing rate of his beating heart.

On the path ahead, another jogger approached and passed him by. Evan's focus didn't waver. He was smiling to himself, thinking of Dana. At six this morning, standing in the half light from the open doorway, he gazed at her profile and dark hair fanned out on the white pillow top. She was in a deep sleep, exhausted from a demanding week ungraciously crowned by last night's ordeal. He had no doubt that her amazing resilience would see her through. Later, when he returned home after his run, she would be up and ready to take on the day.

Further up the path, his mantra changed. *Tra – vis.* After the third repetition, the boy's face came to mind, a dimpled smile bursting over white pearls of baby teeth. Evan's laboring chest filled with cautious joy, checked by an undercurrent of worry. Innocence and vulnerability played at the back of his mind.

Early mornings were the times he reserved for himself, alone in Central Park. In the breaking dawn, Evan would cover two miles or five, whatever his schedule allowed. Never completely alone, he carried his family in heart and mind. Sometimes, despite his intentions, the office jogged along with him. He was apart from his work but never free, his responsibilities merely held at bay.

These were the times he had the best chance of shaking any trifling worries. His life, really, was perfect. His family was at the center. Their voices resounded deep within him as the sweat flowed, soaking the band around his ears and his cotton shirt. His earlier life as a lonely, beer-drinking bachelor was a distant memory, replaced with sure and grounding connections. This exercise regimen was just another sign of his transformation and commitment. For a year now he'd been trimming the spare tire and building muscle. All for them.

Dana might know exactly how Evan's mind worked, what he would be thinking and feeling on his morning runs. Others, his colleagues at the firm, couldn't really know. His reputation for cheerful optimism preceded him. A ready smile and easy manner came naturally and provided his best defense against the tendency to overthink any situation. There'd been tough court dates, tense negotiations, difficult depositions. There'd been Tuesday's deposition. Today's settlement proposal. For Dana, homicide chart and phone calls in the middle of the night.

Later, not now. The morning is still mine.

A subtle dawn pinked the tree trunks to his right. *Da – na – Da – na…Travis.* His rhythm seized up, grabbed by insecurity. Evan felt no more prepared to be a parent at the age of thirty-seven than he felt a decade ago. What kind of world was this for a child? He and Dana had seen enough of the mean streets, the possibilities in human behavior, the threats and hidden dangers. They, better than most people, understood that no one, really, was safe.

Today, Evan didn't have time for the long route. He made his way up the west side of the park but skipped the path around the reservoir and turned back at the Great Lawn, retracing his steps back down to the 70s. In the last few minutes before exiting the park, he liked to go all out, pushing his limits. He sprinted from 77th down to Strawberry Fields and slowed again to a jog as he emerged onto the concrete at 72nd.

Traffic was picking up on the avenue, the rush hour well begun. Evan used the city pavement for his cool down period, decelerating to a brisk walk on his way back home to West End Avenue at 75th. A biting wind cut his cheek and pressed the wet cotton fabric of his T-shirt into his chest, under the sweatshirt. It couldn't be more than forty-five degrees, and in minutes he would lose his self-manufactured heat. The chill was a reminder of the deepening autumn, the shortening of the days. Soon, he'd be running in the dark, but for now there was light, the new day beginning.

He felt an urgency to get home and into the shower. A quick breakfast with Dana and Travis. Instructions for Anneke. Kisses for wife and son. The office.

There were several ways back and he never planned it out, making a random pattern of zig and zag according to whim. Today he took Central Park West, crossed over at 73rd, and walked on the north side of the street. The curb was lined with parked cars on both sides, bumper to bumper. A handful of people bustled east and west, in contrast to a white-haired, stooped man who lingered next to a tree with his leashed, sniffing cocker spaniel.

After crossing Columbus Avenue, partway into the block, a taxi rushed westward, the direction in which Evan was headed. Further up, closer to Amsterdam Avenue, the taxi slowed to maneuver around two double-parked vehicles, a blue and white Crown Victoria and a drab-colored detective's ride. Police activity. Something was going on. The building of interest was a brownstone on the north side of the street, with stairs up to the front door and a basement apartment underneath. A uniformed police officer stood on the sidewalk in front of the stairway, resting a hand on his utility belt as he rocked back and forth, heels to toes.

From about half a block away, Evan saw a woman emerge from the front door of the brownstone and descend the stairs. She was an efficient early riser, dressed in business attire with a brief-case slung across on a shoulder strap. The police officer stopped the woman and showed her a piece of paper. They exchanged words. She shook her head and pointed toward the front door. Perhaps she was indicating that she'd already seen the detective inside.

Evan was nearly to the stairway when the woman and police officer finished their short conversation. From his days in the New York County District Attorney's Office, Evan had gotten to know many of the men and women in blue. But he didn't recognize this one, a young cop with an accessible face and a slim body, almost dwarfed by the uniform. The officer permitted the woman to continue on her way. She turned right and headed west, a short distance ahead of Evan.

As he passed the officer, Evan glanced at him and nodded a pleasant "hello." The officer warily nodded in return. There was no way the officer could know that this sweat-soaked exercise nut was a former assistant district attorney married to a current ADA. Evan felt slightly ridiculous.

He snapped his head straight again and picked up the pace, closing the distance between him and the woman. She was barely a dozen yards ahead, clacking the pavement in new, chunky heels. Evan no longer desired to make eye contact with anyone. Resuming his jogger persona, he intended to pass her on the left without a glance. But then, something caught his eye.

The woman's right heel just missed it, an object lying on the sidewalk where it intersected with the front steps of the next building. The object was so familiar and imbued with tender memory that the sight of it there, forlorn, discarded, kicked and stepped upon, filled his chest with emotion.

The antlers gave it away. Yellow against the dark brown head. Evan came to a halt, the woman forgotten. He rushed to pick it up. If this was the one, the tag would be torn halfway, nearly off... Yes, this was it, Chocolate the Moose.

Evan examined the small stuffed animal, not much bigger than his hand. Maybe it could be cleaned up? Beanie Babies had become collectibles, and this particular character could no longer be found in any of the stores. Yesterday evening, Travis had tearfully related the loss of his favorite toy, yet Anneke couldn't say where he might have dropped it. They'd been to the park that day, as usual.

How crazy was this? To be walking along, and so unexpectedly, to be looking straight at it!

The desire to get home surged anew. In a break from habit, Evan abandoned his cool down period and ran at top speed, as traffic allowed, all the way home.

1 »   *MOTION*

A week earlier
Thursday, November 10, 1994

ONE OF THE JURORS winked at Dana. Number Ten. She pretended not to notice and avoided his eyes. Her adversary, defense attorney Seth Kaplan, couldn't have seen it. Otherwise, he'd be out of his chair screaming, "Mistrial!"

She continued her summation, letting her eyes fall briefly on the faces of the other jurors one at a time, seven women and four men. "Lawrence Kleeger wasn't asking to be a witness to a murder. It was just another day on the job for him. At about three o'clock, Larry pulled the Glass Works van into the service drive at the projects. He was there to install a window in Dwayne Little's building."

Dana sensed the continued attention of the winking juror. Number Ten, the pharmacist, gray at the temples and old enough to be her father. His lips formed a crooked smile. Why now, when the trial was almost over? She'd done nothing to bring this on. Dana strolled along the rail of the jury box and took up a spot on the other side.

"Larry started to unload the van when something caught his eye. Dwayne rushed out the front door with two men chasing him. The men were about the same height, but one was very muscular, the other thin and slight. Larry thought the first guy looked like a 'body builder,' and the skinny one, well, you recall Larry's testimony. He told you, 'I'll *never* forget that face.'"

Dana turned to look at the defendant, and most of the jurors followed her gaze. His face was remarkable. Regular features and tough-guy good looks, but the medium brown complexion was marred with distinct, large white patches, a paint splatter near the mouth and an oversized amoeba next to an eye. A noticeable case of vitiligo.

Tyrone Marshall was the man with the unforgettable face. His friends and enemies alike called him "Stain." He was nineteen years old and belonged to a street gang known as Bred Nation, a fact which the jury was not allowed to know. In pretrial hearings, Seth had convinced the Honorable Jacquelyn DuBois that Marshall's gang affiliation was irrelevant, since there was no evidence of a gang-related motive for the murder. At most, there was an allegation of a personal grudge. Stain was sensitive about his skin condition, and Dwayne Little had dissed him badly about it in front of his peers. The judge agreed with Seth that any reference to Bred Nation would be unduly prejudicial to the defense and precluded that evidence during the trial.

After using the "personal grudge" argument to win his point in pretrial hearings, Seth trampled on it during his summation to the jury at the end of the trial. The prosecutor's theory of motive was ludicrous, he argued. "Sticks and stones." Who would murder someone over a bit of name calling?

Dana silently admitted that the theory was a bit thin. She suspected a gang-related motive but couldn't prove it. What remained, however, was still a very strong case, including her credible identification witness.

"That's right, ladies and gentlemen," she continued. "Larry couldn't forget that face. In broad daylight, from a distance of twenty feet, he had a clear view of this defendant and his friend.

There can be no mistake."

Seth jumped to his feet. "Objection, Your Honor. 'Friend'? 'No mistake'? Counsel is testifying."

"Overruled. Members of the jury, Ms. Hargrove's arguments are not evidence. Your recollection of the testimony is what counts." *And I'm entitled to keep going without these interruptions, Seth!* Judge DuBois may have shared Dana's thought as she instructed the jury in a deep and even tone. Her voice commanded respect, and together with the black robe and her perch behind the elevated bench, created an illusion of a presence much larger than her five feet and one hundred pounds might otherwise convey.

"The defendant and the body builder moved in front of Dwayne, blocking his way to the street. Two against one. They jabbed at his shoulders and chest, pushing and arguing. Dwayne put his hands in the air and shook his head, 'no.' The defendant stepped back, pulled out a gun, and fired twice into Dwayne's chest. *This* was the man Larry saw firing the gun, the man with the unforgettable face." Dana turned and pointed at Stain for emphasis.

Seth turned a blasé eye up to the ceiling. Theatrics. Dana saw the look and could only imagine what else might be going on behind her back as she addressed the jury. Maybe it was good that Seth was preoccupied with his own playacting. Less chance he would notice Number Ten's inappropriate attention.

On the other side of the room, a wellspring of positive energy emanated from the prosecution table. As Dana turned back to the jury, she caught the shining, buttery-brown eyes of Eric Trumble, the junior assistant district attorney who was second-seating the trial. For any junior ADA, second-seating was a great opportunity to gain experience on a major case. For Eric, this was another chance to sit next to Dana at counsel table, where he could smell her perfume and absorb her aura of greatness. Eric was somewhat in awe.

"The defendant ran, but he couldn't hide. Larry's detailed description led the police in the right direction, and two days later, the defendant was placed in a lineup. Larry had no trouble identifying him as the shooter."

Dana was now ready for her next move, to debunk the alibi defense. Marshall had testified in his best schoolboy manner that he'd been visiting his girlfriend "Midnight" in the building next door and left her apartment at about three o'clock. The seventeen-year-old Midnight—true name Janlee Wilkerson—dutifully testified for her boyfriend and corroborated that fact. Marshall claimed that, after he left Midnight's apartment, he was walking in front of Dwayne's building when the shots rang out. Instinctively, like everyone else nearby, he ran.

"This is a case of mistaken identity," Seth had argued to the jury during his summation. "In the confusion of shots and faces and people running, Larry identified the wrong guy. I'm not saying he isn't honest and well meaning. Larry is a likeable window repairman who has no reason to lie. But we all make mistakes, and quite simply, Larry made a mistake. He just got it wrong. We can't convict a man based on a mistake. And even if you're not quite sure whether Larry made a mistake, we still can't convict a man on that basis either. If you're not quite sure, then you have a reasonable doubt, and if you have a reasonable doubt, you *must* return a verdict of not guilty."

Seth's magnetism and sincerity had the power to convince. In the past six years, he and Dana had squared off a number of times in court. Seth was a formidable adversary. But the years had seen a slow change since his days as a rookie. A slight tarnish. A sag in his suit coat. Dishwater blond hair brushing his collar line. Mornings, the face in shadow. A creeping sarcasm. Still, his aqua blue eyes possessed a glimmer of hope and idealism, something Dana tried to ignore with the memory it evoked of that time so long ago, the attraction she'd felt…

"Mr. Kaplan asked you not to credit Larry's testimony. All a mistake, he says." Dana glanced at Seth again, this time holding his eyes for a good second. "But Larry gave the only scenario that makes any sense. It fits the evidence of the defendant's vendetta. Stain never forgot how Dwayne humiliated him in graphic language. This murder is about retribution, pure and simple. But even if you have a doubt as to motive, that isn't a reason to acquit. We can never know what goes on in a person's mind. Motive isn't an element of the crime, and I have no obligation to prove it. Don't let Mr. Kaplan's arguments about motive distract you from the other evidence in this case which has no innocent explanation. It's the evidence that tells you beyond any doubt that Tyrone Marshall is the killer. I'm talking about the previous shooting and the testimony of Darlene Little."

Just two weeks before his death, Dwayne Little had been grazed by a bullet in another shooting. The bullet was recovered from a wall at the scene. A few days after that, Dwayne was on the street with his sixteen-year-old sister Darlene when he saw the defendant and pointed him out. "He's the one," Dwayne said. Darlene testified for the prosecution and was a believable witness, with no reason to lie about her brother's accusation.

The gun itself was never found, and predictably, the defendant denied any involvement in the earlier shooting. But the defense was left without any explanation for the ballistics evidence and Darlene Little's testimony. Why would she manufacture a false accusation? She had nothing to gain by putting the wrong person away.

"What does the ballistics evidence tell us? The same weapon was used in both shootings. The bullets that killed Dwayne Little were fired from the *same* gun as the bullet that grazed him two weeks earlier. Ballistics evidence doesn't lie. It doesn't make a mistake."

A few heads nodded in agreement.

Dana concluded her argument and returned to her seat at counsel table next to Eric. She was satisfied with her summation. The jury had been receptive. A guilty verdict was never a sure thing, but she was feeling optimistic.

The judge instructed the jurors on the law and dismissed them to begin their deliberations. It was lunchtime, and sandwiches would be ordered and delivered to them in the jury room.

The stenographer and the court clerk took a break. The sole spectator in the audience patiently waited. The court officers escorted the defendant to the rail and allowed him a brief visit with her before taking him back to the lockup to await the verdict. After the visit, Stain's mother slowly retreated down the aisle and pushed through the swinging door of the courtroom. Dana knew she wouldn't be going far. She'd attended every day of the trial, maintaining a calm presence in the first pew, her eyes wide and expressive. She would be back for the verdict, and no doubt there'd be tears to go along with it.

When the courtroom was cleared, Judge DuBois chatted with the lawyers at the bench.

"It's been just like old home week, hasn't it?" the judge quipped. They all knew each other well except for Eric, who was somewhat out of the loop. He smiled sheepishly.

"I couldn't have said it any better," remarked Dana.

"I'm not going to comment, Judge," said Seth with a faint smile. "It seems the two of you have more of a history." He wagged his index finger back and forth between the two women for emphasis.

Judge DuBois, former chief of the Special Narcotics Bureau, fondly known as "Jack" to her ex-colleagues, had been a mentor to Dana. But in her fifteen years at the DA's office, she'd also tried several cases against Seth, and they shared a mutual respect. When pitted against Jack, Seth had never been able to win points for his clients by pinning their crimes on poverty and sorry circumstances. The judge was a shining example of perseverance over adversity. She'd pulled herself up from impoverished beginnings as a foster child, worked her way through school on pure smarts, and built her distinguished career in the law, stomping out some of the worst villains from her old neighborhood in Harlem. Her latest accomplishment, an appointment to the criminal trial bench, was the logical progression in her career.

The judge gave a hearty laugh. Gold hoop earrings and a close natural haircut added personality to the neutral black robe she wore. "All I can say is, it's good to have such talent in the courtroom. Nice job, counselors." With a sly smile, the judge caught Dana's eye and gave a surreptitious wink that suggested her awareness of Number Ten's inappropriate attention. The two women felt this shared secret, a very small but unassailable nugget of their former solidarity. In anything that really mattered, however, Jack's rulings from the bench were eminently fair to both sides. Hadn't she given Seth a gang-free trial against a known gang member?

"Robert has your numbers?" The judge was referring to the court clerk.

Seth, Dana, and Eric answered in the affirmative. Mobile phone numbers and office numbers had been left with Robert, who would summon them to return to the courtroom when the jury had questions or arrived at a verdict. Dana didn't mourn the inconvenience of an earlier time in her career when she had to remain glued to her office telephone whenever a jury was out. Now, she was completely attached to her Nokia mobile phone, lovingly caressing the bumps of its number pad as it rested in her jacket pocket. She also used it religiously to keep in touch with home. Travis was always at the back of her mind.

If only there weren't so many dead zones in the Criminal Court building. She had to keep looking at her display to make sure she had a signal.

"Don't go far," said Seth. "Their first question is gonna be, 'what happened to Bounce?'"

"The judge already gave an instruction," said Dana. "But she didn't call him Bounce."

"Right. The body builder."

"I didn't call him that either," said Judge DuBois. "I believe the instruction was that they weren't to speculate as to the whereabouts of the second person allegedly with the defendant at the scene of the crime."

"When you tell them not to speculate, it only invites speculation," said Seth in a sour grapes tone of voice.

"It goes both ways, counselor," the judge retorted. "ADA Hargrove would like me to tell the jury that the DA declined to prosecute Bounce for lack of evidence, and you'd like me to tell them that he's a notorious gang member and suspected murderer being prosecuted by the feds. The middle road is that the jury is not allowed to speculate."

Seth had to nod his head in agreement with the fairness in this.

The young man known as Bounce (given name Brendon Hayes) was an eighteen-year-old gang member currently under indictment in the federal system. Dana had no doubt he was the "body builder," but Larry had been unable to identify him in a lineup, and no other witness had come forward. Under the circumstances, Dana was happy enough that the feds were taking care of Bounce's future by prosecuting him for racketeering in connection with his gang activities, while she prosecuted Stain for Little's murder in the New York State system.

The assistant U.S. attorney had also told her that Bounce was cooperating with the feds to provide evidence against the leaders of Bred Nation, those higher up in the chain. As part of the deal, he would be pleading guilty to racketeering, admitting criminal acts he'd committed for the gang. These were known as "pattern acts" under the federal racketeering statute. If Bounce ratted on enough bad guys before his sentencing date, he would get a break in the amount of time he'd have to serve.

Dana had divulged all of this to Seth, complying with her legal obligation to reveal anything she knew which might be remotely exculpatory. A common defense strategy was to pin the crime on a missing cohort. From Dana's point of view, it was surprising that Seth hadn't adopted that strategy at trial. She guessed that it was the defendant's strategy—against Seth's advice—to present his transparent alibi defense.

The judge and attorneys discussed a few remaining details before going their separate ways to await the verdict. Seth hurried out first, and Dana took a slower pace down the center aisle with Eric at her side. His silence during their conferences with the judge was understandable in light of his junior status and slight insecurity around experienced attorneys, but it stood in stark contrast to his normal loquaciousness and borderline foul mouth. Eric was not one to be shy about his opinion around Dana, and she asked him now for his thoughts on the trial.

"You scored big with that summation. This'll be a quick one for guilty. That sonuvabitch is going down. Can I carry that?"

"No thanks, got it." Dana shifted the handle of her fat briefcase from right hand to left. "I wouldn't say that word too loudly. Mom is waiting outside." They were about to step through the swinging door.

"Always putting my foot in it." He shook his head, hand on the door. "If I had your way with words…"

"Don't slight yourself. You really nailed it with Detective Blake." Dana had asked Eric to handle the direct examination of a few police witnesses, including the ballistics expert Blake, and he'd done a decent job.

Eric looked pleased. They paused in the wide corridor outside the courtroom. Their expressions betrayed awareness of Marshall's mother standing at the far end near a large window, looking down at the street ten floors below.

"Do you want lunch?" Eric asked. He wasn't past attempting to spend every possible moment with Dana, although his former infatuation had been realistically tamed to a sort of academic admiration in deference to her marital status. In 1988, during his year between undergraduate studies and law school, he'd been Dana's trial preparation assistant when she was a rookie. His work as a TPA had been impressive and helped to pave his way into the DA's office upon his graduation from law school in 1992.

Dana fingered her Nokia and pulled it out. Good signal strength. "No, I've got to call home first, then I'll grab something downstairs." She was referring to the hole-in-the-wall coffee shop with shrink-wrapped sandwiches of questionable freshness. She usually bought only a piece of fruit and a protein bar.

"Okay, but hey. You know I have a conflict this afternoon. My CW is coming in at four. It's the only time she could make it."

"Right." Eric was starting a trial tomorrow, an apartment burglary, and he needed to prepare his complaining witness for her testimony. "That's okay," Dana assured him. *The world will go on without you,* she thought with a smile, not unkindly.

"I'll be pissed if I can't be there for the verdict."

"I know, but if you're tied up, I'll give you a blow-by-blow later."

Eric waved goodbye and turned toward the elevator in the opposite direction from Mrs. Marshall. This was Dana's name for her, although she wasn't sure if "Mrs. Marshall" had ever married Stain's father. She was a single mom who looked to be only thirty-six or thirty-seven, four or five years older than Dana. Her son Tyrone, a boy of nineteen, was headed for state prison. Or a walk. Nothing was sure in this business. *Tyrone.* Dana tried to think of him with his given name, to remind herself of the person underneath the external trappings of behavior and street moniker.

Briefly, instinctively, Dana followed Eric, watching the back of his flaxen head and gangling stride as he made his way to the elevator. She took up a spot in the corridor at a greater distance from Mrs. Marshall, on the edge of diminishing signal strength for her Nokia. The courthouse quieted down during the lunch hour, and only a few attorneys mingled in the echoing, broad corridor.

She dropped her briefcase to the floor, leaned against the wall, and pressed the number "1" in speed dialing. After the second ring, Anneke picked up. "Hello? Goodhue residence," said the girl in a Dutch accent.

"Hi, Anneke." Pronounced like "ah-nuh-kuh," although Dana's version didn't quite match the authentic sound of her au pair's accent. *My God.* This trial wouldn't leave her mind. This was the first moment it occurred to her that Anneke was the same age as Tyrone. Two nineteen-year-olds from different worlds. But Anneke had proven her maturity and good judgment a hundred times in the past few months, quelling any lingering misgivings about her age. Next month she would turn twenty, a number that felt better. "How's everything going?" Dana asked.

"Good. Everything's fine. Travis just had his peanut butter sandwich and applesauce. We're going to the park later. Want to talk to him?" Anneke always asked this, and Dana always said "yes" unless she absolutely didn't have a single available minute.

"Want to speak to Mommy?" she heard in the background, followed by toddling footsteps on a hardwood floor and a sudden whoosh of panting breath from the child's mouth pressed into the receiver. "Mommy?"

"Hi, Tug." Travis Ulrich Goodhue. "You having a good day?"

"Mommy!"

"Yes—"

"Mommy, Chockit had choos." Dana understood this to

mean that Chocolate the Moose had been drinking juice.

"Really?"

"My sippy cup."

"Chocolate was drinking from your sippy cup? How nice." Juice on moose and possibly elsewhere. She would be asking Anneke about this later. "Are you going to the park?"

"Park. Bye-bye Mommy!"

"I love you! Hugs for Tug."

There was a clunk, and Anneke picked up the receiver from the floor. "Sorry," she said.

"It's okay. I'm not sure when I'll be home. I have a jury out, so I'll call you later."

"All right."

Dana gave a few instructions about dinner, and the conversation was closed. Without another glance at the mother standing by the window, she picked up her briefcase and continued in the opposite direction, toward the elevator.

There was a call at about two thirty. All three lawyers returned to the courtroom to hear the jury's requests. Bounce was not a subject of inquiry. They wanted a read-back of Darlene Little's testimony and asked to bring the bullets with them into the jury room. Two from Dwayne's abdomen and one from the earlier shooting, pulled out of a wall. In plastic evidence baggies.

"What the hell for?" asked Eric as they walked out again. "The bullets don't mean squat without Blake's testimony."

"Some juries just need something physical," Dana told him. "Makes it real to them. Since there's no gun, the bullets will have to do."

They went back to their offices in Trial Bureau 90, in the state office building across the street from the Criminal Court building, and tried to go about other business while they waited. Eric's office was at the end of the hall reserved for multiple-attorney offices. He'd recently graduated from misdemeanors to felonies and was no longer in a four-person rookie office but still had an officemate, just one, Ernest Chin. Dana's title was senior trial counsel, and she had a private office at the other end of the hall, closer to the offices of Bureau Chief Patrick McBride and Deputy Bureau Chief Michele Seidman.

Dana loved this place, TB 90, where she'd been initiated into the world of criminal law in the fall of 1987. In 1988, she'd been transferred—involuntarily—to the elite Financial Crimes Bureau, and after a two-year stay, asked for a transfer back to her original bureau. The work on complex money crimes had been valuable, but the investigations were paper intensive and slow moving. In the end, Dana came to realize that she thrived on the constant activity and pressure of street crime, even with all the extra aggravation and frustration that came with it.

Big changes were in the offing. Their highly revered chief had just won the election for district attorney. Come January 1, Patrick would be taking over his new digs, an immense office on the eighth floor of the Criminal Court building. Everyone assumed that Michele would be bumped up to the head spot in the bureau, leaving her position vacant. Any senior attorney hoping for a long-term career path within the office had an eye on the deputy spot.

At four forty-five, the second call came into Dana's office line. "This is it," Robert said. She bolted out of her chair. Depending on the traffic in the elevator banks of the two buildings, she'd be back in the courtroom within three to five minutes.

On her way out, she passed Eric's office and glanced through his open door. His officemate was gone, but a middle-aged woman sat across from him at the desk with her back to the door. Eric turned his eyes up to meet Dana's. He gave her a shrug and a chagrined look. She responded with her own shrug and a quick wave.

Back in the courtroom, the participants were beginning to assemble. Dana walked up the center aisle in her two-inch pumps, the sound magnified in the stillness. Mrs. Marshall was the lone spectator, sitting in the front pew, her head and shoulders visible above the back of her seat. She wore the same conservative taupe-colored suit she'd worn every day of the trial and sat with erect posture, head held high.

Seth had already taken his seat at counsel table. Dana pushed through the gate into the area reserved for the participants, nod-ded at Seth, and placed her briefcase on the prosecution table, the one closest to the empty jury box. The elevated bench was cold and vacant. The stenographer sat at her machine, feeding in a new accordion-folded stack of paper. Robert was at the clerk's table to the side of the bench, ready to use his desk phone to call Judge DuBois when everyone was assembled. Dana said to him, "Did you speak to Mr. Trumble? He's unable to make it. We can go ahead without him." Robert nodded his assent.

A side door opened and Tyrone Marshall entered, his hands cuffed in front of his body. A court officer held one elbow and another officer ambled behind. Over the past few days, Marshall's "gansta" strut had slowly transformed into a stoop-shouldered shuffle in moments when he appeared defeated. He would drop his head and move his lips in speech, silently muttering to himself. He showed these behaviors now. As he approached the defense table, his head bobbed up. He glanced at his mother and gave a fleeting smile. The whites of his eyes were pink and suggested a hint of the fear underneath his play at nonchalance.

One of the officers removed the cuffs, and the defendant sat down. Seth bent forward in his seat, looked up into his client's eyes, and placed a hand on his back. A few words were whis-pered. Seth was an excellent lawyer, but the most prominent feature of his lawyering was the personal concern that beamed from his face. He genuinely cared about his clients.

Robert picked up the phone, and seconds later, the judge strolled in. "All rise," intoned the clerk. Judge DuBois ascended the bench. "Bring in the jury," she said.

They remained standing as the door to the jury room opened. This was the moment of truth. Most experienced lawyers could predict the verdict from the jurors' behavior as they filed into the courtroom, even before the foreperson spoke. A light mood, smiles, a sense of relief, and the temerity to glance at the defendant most often preceded the words "not guilty." A somber mood, clenched jaws, and a dogged refusal to meet the defendant's eyes most often preceded a declaration of "guilty."

This jury was very somber indeed.

One by one they filed in, seven women and five men, each one wearing blinders on the way to his or her seat in the jury box. Number Ten had completely forgotten his attraction to Dana.

A half dozen were seated when Dana heard the clunk of the courtroom door behind her and the scuffle of footsteps. She turned to see Eric rushing up the aisle, piece of paper in hand. He pushed through the gate and handed it to Dana just as the last juror took her seat. Everyone sat down.

Eric was out of breath, and his boyish brow was crunched in worry. She looked at him with a puzzled expression on her face. Everyone looked at him. Then Dana's eyes fell to the paper and she read the brief note written there.

The judge waited for the word before proceeding.

Time stood still while Dana made her decision. She had a choice, and there would be dire ramifications either way. She'd seen the looks on the jurors' faces and felt the tense expectancy in Eric's body at her side. Her heart pounded out the seconds. Five beats.

The judge raised an eyebrow. "All is well?"

"Yes, Your Honor, I'm sorry for the interruption."

The judge turned to Robert and nodded the go ahead.

Dana felt a hand on her forearm. Eric seemed to disagree. But she didn't look at him, and he removed his hand. She knew he wouldn't do anything else to interrupt.

"Will the jury please rise," instructed the clerk.

The jurors complied.

"Will the defendant please rise and face the jury."

Tyrone did so.

"Madam Foreperson, has the jury agreed upon a verdict?"

"We have."

"What say you on the count of murder in the second degree, guilty or not guilty?"

"Guilty."

A cry escaped the throat of Mrs. Marshall.

The defendant turned to his mother and dropped to his seat.

Mrs. Marshall gave her son a single, intense pain-filled look, but did not stand or protest further. Her proud posture sagged, and she lowered her face into a handkerchief, sobbing quietly.

Seth asked the court to poll the jury. One by one, each juror was required to say the word "guilty." When the verdict was indelibly recorded, Judge DuBois gave a brief speech, thanking them for their service and telling them they were free to go.

After the jurors filed out through the side door and it was closed behind them, Dana rose. "Your Honor."

"Yes Ms. Hargrove."

"This is somewhat irregular, but I have a post-trial disclosure to make."

Seth stood. "Disclosure? *Now?* If this is about that mysterious note, Your Honor asked Ms. Hargrove what was up the moment Mr. Trumble walked in. She said it was nothing."

"I don't believe I said it was nothing."

"What do you have?" asked the judge.

The paper was now wet and crumpled in her hand. She did

not need to refer to it. A muffled expletive slipped from Eric's lips. Dana squared her shoulders. "Brendon Hayes, the man allegedly with the defendant at the scene of the murder, pled guilty today in federal court to the charge of racketeering."

"We were aware of his impending guilty plea," said Seth.

"But the indictment had been sealed. We didn't know the pattern acts in support of the racketeering charge. This afternoon, Hayes admitted that the shooting of Dwayne Little was a gang hit, and that he, Hayes, was the one who fired the gun."

Mrs. Marshall jumped to her feet. "Bitch! You bitch let this jury—"

"Mistrial!" yelled Seth over the mother. "My client is innocent of this charge."

The judge banged the gavel. "The trial is over counselor. You can't move for a mistrial—"

"We move to set aside the verdict on the ground of newly discovered evidence. This evidence proves my client's innocence. He must be released—immediately."

Dana was trying to get a word in edgewise when the courtroom door behind them opened and two burly men in navy blue nylon jackets marched forward in the aisle. There! They would be the ones to set this straight.

Judge DuBois banged the gavel again over the din. As the two men passed through the gate, she asked them to state their business with the court.

"Special Agent David Bergin, FBI, Your Honor. I have a federal warrant for the arrest of Tyrone Marshall on the charge of racketeering."

2 »   *ANNEKE*

WHEN DANA CALLED, Anneke was clearing away the lunch dishes on the dining table, and Travis was in the playroom, a small alcove off the living room. The boy had turned two in August, the week Anneke started this job. He got into absolutely everything, and she had to watch him closely. She could leave him on his own for a few minutes in the playroom, the only place in the apartment that Dana and Evan had fully baby-proofed.

The dining area was a rectangle of hardwood floor between the kitchen and the carpeted living room. At lunchtime, Travis always sat up to the table in his booster seat, placed on top of a regular chair. Getting the food precisely into his mouth was a challenge, as well as keeping it off the floor and his clothing, face, and hair.

This lunchtime, against house rules, Anneke had allowed Travis to put Chocolate the Moose on the table next to his plate. She'd regretted her laxness the minute he lifted his sippy cup to Chocolate's lips and tipped it up to give his friend a swallow. Gently, she took the moose away, and the boy didn't cry for long. Anneke prided herself on a soft touch and maintained a conscious vigilance over her behavior. Her own mother had been rough.

Occasionally Anneke would pretend Travis was her child. Not often. But it was helpful at moments when he was especially trying, and it felt natural at moments when he was especially lovable.

No one could possibly think they were related. Travis had inherited Dana's dark brown hair, eyebrows, and lashes, and Evan's blue-gray eyes with flecks of gold, an arresting combination to go along with his pudgy, dimpled cheeks in olive skin. Anneke had an unruly mop of coarse, strawberry-blonde curls, green eyes, a few freckles across her chubby nose, and pale skin that went ruddy-cheeked and blotchy in a cold wind.

Dana always called around lunchtime, never a specific time, and would try the landline first, although she'd given Anneke a mobile phone as a backup. Anneke would spend the noon hour in anticipation of the call, postponing any afternoon outing until she received it. There was always a chance that one of them would be out of range on their mobile phones, causing unnecessary anxiety if Dana couldn't get through. One day, they failed to connect, and Anneke could hear the tension in Dana's voice when they finally spoke, late in the afternoon.

Perhaps there were times, like today, when Dana could discern from the noises over the line that Travis was not under a watchful eye at the moment of the call. Anneke picked up the cordless phone in the kitchen where she'd just placed the dishes in the sink. As she talked, she went back to the dining area before she called out to Travis, who came running across the carpet of the living room and onto the hardwood floor. The receiver was too large for his little hand. She helped him to hold it to his ear and stood helplessly by as he made his confession about the "choos" before pushing the phone away, causing Anneke to drop it.

She wasn't too worried. The Goodhues were excellent employers and tolerant of her small mistakes and slip-ups. But she was still adapting to this new life abroad and her first full-time job. August, September, October, and now November. Going into the fourth month.

Anneke had replaced a middle-aged woman, a live-out, who'd been wonderful with Travis, but not very punctual, making Evan or Dana late to work several times. The family lore now included a few colorful anecdotes about cases thrown out of court owing to the former nanny. They decided that a live-in au pair was the sensible solution and were "so happy" to have Anneke with them. This is what they told her.

The arrangement was somewhat awkward. Not for Travis, of course, who loved human contact and thrived on extra attention. But this modest three-bedroom apartment on the ninth floor was a bit cramped for four people. Anneke's room was the smallest one, but she was used to tight quarters. The apartment she'd grown up in and shared with her younger sister and parents was a converted single floor of an old house on a canal in Amsterdam.

In her new home, she was well past the initial shock of her confinement with strangers and their slowly-revealed habits. Now, it wasn't so much the limited space but her awareness of unspoken thoughts that made everything so awkward. Daily, she felt the tension between her need for privacy and the desire to know and understand her new family. But if outward appearances were any indication, they were getting along just fine.

All in all, Anneke counted her blessings. She'd heard a few stories from other au pairs she knew in Manhattan, contacts that the agency had given her when she started the job. Marije, a girl of twenty from Holland, was having a very difficult time with her employers in an apartment several blocks north, on 85th Street. The mother was constantly breathing down Marije's neck, calling her two, three and four times a day, asking detailed questions about their eighteen-month-old Elise, a toddler with spontaneous sunny smiles and equally spontaneous blood-curdling tantrums.

There were days when Anneke and Travis would be alone together for ten hours at a stretch. There were days when Anneke experienced small flashes of panic and instants of crushing loneliness. But everything could have been much worse. By the luck of the draw, she'd ended up with Travis and Marije got Elise. Daily, Anneke reminded herself of her good fortune, blocking out other things. She made an effort to keep the mood lively, even if the effort tired her.

"Come on, Travis. Let's get ready for the park."

"Park!" He hurtled into her presence and halted at her feet, taking up a rhythmic chant as he rocked right and left and back again: "Vitt-a bloom-in, road-a bloom-in, blou-a bloom-in, hail-a bloom-in."

Oh, she was so proud of him! Reciting the Dutch she'd taught him during their late summer outings in the park. *Witte bloemen, rode bloemen, blauwe bloemen, gele bloemen.* It was their own little game.

"*Heel goed*, Travis. Do you remember what all those words mean?"

"Flowers."

"Right. Do you remember the colors?"

"Red ones."

"White, red, blue and yellow. But the flowers are all gone now." Anneke's English was excellent, with a few, endearing mispronunciations. Her "th" was more like a "d," and "gone" sounded a bit like "con." But like all well-educated Dutch girls, she was fully bilingual. English was a staple of the school curriculum every year from age six through eighteen.

"Come on, then, we'll get your coat." Chilly outside, but still fine enough for a walk to the park. She dreaded the days with pouring rain when they had to stay inside all day. Even then, she tried to find a way to get outside. There was an indoor play area just two blocks away if she could get to it. Colder weather would be here soon, but the Dutch were hearty folk, walking and cycling daily on the cobblestone streets of Amsterdam. Anneke was sturdily built and thick-boned. She would make Travis into a true little Dutchman, at least as far as the weather was concerned. It was good for him.

He followed her to the foyer, where she grabbed his puffy, hooded jacket from the coat closet. She crouched down to his level, aimed a sleeve toward an arm, and pushed it through. Her senses were alert. Intuitively, she determined that no other item of dress was needed since she'd changed him after lunch. Travis was not potty trained — yet — but Dana had promised they would start "working on it" soon.

Anneke pulled on her own pea coat and grabbed her mobile phone from the little table in the foyer, dropping it into a coat pocket and patting the outside. She grabbed the collapsible umbrella stroller from the coat closet as well.

"Want to get Chocolate?"

"Chock-it!" Travis spun around, looking blimpish and bundled as he ran to the playroom. She heard him thrashing about, calling for his friend, and then she remembered.

"I've got it, Tug." She raced to the kitchen and grabbed the moose from the counter where she'd cleaned its mouth after the juice incident. "Come on, now. I've got Chocolate."

He came running and watched as she tucked the small moose into a pocket on the back of the fabric seat of the stroller. They were ready to head out.

Down nine floors in the elevator and into the lobby they walked, Anneke holding Travis's hand with her right and clutching the curved handles of the folded lightweight stroller with her left. They took it slow. She always made him walk as long as possible before giving in to his inevitable fatigue, popping open the stroller, and letting him ride.

She said hello to the doorman, who sat on a stool by the front door. Seeing her hands full, he jumped up to open the glass door. "Thanks, Bashkim," she said.

"You're welcome, Miss. But it's Endrit."

"I'm sorry, Endrit."

He laughed, a gold tooth flashing in his top row of teeth toward the back. "I know, I know. So impossible." He had black, wavy hair and a brilliantly happy smile in a craggy face of mismatched features.

Anneke laughed too. She could never tell them apart, the Albanian brothers, Bashkim and Endrit. It had taken her long enough just to learn their names. She could swear they were twins. Perhaps only Endrit had a gold tooth. She would have to look more closely at Bashkim's mouth.

Endrit crouched a bit and waved at Travis, who returned the gesture.

Outside, a gust of wind knocked into them and vanished. It felt good to be released from that apartment, to shrink into insignificance within a world of tall buildings and pavement. The city trees had lost half their leaves. The sky was bleak. A car horn sounded. Peering down the street, she found the sidewalk strangely empty and quiet, an endless path of concrete. Skyscrapers loomed, hovering overhead, closing her in. It was a vast landscape, yet so confining, pressing in on all sides.

Anneke froze, crushed alive in a transparent, soundless vacuum. Where had everyone gone?

Reflexively and unthinking, she tightened her grip on Travis's hand. *What am I doing here?* She twisted back to the left and saw two teenage girls at a distance behind them, twisted again and saw several more people across the street. Strangers.

Travis pulled at her hand. Sound rushed into her ears, and she heard voices behind her. The teenage girls.

"Okay." She forced a laugh. "It's okay. Let's go, Travis." The girls passed them by at a quick clip.

"Vitt-a bloom-in." Travis started his chant to go along with his plodding, rhythmic footsteps.

They made their way eastward, one step at a time, toward

the park. Alone together, a teenage girl and her two-year-old, unknown to every passerby.

Anneke's mind fell into a dull, blank, numbing hum.

This was a day without toddling playmates. Anneke didn't have the energy to go up to the playground on 81st and seek them out. She loitered here and there at the edge of the park, pointing out to Travis anything that seemed noteworthy, providing comments with appropriate, excited inflection in her voice. A Lhasa Apso on a leash. A very fast rollerblader. A man with knobby calf muscles speed walking in a tipping gait.

Already she could feel it coming. A dwindling of life, a darkening of days. There was less activity in the park today than there'd been in October, and far less than September.

On the way home, Travis was lucky to ride all the way in his stroller. It was nearly three o'clock, nap time, and his head started to droop.

As they entered the front door, Endrit stopped her. "Here, Miss. This comes for you." He seemed to be handing her an envelope. Before taking it, she gazed at the small, square item for several seconds, finding the paper startlingly white against Endrit's light brown skin. His thumb covered whatever was written on the outside. How strange... Who had sent this? Yet, somehow, it wasn't entirely unexpected.

"For me?" She took it from him. "Who...?"

"A man comes. A man with a little girl."

Yes, of course. Endrit gave it away, even before she saw the writing on the envelope. Her name, "Anneke Zonneveld," was written there by a hand well known to her.

In her young life of nineteen years, like every other young woman her age, Anneke had experienced exultant highs and crashing lows, intense emotions that were both crazily good and devastatingly bad. If it were possible to combine every such moment of her life into one, this would be the result, the blinding splash of confusion she now felt.

3 »   *DEFAMATION*

Evan sat at his desk in the offices of Belknap & Rose, PC, reading the final lines of *Dumpster Grave* by Tina Delmonico. He slapped the paperback shut with a laugh and a shake of his head. Perhaps he should try his hand at fiction. If Delmonico could score a huge book contract with this gem, possibly anyone could.

Just then, Steve Belknap walked past the open door and stuck his head in. "Hey, I see you're having too much fun in here again."

Evan's blue-grays lit up in merriment. "If torture is your idea of fun. Remind me to thank you properly for this assignment."

"I expect a full report on the storyline. I'll see you later in my office."

"Sure. Anything to save you from reading this masterpiece." He waved the "masterpiece" in the air.

Steve laughed, sending a gentle flush into his pale skin to the roots of his pure white head of hair. With a two-fingered gunshot and a spry turn of the heel, the sage septuagenarian disappeared from the doorframe.

Evan enjoyed the repartee. Partners Steven Belknap and Gregory Rose were the absolute best fellows to work for. And Evan was well used to his superiors and colleagues teasing him about his public "habit" of engaging in "recreational reading" on the job. Anyone walking past his open office door might glance in to see him goose-necked over a curled paperback with his feet propped up on the desk. "Racking up those billable hours?" a colleague might ask, faking a beleaguered tone of voice.

But they all knew this was real work. Sometimes fun, sometimes not. Evan regularly vetted galleys and advance paperback copies of upcoming releases for the firm's client, Mysterion Publishing. His mission was to spot potential lawsuits for defamation, copyright infringement, and the like. The task was less enjoyable when, as in this case, the novel was embarrassingly bad, it was already on sale, and a lawsuit was well underway, in the midst of a nasty discovery war.

More than two years ago, when *Dumpster Grave* was in galleys, an attorney at another law firm had screened the novel for Mysterion, finding no problems. A month after its release, a woman named June Tinker sued Delmonico and Mysterion for defamation. To defend the lawsuit, Mysterion immediately hired Belknap & Rose, a major name in litigation. Soon after that, Mysterion decided to switch all its business to B & R, including the vetting process.

To be fair to the poor slob who missed the lurking problem, it was virtually impossible to predict a potential "of and concerning" defamation lawsuit, something even the best attorney could miss during the screening process. There was no way to know what had gone through the author's mind while writing the novel, no way to know the identities of the author's acquaintances, friends and family. The author's full disclosure to her attorney was needed, but even then, there was never any assurance against a lawsuit.

Tina Delmonico's name was big in mass-market paperback crime fiction. *Dumpster Grave,* a novel that took place in a suburban New York high school in the late sixties, was her fifteenth published work of fiction. June Tinker alleged that she and Delmonico had both attended the sprawling Ellsworth High School on Long Island, graduating in 1968. Her theory was that

Delmonico had portrayed the fictional protagonist in *Dumpster Grave*, "April Taylor," in such a way that people would recognize the character to be Tinker and would believe that Taylor's misdeeds were really Tinker's. In other words, the novel was really "of and concerning" Tinker, a thinly disguised attack on her character.

Lucky for Evan, it was virtually impossible for a plaintiff to prove this kind of claim. The similarities between the plaintiff and the fictional character had to be pervasive and striking. On top of that, the content of the book had to be false and defamatory of the plaintiff in order to prove libel. Truth was a defense. And Mysterion was protected by the disclaimer in the book that any resemblance to persons dead or alive was purely coincidental. Even so, there were plenty of frivolous lawsuits to go around, wreaking havoc on lives and wallets.

Shortly after Evan was handed the assignment, before making any investigation of its allegations, he made his first telephone call to the author. In a diplomatic tone, he asked if she might recall a person named June Tinker from high school days. Delmonico shrieked her response in her distinctive, high-pitched New Yorkese: "I swear to God, I never heard of this woman in my life!"

Soon afterward, Evan confirmed the truth of Tinker's allegation that they'd attended the same high school. Was Delmonico lying about not knowing her? Certainly, it was possible to remain unaware of a few classmates in a very large high school, or to have a foggy memory of names and faces decades later. Quite possibly, June Tinker was a gold digger who never knew Delmonico when they were in high school. After reading the novel, she might have discovered that she bore some slight resemblance to the character April Taylor and thought she had a chance to profit from it. April Taylor and June Tinker. Tinker, tailor, soldier, sailor… Pure chance that June Tinker, in

1968, had a chestnut-colored half-ponytail, brown eyes, a small pixie nose, and daily wore white go-go boots, paisley miniskirts, Twiggy lashes, and Slicker lipstick. So many teenagers of that era copied that look.

Evan was reflecting on these points when junior associate Mineko Inoue walked into his office, carrying her copy of the novel and another, larger book underneath.

"Finished?" she asked.

"Yup, just now."

"How'd you like the scene with the garbage bag and the dumpster?"

"My favorite part."

"Oooo, gross out, Evan!"

"I knew you'd like it."

"I'll have nightmares tonight."

"But it was all so fake."

"Not to me," said Mineko. "I take everything literally, and I hate gruesome stories. Anyway, we can use your opinion in court. It might be a winning tactic."

"How so?"

"We'll argue that the plot is so fake and ridiculous that no one would find it defamatory. Everyone will just think it's a joke."

With natural ease, they fell into comfortable laughter. Their collegial relationship dated back to their days in the district attorney's office, when Mineko was a trial prep assistant and Evan a senior trial counsel in the Financial Crimes Bureau. In the fall of 1988, Mineko started law school, graduated in 1991, and took a prestigious clerkship with an appellate judge for the year following her graduation. Meanwhile, in 1990, Evan left the DA's office for the private firm, and in 1992, he recommended Mineko for an available associate position. It was a good fit, and the partners at B & R were more than pleased with Mineko's work.

Evan had been quick to enlist her help in the litigation *Tinker versus Delmonico*. Among the available associates, she was the perfect choice for this one. Besides Mineko's obvious intelligence and legal talent, her quiet confidence and calming presence would be assets in dealing with the screeching defendant Delmonico as they prepared her for an upcoming deposition, to be held next Tuesday. Evan also sensed that Mineko, with her unique style of feminine professionalism, would find subtle ways to tame and groom Delmonico for trial, smoothing down the threatening, sharp edges.

"Is that what I think it is?" Evan asked, eyeing the large book in Mineko's hands.

"Success." She handed it to Evan. "My crowning accomplishment. I think I deserve a raise."

"Watch it, Minnie. Showing your pushy side again." He grinned at her, laid the book on his desk, and dropped his eyes to the cover. A hand went to his forehead and ran back along the short-cropped sparse coating of sandy hair, over the bald area in the middle of his head, coming to rest at the nape of his neck. This habitual gesture was Evan's subconscious reminder that the porcelain spot, which had been the size of a sand dollar in the days Mineko first knew him, had grown to dominate half his head. "*This* is amazing," he exclaimed.

"Didn't I tell you?"

"Where'd you get it?"

"A secretary at the school district let me rummage around in a back room of the administration office. She said they'd hung onto some yearbooks, but there was no guarantee it would be there. I lucked out."

Evan opened the book and scrunched up his nose.

Mineko nodded in agreement. "A little musty, right?"

"A lot musty. Sitting in a damp corner since 1968. Wait, here we go." He was leafing through the pages of senior portraits. "What a face. Tina Delmonico. Varsity cheerleader, junior and senior years. That's it, nothing else. No literary pursuits noted."

"But she has a literary mien, don't you think? With those glasses?"

"Mean is right, but not so bookish. I like the pointed edges on those glasses, like shark's fins." He turned more pages. "Hundreds of kids between Delmonico and Tinker."

"No wonder she never heard of her."

"'*I swear to God, I never heard of this woman in my life!*' Here we go. 'June Allison Tinker.' June's mother must have been a fan of the movie star June Allyson. Look at that cute half-ponytail and elfish nose. Her lips look dead from that silver lip gloss. I don't see any Twiggy lashes though."

"I'm sure the school photographer told her to remove them. What would her mom say?"

"I bet she wore those twigs when she was marching and playing her flute. She was in the band her freshman through junior years. Not senior year. That's consistent with her allegations in this lawsuit. She couldn't have completed band her senior year."

"That was the fateful year in *Dumpster Grave*," said Mineko, her voice full of drama. "She got pregnant and dropped out of school near the end of the year."

"Maybe the tuba player was the father. Hey, what do you get, crossing a flute and a tuba?"

"Very funny."

"But here's something that isn't funny. Tina was a cheerleader. Wouldn't she have run into June on the football field?"

"I don't know about your high school, but at mine, the cheerleaders wouldn't be caught dead hanging out with the dorks in the band."

"Even a cute girl with Twiggy lashes playing the flute?"

Their conversation was interrupted by the ringing phone. Evan picked up and received word that Tina Delmonico had

arrived. "Can you show her into the small conference room?…
Thank you." He hung up and turned to Mineko. "Are we ready
for her?"

"You bet." Mineko's eyes, the solid, near-black irises,
sparkled in understated jest. Her face had matured since their
days in the DA's office, and the scrim of bangs was gone from her
forehead. Most days, like this one, her shiny black hair was pulled
into a bun close to her head, accentuating the high cheekbones.

Evan handed her the yearbook and told her to bring it along.
Side by side, they made their way down the hall, past the offices
of a dozen attorneys. B & R was a "small" firm by Manhattan
standards, a mere fifty-three attorneys and a support staff of
twenty. Evan, Mineko, and ten others made up the core litigation
group.

When they entered the small conference room, Tina Delmonico was seated in one of the eight chairs at the table. A
receptionist was setting a cup of coffee, cream and sugar in front
of her on the table.

"Ms. Delmonico," Evan said, extending his hand over the
table. The author did not rise from her chair but gave a limp-
wristed shake to Evan, and then Mineko.

"Thanks, Cindy," Evan said as the receptionist left the room.
The attorneys sat down across the table from the author.

Tina Delmonico regarded them warily before turning her
eyes to the creamer, pouring a healthy dose into her coffee, and
depositing three lumps of sugar. The paperback queen was a
slight woman in her early forties with pinched features giving an
older appearance than the airbrushed photograph on the back
cover of her novel. Every color and shape clashed. She was
wearing a textured wool, short-sleeved dress in chartreuse. She
sat with hunched shoulders under a stiff pile of highlighted
brunette hair. No glasses, but the irises were an unnatural
turquoise blue, suggesting colored contact lenses. The painted

black lashes were spidery, the lips crimson and large. The mouth emitted a big sound.

"I don't know what I could tell you. This is all such a crock." She spoke to her coffee cup, stirring it.

"Yes," said Evan, "that may very well be, however—"

"I never heard of this woman in my life. Why would she want to sue me?"

"Think of it as a form of flattery," said Evan. "A price many celebrities have to pay."

"And, as a novelist, you're an observer of human behavior," said Mineko, in a deferential tone, "with insight into motivation and temptation—"

"Of course."

"So, I'm sure you can discern the reasons that someone might want to sue you."

"Everyone is out to get a buck. This is the crass society we live in. No respect for an artist. My artistic integrity is at stake here."

Evan could guess Mineko's thoughts on that one, but he kept a straight face. "The biggest challenge we have, Ms. Delmonico, is the allegation that you must have known June Tinker because you were in the same high school graduating class. You'll be fielding questions on that topic during the deposition next week."

The author rolled her eyes to the ceiling. "There were six hundred and twenty-nine people in my graduating class." The large, bright lips distinctly formed and exaggerated each syllable of that number. "I'm supposed to know them all? Every girl with Twiggy lashes? Impossible!"

The first red flag went up. Such an exact number, stated without hesitation. Did she pull that number out of a hat, or was it the result of preparation, a calculated defense? Evan would check on its accuracy later.

"Opposing counsel might confront you with the proof of this

connection to test your reaction." He glanced at Mineko. "Ms. Inoue has something here I think you should see. How long has it been since you looked at your high school yearbook?"

Mineko opened the book to the beginning of the senior portraits and slid it across the table. Delmonico quickly flipped the pages to her own picture. A laugh spurted from her throat, ending in a piggish snort. "*Love* those glasses. I haven't seen this for years." She lingered on the page and lowered her face to it, lips twisted in a smile.

After a good, long look, she moved on, reluctantly turning the page. She slowly scanned the left-hand leaf and the right, turned the page again, and made another slow scan. Without warning, she picked up the pace. "I don't remember *any* of these people," she said, flipping page after page. The onward rush gave the appearance of familiarity, a deliberate path to the endpoint, but her precision could be blamed just as easily on the guidance of the alphabetical listing. There was a distinct, pregnant pause on the page just before she reached her destination, embellished with another, "I just don't know any of these people." A deep breath, and the final turn.

Evan saw it—the flit of Delmonico's eyes onto Tinker's portrait in the middle of a dozen on the page, a momentary flit away, followed by a deliberate show of searching the page and seeking it out. "So, *this* must be her," she said, shaking her head. "The plaintiff from hell. June Allison Tinker."

Mineko looked at Evan, who gave her a nod. "Looks like you remember her," Mineko said cheerfully. Accepting and open, Mineko was someone a client could confide in.

"Are you kidding? Who would remember *that* face? Never have I..." Delmonico uttered a sound of disgust, closed the book and pushed it across the table to Mineko.

Uh-oh, Evan was thinking. We're in for a rough ride. The lawsuit from hell.

* * *

Later that afternoon, Dana called Evan in the middle of his ruminations. He was letting his imagination run wild into the territory of every possible undisclosed truth. By the end of their session, Evan, Mineko, and Tina were on a first-name basis, but Tina had not conceded much else. Dana's call was a welcome distraction. "My jury is still out," she said.

"The waiting game."

"I'm sure you don't miss it."

He didn't want to admit that he did. There were times when Dana's career seemed far more exciting and important than his. But this was the tradeoff. For his family, he'd left the frenetic pace and low salary of a public prosecutor for the bigger bucks, longer hours, and swankier office of a private law firm.

But he couldn't say that his work was uninteresting. How many lawyers had the privilege of defending the likes of Tina Delmonico, a character, an artiste, a client who wasn't (he believed) telling him the truth? Evan also had the opportunity, occasionally, to experience the excitement (less dramatic than Dana's) of delivering a summation and awaiting a jury verdict in a civil case. Just a lot less frequently. The vast majority of his cases settled before trial. "Most days, can't say that I do miss it," he replied. "What're the odds on the verdict?"

"Good chance it's guilty. They just asked to see the bullets and to hear a read-back of the sister's testimony. I didn't see any seriously troubled looks on their faces. One of the men on the jury... Well, I'll tell you later."

"One of them what?"

"Was looking at me during summation."

"Looking?"

"Eyeing."

"I see." And he did. His wife was an attractive woman. Did Evan deserve her? Maybe not based on his looks alone, but what about that personality? In moments of self-doubt, this was his recurring internal joke. "I'll come downtown and beat him up, but I'll wait until the jury comes in with the guilty verdict first."

"Those workouts are paying off. You have the muscles for it. You'll lay him flat."

"All for my woman."

"Well, the woman might be late getting home. What time can you make it?"

"I'll try for six-ish." It would be tough, but Anneke had to be relieved. Ten hours with a two-year-old was more than enough for anyone. Evan and Dana did their best to juggle late nights so that one of them would always be home around six. At least Evan had a logistic advantage; his midtown office was a shorter subway ride home than Dana's office downtown.

"You think Anneke's doing all right?" asked Dana. Her tone was wistful, seeking reassurance.

"Why do you ask? Something happen?" They'd had this conversation before, but the anxiety resurfaced from time to time.

"No. I don't know. Must be so hard to be away from home, but she always has a smile on her face. Sometimes I have the feeling there's a little bit of sadness underneath."

Evan thought of that sunny face, rugged and strong. "She says she loves being in New York. It's an adventure when you're nineteen, even if you have to take care of a toddler to do it. But we can never know everything that goes on in a mind."

"Sometimes she seems too good to be true."

"Maybe that's because she's doing such a great job, and we have it so easy, compared to last year. I know I'm glad we don't have to worry about being late to work." Under the circumstances, a live-in au pair was the right choice. They would have preferred to place Travis in the care of a grandparent, but that option was not possible—for now. Dana's parents would have loved to care for their first grandchild, but they lived in New

Jersey and were both still working full-time. Evan's mother, a young widow of sixty-two, lived closer to them, in Westchester County. She was currently caring for Evan's niece and nephew, the kids of his older brother, during after-school hours. Kelly was thirteen and Ian was eleven. As the children got older, their after-school hours filled with sports and activities, and Brenda Goodhue's involvement in their lives had changed. Dana and Evan held out the hope that they could soon persuade her to start caring for Travis instead.

"You're right," said Dana. "I shouldn't go looking for problems. Let's enjoy our good luck. Tug absolutely adores her."

"No question."

"And she's reliable."

"From day one."

"Okay, I'll stop worrying about Anneke and concentrate on my murderer."

"A lot more fun."

"Gotta go."

"Love you."

"Love you too."

4 »   *FAMILY*

THAT EVENING, ANNEKE ate dinner with Travis at five thirty. She reheated food that Evan had made earlier in the week, selecting two slices of meatloaf and small portions of roasted potatoes and peas.

Evan arrived at six twenty, anxious to play with his son for at least fifteen minutes before he could even think of eating. Dinnertime on weekdays was a scattered, unpredictable event because Evan and Dana showed up at different times and Travis was always hungry long before they got home. Anneke was not expected to cook for the family. "That's not your job," insisted Dana. "Tug is your only concern."

As a result, no one seemed to eat together. Evan and Dana shared the cooking duties and were equally proficient. On weekends they prepared extra portions which could be reheated throughout the week. Some evenings, when one of them got home very late, the other would not be able to wait for dinner and would eat alone.

All of this took some getting used to for Anneke, who'd always eaten at six sharp with her parents and younger sister. Mealtimes in Holland traditionally varied little in scheduling or content. There were the two "bread" meals, breakfast and lunch, and the one hot meal, dinner with the family around the table. Breakfast at seven, tea at ten, lunch at noon, coffee and sweet snack at three, dinner at six.

She had explained some of this to the Goodhues, including a demonstration with the jar of *hagelslag* she'd carried in her suitcase from home—chocolate sprinkles she liberally applied to buttered bread in the morning for breakfast. Not just chocolate, but Dutch chocolate. Dana took a bite and laughed with pleasure before she asked Anneke not to share this culinary custom with Travis.

In her new life, the only meal schedule that Anneke could arrange was dinnertime with Travis between five thirty and six, consisting of heated leftovers, or if none were available, something simply prepared. It was easy enough for her to fix Dutch *stamppot*, potatoes mashed with green vegetables, or *hutspot*, potatoes, carrots and onions. Once the Goodhues had made it clear that they approved of her having an early dinner with Travis, she no longer worried about it. Still, something seemed to be missing from her quiet evening ritual.

Anneke was permitted to retire to her room or to the living room when one of the parents came home. She was also free to go out if she liked. On this particular evening, none of these choices appealed to her. She felt stir crazy but would not go out, not after reading that message she received this afternoon.

She entered her bedroom and picked up the novel she was reading by Dutch writer Harry Mulisch. Stuffed inside was the latest five-page letter from her little sister, Betje. She pulled it out and placed it on the little table next to her twin bed. She'd already read it three times, but perhaps she would read it again tonight at bedtime.

Her room was tiny and seemed unbearably claustrophobic just now. Pulling back the curtain on her small window, she looked down at the street below. Miniature people scurried along, and the faint sound of traffic floated up. She took her novel into the living room and claimed the easy chair in the corner farthest from the dining area, across from the alcove/playroom where Evan and Travis were tumbling on the carpeted floor.

The living room, with its attached dining area, was the center of the home, with open doorways to the playroom, kitchen and foyer. Nearly everything could be heard and seen.

Along with the roughhousing came Travis's giggles and squeals of delight. "More, Daddy. Do again!" There were new rounds of tickling and bouncing and bubbling laughter.

Anneke turned a page of her novel and flipped it back again, not remembering what she'd read. The page disappeared. In its place was the white notepaper with that familiar handwriting in black ink: *Ik zal je morgen bellen, nadat ze vertrekken. Niels.* I'll call you tomorrow morning after they've left.

She looked up at the antics in the other room. They hadn't noticed. She looked down again and saw only an open book in her hands.

The gymnastics came to an end. Evan said, "Come on, buddy." He took Travis by the hand, and they walked to the kitchen. After they disappeared inside, Anneke heard Evan open the refrigerator. He removed plastic containers and tossed them onto the counter, making dull sounds. He opened a cabinet, removed dishes, and placed them on the counter more carefully, making brighter sounds.

At six forty-five, Dana walked in the front door. At that moment, Evan was using the microwave while Travis remained underfoot. Anneke had turned another page of her novel and was staring at it blankly.

Travis heard the front door and ran out of the kitchen. Anneke's head was tipped down, but she saw enough from under her brow. In the foyer, Dana dropped her briefcase and swooped up her child. "How's my big boy?" She smothered him with kisses and glanced up with a turn of the head. "Hi, Anneke."

"Hello!" She put on a cheery voice.

"How'd everything go this afternoon?"

"Perfect. He was a little doll."

"Isn't he though?" She laughed and carried Travis into the kitchen. Anneke heard, but could not see, the kiss that Dana gave Evan.

"What was the verdict?"

"Just what we expected."

"Congratulations."

By now, Anneke had caught onto the style of communication between Dana and Evan whenever Travis was awake and within earshot. Graphic details, names of crimes, and certain legal terms were edited out. They even refrained from using the expressions "guilty" and "innocent." As a result, Anneke had developed the skill of reading between the cryptic lines. She respected this parenting decision and adopted it for herself. *Kleine potjes hebben grote oren*. Small pots have big ears, went the Dutch saying. Small children will pick up everything.

Anneke had figured out enough about Dana's current murder prosecution to know that the jury must have delivered a guilty verdict today. But Dana's tone wasn't entirely positive, and she spoke now in a way that suggested a problem.

"You remember Hayes?"

"Right."

"He pled today in the federal case."

"I thought you said that was the plan."

"But I didn't know that my case was one of the pattern acts."

Anneke didn't understand the term "pattern act," and it seemed to take Evan a moment to understand as well. Before he could respond, Travis interjected, "Mommy, Mommy! Can I have some?"

"Didn't you have a nice dinner already?"

"Mommy, have some?"

"Okay, just a minute."

Evan said, "He pled to…to being the one?"

"Yup. And Seth moved for a directed verdict. The judge ordered a hearing and it starts tomorrow afternoon, so I'll have to prepare in the morning. It's going to get in the way of everything."

"But you're not on the chart for a while, are you?"

Anneke understood this code word. The "chart" was homicide chart, when Dana was on call day or night to respond to crime scenes. Murder scenes. She never spoke of it in front of Travis, and said very little even in front of Anneke, who could only imagine how horrible this aspect of her job must be. Or how exciting. The main impact on Anneke was the possibility they would ask her to work late. Once, there'd been an evening when Dana had been the early parent home but was immediately called out again, and Evan could not break away from work. Anneke was left alone with Travis until eight thirty.

"Next Wednesday."

"Let's hope the guardian angels are hovering over the city that night."

"Yup. We'll pray for no new cases."

The chatter went on over the sounds of dinner preparation, clattering silverware, and Travis's random contributions. Family, comfort, togetherness, home.

The sounds carried Anneke across the ocean and back in time. At a sturdy square table, she sat across from her mother, and Betje sat across from their father. Mama passed the bowl of steaming potatoes, offering the food with a straight-line smile on her lips and flyaway wisps of gray at her temples. There was no judgment in her eyes, not at this remembered dinnertime. Papa and Betje were bantering on about something. It didn't matter what. They were the cheery ones in the family, always finding something to be happy about.

In the kitchen, Evan and Dana were laughing too. They were laughing even though Niels was in New York and had spoken to their doorman about her. They were unaware of this intrusion. They were safe, and they had each other. They had nothing to worry about in their lives, but Travis didn't know this and he started to whine. It was the end of the day for him, and the sound of his voice was a mixture of fatigue and excitement from the long-awaited family intimacy.

Niels had been out on the street, watching this building, getting up his nerve to leave a note with the doorman. Maybe he'd been watching her with Travis, even following them. But it was nighttime, and he wouldn't be watching right now, would he? Not with the little girl. It was too chilly. They would be inside somewhere.

She had to get out.

She stood up, surprised to see the three of them sitting around the table. When had they done all this? They'd set the dining table for three, placing the child-size silverware in front of Travis, who was sitting in his booster seat. The food was on the table. After all, the baby would be having a second dinner, a family dinner, even if his mom and dad only allowed him a bite or two.

"Did you get enough to eat, Anneke?" Evan was asking. "Would you like something?"

"No, thank you, I'm fine. I think I'll go out for a walk." No surprises here. She often took an evening walk.

"It's good to get out for some fresh air," said Evan.

Anneke walked past the dining table toward the foyer.

"Just one thing," said Dana, twisting around in her chair, "in case we don't catch you later." Anneke paused mid-step. "Did I tell you about Saturday? We decided on a time."

"Any time is okay."

"We're going to leave at six thirty. Can you feed Travis dinner while we get ready?"

"Sure. Not a problem."

"Great. Thanks so much, Anneke." Dana turned back to the table, back to her family.

With her head low, Anneke slid out the front door when it was held open for her. The uniformed man on duty was neither Bashkim nor Endrit. A few doormen rotated on the night shift, and Anneke had exchanged more than mere pleasantries with some of them, but tonight she didn't want to see anyone or to be seen.

The temperature had dropped sharply since three this afternoon. She pulled up the sides of her collar around bare neck and tilted her forehead down against the wind, eyes shifting nervously right and left. There were many dark corners under awnings and between buildings, but he would not be there. No, he would not.

She forced her eyes straight ahead and walked at a brisk pace, hardly noticing her surroundings. She stuck to the well-traveled streets and avenues. It was only a bit past seven, and the Upper West Side was brimming with activity, people still coming home from work, eating at restaurants, and grocery shopping. She'd been out in the city at night plenty of times, enough to know she should avoid walking alone in the park, either Riverside Park or Central Park.

Soon, her heart was racing. From the exercise or her thoughts? She couldn't shake the image of his eyes watching her.

Ik zal je morgen bellen… He'd gotten the address and the home phone number. He couldn't possibly have the mobile phone number. No one but Dana and Evan knew it.

He would be waiting and watching until they left in the morning. Or maybe he already knew their schedules. Had he watched Evan on one of his morning jogs? Followed Dana to the subway? Spied on Anneke and Travis in the park?

Would she stay glued to the phone until he called? Tomorrow was Friday, a workday, and she was taking care of Travis and could not possibly talk to him. She would say hello and be perfectly pleasant and neutral, and then she would request that he never call again. It was the Goodhues' home, their telephone, their territory. She could not possibly see him. She did not want to see him.

Saturday and Sunday were days off, but she would be giving Travis his dinner at five thirty or six on Saturday and babysitting while the Goodhues went to the theater. These occasional weekend nights were part of their understanding, to be negotiated and exchanged for certain weekdays off, whenever Evan or Dana had vacation days or arranged to be home.

She didn't mind at all. In fact, she looked forward to these extra nights on duty, the few times she was allowed to tuck the pajama-clad toddler into his bed, stroke his baby-soft hair, and tell him a bedtime story, or sing him to sleep. The bedtime hour was so full of wonder. There were those adorable sleepy eyelids, the drifting off into slumber, and the chance to create a special closeness. In that gray zone between wakefulness and sleep, Travis would hear her voice and feel her tender caress.

She hoped for more of these nights in the coming days. She hoped for the strength to say "no." The more time she was tied to Travis, the more excuses she would have. She could not possibly see him. If they met, there was no telling what might happen.

Perhaps she should tell Dana? No, it would be better to tell Evan.

But it was too early to panic. She would wait to see what he had to say.

5 »   DEPUTY

DANA SAT ACROSS from the district attorney-elect and asked him, "What am I going to do without you?"

Patrick McBride's rugged fifty-year-old face betrayed heartfelt affection. He and Dana had a professional relationship that could only be described as rare. "I'm not going to Timbuktu," he said defensively, scratching his head. The thick cushion of russet-colored hair was sprinkled with gray.

"Might as well."

"It's just across the street."

"I'll have to take a number and stand in line."

"You can call me anytime you want to talk. About anything."

She remembered the last time he'd said those words. It had been 1988, on the occasion of her unexpected transfer to the Financial Crimes Bureau. That time, she'd been the one to move across the street to an office in the Criminal Court building. And Patrick had made good on his promise, opening his door to her and bestowing lifesaving advice at a critical low point in her career.

Now it was his turn to leave. With the support of the retiring district attorney, Patrick had easily won the recent election. Come the first of the year, he would be taking up residence in that monstrous, ceremonial office across the street on the eighth floor. His time would be scarce and valuable. He wouldn't interrupt a meeting with, say, the Mayor of New York City just because a senior trial counsel needed his attention.

"Okay," she said. "I'll be sure to call you any old time. I like listening to Muzak."

"Very funny. Let's not dwell on the distant future. We need to talk about the immediate future. The Marshall case. What the hell happened?"

There was a knock on the door, and Eric stuck his head in. "Good. Just who I want to see," said Patrick. With his characteristic energy and quickness, he twitched his fingers, beckoning the young attorney inside.

It was the lunch hour, and Dana had left a message for Eric to join them in Patrick's office if he could break away from his burglary trial.

"How's it going?" Dana asked as Eric took a seat next to her, opposite Patrick at his desk.

"I'm going to see if I can get Michele in here," interrupted their boss, lifting the phone receiver. "We need all the great minds we can get." Patrick speed-dialed Deputy Bureau Chief Seidman, who sat in the office next door.

Eric answered Dana's question. "I barely survived the suppression motion. The judge didn't like the search, but I convinced him that the cops didn't need a warrant. That case law you gave me was right on the money. Thanks, Dana. We started picking the jury and have four in the box so far. We should get the full jury by the end of the day."

"Michele's on the way," said Patrick, hanging up the phone. "How does your complainant feel now, after what happened yesterday?"

"Mrs. Deely is a nice lady," said Eric. "She'll be here on Monday, no problem. But I didn't make the best impression, running out on her in the middle of our trial prep." In a business where complaining witnesses can be flaky, unreliable, or too intimidated to show up, a steady, dependable, and credible CW was everything a prosecutor dreamed of.

Michele Seidman walked in. "Hello everyone. I understand you have a little problem."

"To put it mildly," said Dana.

Michele took the last empty chair next to Patrick's desk.

"Perfect timing," said Patrick. "Eric was about to tell us the story of his dramatic entrance into the courtroom of Judge DuBois."

Michele crossed her legs at the ankles just above her blocky pumps and leaned forward in her chair, with fingers laced across her abdomen. Not overly concerned with fashion, Michele hadn't swapped out her collection of gray, brown, and taupe skirt suits for several years, and the gradual spread of middle age was stressing the seams. At forty-six, the likely heiress to the position of bureau chief had an abiding curiosity and a sharp mind. "I'm dying to know everything," she told Eric directly with a spark in her small, gray eyes.

"Well," Eric shifted in his seat, a sign of his discomfort. Exposing himself to the judgment of three of his esteemed superiors was more disquieting than facing a judge and jury. "Dana walked by my door on her way back to the courtroom, and a minute later, the court clerk Robert called me. I told him I wasn't able to make it for the verdict. I still had a lot to go over with my CW. About five minutes later, the phone rang again, and I was thinking of letting it roll, but with the jury coming in, I thought…" He cut his sentence short.

…maybe Dana needed something and was calling me. Dana mentally supplied the rest of the sentence and glanced at Patrick, noticing the tiniest hint of a smile on his lips.

Of course, Eric couldn't know who was calling before he picked up the receiver. Wouldn't everything be so much easier if they could get the new technology for caller ID? Evan's firm had just installed it and Dana was jealous. The public sector always lagged behind private business when it came to upgrades in technology.

"Anyway, I answered the call, and it was Assistant U. S. Attorney Alan Prendergast. He said that Dana wasn't picking up her phone, and could I give her a message? 'Tell her that Bounce just took a plea on the racketeering charge.'"

For Michele's benefit, Patrick explained. "Bounce is the street name for Brendon Hayes, the gang member who was with the defendant during the shooting."

Michele nodded. She had a general familiarity with the evidence.

"The AUSA said, 'I just thought you might like to know that Hayes admitted to shooting Dwayne Little.'" Eric added a nasal inflection to his voice, revealing his disdain for this Prendergast fellow.

"How nice of him," said Michele.

"Oh, we love this guy," said Dana. "I kept him completely in the loop about our prosecution and asked him to do the same for us. His racketeering indictment was sealed. We didn't know that the Little shooting was one of the pattern acts. He could've given us a heads-up."

"I asked him," continued Eric, "if he meant that Bounce was with Stain during the shooting. He said, 'No, Hayes pulled the trigger. Your guy gave him the gun.'"

"But *your* eyewitness testified that Stain pulled the trigger, right? This is interesting," said Michele.

Patrick nodded in agreement. "During the plea, did Bounce give any more details? When did Stain hand him the gun? What did they say to each other?"

"I...don't know."

"You didn't have a chance to ask Prendergast, did you?" asked Dana, trying to help him out.

"I have to say, maybe I freaked the minute I heard that Bounce was the shooter. It seemed to me this was obvious *Brady* material." Eric was referring to *Brady versus Maryland*, the seminal U.S. Supreme Court case that established a criminal defendant's constitutional right to receive any exculpatory evidence known to the prosecutor. "I didn't ask him any more questions and just scribbled down what he said like a maniac. Mrs. Deely was looking at me like…" Eric did his best facial imitation of shock and motherly concern. "I was practically out the door when I started apologizing and asking her to hang out for a few minutes until I got back. Turns out I was gone for half an hour."

"And the entire assemblage was poised for the verdict when you burst in," said Patrick.

"No kidding. I didn't say anything but gave the note to Dana, and then…"

"Go ahead," Dana teased him. "You can say it. You would've handled it differently."

"I was happy to let you decide," admitted Eric. "The choices were all impossible," he added—in sweet defense of her, she thought.

"How did *you* see it, Eric?" asked Michele. She loved to glean everyone's thoughts before coming out with her own.

"Like I said. It was *Brady* material. I was worried that the case would tank if the jury said 'guilty' before we disclosed this information."

"The case would 'tank'?"

"I mean, it would be thrown out. Judge DuBois would dismiss the indictment, and we wouldn't be able to retry the case. It would be double jeopardy."

"Ah-ha," said Michele.

"Ah-ha," mimicked Patrick and Dana.

"Double jeopardy," said Michele. "Think about *that*."

"I read your note three times while the judge and jury

waited," said Dana. "And then it occurred to me."

Michele kept after Eric, using the opportunity as a teaching moment. "What would have happened under your plan? If we revealed this information *before* the jury announced the verdict?"

"Maybe the judge could've reopened the trial for new evidence?" He looked at their faces one by one. "I guess not."

"The jury had already deliberated. It was too late to reopen the evidence."

"Well, then, I guess Seth would've moved for a mistrial, and…" Eric was beginning to understand.

"And Judge DuBois would have granted it because, at the very least, this new evidence has to be explored."

"And double jeopardy would bar a retrial. But this way, *Dana's* way…" He looked at her with the dewy eyes of renewed admiration.

"The jury finished its job," said Michele. "We have a verdict. Seth makes his motion. If he wins and Judge DuBois sets aside the verdict, we can appeal. If we get a reversal, the guilty verdict is reinstated. No need to retry the case, no double jeopardy problem. Let's say he loses before Judge DuBois. Same thing. The verdict remains untouched."

Dana finished Michele's thought. "But let's say all of this happens *before* we get the verdict. If Seth wins the motion, the case is dismissed, we can't retry it, and we can't appeal. An appellate court wouldn't touch it because, even if the ruling is reversed, there's no verdict to reinstate, and a retrial is barred by double jeopardy."

"Okay," said Eric. "But what if he lost the mistrial motion before the verdict came in? At least we were upfront and told the court what we knew. After that, we let the jury go ahead and deliver the verdict."

"What do you say to that, Dana?" asked Patrick. He was enjoying this teaching moment just as much as Michele.

"Even if Seth lost the mistrial motion, he would still win."

Eric scrunched his milky brow under the crown of cropped yellow curls. Dana explained. "The new evidence has to be explored in a separate hearing. Witnesses have to be called. We couldn't ask the jury to wait that long to deliver its verdict. The jury would be dismissed, and that's really the same as winning the mistrial motion, because we can't retry the case."

Eric nodded with an enlightened expression on his face.

"Looks like Ms. Hargrove is right again," said Patrick.

"Then let's get to the really interesting thing here," said Michele. "What on earth actually happened at the murder scene? Who's the shooter? Who's right—Bounce or your eyewitness?"

"And if Bounce is right, how does that affect the guilty verdict?" added Patrick.

Dana knew what he was getting at. "It *does* affect the verdict if, for example, Stain gave him the gun for no specific purpose a month before the murder. If that's the scenario, well, then..."

"We're blasted out of court," said Eric, shaking his head. "Stain wins the motion because he can show that he didn't have the intent to murder Little."

"But it *doesn't* affect the guilty verdict," continued Dana, "if Stain handed Bounce the gun at the scene of the crime, or even if he gave it to him sometime earlier, with an instruction to use it to kill Little."

"Right," said Eric. "Either way you look at it, Stain is guilty. Pulled the trigger like Larry testified, or gave Bounce the gun with an order to kill. He's an accomplice to murder." Eric's face revealed his intellectual efforts, but in the next moment, showed confusion again. "You know, it *would* have an impact on the verdict."

"How so?" asked Michele.

"If I was on the jury and heard both versions, I would be so mixed up about what really happened that I wouldn't know what to believe. These are two completely different theories. I might have a reasonable doubt and have to acquit."

"Good point, Eric," said Patrick. "Right now, it's too hard to call because we don't know the details about the supposed hand-off of the gun. Hopefully that will come to light at the hearing. But aren't we forgetting something here?"

Dana and Michele smiled. Eric looked puzzled. Dana explained. "Everything we've said so far is based on a shaky premise."

Patrick and Michele each indicated assent with their own unique mannerisms. Patrick: a two-eyed, fleeting wink. Michele: a tip of her head downward to hide the grin. Eric just continued to look puzzled.

"We've been assuming that Bounce told the truth during his guilty plea. But these two thugs are gang members. They lie whenever it suits them. The real question we have to ask is, why? Why did Bounce make this so-called confession in federal court? What's in it for him? Looks to me like he's trying to pay off a debt to his buddy who's on trial for murder."

Now all the heads were bobbing.

"And *that's* what your hearing is going to be about," said Michele. "To get to the truth."

"It ain't gonna be easy," said Patrick.

"Especially against Seth," said Dana.

Eric gave Dana a chagrined look. "Sorry I got you into this. I was an idiot running into the courtroom like that. I should've just waited until you got back—I practically botched everything."

Patrick swiveled in his chair to regard him straight on. "Eric," he said, in a forceful, compassionate tone. The young attorney lifted his eyes to meet those of his mentor. "You did the right thing going to the courtroom with this information. Absolutely. You did the right thing."

Said like that, no one could dispute Patrick's opinion.

He's going to be an amazing district attorney, Dana thought. What on earth am I going to do without him?

Just as they all stood up, ready to leave, Patrick said, "Dana, hold on a minute." Michele headed back to her office, and Eric returned to his burglary trial.

She waited but remained standing with her hands on the back of the chair, using it as an anchor. She felt antsy. She needed to get going, to prepare for court. Judge DuBois expected them at three thirty for a preliminary plan of action.

"As you can imagine, Michele is a shoo-in to replace me as bureau chief. I've recommended her, and the front office will rubber-stamp the appointment. That leaves the deputy spot open."

Dana looked at him and rolled her eyes.

"Okay," he said. "I don't have my head in the sand. I know you're aware of this."

"Like every other senior trial counsel in the bureau."

"All of you are champing at the bit. Next week I'll be making a formal announcement and soliciting applications for the spot. After that, I'll have to make a decision by the end of the month. I'm hoping you'll put your name in."

"Don't know, Patrick."

"You'd be an outstanding candidate for the job."

"Really don't know."

"Just the way this meeting went today tells me as much. You have a lot to share. A lot to teach your junior colleagues."

"I really appreciate that Patrick, but you probably know that I really love the trial work. It took me a couple of years to get into it, but now…"

"Now you're in your stride, I know. And part of me wants to see you continue down that road."

"I love it, but it can be stressful, especially now that I have Travis to worry about."

"That's something to think about. The stresses are different for a supervisor, but I ended up having more time with my kids as soon as I was off homicide chart."

"I do see Michele working long hours…"

"That's partly Michele, but, yes, the hours are long. Hard work, but a different quality of work. There isn't the constant worry about your witnesses coming in, and you don't have to answer calls in the middle of the night."

"Except sometimes."

"Sometimes, right." On newsworthy or political cases, the deputy might be called out along with the homicide ADA.

"Give it some very serious thought. I can see you as bureau chief one day, and this is the stepping stone."

"Thank you, Patrick. I *will* seriously consider putting my name in." She turned to go. At the door, she paused. "Have you given some thought to Denzel?"

"Of course," said Patrick. "He's at the top of the list, your biggest competitor."

Jared Browne, also known as "Denzel," was Dana's closest friend from rookie days, when they shared their office with two other rookies, Ellen and Tom, and all four of them shared Eric as their trial prep assistant. Ellen and Tom had since left the office for private practice, while Dana and Jared had weathered the ups and downs of criminal prosecution, climbing the ladder from low-level felonies to homicide chart.

This place threw everything at you. Hard work and heartbreak. Fear and reward. Futility and justice. This was the toughest job in the world, a place that forged resilient bonds among colleagues and shared memories of defeat and triumph.

Denz was her buddy. They'd had some laughs over the years. She thought of him now as the perfect candidate for the deputy spot. He was rational, even-keeled, intelligent, personable, and well-liked by all. She thought of their early days and his occasional uncertainty and the way his insecurities had melted away over the years, revealing a glossy, tough patina underneath. Recently, the juggling of home life and work had become more of a challenge for him. Jared and his wife had a three-year-old boy and just had their second baby, a girl.

"Good," she said to Patrick before walking out the door. "Keep him at the top of the list. The bureau will be in good hands if—or *when*—I decide not to apply for the job."

"Get back to work," he said, pretending disgust. There was a big smile on his face.

Speaking of Jared, there he was, walking straight toward her in the hallway after she left Patrick's office, giving her one of his big, Denzel Washington smiles.

"Hey, Dorothy." He didn't have to say the next line. It was understood.

"Eric's across the street on a burglary trial," she said, stopping him in his tracks. They stood face-to-face, little room between them.

"So, you've lost him. What'll you do without your sidekick?" This was all in good fun, and even Eric knew about it and didn't mind. He could tell they loved him. Adored him. But now that Toto had run away to take care of his own caseload again, Dana would be going solo against Seth and his little post-trial motion.

"I'll just have to do without him. He was a big help at the trial, but I'm on my own for the hearing. You heard about it?" She crossed her arms against her suit jacket and looked him directly in the eyes, second nature. He stuck his hands in his pants pockets and returned the look. Their postures bespoke ease and comfort with each other.

"Who didn't? You and Eric are now legend, if you weren't already."

"It's a huge headache. A minute ago, Patrick and Michele were being a two-headed Socrates with me and Eric."

"Sounds like fun."

"Someday soon you could be on the giving end instead of the receiving end of one of those exchanges."

"How so?"

"The spot."

"Right, the spot."

"You're still interested, aren't you?"

"Anything to get off the chart. It's killing me. Murder by homicide chart. I'm trying not to get my hopes up for the spot, though. How about you?"

"I'm not so sure I want it. Not for a while anyway. Patrick says he's announcing the opening next week, so dust off your résumé. I put my two cents in and said you'd be great—"

"No..."

"—but he already knows it."

"You did that for me? Thanks, Dana. You have a minute now? I've got some great new pictures of Lena in my office."

"Gotta run, Denz." She backed away. "Have to get ready for Jack." She needed to check the status of her rush order on the transcript of Bounce's guilty plea in federal court. More important, she wanted to make her midday call to Anneke. "But I'll come by later and see if you're still there." She was five paces away, heading toward her office, when she thought to add, "I'll bring my new pictures of Travis."

6 »   *UNEXPECTED*

ANNEKE PICKED UP the phone on the third ring. The clock on the kitchen wall said ten thirty-five. He'd waited, a sign of nervousness. He could have called earlier. Dana had left at eight and Evan at eight thirty.

She almost spoke in Dutch but stopped herself. Maybe it wasn't him. "Hello? Goodhue residence."

He hesitated only slightly. *"Groetjes Anneke. Mijn Anneke."* His deep voice was tender, just like the old days, with a rough underlayer of tension. At times they'd been able to pretend it away, but the disquiet always simmered beneath the surface.

They continued talking in their native tongue.

"Niels. I don't understand. Why are you here? Why are you calling?" As she spoke, she walked back to the playroom from the kitchen where she'd picked up the cordless receiver. Blinded by emotion, she nearly stumbled over Travis. He was trying to fit the triangle block into the round hole on the board. She dropped to her knees, sat on her haunches and stroked his soft crown with her left hand while holding the phone with her right.

"I'm here to see you. *We're* here to see you."

"What do you mean 'we'?" She knew exactly what he meant. Her heart pounded like it would burst out of her chest. Dizziness rushed to her head. She fought back by keeping her hand on the child in her care. A grounding connection. Travis found the slot for the triangle, dropped the block in, and picked up the square.

"I'm here with Kaatje."

For a stunned moment, she allowed the name to hover, closing the distance between her and Niels at his mystery location. "Why did you bring Kaatje here? Is Renske with you? How did you get my address and phone number?"

Silence. When he spoke again, it was in a quiet voice. "I have to see you. I'll explain everything then."

"I can't. I'm working."

"Don't you have a day off?"

"I…I can't. I just can't." She envisioned little Kaatje in the room with Niels, wherever that room happened to be. Perhaps she was playing nearby, or even sitting on his lap as he spoke on the phone. The girl was Travis's age, only two months younger.

They didn't belong here in Anneke's new world. The voice on the telephone didn't fit. The familiar but incongruous sound evoked an eerie, ever-shifting landscape. She was, at once, sitting on the playroom floor next to Travis and having a conversation with Niels in his studio on the Keizersgracht in Amsterdam. His unexpected arrival in New York had released a tiny realization. She'd been hearing his voice all along in the background, during conscious hours and countless nights of dreams she'd forgotten or remembered and shoved out of her head in the morning.

And the child. Unseen for two years, Kaatje would now be as big as Travis. Distance and time and a whitewashed mind hadn't kept a child from growing, from existing, from demanding a place on this earth.

"Would you like to talk to her?"

Oh no, God no.

"Here, *schatje*, say hello." There was a rustle as he shifted the phone to the child's ear.

A tiny, sweet voice greeted Anneke, faintly arriving from the end of an infinite channel, speaking babyish phrases in Dutch. At the same moment, next to her, Travis shook himself away from her hand. "Ah-nuh-kuh!" he exclaimed, much louder than the small female voice that correctly pronounced her name in her ear. She'd been clutching Travis too hard, and now he was running to the other side of the room.

Niels came back on the line. "You see, she wants you to come and visit."

"This is impossible. How did you even find me?"

"Anneke." He stopped. She heard him breathing and felt the tense emotion building toward what he was about to say next. "*Ik hou van je nog.*"

At one time, those were the words that kept her alive. "I still love you." How could he be saying that now? Did he really expect her to return the feeling? She remained mute.

"Tomorrow is Saturday. They couldn't want you to work on the weekend. You can come and visit us."

"I'm babysitting tomorrow, a special favor."

"All day?"

She didn't answer and wondered why she was unable to press the "end" button on the phone. Her finger wouldn't do it. Something told her she'd regret hanging up. Travis was calling her name, holding up a crayoned page he'd ripped from a coloring book. "That's nice, Travis."

"Then I'll have to come and visit *you*," Niels declared in a new, shaky voice, a bit louder. Very insistent. He'd used that voice only once before, a time she wanted to forget. "I'd like to meet your employers and see how they're treating you. And maybe Kaatje would like to meet the little boy and have a playmate."

Panic rose in her throat, jolting her senses alive. This was a grave threat. He had to understand the need to stay away. "No, no, you can't come here. You cannot! This is *not* my house. You have no right. You shouldn't even be calling this number."

Travis started mimicking, "neigh, neigh," like the sound of a horse in one of his favorite fairy tales. Luckily, he couldn't understand the rapid Dutch she fired into the phone.

"Kaatje and I can visit like anyone else," said Niels in a conversational tone. "Yesterday we stopped by and got to know your doorman. A very nice fellow with a gold tooth. He tickled Kaatje under the chin."

"This is impossible. You can't come here. Of course I'll come meet you, but don't come here and don't call again." Without pause she added, "If you really loved me, you wouldn't dare to come here." Instantly she regretted the mention of love. What they'd had was never that. What they had now was nothing.

"Okay, then meet me tomorrow."

"Tomorrow, no. I'm babysitting." How long could she use that excuse? "Sunday, maybe. I have a day off on Sunday."

As soon as she'd made this concession, the rest of the conversation proceeded automatically, in a smudgy dreaminess. She walked back to the kitchen for a pencil and notepad. He recited the address and the time, and she dutifully wrote everything down, obeying him just like she used to during their long afternoons in his studio. *Don't move. The light on your face is just so, like that.*

She agreed to come. The address was only a few blocks away. A sublet, the apartment of a Dutch expat who was away for two months, visiting his family in Holland. The place was fully furnished, equipped with the phone Niels was using to call her. She asked how he'd managed to find a place so close. There'd been a number of listings, he said, but ultimately, "It was meant to be, don't you think?"

Serendipitous. He'd found her, and he'd found a place nearby, and everything had simply fallen into place because it was fated that they meet again. He would explain everything when he saw her.

"Yes, Niels, of course."

"It's for the best, you'll see." The edge to his voice was gone. The renewed tenderness was a sign that he'd gotten what he wanted.

Finally, her thumb went to the "end" button.

He *had* gotten what he wanted.

In the beginning, when she first knew him, the opposite had been true. At least, that was her belief. She'd gotten what she wanted, a fantasy brought to life.

A small hand was shaking her shoulder, speaking her name. She was sitting cross-legged on the playroom floor, not sure how she'd arrived there again after making the trip to the kitchen for paper and pencil. Looking into the boy's eyes, she remembered the scrap of notepaper. What had she done with it?

Travis plopped down in the diamond-shaped space between her knees. "Read this?" He had brought over a book, one of his favorite stories, *The Little Engine That Could.*

"Okay, Tug." She arranged him more comfortably with her arms around his shoulders and the book in front of them both. She started to read.

The scrap of paper wasn't necessary. The place and time of the appointment were indelibly written on her mind. But she had to make sure that the paper wasn't left out where Dana and Evan could find it.

She held the book open with her right hand and used her left hand to search her jeans pockets, front and back, on the left side. Nothing. She switched hands and repeated the search on the right side. Success. She'd shoved the crumpled paper into the back-right pocket.

She left it alone for now and relaxed into the security of Travis sitting in her lap, so dependent upon her. She wasn't losing her mind, and the story was just getting interesting.

* * *

Lunch had been finished an hour ago, and still no call from Dana. The walls were closing in on her, and she had to get out. She saw his face everywhere and felt afraid. The thought persisted that the world outside this apartment was no longer safe.

But inside was just as bad. There'd been his note, his phone call, and his threatened visit.

She couldn't leave the apartment until mother and child had their usual ten second conversation on the phone. Anneke was suddenly annoyed at this habit, an unspoken rule that kept her tied to her post. If she didn't wait for the call, it was a sure thing that she'd be out of range behind a tall building blocking the signal for the mobile phone. Then there would be panic on top of the panic she already felt.

It didn't matter. Maybe they shouldn't go out today. Niels could be anywhere, watching and waiting. They would just stay inside this afternoon and make the best of it.

The phone rang. She hesitated just a moment before answering.

"Hello. Goodhue residence."

"Anneke. Sorry, I got tied up and couldn't call sooner. How's everything going?" Dana's apology sounded familiar and worn out. How could the schedules of two women be so different? But Anneke was not a woman yet. Not a woman like Dana.

Of course it was a horrible day, but she said, "Just great."

"How's my Tug?"

"He ate a good lunch. Grilled cheese. We were about to go out. Here, you want to talk to him?"

Would you like to talk to her? She heard his voice again, full of love and tenderness and the desire to make the connection.

Anneke put the boy on the phone for his few words with Mommy, and the rest of the call was soon completed with Dana's promise about the time she'd be home.

As soon as she hung up, Anneke got their coats and hustled

to get them ready for the park. They needed the fresh air. But just as they were about to walk out the door, the intercom sounded. She pressed the button. "Yes?"

"Excuse me," said the doorman. It was Endrit, or perhaps Bashkim. They sounded just alike, especially under the static of the intercom. "Goodhue apartment?" he inquired.

"Yes, this is Anneke."

"That is who I'm calling." Endrit was always so tentative about her name. As if she didn't quite exist or belong in the Goodhue apartment. "The man here, he wants Anneke Zonneveld."

"Man?" Her pulse accelerated.

Over the speaker, she heard Endrit talking to someone in the vestibule near the intercom. The doorman's voice came over again. "He says his name is Timmers."

A Dutch surname, but not one that she knew, unless…no, Niels couldn't be giving a false name. This had to be a new, unexpected visitor. In any case, she couldn't allow anyone to come up here to the apartment. "I was just coming down. I'll meet him in the lobby."

"Okay."

With beating heart, she gathered up the umbrella stroller and took Travis by the hand. The elevator came too quickly and delivered them to the lobby before she was ready. The doors opened on the waiting area for visitors, which had a leather couch, two chairs, and end tables with vases of silk flowers. A square rug on the marble floor delineated the area, color coordinated with the furniture in beige and black.

She could see him sitting in one of the chairs, a nervous bounce in his knee. A small man she didn't know, about thirty-five, with sandy hair, wearing a tweed cap and jacket. When the elevator doors opened, he looked straight up at her, his face frozen in a still frame. He jumped to his feet. Yes, his demeanor seemed to say. She was the person he wanted.

She glanced around, seeking protection. Beyond the man, in the glass-enclosed vestibule, she saw the back of Endrit's head with its thick black hair. He was perched on his little stool by the front door, looking out into the street, oblivious to anything taking place in the lobby behind him.

"Anneke Zonneveld?" said the man.

She nodded, leaned the stroller against a chair, and stooped to pick up Travis. In a natural move that was familiar to them both, the child straddled her hip and hugged her around the neck. She felt slightly ashamed, as if little Travis was her shield instead of the other way around.

The man spoke to her in Dutch, starting out with an introduction. His name was Jan Timmers, and he was hoping she could provide him with some information. Their conversation had to be held in confidence. He handed her a business card with the word "Investigations" and a phone number printed under his name. Another phone number with a New York area code was hand-written below.

"What are you investigating?" she asked.

"I'm looking for two missing people." Before she could have time to react, he removed a photograph from his inside jacket pocket and showed it to her.

If the day hadn't already required an extraordinary amount of self-control, her face or voice might have revealed her inner distress. As it was, holding Travis close, focusing on the photograph in the investigator's hand, she was able to maintain a passive expression. Or so she thought. Before seeing the photograph, she'd already guessed the identity of the people depicted. But her intuition afforded little preparation for the shock she felt, seeing those two faces together.

So, this was Kaatje.

Timmers scrutinized her countenance as she looked at the photograph. "You know these people of course?" It was not a question. He knew. He'd been given the assignment. He'd studied the picture of Niels and Kaatje, and now he was studying her.

She didn't need to confirm his knowledge. Instead, she asked, "Why do you say they're missing?"

"Renske Van Leeuwen is very interested in finding them. They left home a few days ago and haven't returned. Have you seen them here in New York?"

"No," she blurted, the literal truth. She had not seen them and didn't want to see them.

Whether she should say anything more to Mr. Timmers was another matter. There was something about him she didn't like. And if she kept her upcoming appointment with Niels, her purpose in seeing him would be to convince him to go home. She had some belief in her ability to do this. She could send him back to Renske on her own, without the help of this strange little man, and without involving anyone else, important people like her employers.

He looked at her as if he suspected a lie, but he said nothing of the sort. "All right. Keep my card and give me a call if you hear from him. I'm at the New York exchange written on the bottom. Please keep this confidential. Don't let him know I'm looking." He put the photograph away in his inside jacket pocket as she put his card in her back jeans pocket. "Cute little boy," he said, jutting his head forward into Travis's face. The child pulled inward, tightening his grip around Anneke's neck.

Mr. Timmers knew better than to attempt any further interaction with the boy. He stepped back and said, "Please call if you hear anything. I'll check back with you in a day or two." So, this was not the end of it. She'd be hearing from him again. He turned and walked through the lobby. In the vestibule, he glanced at Endrit, touched the tip of his hat, and left the building.

She froze, startled by a new thought. The doorman. She had to find out what he knew.

Anneke put Travis down and took hold of the handles of the stroller. The boy had been so well-behaved. Not a single word, just a wary look at the stranger as he clung to his nanny. "Let's go say hello to Endrit," she said, taking him by the hand and leading him to the vestibule. Travis mimicked the name with a gleeful squeal. He seemed to be just as relieved as Anneke to be rid of Mr. Timmers.

"Hello," Anneke greeted the doorman.

"Hello, Miss."

"That man who just left…"

"Yes, Miss."

"Did he ask you any questions?"

"Oh, yes. So curious, wanting to know if I see these people."

"What people?"

"A man and a little girl. He shows me a picture."

"And you told him that you saw them?"

"Saw them? Why, no Miss. I never see them."

"But, I'm sorry Endrit, I thought…"

"Bashkim, Miss."

"Oh, pardon me, Bashkim."

And then she saw that, of course this was not Endrit. The brothers looked very much alike, but the knowledge of her mistake made her aware of the noticeable differences in their appearance. Bashkim was a bit taller and thinner. No gold tooth, and as if to match this absence, his smile was merely pleasant, not brilliant.

"It's okay, Miss. My little brother."

"So, he's the younger one?"

"Yes, but people get confused."

"I almost thought you were twins."

"Yes, I'm used to it."

They wished each other a good afternoon, and he held the front door open for her.

With a quick look right and left and across the street, she directed her charge toward Central Park.

When Dana walked into Jack's courtroom at three thirty, she was met with another unexpected development in the case of *People versus Marshall*. The scales had tipped from right to left. She'd lost Eric, and Marshall had gained an extra lawyer.

Sitting at the defense table next to Seth was attorney Vesma Krumins. Dana and Vesma had a memorable history. Two and a half years ago, when they were both noticeably pregnant, they'd battled it out on a high-profile murder case against a late-term abortionist. Two counts of murder were charged, and the jury came in with a guilty verdict on one, not guilty on the other. A grisly case, emotionally draining for both women.

Walking up the aisle of the spectator section, Dana scoped out the scene. Mrs. Marshall, wearing the same suit she'd worn throughout the trial, was the lone spectator sitting on the left side, behind the defense table. Passing by, Dana made no attempt to meet her eyes. Behind the bar, Robert was at the clerk's table and a stenographer was at her post. The bench was empty, and the defendant was still in the pens, waiting to be brought in. Vesma and Seth were conferring in low tones, while Vesma jotted notes on a legal pad between them. Dana noticed, and remembered, that Vesma was left-handed.

"What's up counselors?" Dana asked as she passed through the gate.

Seth handed her a slender sheaf of stapled papers. "Consider yourself served. This will explain it." He shook his head and rolled his eyes in an understated show of disgust.

Dana took a seat at the counsel table on the right, the one closest to the jury box, and started to flip through the offering. On top was a two-page affirmation signed by Seth, seeking the court's permission to be relieved of his assignment as Tyrone Marshall's attorney. At the hearing on his post-trial motion to set aside the verdict, Marshall would be calling Seth as a witness, and it violated the professional code for Seth to represent him and testify in the same proceeding.

Underneath Seth's affirmation was a three-page sworn affidavit, signed by Marshall. He claimed that Seth had railroaded him into testifying, had told him that an alibi was the only possible defense. He claimed that he'd told Seth about a witness who had seen Brendon Hayes shoot Dwayne Little. He claimed that Seth had told him this witness was not credible and should not be called to testify. He claimed he was innocent of all charges, Seth had gotten him convicted, and now the truth had finally come to light—Brendon Hayes was the murderer.

It took Dana only two minutes to read the papers. In the background, Robert was whistling "New York, New York." She looked up, and her eyes met Robert's under his drooping, gray eyebrows. A thirty-year veteran of the criminal justice system, the court clerk had seen everything. His lips were puckered with musical notes, but his eyes gleamed in jest. He knew. He'd just received a copy for the judge, who was reading the papers in her chambers.

"Seth, you bad boy," said Dana.

"Save that for your two-year-old."

"I would, but Travis is never this bad."

"Okay you two, maybe I'd better call the judge," said Robert.

"Sure," said Seth. "Just what I need, another…" He muttered something under his breath, but Dana could guess. Another ADA, or ex-ADA, against him. It was a joke, but one that he dared not say out loud because it skirted the line too closely.

"Want to wait before we get the defendant?" asked Robert.

"Yeah. We have to see the judge first," said Seth.

Robert picked up the phone receiver on his private line to

chambers. Dana turned to Vesma, who'd been sitting quietly with an amused look on her face. "You sure you want to take on this case?" Dana asked.

"I was the logical choice. I have some free time," said Vesma. The possibility floated in Dana's mind that Seth had orchestrated his replacement. Vesma was an able competitor, having come out even against Dana in the past.

"You might have a difficult witness on this one," Dana replied.

"Brendon Hayes?" asked Vesma, tongue in cheek.

"Him too."

"Don't worry. I can handle both of them," said Vesma, giving Seth an oblique look.

"All rise," intoned Robert. Judge DuBois walked in from the side door, and the stenographer perked up. Robert called the case name and docket number.

The attorneys remained standing as the judge ascended the bench. Even before taking her seat, the judge started talking. "This is a pretty mess, isn't it? I've read the papers. You don't need to tell me a thing. Application granted. Mr. Kaplan, you're relieved of the assignment and I'm assigning Ms. Krumins as your replacement."

"Thank you, Your Honor," said Seth.

"As I understand it, Ms. Krumins, your client is now asserting three grounds for setting aside the verdict. One, the prosecution withheld exculpatory evidence. Two, if this evidence had been introduced at trial, the jury would have come in with a 'not guilty' verdict. And three, Mr. Kaplan supposedly rendered ineffective representation, violating the defendant's constitutional right to counsel. That about it?"

"Correct, Your Honor," said Vesma.

Standing within a few yards of opposing counsel, Dana was conscious that Vesma's stature was nearly equal to her own, maybe an inch shy. She glanced down briefly and noted the three-inch heels on Vesma's feet, bringing her close to Dana's height of five eight. Unlike most Legal Aid attorneys, Vesma was a stylish dresser. She wore a skirt suit of an unusual, deep charcoal color with a snug fit, suggesting more of her body than Dana's brown skirt suit suggested of her own. The suit color was accented by a peach blouse of a fine material, and the three-inch sling-backs on her feet were a darker peach, almost orange, setting off the ensemble. Her mode of dress contrasted with the tough, plain features of her face and the ash-blonde hair falling to mid-back, untrimmed, not styled.

"Where are we on this?" asked the judge. "Can we start testimony on Monday?"

"I have a writ prepared for Your Honor's signature, with an order to produce Brendon Hayes from federal custody for a court appearance on Monday." Vesma handed the paper to Robert, who delivered it to the judge on the bench. "I have to say," continued Vesma, "I'm not as experienced with the procedures in the federal corrections system, but I'm told this is the correct writ."

"Shouldn't be a problem," said the judge, looking it over. "But if there is, we can always start with the ineffective assistance of counsel claim, can't we? The defendant and Mr. Kaplan can each give their testimony of the events. Mr. Kaplan, make yourself available for testimony on Monday morning, ten sharp."

"I look forward to it." Everyone could hear the sarcasm.

"Ms. Hargrove, do you plan on presenting any witnesses?"

"Not at the moment, but I'd like to know the identity of the eyewitness mentioned in the defendant's affidavit. If the defense plans to call this mystery witness at the hearing, the People are entitled to disclosure."

Seth laughed and started to speak.

"Mr. Kaplan," said the judge, "since you're no longer of counsel here, I would ask Ms. Krumins to respond."

"Judge, we have no such witness for the hearing. No bona fide witness, that is. And if the assistant district attorney insists on pressing this issue, we ask that she recuse herself. The defense wants to call her to testify about when she became aware that Brendon Hayes was the trigger man."

Dana cut in. "Is that a new legal term? 'Bona fide witness'? Either there's a witness or there isn't a witness. The People were never aware of any eyewitness other than Lawrence Kleeger, or I would have disclosed that fact to the defense. Now that I'm hearing for the first time about a new eyewitness, I'd like to know who that is. Second, I object to the suggestion that I recuse myself. Mr. Kaplan and Your Honor are aware of the precise moment that the People learned of Mr. Hayes's guilty plea in federal court. Up until that point, everyone knew he was under indictment. A sealed indictment."

"With no disclosure between the federal prosecutor and the DA's office? I find that hard to believe—"

"Mr. Trumble can always be called as a witness to verify—"

"Counselors," interrupted the judge. "I see no need for ADA Hargrove to recuse herself. We were all here, except for you, Ms. Krumins, when Mr. Trumble delivered the news. As for the mysterious eyewitness, I assume you will be elaborating on that allegation during your examination of the defendant and Mr. Kaplan on Monday?"

"Correct, Your Honor."

"And your client will be waiving the attorney-client privilege so that Mr. Kaplan can testify freely?"

"Yes."

Dana's suspicions were confirmed. Her application for disclosure had been a test. Either the witness was a figment of Stain's imagination, or Seth had truly followed up on a lead, only to learn that the "witness" was someone under Stain's thumb, coerced into giving a story—or else.

"All right then. There's nothing further to discuss. Are we ready to bring the defendant in and give him the news?"

"By all means, Your Honor," said Vesma. "I will be making a bail application when he's here."

"All right," said the judge. Dana could guess how that would turn out.

Robert sent the word. Seth left counsel table and took up a seat in the audience, two rows away from Mrs. Marshall. No telling how the defendant's mother felt about Mr. Kaplan right now.

Two court officers escorted the defendant into the courtroom. His hands were cuffed in front of him, and his eyes went briefly to his mother. He was directed to stand on the left of his new attorney, who served as a buffer between him and the prosecutor. Vesma leaned toward him and explained a few things in a low tone.

Judge DuBois addressed the defendant directly, bringing him up to date on the status of his motion. "You realize that Mr. Kaplan is entitled to respond to your allegations at the hearing? Did Ms. Krumins explain that to you?"

"Yes," said Marshall.

"You're opening up for disclosure everything that went on between you and Mr. Kaplan, including communications that are usually protected by the attorney-client privilege. Do you understand?"

"Yes."

Oh boy, thought Dana. Another "he said/he said" to add to the one between Bounce and Stain. Where was the truth?

"In order to proceed, I will need a formal waiver of the privilege by Monday."

"I'll prepare the paperwork, Your Honor," said Vesma. "At this time, in light of this new evidence that my client did *not* shoot Dwayne Little and wasn't even at the scene of the murder —"

"We don't know that, counselor," interrupted Judge DuBois.

"Judge, another person admitted to killing the victim. My client wasn't even there."

"Hayes said nothing about his location, not that I'm aware."

"Hayes admitted to shooting the victim, and it's our position that this is strong evidence of my client's innocence. It's unconscionable to keep him incarcerated. We ask the court to release him on his own recognizance or to fix a reasonable bail pending the hearing on his post-trial motion."

"A jury has found him guilty of murder," said the judge.

"Without hearing all the evidence."

"Application denied. At this point, I'm not convinced. Remand the defendant." The judge stood quickly, still speaking, cutting off any chance for response. "See you all on Monday morning."

"All rise," said Robert too late, when the judge was nearly out the side door.

The only two people not already standing got to their feet. Turning to go, Dana observed the awkward exchange between them. Seth's eyes inadvertently moved to Mrs. Marshall's face. He gave her a tepid smile and stepped in her direction. The young mother of the teenage convict responded with a hateful gleam in her eyes and a snarl on her lips. Seth turned away and found the center aisle, making a hasty retreat.

Mrs. Marshall remained in the courtroom, hoping for a few words with her son.

7 » *BROADWAY*

SATURDAY MORNING, TRAVIS sat on his Aunt Cheryl's knee at the dining table while Dana brewed coffee in the kitchen. Evan was out on a long run, a luxury he afforded himself on weekend mornings.

Anneke might have been behind her closed bedroom door — or not. Dana couldn't be sure. The door was usually shut, and the silence behind it could mean sleep, quiet activity, or emptiness. An awareness of that tiny bedroom, and the presence or absence of its occupant, could always be felt in the small household.

But Anneke's whereabouts weren't Dana's concern. Or shouldn't be. On weekends, the au pair was off duty except by special arrangement. Today they didn't need to see her until Tug's dinnertime, when they would be getting ready for the theater.

"Bounce-a-bounce-a-bounce!" Holding a small hand in each of hers, Cheryl made these rhythmic exclamations with each bumpy jolt of her knee, sending Travis into fits of giggles. The child adored his sunny, vivacious aunt, Mommy's younger sister.

Dana walked in with two mugs of coffee and plunked them on the table. They both liked their coffee black. "Think you can let go of your nephew long enough to have some of this?"

"Absolutely. I need it. Hey, my little Tug." She bent to kiss him on the cheek, letting her full, loose, chestnut brown hair fall over his head. She sat up again and raked the tresses back with the long-nailed fingers of her right hand. "Give auntie a quick break." She twisted to the table and picked up the cup.

"Some?" He reached for it as she lifted the cup to her lips.

"No sweetie. Only for grownups." He kept reaching. "Have you been caffeinating this child, Dana?"

"You know he just wants anything you touch."

"Juice?" said Travis.

"Not juice. Look inside." Cheryl arranged him so that her left arm snugly circled his entire torso, including both of his arms, before she lowered the cup to give him a look inside. Dana marveled at this display. How did the childless Cheryl so easily and intuitively take these precautions? One quick movement from a two-year-old could launch scalding liquid over them both.

"See, Travis? Yucky black coffee."

"Yucky!" Aunt and nephew scrunched up their features, making appropriate yucky faces at each other. Cheryl took another big gulp.

Dana walked back to the kitchen and called out, "Want anything else?"

"No, I'm good."

Dana needed something. Toast would be just right before class. "I don't know how you do it. I can't exercise on a completely empty stomach." She looked at the kitchen clock. It was nine fifteen, and class started at ten thirty. Enough time to digest. She popped a slice into the toaster. While she waited in the kitchen, Cheryl kept talking to her from the other side of the wall.

"It's the after-show pasta at midnight that does it. I'm still full. Matter of fact, let's walk down today. I could use the extra air."

"Walk to the studio?"

"It's just a short walk."

"On top of everything else?" Broadway Dance Center, at Broadway and 55th Street, was more than twenty blocks from

Dana's apartment. "You're going to walk all that way, take an hour and a half jazz class, and be a Pink Lady tonight?"

"You forgot warm-up class before the show."

"And warm-up class, which is probably a lot harder than advanced beginner jazz."

Dana was grateful for the sacrifices her little sister made for their Saturdays together. As a professional dancer, Cheryl had to lower herself to the advanced beginner level for Dana's sake. A sign of true commitment to their relationship. For Dana, the class was tremendously fun, but also very challenging and a vigorous workout. Cheryl, on the other hand, effortlessly kicked and pirouetted, never breaking a sweat.

Dana found the strawberry jam in the fridge as she tried to remember the dance combination from last week, marking it out in miniature steps on the kitchen floor. Kick ball change, pas de bourrée, fan kick, inside pirouette, step touch, step touch with a cool snap of the fingers, and… Her mind went blank.

It was show jazz, Cheryl's favorite style, but not something that came easily to Dana. On weeknights after work, when she had the time to take class, she preferred to stop off at Dance Space downtown. The styles of jazz dance suited her personality better, and there was a healthy emphasis on gentle, anatomically correct warm-up of the body. Exactly what she needed after a stressful day in court.

"I love Billy's class," Cheryl said, referring to their Saturday morning teacher, a Broadway icon known for his choreography. "That's the good thing about dance. Even advanced dancers can get a lot out of a lower level class. It's a perfect start to the day. Isn't that right, Travis?" Holding Travis close, she stood up and extended his arm into ballroom position. To the child's delight, she waltzed him around the room, lowered him to the floor, and showed him the hand jive from *Grease*.

"Slap, slap," said Travis, patting his thighs.

The toast popped up, and Evan walked in the front door. "Hey all."

"You sound pumped," said Dana from the kitchen. "Ooo, sweaty! Wait, I have to butter the toast."

"Got some there for me?"

"You sound *just* like your son."

"Don't worry. I have no designs on that lonely little slice. I'll get lost." Evan walked into the dining area. "Just in time for the hand jive!" He slapped his knees, bumped his fists together and sliced his hands in midair, all in the wrong order.

Cheryl glanced up from her lesson. "Ooo sweaty is right."

"Not coming a step closer."

"Daddy!"

Evan crouched for the imminent collision with his running toddler. "See here? My son still loves me." Travis flung his arms around Evan's neck, turned his face to the side for a kiss on the cheek, and was off again, like a rocket. "Okay, even Travis has something to say. I get the hint."

Dana walked in with her toast. "Go take a shower," she ordered. "You have the time." Evan scooted off down the hall, dutifully.

"So, I guess we're not walking then?" asked Cheryl with a twitching smile on her lips.

"Nope. By the time he gets out of the shower it'll be too late. We'll have to take the subway."

The changing of the guard often required fine adjustments in plans. But in this case, Dana really didn't mind.

Completely unlike herself, Anneke slept in. On weekdays she was up by six thirty, weekends by eight, but last night, she'd been unable to sleep for many hours. After turning out the lights, she'd stared into the dark for an eternity before dropping off the end of the earth.

Her absence had been deep and black. Thankfully. Opening her eyes on the bedside alarm clock, she saw "10:46" in red digital numbers and resisted a full return to the truth.

Curled up in the covers, still as a cat, she slowly brought the room into focus. With the curtain closed on her small window, the walls were cast in gray from the diffuse light. There wasn't much to see. Her allotted space in this home was eight feet by ten.

The apartment was quiet. No voices, no footsteps, no running water. Within several seconds, she knew. She was alone.

This was her opportunity to jump in the shower. There was only one. The apartment had one full bathroom with a toilet, sink, bathtub and shower, and a separate WC, or as the Americans called it, a "powder room." Use of the shower was an awkward circumstance of their household arrangement, involving a delicate, tacit sensing of schedules. Anneke would take a shower now, unsure of what Evan and Travis were up to and when they would return. Dana was taking a dance class with Cheryl, that much she knew.

She sat upright, thinking of the shower, and thinking of the time. Six hours ahead in Holland made it almost five o'clock. Betje still lived at home while attending the university, but she was out of the house as much as she could get away with. Joining their parents for Saturday dinner was expected, and at five thirty, she would certainly be at home, helping their mother get dinner on the table.

That made time for a shower before the phone call.

Anneke was allowed, and encouraged, to make an overseas call on the weekends, using the Goodhues' landline. Letters went only so far. She'd read the six pages of Betje's latest letter over and over again, the final time right before turning out the lights last night. The blue paper was thin, the handwriting even and orderly, made with the pleasing fluidity of a fountain pen.

Betje was just fourteen months younger than Anneke, her closest friend and a true confidant. She was the only person who knew—everything. But, for more than a year now, they'd been silent on that big subject from the past. They'd buried it, and whenever the conversation threatened to turn that corner, a transparent wall conveniently rose between them. They would look at each other, knowing what was behind their blank expressions, pretending it all away. It had never happened. Betje understood Anneke's need for this.

But if Anneke reopened that tomb, her little sister would be willing to remember. Betje could keep a secret. She'd proven her trustworthiness. She would listen and understand and maybe have some valuable advice to give. At the very least, she'd offer comfort and acceptance. It was a tempting idea to call her and let everything tumble out into a receptive ear, to unload some of this weight.

That temptation had to be resisted. If everything went as planned tomorrow, if all her troubles with Niels were to disappear, talking about it today would be for naught. Betje was such a happy girl. Why should she trouble her? It would be enough simply to hear her voice, to find out what they were cooking for dinner, how she was getting on with her boyfriend, and whether she was enjoying her classes. The lucky girl was following the path that had been chosen for Anneke, before the detour.

Jealousy wasn't a factor, and Anneke didn't begrudge her little sister's success and happiness. She could have had that life. Not living it had been her own doing. She had no one to blame but herself.

After the performance and a visit with Cheryl backstage, Evan and Dana sat across from the Avendaños at a restaurant in the theater district. Evan's suggestion to go out for cocktails was considered, but they ended up agreeing that something to eat sounded a whole lot better. Late night partying, drinking and hangovers were a thing of the past for these two young couples with children.

"Your sister is absolutely magnetic on stage," Melanie said. "She's going to make it big, I can just feel it."

Noel nodded in agreement. "The whole show was excellent. The dancing, singing, and acting. I might have to go out and buy the soundtrack. Does the recording have Cheryl's voice in the chorus?"

Dana laughed. "I think so. But I didn't figure you for a fan of *Grease*, Noel. It's not exactly high culture." She imagined that Noel would much rather be reading a novel of magical realism by a South American writer than watching a Broadway musical.

As the two couples talked, the spirit of Noel's proud little Spanish bookstore in Queens, now long gone, hovered over them. Behind that lovely image lurked darker visions—the outcome of the Colombian narcotics cartel investigation of 1988. For tonight, the four friends had suppressed these troubling memories and were fully in the moment, enjoying their time together.

"Wait a minute," Evan cut in. "I'd say fifties rock and roll is the highest in American culture."

"North American," corrected Noel.

"Right you are."

"My point exactly," said Dana. "Not exactly high, but the highest we've got here in North America."

"You're so funny, baby." Evan grabbed the nape of her neck and gave it a short massage. "So funny, even on ginger ale."

"Har-dee-har." Dana grudgingly agreed. She was not known for her scintillating wit and repartee.

"Admit it, Dana," said Melanie. Her hazel eyes danced. "You love this kind of high culture. I saw you snapping your fingers and lip syncing." As her lifelong friend and college roomie, Melly knew Dana better than Evan in some ways. Six years ago, their friendship had been put to a test that few women could have endured. They made it through, scathed and battered and down for months, but they'd clambered back up to the top, coming out stronger than before. Keeping in touch required real effort now that they had children and Melanie no longer lived in Manhattan. But their friendship was sacred, and they weren't going to let it go.

"You're right. I—"

"Maybe we'll see you on stage someday?" asked Noel. "All those dance classes?" He did a little rhumba with his shoulders above the table.

My stage is the courtroom, she could have said. "I'm living the life vicariously. Cheryl's having a blast, isn't she? And you're right, Melly. I do admire those performers. All that talent…"

"Cheryl's talent," said Evan.

"Right, my little sis. She's living her dream."

"And still in high school," said Evan in a squeaky voice. They all laughed.

"She's, what, twenty-five now?" asked Melly.

"Twenty-six," said Dana. "She says all the actors in the show are in their twenties and even their thirties."

"Part of the acting challenge," said Evan. "To be forever young, a perpetual teenager."

His words delivered a small jolt. Forever young. Frozen in memory as a teenager.

Dana knew that Evan hadn't meant to evoke the specter of the cartel investigation, but she scanned the faces of those present to see if anyone else had picked up the thought. No one noticed, or maybe that was an illusion as well. She took in Noel's mysteriously sensitive features and imagined the pain buried deep inside, something he shared only with his wife in private moments.

But the past was over and done with, and Dana's friends

were now making a good life for themselves in a suburban town in New Jersey. They were safe and happy, living their dream of building a big family, making a good start with two little ones, Patricia age three, and Rafael age one. Melanie was staying home with the kids for now, and Noel was supporting them, barely, in his job as a manager of a large bookstore, an outlet in a national chain. Not his own shop, but, well, weren't they all making sacrifices for their families?

After a long, lingering midnight snack, the two couples paid the bill and emerged into the bustling nightlife on the avenue. Each person took a turn with half of the other couple for a good-bye hug and parting wishes.

When it was Dana and Melly's turn, the hug lasted a long time. Dana's cheek pressed into the silky, honey-colored hair, and she whiffed the familiar fragrance that Melly always dabbed behind her ears on special nights. Even through the layers of their autumn coats, Dana could feel the extra ten pounds on her friend, the remnant of two pregnancies, comfortably worn by the stay-at-home mom and gourmet cook. It was so clear that Melly was happy. So clear that she held no rancor against Dana for what had happened in those dark days of 1988. Oh, what a cherished friendship!

"Let's get together soon with the kids," said Dana.

"I'd love to."

"No excuses."

They exchanged kisses on cheeks and said goodbye. The Goodhues flagged down a taxi, and the Avendaños walked to the garage to pick up their car. Going their separate ways, they headed for home to babysitters and sleeping tots.

It was near one in the morning when Dana and Evan walked in the front door. They didn't expect Anneke to be awake, but they found her in the living room, pushed back in the easy chair, reading under the light of a solitary standing lamp. They made small talk before saying goodnight. Anneke stayed just where she was, looking very solidly ensconced, when they left her and walked down the dim hallway to Tug's room.

His door was halfway open, and they could see the glow of the nightlight plugged into a wall socket. The red dot of the baby monitor shone in the dark from the crib-side table. The receiver was in their bedroom, always in the "on" position at night.

They entered and stood at the crib with their hands on the top rail. They'd promised their son that, very soon, he would be getting a "big boy bed." Little Travis was wearing his footed, cowboy PJs and slept on his side, hugging his nighttime animal, a soft teddy bear. Every breath could be heard, every dream imagined.

First Dana, then Evan, gently touched his forehead before they quietly retreated to their bedroom at the end of the hallway.

Closing the door softly behind them, Evan turned to Dana, who was standing in the middle of the shadowy room, waiting for him. The curtains were open, and light from the street rose upward.

He found her and took her in his arms. Their mouths joined in a deep kiss.

When their faces parted, he whispered to her. "Dana, my love."

"Evan."

"Tug was so sweet."

"Our little baby."

"Are you…do you…?"

"Yes, darling."

He touched the bridge of her nose with one finger and drew an outline across her eyebrow and down her temple. "I was thinking," he began.

She waited.

"I was thinking that the Avendaños seem very happy."

"They are."

"With their two little ones."

"Two," she repeated, choosing the right word.

"Yes."

"I was thinking the same thing," she said. "I've been thinking about it for a while now."

"Have you?" His eyes sparked in the faint light.

Still hugging, they sidled over to the bed and dropped sideways onto it. They inched up to the middle.

He stroked her hair away from her eyes, kissed them one at a time, and whispered, "I'll be quiet."

"We'll do our best."

8 »   *KAATJE*

THE APPOINTED HOUR was soon upon her. Sunday, ten o'clock. At nine forty-five, she started out on her short walk. Her mind threatened to go blank, and the scrap of paper was jammed into her pocket for security. A few blocks away, Niels was waiting for her. Kaatje would be quietly playing, or tugging at him for attention, or crying for her mother, confused by the strange apartment in a strange city.

Sweating in the cool air, Anneke followed the concrete path toward her fate. In her mind, she'd composed sentences and had practiced them in whispers, late at night. Helped by the darkness, her imaginary scenes became real. She made practical points, and Niels responded sensibly. Her arguments were irrefutable.

An investigator came, she tells him. Renske is looking for you and Kaatje. You have to think of the little girl, what's best for her. Nothing else matters.

Yes, of course, you're right, he replies. I only wanted to see you, to introduce you to Kaatje. It's time now to take her back to her mother.

But reason and emotion were not the same. Doses of irrationality sabotaged her practice sessions. She would be talking sensibly when, suddenly, he'd snap back with harsh words, lapsing into those behaviors she loathed, almost feared. He was headstrong, righteous, and impetuous. He fiercely resisted authority.

You've met with Renske's investigator, he accuses her.

I haven't said a word, she assures him.

Then don't! I searched for you. I traveled the ocean to see you. I left everything behind for you. And you're sending me back? After I made such a sacrifice?

These were the words she imagined. The story was yet untold.

Ik hou van je nog. A ridiculous sentiment.

As she walked, she remembered.

At seventeen, Anneke was in her last year at the Amsterdam Lyceum, the most rigorous academic high school, working for her VWO diploma to qualify for university study. She lived her life in books, immersed, body and soul, in the excitement of ideas. Culture, art, literature, sociology, psychology, language, classics, history, philosophy. She wasn't attracted to practical subjects, business, politics, economics, or science. Theories of human inter-action and the evolution of society thrilled her, and she thrived on the emotional impact of art and literature.

Lofty contemplations provided an escape from the borders of tiny Holland and the limits of her home life. Her parents, espe-cially her mother, were devout Lutherans, provincial and narrow in their views, tied solidly to routine and tradition.

Anneke's circle of friends was small. She had three very close girlfriends, Tonia, Sofie, and her sister Betje. She had no boyfriend and did not long for one. The boys she knew were uninteresting, lacking in depth. Their social development had arrested at the stage of flitting eyes and inane shows of maleness—the only methods they seemed to have for communicating attraction, male to female. She would have none of it, except to engage any particularly smart boy in debate during philosophy or literature class. These were the boys with valuable minds who shared her excitement over ideas and clashed with her vigorously in theoretical arguments. These were the boys who weren't much good for anything else.

Of the popular teachers, Niels Van Leeuwen was at the top of the list. His enigmatic personality could shift abruptly from dark brooding passion to magnanimous gestures of humanity and warmth. Tall and commanding, Mijnheer Van Leeuwen directed his classes in art history and philosophy with ease and control. His gift for teaching transformed ancient events into today's explanations. He seemed to live simultaneously in the past and the present, a man who could be at home in any era. The walls of his office at the Lyceum were covered with prints of Dutch painters from the Golden Age, Rembrandt Van Rijn, Frans Hals, Jan Steen, Johannes Vermeer.

Anneke would never forget the first day of art history class. She sat in the front, on the far right. Mijnheer went around the room, engaging the students one by one. Each was asked to state his or her name and the name of his or her favorite painter, from any era or country. He snaked his way around the classroom, starting with the student in the front on the left, going down the row from the front of the room to the back, over to the back of the next row and up to the front, and so on. In this pattern, Anneke ended up being the last person to be called on.

She had plenty of time to think of her answer, the time it took to go through twenty-five or thirty people. Most of the students were nervous to be called on so unexpectedly, and those who were not culturally sophisticated invariably picked Rembrandt, the painter everyone knew.

When it was Anneke's turn, Mijnheer rested his eyes on hers. They were deep-set, a dark cobalt blue. Her planned response got tangled in a beating heart. "My name is Anneke Zonneveld," she said, stumbling a bit and clearing her throat. "My favorite painter is Johannes Vermeer." His gaze did not waiver, as if he knew of her desire to add something else that would distinguish her. She sat up taller before delivering the line she'd been planning: "And the painting I love the most by Vermeer is *Girl Reading a Letter at an Open Window*." She did, indeed, feel very passionately about her opinion, although she wasn't quite sure of the reason.

He stayed with her. At first, she was worried that he might ask her to explain. But he said only, "What an *excellent* choice, Anneke," with such genuine feeling in his voice that her whole body glowed. His eyes went briefly to the tumble of curls on her forehead before he shifted his attention to the class as a whole.

After that, everything between them was all her own doing, not his. She remained convinced of this, even later, after he hinted that there'd been others before her.

It began with her visits to his office. He told his students he was "always available." At the top of her class, Anneke had no need for after-hours help with assignments. She had another reason for visiting. In her conscious mind, she was testing a brave new idea, her ability to hold her own in a discussion of art with a scholar, a man twice or more her age. This was the justification for her actions. She did not want anyone else around during this experiment.

"Why do you suppose you're so attracted to that painting by Vermeer?" he asked the first time.

"It must be that open window. She's enclosed in the house, but the letter has the power to transport her outside. Or maybe the writer of the letter is suggesting that possibility to her."

"Sounds like you've read the commentaries on this painting."

"No, I haven't."

"So, these are your own ideas? You saw all of this in the painting, just by looking at it?"

"Yes, I did."

He considered this and seemed impressed. "You saw the symbolism. Her desire to leave the home."

"Probably because she's so engrossed in the letter. It seems clear to me that the writer is someone very important to her—"

"Who do you suppose wrote to her?" he cut in.

"Oh, I don't know, but she's standing by the open window, wanting to go to him…"

"The writer must be a man then? Perhaps a lover?"

She was aghast to hear a teacher use that word with her. She laughed in embarrassment, feeling a parallel reality growing between them, right there in his office. "I hadn't thought of it. But yes, it must be a man. She wants to go to a man."

To her continued embarrassment, he launched into an exposition of the symbolism of the fruit in the foreground, the peach split in half to reveal the pit. Finally, in a voice she would come to love and obey, he directed her to "turn sideways." She complied without thinking, and what he said next did not come as a surprise. "You know that you resemble the girl at the open window?"

She turned back to look at him head on but did not answer his question.

"This may be another reason you're drawn to the painting."

"I hadn't thought of it."

"Often, we form our opinions without thinking, don't we? Just because we know things and sense the reasons for them."

After their first conversation in his office, she became a regular visitor. Her purpose was to discuss art, she told herself. One afternoon, he revealed his private passion, the art he created in his own studio off campus. With endearing shyness, almost deferentially, he asked if she might have an interest in visiting his studio on the Keizersgracht. Without hesitation, she agreed. Immediately, they went.

The studio was an attic space with a slanted ceiling and a

window looking out over the canal. The space was filled with his original works of art, sketches and oil paintings. Originals, she believed, but oddly, they mimicked the style of the Golden Age and were reminiscent of the masters, even her beloved Vermeer. In her opinion, these works were nearly every bit as good.

A small pedestal with a chair atop was placed near the window, where the light would stream in at certain times of the day. A couch-bed was tucked into the darkest corner. She would come to know both of these areas very well.

On that first day, as she slowly shuffled through the room, stopping to gaze in awe and wonder at each creation, she felt his eyes on her profile. She did not turn to look at him. She remained in his spotlight, which he trained on her, focused and controlling. With a flush of pride, she realized her real purpose in visiting his office at the Lyceum, and her real purpose in following him to his studio on the Keizersgracht. Her cheeks burned, not from embarrassment but from the excitement of her discovery.

The coming year was laid out before her, a year in which she would refine her façade of the self-actualized woman. She would be with him completely, believing that her actions were a matter of choice. She might do anything he asked of her, as long as what he was asking could be given by a woman fitting this image, the paradigm of her ideal. She might suspect her naïveté, but she wouldn't allow that suspicion to develop into alarm or shatter the dream.

She had arrived. On the north side of 73rd Street, after crossing Columbus Avenue, she found the address a few buildings in. His apartment, the sublet, was inside a four-story, converted brownstone. Ten steps led up to the front door, with basement apartments underneath the stairway.

She took the stairs slowly, wishing that the last three years could be erased. This brownstone, this set of stairs, had not been the envisioned endpoint of her constructed universe. At the top she came to a heavy wooden door with a centered, oval panel of frosted glass. On the stone wall, to the right of the door, she found the panel of buttons with the intercom.

Ten numbers on a little rectangle. The even numbers and their buttons were on the right, and the odd numbers were on the left. The number "7" was on the top left. Perhaps she should have been sitting on the left at the front of the class. She would have been the very first student he called on, a student later forgotten.

At the very bottom were B1 and B2 for the basement apartments, 1 and 2 in the next row up, and so on to the top, apparently following the internal placement of the apartments in the building. There were two per floor.

She pressed the button for 7 and waited, feeling the moment to be longer than it truly was. No voice came over. The next thing she heard was the loud buzz of the front door, announcing the release of the lock. Was he unable to speak? She pushed the heavy door inward.

In the lobby, the stairwell confronted her. The door to apartment number 1 was on the left, and number 2 was on the right. She started up, her breathing shallow and rapid against the echo of the stairwell. One flight up to 3 and 4, the next flight to 5 and 6, the final flight to 7 and 8. A minute or more had passed since he'd buzzed her inside, and still, the apartment door on the left side of the landing remained closed.

Anger rose in her chest. It was just like him to summon her and make her do all the work. In her days at the Lyceum, an invitation to his office would be implied, but when she arrived and knocked on the door, "come in" was yelled from inside, the voice vaguely annoyed. When she entered, he would be behind his desk, reading or writing or on the phone. He wouldn't look up right away, pausing several seconds to don his ostensible availability. Then, he'd lift his cobalt eyes with a look of mild irony, letting her know of the privilege he was affording her.

Always, everything that happened afterward would be so dramatic, heady, and reckless that she would immediately forget, or at least forgive, the predictable prelude. His shift from the outside world to their intimate universe would be sudden and intense, his attention exclusive and all encompassing.

But now he surprised her. With her knuckled hand poised to knock, the door quickly dropped away, opening completely in one forceful movement. Framed by the doorjamb, the two of them appeared before her, a picture not unlike the one Mr. Timmers had shown her.

Niels was the same and not the same. His face was still handsome, narrow, and aristocratic, but the cheeks were a bit narrower and hungry looking. His fine, black hair was not as short and tight to his head as he used to wear it, but was pushed here and there, as if he'd just gotten out of bed. Above the sharp cheekbones, puffy, purplish shadows underlay his probing eyes, which now held more of the dark, brooding side of his personality. Gone also was that little spark of mirth, the irony of the artist pretending to be interested in mundane, daily existence.

He was not a free man. He had obvious responsibilities. He was holding a toddler in the crook of his left arm as his right hand clutched the doorknob.

The baby spoke first. "Anneke!" He'd instructed her well.

Anneke's right hand went instinctively to her abdomen, clutching it with remembered feelings of heaviness, emptiness, and loss. Father and daughter looked nothing alike—at least, the resemblance was not immediately apparent. Daughter was a miniature version of mother.

"*Even binnenkomen*," Niels bade her. She complied, taking the few steps needed to enter. He closed the door behind her.

White noise filled her head, shutting out all thought and any perception of her surroundings. Her eyes were on the girl, entranced by that little face, enclosed within a viewfinder like a black halo that encircled and focused her vision.

She needed to turn and run. That was it. Just turn and get out of here, if she could.

But before her frozen limbs could thaw, Kaatje leaned dangerously forward in her father's arms, reaching out over the chasm and risking a fall to the floor. Anneke couldn't hesitate. She had to take the child. Immediately.

So easily they came together. The child's slender arms circled Anneke's neck, little legs straddled her hip, and the head of soft, strawberry-blonde curls pressed into her cheek.

"I've left Renske," Niels declared in defiant Dutch. "I've left her, and I won't go back. I want you with me. You belong with me and Kaatje."

Anneke's hand went to the little girl's head, and she buried her face in the silky soft crown. Niels was speaking in his dramatic, ridiculous way. An invisible barrier rose, shielding her from his words as she held and protected her living, breathing, sweet-smelling child. She didn't understand a word he was saying.

Afterward, she sat with Marije in a coffee shop, waiting for the waitress to bring their lunch. Anneke couldn't recall what she'd ordered and didn't much care. She would simply accept whatever was placed at her spot on the table, hoping she could eat it.

Marije was describing her latest humiliation, little Elise melting down in a crowded market on Broadway. Unlike the Goodhues, Marije's employers regularly gave her shopping lists and errands, which she was expected to complete cheerfully with the eighteen-month-old in tow.

Anneke was usually sympathetic, but today, Marije's travails and complaints floated about her head like persistent, swarming gnats she wanted to bat away. Something dark and threatening and far more serious loomed. Couldn't Marije see it?

She stared blankly at Marije's face, the lips moving in the shapes of their native Dutch. The cheeks were bony and hollow, the nose sharply pointed, the forehead high and concave at the temples, the limp hair a dusty color. So grateful to have, at least, one good friend in the new world, Anneke had always been indifferent to her appearance.

Like Anneke, Marije was well educated and enjoyed discussing lofty ideas, books, and culture, along with all the reminiscences they shared about their home country. Today, however, Marije seemed unusually unattractive, hard, and uninviting. Her usefulness had already been spent—their lunch date had provided a convenient excuse to get away from Niels.

"That sounds so awful and embarrassing," Anneke said in the tone of an automaton.

"I don't know if I can stand it. I don't know if I can do this much longer."

"You think it was a mistake to come here? To be an au pair?" Anneke's questions hung in the air as the waitress arrived with their food. She was surprised to find a roast beef sandwich plopped in front of her, something she never would have ordered. Niels always liked meat on his sandwiches.

The server retreated. Marije picked up a spoon and started on her soup, head bowed over the bowl. When she looked up, tears were in her eyes. "Yes, maybe it was a mistake. I didn't know this could be so difficult."

The feebleness in Marije's voice annoyed Anneke. Children were allowed weakness, but not their caregivers. "She's a baby," Anneke said tersely. "Be patient with her."

"Sometimes I can't."

"Of course you can."

"But, this one... You don't know her."

"Babies are helpless. You have to protect them. You have to be patient. Anything you say or do could destroy her!"

Marije's eyes widened. She dropped her gaze to the soup bowl, shocked into silence.

Now fully awake and on edge, Anneke was on the verge of spilling her truly sordid tale, something with real sorrow and pain and the weight of all the misery in the world. What would Marije say then? But, no. It was hopeless. More than that, it was dangerous, because what, really, did she know about Marije, a girl she'd met four months ago?

Anneke stared at her hands, stripped a crust off the bread and nibbled at it, her stomach sour. She couldn't eat this food and was finding it difficult to sit here much longer. But neither did she want to return "home" just yet, to that happy apartment, the smart lawyers and their wonderful life with their happy, happy boy. She had another alternative, but it was something far worse. She could *not* retrace her steps to Niels. Not today. She really had nowhere else to go.

Through the awkward silence, Anneke dared to look up and see her friend anew. Marije was slumped forward, listlessly stirring her soup as beads of water dropped from her eyes into the bowl.

With sudden regret, Anneke took a deep breath and exclaimed, "I'm sorry, Marije."

The weeping girl grabbed a napkin, dabbed at her eyes and blew her nose. "It's okay."

"No, it's not. I made you cry."

"Don't worry about it."

"I don't know why I snapped like that. I guess the job is getting to me too." She attempted a smile.

Marije sniffed and returned the smile, putting the napkin to her nose again and blowing loudly, making a silly honking noise. She laughed, sending that lovely light into her eyes, her most pleasing feature. Anneke laughed along, and soon, she thought of a funny story to tell and completely switched the path of their conversation.

It was better this way, to laugh and to just forget.

9 »   *HEARING*

Monday morning at ten, all parties were assembled in court for the hearing on Tyrone Marshall's post-trial motion. Vesma Krumins sat with her client, a.k.a. Stain, at the defense table. Dana was at the prosecutor's table, and the court officers, court clerk, and stenographer were at their posts.

The single, indispensable observer from the public, Mrs. Marshall, sat quietly in the first row of the audience section, her posture erect, hands in her lap. Attentive and alert, she was ready to record every detail of the proceedings through the windows of her luminous brown eyes.

Before the judge walked in, Dana leaned to the left and asked Vesma, "We can get through this today, can't we? You have just the two witnesses?"

"I'll need an adjournment to bring Hayes in—"

"What? Why?" Dana could only guess that Vesma had botched the procedure for getting her star witness out of the federal pen for the day. Without Hayes, they had only Seth Kaplan. As far as Dana could tell, Seth was merely a diversion and a long shot for the defense.

"All rise."

Silently seething, Dana held her tongue as Judge DuBois ascended the bench. *People versus Marshall* was threatening to ruin another week, just when she was scheduled for homicide chart on

Wednesday night.

They all took their seats for the judge's opening remarks. "This is on for the defendant's motion to set aside the guilty verdict on the ground of newly discovered evidence. The defendant has the burden of proving there's new evidence he couldn't have discovered in time to introduce at trial. He also has to prove that he probably would have been acquitted if the jury had heard this evidence. Sound about right to everyone?"

Vesma stood to address the court. "Correct, Your Honor, but we also have two other grounds as well."

"Right. Ineffective assistance of counsel, and ADA Hargrove's alleged withholding of exculpatory evidence. I've read the papers, and I have your client's written waiver of the attorney-client privilege. Mr. Marshall, have you discussed this waiver with your new attorney?"

Stain had been fidgeting in his seat until now, his eyes rolling and lips moving with silent mumblings and admonitions to himself. He looked up from his hands, glanced at Vesma for her approving nod, and said, "Yeah, she told me."

"You're willing to have Mr. Kaplan disclose everything you discussed in this case? All of your trial strategies?"

"Yeah...I mean, yes, Your Honor."

"All right, the waiver is accepted. I have your witness list. Two names in addition to the defendant. Call your first witness, Ms. Krumins."

Vesma wobbled slightly, looking less than solid on her three-inch heels. She scooped up a handful of ash-blonde hair, tossed it over her shoulder, and cleared her throat. "First, Your Honor, if I might beg the court's indulgence, I have an application..."

"So soon?"

"Brendon Hayes, our main witness, has not been produced from federal custody today. I've just learned that service of the writ on Friday afternoon was insufficient notice. We can start today with Seth Kaplan's testimony, but we need an adjournment to continue the hearing."

"You'll have him tomorrow?"

"Well, no. I've been informed that the earliest is Wednesday."

Dana was livid but unable to object. It was in her interest to cooperate with the defense in getting Hayes, a.k.a. Bounce, into court. She had to explore his motive for stating that he shot Dwayne Little, and she had to flesh out his story about Stain giving him the gun. If she didn't cross-examine Hayes, she risked losing the motion. The transcript of his guilty plea in federal court was so sparse that his words could be construed to support Stain's alibi. "Tyrone Marshall gave me the gun," Bounce stated on the record. "I shot Dwayne Little." Not much more.

The judge had a suggestion. "There's another option here. I can decide the motion without getting Hayes in here to testify. The People have provided the transcript of the guilty plea and Eric Trumble's affidavit about his conversation with the federal prosecutor. These materials are enough to decide whether there's any 'newly discovered evidence' under the law."

Sensing an objection, the judge looked at Dana even before she stood up. "I take it you want to cross-examine him?"

"Yes, Your Honor. Hayes is less than clear in this transcript about what supposedly transpired."

"Just an idea. Okay. I'll grant the continuance. We'll do part two on Wednesday. Meanwhile, I take it Mr. Kaplan is here and ready to go?"

"Yes," answered Vesma.

Seth was waiting outside. Before entering the courtroom, Dana had seen him in the corridor cooling his heels, apparently displeased about this state of affairs. Judge DuBois gave a signal to a court officer, who jumped to retrieve the witness.

Seconds later, Seth strolled calmly up the aisle, avoiding any eye contact with the mother and her son. Days ago, he'd been their only hope, a potential savior. Today, he was their target for a legal malpractice lawsuit. Dana didn't envy him. The risks a prosecutor faced were bad enough. She was glad she'd never have to deal with the stress of a client turning against her.

In Dana's experience, criminal defendants rarely succeeded in their claims of ineffective assistance of trial counsel. These motions were usually dismissed outright on the papers. Affidavits of disgruntled convicts were plentiful. After the fact, when the trial strategy hadn't panned out as hoped, it was easy enough to fabricate allegations that "my lawyer told me this," and "my lawyer told me that." If there was no independent evidence to support the defendant's self-serving allegations, a hearing wasn't required. The trial judge could evaluate the competence of his attorney simply from the record of the court proceedings. No need to subject the attorney to cross-examination.

But this case was different. This case was unusual because of the tandem prosecutions, Bounce's in federal court and Stain's in New York State court. Dana believed in her eyewitness Lawrence Kleeger and the accuracy of his observations. She was convinced that Stain was the shooter, and that Bounce had lied in federal court. But the federal case had raised a little worm of doubt. If there was any chance that another witness had seen it go down a different way, any chance that Stain was wrongly convicted, then that possibility had to be explored.

After raising his right hand and swearing to tell the truth, Seth took a seat in the witness box where he'd grilled so many police officers and prosecution witnesses in the past. Dana saw no hint of discomfort but sensed a large dose of humility. Seth had cast off the usual combative posture he assumed when fighting for the underdog. His own integrity was on the line, competing with the interests of his former client. Before he could say a word, his understated confidence told Dana that Marshall's allegations were pure baloney. Whatever else she thought of Seth, he was an excellent attorney who worked within the confines of the professional code of ethics. Marshall had been lucky to draw him as his court-appointed counsel.

Vesma stood to inquire. "Mr. Kaplan, let me direct your attention to March of this year, when you were assigned to defend Tyrone Marshall against the charge of murdering Dwayne Little. Do you recall discussing the defense strategy with him?"

"Yes, I do."

"Could you please relate the substance of your conversations?"

"Yes. He said that he didn't commit the crime and he had an alibi. Just before the shooting, he'd been at the apartment of his girlfriend Midnight—that's Janlee Wilkerson. He was leaving her building when the shooting occurred, right in front of the building next door."

"Did you come to a decision how to present his alibi defense?"

"We agreed that Ms. Wilkerson should testify."

"Isn't it true that you also advised Tyrone to testify in his own behalf?"

"No, I did not."

"Didn't you insist that he take the witness stand because he had no other chance of beating the charge?"

"Absolutely not." Seth's pointed look at Tyrone arrested the fidgeting and the eye rolling, but the underlying distress remained. Their eyes locked for several seconds before Seth turned back to Vesma. "Tyrone was directing the discussion," Seth explained. "He told me he wanted to call Janlee as a witness, and he also wanted to testify. I explained the risks. He was opening himself to impeachment. The assistant district attorney would try to show that he wasn't worthy of belief by cross-examining him about his criminal record. So, I strongly advised against it, but I also explained that the ultimate decision about testifying was his to make."

So much for Marshall's allegation that Seth "railroaded" him into testifying. The answers to this line of questions had been predictable, and Vesma did not appear to be thrown by the fact that she'd just lost the first round. She went on to the next allegation in Marshall's affidavit.

"Do you recall having any discussions about another potential defense witness?"

"Yes, Tyrone said that he knew a witness who was talking up the murder, telling everyone at the projects that 'Stain didn't do it.'"

"Stain?"

"That's Tyrone's nickname. Rather unkindly, people tagged him with that name years ago because of his incurable skin condition, vitiligo. But Tyrone kept the nickname as a sort of badge of pride, in defiance of the people who made fun of him."

Well, maybe Seth hadn't completely stepped off his soapbox. "Nickname" and "badge of pride" instead of "street moniker" or "gang identity." Dana wouldn't object to any of this—Judge DuBois could easily see through it.

"What else did Tyrone tell you about this witness?"

"The witness was saying he'd been at the projects that day and he'd seen Bounce pull out a handgun and fire two shots into Dwayne Little. Bounce is the street name for Brendon Hayes. This witness claimed there was no one else at the scene, and that Stain was next door with his girlfriend Midnight at the time of the shooting."

Dana glanced to her left and saw a transformation in the defendant's expression, a smug turn of his lips. His eyes were trained on Seth, and he was no longer mumbling to himself.

"According to Tyrone, how did the witness know he was with Midnight?"

"Tyrone said the witness visited him and Janlee in her apartment that afternoon, shortly before the shooting."

"Did Tyrone give you the name of the witness?"

"Yes, he said it was Jeremy Grant." Dana perked up. A familiar name.

Vesma took a step toward the witness box. She made an impression in her navy-blue suit with a fitted skirt under the waist-length jacket, her light hair against the dark material, thick and messy and free. Red lipstick. "Did you follow up on this information?" she asked. In contrast to the striking picture she created, Vesma's tone was noncommittal, almost lackluster. She was posing the expected questions without betraying any hint of a secret revelation to come, something to prove that Seth had royally screwed up.

"Yes, I did follow up. I got Mr. Grant's phone number and address. I went to his apartment and interviewed him."

"After this interview, did you make a decision whether to call Mr. Grant as a defense witness?"

"I determined that he wasn't reliable or truthful. I advised Tyrone that Grant should not be called as a witness because it would backfire badly."

"But isn't it true that Tyrone still wanted him to testify?"

"That's correct."

"And wasn't that because Grant was claiming he'd seen the shooting and he'd seen Brendon Hayes fire the gun?"

Seth didn't answer immediately. A smile tugged at his lips. "Yes. That was the reason Tyrone gave me."

Vesma turned to the judge. "No further questions." She retreated to counsel table without glancing at her adversary.

So, *this* was the big closing point. Privately, Dana reveled in glee. Vesma's omission was obvious. She'd asked no questions about Jeremy Grant's untruthfulness. There could be only one reason—any further examination on this subject would prove that

Seth had not blundered.

If, in fact, Jeremy Grant had seen Brendon Hayes commit this shooting, Seth—or any defense attorney—would have presented this witness at trial, even if he had two heads and a criminal record a mile long. Grant was likely a person in the latter category, since his name regularly popped up on lists of suspected Bred Nation gang members. But his criminal life couldn't be the only reason that Seth found his story to be unbelievable.

With a flash of insight, Dana understood the crazy phrase Vesma had used in court last week. The mystery eyewitness was not a "bona fide witness" at all.

Dana stood up to begin cross-examination. Her intuition was so strong that she was about to do what every trial attorney called "the ultimate mistake"—to go in blind, asking questions without knowing the answers.

Six years ago, when she and Seth had been novices, naïve and idealistic on opposite sides of the spectrum, they'd questioned each other blindly, not in a courtroom, but over drinks during a happy hour that hadn't turned out so happy. A wiser person might have been prepared, but Dana had been shocked by Seth's answers. Today would be different. They were older, with years of courtroom experience under their belts. On top of that, Vesma and Seth had both, in their own ways, given Dana the nod to go ahead.

"Mr. Kaplan, Jeremy Grant told you that he'd been outside Dwayne Little's building on the afternoon of March 19 of this year, correct?"

"That would be correct."

"And I'm sure you asked him to give you the details of his observations?"

"Yes. First, he gave me an overview. After that, I slowed it down and went through the shooting, one step at a time."

"Did you ask him where he was standing at the time of the

shooting?"

"Yes. In his first narrative, he said he was directly in front of the building, near the main entrance. But when I asked him to describe where he was standing in relation to Little and Hayes, it seemed he was in the line of fire. So, I asked him to be more specific. He changed his story and said that he'd been across the street at the time of the shooting. He quickly added that he had a clear view of it."

"Were there other inconsistencies in his story?"

"Well, yes. Grant said that Hayes came out of the building behind Little and just shot him immediately without any provocation. From the description, he seemed to be saying that Hayes fired into Little's back. I questioned him further, without revealing the fact that the bullets actually entered from the front, in the abdomen. Grant changed his story again and said there might have been an argument between them right before the shooting. There were other inconsistencies involving the handling of the gun and whether Hayes was already holding it when he came out of the building, or whether he pulled it out of a jacket pocket."

"Did you ask Grant anything about his membership in the gang Bred Nation?"

"I did. He denied it."

"Do you have information from any other source that Grant was a member of Bred Nation?"

"Objection, hearsay," said Vesma.

"Withdrawn," said Dana, before the judge could rule. "Did you ask him if the defendant, Tyrone Marshall, had instructed him what to say about the shooting?"

"I did. He denied it."

Dana would bet that Grant owed Marshall for something having to do with the business of Bred Nation. That's what this was all about. But she didn't expect Seth to fork over the proof for free. It was time for her to explore the cave, to dig out the surprise tucked into the black hole. Blindly, she'd groped her way inside and was deep enough now to become accustomed to the dark.

"Mr. Kaplan, didn't these inconsistencies in Grant's story make you suspicious that he hadn't been at the scene of the shooting at all?"

"It certainly crossed my mind as I was talking with him."

"So, you investigated and found out that he *wasn't* standing in front of Little's building on March 19 like he said. Isn't that right?" There. She'd gotten it out, fingers invisibly crossed.

"Yes," was the answer, bold and beautiful.

The courtroom jelled in a wobbling second of silence. *Yes.* The ultimate fact was so easily confirmed, although she'd known it merely from intuition and logic.

"Tell us, please, where Mr. Jeremy Grant was on the afternoon of March 19."

"In this courthouse, down the hall, in Judge Archibald's courtroom. He'd been arrested in January on a drug possession charge and was at liberty after making bail. On the afternoon of March 19, his case was on the court calendar. I confirmed that he showed up by looking at the docket sheet. I also called his attorney, who said they were in a suppression hearing from about two until three thirty that afternoon."

"Objection," Vesma interjected.

"What grounds?" asked the judge.

"Hearsay. The prosecutor would like this court to believe the truth of what Grant's attorney told Mr. Kaplan."

With raised eyebrows, Judge DuBois looked at Vesma as if to say, *Are you nuts?* Out loud she said, "I'll sustain that as technically correct, but Ms. Krumins, are you going to continue to pursue this claim that Mr. Kaplan rendered ineffective assistance of counsel?"

"Well, yes, Your Honor, if I might inquire further of the

witness..."

"I haven't finished cross-examination," Dana reminded them.

"—and go *where* with this, counselor?" asked the judge, still engaging Vesma. Without waiting for an answer, she turned to Dana. "Proceed."

"Did you inform Mr. Marshall of the fact that Jeremy Grant was not at the scene of the shooting?" Dana asked.

"I did. He said it must be a mistake, because Grant told him he'd seen the shooting. Tyrone still wanted him to testify at trial."

Dana nodded and considered. The next question would be one too many. She turned to the judge. "No further questions."

"Redirect?"

Vesma declined.

"You may step down, Mr. Kaplan."

"Thank you, Judge."

Vesma turned to whisper to her client as Seth was making this parting remark to the judge, letting his gaze linger long enough to hope for, and maybe imagine, a flicker of approval in her eyes. But Judge DuBois retained her neutral expression, calmly at the helm of her courtroom.

Seth was in no hurry to leave. He crept at a snail's pace between the two counsel tables toward the audience section, tacitly keeping an ear open. Again, he avoided Mrs. Marshall's eyes.

"Is the defendant going to testify on this part of his motion?" asked the judge.

"No, Your Honor."

"Do you have an application?" The judge was drumming her fingers on the desk in an audible five-digit rhythm.

Vesma did not respond immediately, and Dana jumped into the silence. "At this time, Your Honor, unless the defense plans to withdraw the claim of ineffective assistance of counsel, I'd ask the court's leave to call Jeremy Grant's attorney as a rebuttal witness—"

"I don't think the defendant wants this court to waste the time of another attorney. In lieu of that testimony, Ms. Hargrove, you may submit an affidavit from Grant's attorney, documenting the court appearance on March 19. Meanwhile, unless an unlikely surprise crops up in that affidavit, I'm denying this part of the defendant's motion. The court finds that Mr. Kaplan rendered *excellent* assistance of counsel, far exceeding the constitutional minimum."

Both attorneys gave their thanks to the court. Dana's voice was a bit livelier.

The gavel came down hard. "I'll see everyone here Wednesday morning for part two. Ten o'clock sharp."

Dana heard a squeaking hinge and turned around to see the back of Seth's head, the unkempt hair brushing the collar of his elbow-patched jacket, before he disappeared behind the swinging door into the corridor.

10 »   PLAYMATES

IT WAS HIS RIGHT to visit the park like anyone else who wanted to come on a chilly Monday afternoon. Kaatje needed the air, and she needed to see her mother.

Wherever they went in this city, Niels always held his little girl close to his chest, her arms tightly wrapped around his neck. Kaatje felt as light as air, and he didn't mind carrying her whenever she couldn't or wouldn't walk. He hadn't brought a stroller with him from Holland, and he hadn't purchased one since arriving in New York a week ago. After all they'd been through, it was best to stay tightly connected, breathing as one. Father and daughter needed each other, and now Kaatje needed her real mother.

Kaatje was Anneke. She looked nothing like Niels even though she was his, born of his seed. He'd been convinced of their lack of resemblance from the very first day he saw her as a newborn. Based on that certainty, he'd taken a monumental risk. His perception became so engrained over time that he simply didn't understand what went wrong. What, exactly, had Renske seen—and when?

These thoughts buffeted him with every gust of wind as he kept up his brisk pace. *"Papa, niet doen!"* Kaatje's cry was squeezed from her lungs, breathless. He pulled back to look at her face. Had he done this? Had he muscled her into his chest so tightly that he made her cry? "*Sorry, schatje, het spijt me erg.*" He planted kisses on her tear-stained cheeks and on the tip of that cold little button of a nose. She didn't ask to be let down, and he wouldn't let her go. Under his kisses she started to laugh again. She wanted to stay in his arms, he was sure of it.

A memory came to him. Age two? Much too young. Maybe he was three, not much older. As a small child, he'd been just this way, wanting to be held. His mother, time and again, would sweep him up and he would hang on tight while she ruffled his hair with one hand and kissed him all over his cheeks and nose.

Later, as an older boy, he knew exactly how to get what he wanted. A certain look. Whenever he needed that closeness, he would play his eyes in the way that softened his mother. She couldn't avoid him then. She would bend over and grab him, pull him up by her side on the sofa or take him into her lap on the easy chair, holding him close. He remembered the scent of her clean, warm skin, his nose tucked down into the soft fold where her neck ended at her shoulder.

She'd been dead now these many years.

Motherless from the age of twelve, he craved female attention and had a constant string of girlfriends. As he grew older, the girls did not. There was only one woman his own age he stuck with. Renske. She was almost mannish in her maturity and the only acceptable person to marry. With her, he never used his childish manipulations. Over time, his tricks developed into the subtler techniques he used on others.

He was aware of his behaviors but detached from them, observing himself from the outside, like watching a movie. He knew about his aloofness and indifference, his oblique glances, the affected professorial sagacity, and the understated virility. These were the ways he discovered the willing objects of his need, the ones who responded. Anneke had responded. But then she surprised him, turning out to be different. He stopped thinking about anyone else. Without asking or doing anything special, she put a halt to his tramping about.

Now look at her. What had happened? How could she turn the tables on him like this?

He entered the park at West 72nd Street and headed north toward the playground at West 81st. Anneke and the little boy could be anywhere along the way. He'd followed her one day and knew her likely route.

It had been difficult with Kaatje. She'd been patient sometimes and other times not. Directly after arriving in New York, he loitered off and on across the street from the West End apartment, holding his baby in his arms, considering the best way to approach Anneke. On the afternoon of the third day, he had the good luck of catching her as she left the building with her spoiled little charge. The street was busy enough that she didn't notice him. With Kaatje tight to his chest, heart pounding, eyes streaming, he followed them from the apartment, all the way to Central Park.

That must have been the day before that runty little investigator arrived. News of the man named Timmers had sent Niels into a tailspin. Yesterday, Anneke related the details of his visit, describing his appearance from the top of his tweed cap down to the scuffed Hush Puppies he wore. It was pure chance that the private dick had failed to run into Niels on the street.

Why had Renske gone to these lengths? She knew he wouldn't like it, this attempt to track him down. Wasn't she glad to see them gone? Hadn't she tossed them out?

Kaatje was crying again, gibbering in her limited speech. "What is it, sweetheart?" he asked. "Are you cold?" He pulled the hood up over her head and tightened the drawstrings to make it snug. "We're going to see Anneke."

"Mama," the girl cried in a familiar refrain. Just when he managed to distract her, she would renew her plea for the false mother.

Oh, the lies they'd told. For two years they'd deceived little Kaatje. One day, he would straighten it out and she would know her real mama, the red-haired *Girl Reading a Letter at an Open Window*. The girl who wanted to escape but belonged at home. His sturdy, ruddy-faced Dutch girl, so like the faces in paintings by the masters he admired, the faces he tried to capture with his own amateurish attempts at oil on canvas. Anneke's face. He thought of the hours she sat on his pedestal, her profile and body gently outlined in the stream of afternoon light from the attic window. And afterward in the dusk, warm and groping and urgent…

Every new day of her young life, Kaatje looked more like her mother. Niels began to miss Anneke a little bit more each day, saw a little bit more of her in the child, and rued that much more his mistake in giving their child to Renske. He hated himself for it. With sick melancholy, he envisioned Anneke left behind at the open window, reading that letter she'd written to him before sending it off. He should have acted on that letter. Was it too late? No, it wasn't. He would make things right.

Making his way through Strawberry Fields, his eyes scanned every face along the path. The ground beneath him shifted. Maybe the earth was falling off its orbit, or maybe the trees were swaying from his unsteady gait, pitching him from side to side. Day and night, ever since leaving Renske, the world had been off kilter. Only a week ago he'd been securely planted in his mundane routine. In a day's time, everything was left behind.

On the airplane with Kaatje he acknowledged, finally, the significance of the moment. It was, he saw then, the culmination of months of planning, all of it hidden from others, from Renske, and even from himself. Deceptive inquiries to unearth Anneke's employer and address. Casual shopping for a sublet in New York. A passport for the little one. A bit of evidence negligently tucked into some papers on the desk of his home office.

He wanted Renske to find it, he saw that now. Why else had he kept that letter for two years, if not to hold onto a dream and make it happen? It became the daily reminder of his mistake. He understood the reasons he went wrong. He wasn't supposed to regard Anneke any higher than the others in his chain of young girls. He understood his motive. There was a façade to maintain and a false sense of high purpose about Renske and respectability. But he shouldn't have let Anneke go. It would have worked. She was not a girl but a young woman, more mature than any woman twice her age.

Renske's reaction to the evidence revealed something to him. He'd been sloppy. He'd left other clues. She didn't show the white face of shock. She was enraged, in a red-faced fury, but she wasn't surprised. Retreating behind a closed door, she voiced the sickening wail of her grief. The hours of her incapacitation provided the time and the cover he needed for his escape.

Slowly, he was coming around to these subtle workings. Years of planning, really, all of it just beneath the surface. Yet, he picked up and was gone in a day, making a belated effort not to sabotage a possible return. He made a call to the Lyceum, giving an excuse about a family emergency. Could a substitute be arranged? Everything was left behind, his studio, his students, his wife, his country. His wife was the only one he'd left for good.

Unmoored and despondent, he lurched through this strange metropolis, growing ever more desperate against an unexpected wall of resistance. Yesterday. Anneke was melting for Kaatje but impervious to him. Her new, surprising strength was tipping the scales. Where was the old balance between them, his natural dominance and command? How could she prefer a life of slavery to a strange family and a little boy not of her own blood? Her first and only reaction should be to run from them into the arms of her real family, her own little girl and the man who wanted them both.

He would find a way to go back. But he wouldn't go back without her. The three of them were meant to be together, or there was nothing left for him.

Kaatje was too young to know it now, but she'd thank him one day. She was a miniature Anneke, not just in her looks, but in the fiber of her being. The child was nothing like her adoptive mother. Tall and severe, Renske was more olive-skinned than a typical Netherlander, owing to that single feature inherited from her Basque grandfather. She was too mature and even-keeled to embrace passion, too independent to be of service to him, and too muscular and athletic to be truly motherly, although she'd yearned from the start of their marriage to be a mother.

"We can't see Mama right now," he told his little girl. "But we're going to find Anneke. You remember Anneke? And there's a little boy. You'll like him, wait and see. A new playmate." They were coming up to the playground now.

"Where's the boy?"

"I'm looking for him now. His name is Travis. Let me see…" And just as he said this, he spied them. What good fortune to see them at the same moment he was trying to distract Kaatje with the thought of a new playmate.

As a precaution, Niels scanned the environs quickly and completely. No tweed cap. Anneke was pushing Travis gently on a swing with a basket-type seat designed for very young children. She had not seen them. Not yet.

With Kaatje still hanging from his neck, he stepped onto the soft wood chips cushioning the play area. A climbing structure and slide over there, the swings over here. Because of the cool weather it wasn't crowded, but there were other children and nannies and mothers. No fathers. Anneke was concentrating on the boy.

Niels came close enough to call her name gently. She turned her head to look at him, caught her breath and grabbed the ropes on the next upswing, arresting its movement. With their eyes locked, Niels crouched to let Kaatje down. Looking at him, Anneke remained rigid until the child ran to her, calling her name. Her eyes dropped and her face softened, but her expression turned tragic and despairing when Kaatje grabbed her leg in a bear hug. The toddler clung tightly as Anneke slowly let go of the swing and awkwardly lifted Travis out of the seat. Holding the boy's hand, she peeled Kaatje away with her other hand, crouched down, and introduced the two children.

"Travis, say hello to my friend, Kaatje."

Travis was a few inches taller. He looked down into her eyes with a shy smile and reached out to touch a curl on her forehead, where it escaped the snug-fitting hood. "Hair!" he exclaimed, turning his head up to look at Anneke. Without prompting, he flung his arms around the little girl, and they both fell to the ground in a rolling tumble.

In a moment, the children pulled themselves up to sitting and started to giggle. "Come on," Travis said. Although Kaatje didn't speak English, the tone and gesture conveyed the message. Travis got up and started to run toward the play structure, and Kaatje followed.

Niels came up behind Anneke as she watched the children climb the stairs of the wood structure. "They're great friends already," he said.

"You shouldn't have come. I told you. Take Kaatje back to her mother."

"I *have* taken Kaatje to her mother."

"How can you do this, Niels? You've taken a child away from her mother."

"Don't you want to know her? Don't you want to be with her?"

Anneke wouldn't look at him. She was staring straight ahead at the children, her jaw set, her profile angry against the gray

November sky. "I have to watch them. They're too little. The older children will run right over them." She started toward the play structure.

Niels held back and watched her. She was so natural with the children, unlike Renske, the awkward giraffe with stilted speech and a forced laugh that children regarded suspiciously. From a child's perspective, Renske's hard core of strength from years of athletic training must have been threatening. She always seemed to be pushing herself on Kaatje, wanting too hard to be her mother and lacking any sense of ease or natural entitlement.

That's how Niels saw it. Kaatje must have sensed all along that Renske wasn't her true mother.

Dana walked in the front door and called out, "I'm home."

Travis came running. "Caught ya!" he yelled gleefully as he crashed into her legs. She dropped her briefcase and picked him up. "No, I caught *you*."

Dana couldn't know what Travis was really saying, but Anneke still felt unnerved to hear the girl's name spoken in a childish American accent.

"Caught ya, caught ya!" he said over and over again. This was precisely what Anneke had feared all afternoon. Travis was so taken by his new little friend that her name was bound to pop up at home.

"What's all this, my big boy?" Dana carried her child past the open kitchen door, craned in and greeted Evan with "Hello, darling," and a few kisses in the air, and continued into the dining area, where Anneke was setting the table for Evan's late dinner with Dana.

"We were playing that in the park," said Anneke with forced brightness, looking away. The nervous thrum in her head wouldn't stop. Out of a need to keep busy, she'd volunteered to help this evening, but the activity wasn't soothing. She was still going out of her mind. It was late, near the child's bedtime, and Evan had accepted Anneke's offer to change Travis into his PJs when the parents sat down to eat.

"Mmm, smells good. What are we having?" Dana spoke to Evan from the other side of the wall between them. Anneke glanced at Dana and they shared a smile. "Is it leftover stew, or is it leftover stew?" Dana winked at Anneke and walked into the kitchen, still holding Travis.

"You were right the first time," Evan said. "Specialty of the house."

Anneke finished setting the table and had nothing else to do. Evan wasn't ready with the dinner, but she couldn't enter the kitchen to offer help when the family of three was in there. She went to sit in the easy chair, twenty feet away, and stared at the ceiling. Every word coming from the kitchen was audible.

"Sorry I'm later than I said."

"No problem. Gave me time to get this going. Anneke said she'd change Travis while we're eating."

"Speaking of 'caught ya,' Patrick caught me on the way out the door this evening. He formally announced the job opening for deputy today, and he asked me again if I'd be throwing my hat in. What do you think?"

"Some?" Travis persisted in his demand over Dana's voice.

Anneke heard the sounds of shuffling feet and the fan in the microwave and the beep when its cycle came to an end. Evan opened the door and extracted the food.

"No, no, don't touch. Here you go, Tug." Dana must have given him a bite of something because he quieted down.

"I'd say it's up to you completely. What do *you* want?"

"I want to be in the courtroom."

"There you go, end of story."

"But it might be easier to be a supervisor. It's a better fit with family obligations and everything…no, honey. That's hot."

"Want to…down!"

"Okay, go on then. Go see Anneke." Travis ran out of the kitchen and climbed up into the easy chair, onto her lap. She heard Evan say, "We have things covered at home." Yes. Anneke was the coverage, their peace of mind.

"But the chart adds so much stress and the odd hours," said Dana.

"Book?" Travis asked Anneke.

"Okay, go get a book." He climbed back down and toddled to the playroom.

She heard the last part of Evan's response: "…the attraction for you. There's all that excitement."

"Losing sleep, going out in the cold, in the dark, hanging out with a bunch of cops and the B.A.G.?"

Anneke had heard these initials before and believed they meant "blood and guts."

"Watch it. You're making me jealous."

A smacking kiss on the cheek could be heard.

Travis was back, struggling harder than before to climb up into the chair because he was holding *The Little Engine That Could* in one hand. He made it onto her lap and settled in.

She opened the book and started reading it for the hundredth time. Because the words of the tale were so familiar, her mind had room for the incessant repetition of her conversation with Niels in the park that day.

I'm not going back without you.

What happened? You wouldn't leave her when we were together.

She guessed everything. Even before she saw the letter. But then she knew for sure.

What letter?

The letter you wrote me from the hospital.

Oh my God. Niels. You kept that letter? For two years you kept it?

It was so beautiful, Anneke. How could I ever let it go?

I told you to…

How could I ever let *you* go?

"Anneke! Say it!" Travis insisted. "'I think…'"

"'…I can.'"

Evan and Dana were walking out of the kitchen with steaming dishes in their hands. They arranged the food on the table and pulled out chairs on opposite sides. Tug suddenly lost interest in the book. He jumped from Anneke's lap and bounded off to be with his mommy and daddy.

Chattering, hugging, eating, laughing.

Their noises receded into the background. In her mind's eye, Anneke was focused on the children in the playground. Kaatje, her miniature clone, was prominently featured. The girl had Anneke's unruly mop of strawberry-blonde curls, but finer and softer. A few snarls poked out the sides of her snug hood. She had the same green eyes and chubby nose with freckles strewn across it, more densely arranged than Anneke's. She had the same pale skin that went ruddy-cheeked in the wind.

An apparition? A dream? This was the impossible child she'd tried so hard to forget, forced herself not to imagine. Here was the child, so like her, so completely of her. To think that this child could have been aborted… The thought was too horrible. Niels had suggested it, but Anneke had never considered that possibility at a time when it was still possible. During the months of her pregnancy, she'd been sick and depressed and elated all at once, dreaming the time away in her fantasy of a life with the child's father. Meanwhile, the fetus grew inside her until it was too late…

Returning to her thoughts of the playground, Anneke saw Kaatje descending the play structure and toddling away over the wood chips, oblivious to the older children running right and left around her. There was something familiar about the child's posture and the way she moved. Her feet were slightly pigeon-toed. Unlike Anneke, the child was frail and small-boned, petite for her age and noticeably smaller than Travis. She took up a stance at a short distance from the jungle gym and watched the boy as he cavorted and showed off for his new friend. She stood in a way that Anneke had seen before. Her legs were slightly apart, her lower back was gently swayed, her right arm was bent at the elbow, and the hand, in a soft fist, rested in the curve of the small of her back.

In these ways, the walk and the stance, the child was not Anneke. Whether these traits were innate, learned, or genetic, they were entirely her father's. She was the child of Niels. There was no mistaking the resemblance.

Tomorrow would come. No way to avoid it. Would she take Travis to the park again? Would she wait there, knowing that Niels and their little one would be coming to meet her?

She couldn't hide from them. She would call up the strength to convince him to leave her alone, to do the right thing, to take the child and go home. And if he continued to ignore her, she would find the strength to summon the help she needed to send them away.

11 » *DEPOSITION*

ON THE MORNING of her deposition, Tina Delmonico made her return appearance at Belknap & Rose wearing a suit of singular design. The fitted jacket displayed a pop-art web of alternating black and white saw-toothed diamond shapes, set off with large plastic, rhinestone-edged black buttons. Her earrings were exact copies of the jacket buttons. Her nails, lipstick, and heels were blood red.

She may have believed she was following instructions. On her first visit, Mineko had tactfully suggested that a conservative suit would be appropriate for the deposition, without mentioning the reason why. There was no dress code, but Evan and Mineko had privately agreed to use the occasion to judge how the author of *Dumpster Grave* would impress a jury if the case went to trial. Now it was clear that Tina Delmonico was guided by her own personal definition of the word "conservative."

The plaintiff, June Tinker, would also be deposed later in the day. Each side wanted to depose the party on the other side, and so they'd flipped a coin to settle on one location for both depositions, coming up with B & R. The timing was arranged to avoid a face-to-face meeting between plaintiff and defendant, Tinker and Delmonico.

Fifteen minutes before her deposition, Delmonico was shown into Evan's office to receive his last-minute advice. The sight of her in his open doorway was jarring. Evan uncrossed his eyes and greeted her. "How are you, Tina? Have a seat." His usual big smile froze into a taut citrus wedge as he looked into her eyes. The long spider legs of black lashes now bordered irises of a vacuous, milky gray hue. No longer were they turquoise blue. Apparently, she'd chosen a more "conservative" shade of contact lenses for the occasion.

Evan reminded his client that the plaintiff's attorneys would be questioning her first. Lead counsel Rajani Choudhary would likely do all the questioning for the plaintiff's side, but she was bringing along an associate, Douglas Teague, just as Evan had asked Mineko to assist him. After Choudhary's direct examination, Evan would have a turn.

"Answer the questions honestly and concisely. It's best not to volunteer any extra information. Everything you say can be used later in a summary judgment motion or at trial."

"Humph," Delmonico uttered disdainfully. "What'm I going to say? I never heard of Tinker before this lawsuit. Let's see if they can twist *that* into something."

"I don't think they'll 'twist' anything, but certainly they'll be looking for whatever might help them." Choudhary was a well-respected, successful attorney who'd never shown herself to be underhanded or unfair. With this in mind, Evan was less worried about his adversary than he was worried about what might slip out of his own client's mouth.

Minutes later, six people assembled in the small conference room where Delmonico had first met her attorneys a few days earlier. The group consisted of the four attorneys, the witness, and the court reporter, a young woman named Marta Juarez. Coffee and pastries had been set up on a side table, and Delmonico was invited first to indulge her requirements before she took her designated seat at the head of the conference table. Juarez sat nearby but slightly apart from the table with her steno machine at her knees. As the attorneys served themselves with coffee and made small talk, the witness sipped her sugary hot drink, light beige in color from all the cream. She left her mark behind—a noticeable red mouth print on the edge of the white cup.

The participants settled in, plaintiff's attorneys on one side of the table, defendant's attorneys on the other side. Juarez administered the oath, Delmonico swore to tell the truth, and they were underway. Everyone remained seated.

Rajani Choudhary, a woman of about fifty, conducted the direct examination in a civil, professional voice with a faint British accent, lending her an authoritative air. At her side, the clean-cut junior associate Douglas Teague remained silent, but he exuded such youthful eagerness in his posture and gestures that the main impression was one of inexperienced zeal. He was clearly a recent law school graduate, a new hire in training. He alternately clutched a manila folder and opened its cover to look at the papers inside. With wide eyes, he nodded vigorously whenever his superior leaned in for a short, whispered consultation.

By contrast, the team of Goodhue and Inoue had a stronger appearance of unity. Mineko was far more experienced than Teague and displayed a cooler exterior, which accurately reflected her interior plane of confidence. Evan was in the lead, but Mineko was sharp enough to pick up anything he might forget.

There wasn't much that Evan could do to control Choudhary's direct examination. Fewer objections were allowed at depositions than at trials. Only the most egregious errors would be cause to preclude a line of questioning until a judge could make a ruling. If Delmonico ignored Evan's advice to give terse replies and went off the grid with her answers, he would be faced with a dilemma. He could halt her testimony by objecting that it was not responsive (inviting the criticism that he was hiding damaging evidence), or he could allow Delmonico to continue unrestrained (creating a messy record to be explained later at the jury trial).

An experienced litigator, Choudhary boldly focused her dark eyes on Delmonico's faux milky grays. A pair of reading glasses rested on top of the attorney's head in the thicket of pure black, wavy hair, cut short to the nape of her neck. The contrast between the two women in voice, character, and appearance was striking.

Quickly and easily, Choudhary covered the preliminaries of Delmonico's background and her publishing credits in mass-market paperbacks before launching directly into the meat of the lawsuit.

"Ms. Delmonico, you were a member of the 1968 graduating class of Ellsworth High School, isn't that correct?"

"Yes."

"And you're aware, are you not, that my client, June Tinker, was also in the 1968 graduating class of your high school?"

Delmonico didn't answer immediately, glancing first at Mineko before turning back to her inquisitor with an upturned nose. "I've been made aware of that, yes."

"You were made aware of it? When was that?"

"Just recently, when I saw her picture in the 1968 yearbook."

"You recently looked at your copy of the yearbook?"

"No. I don't own a copy of the yearbook."

"You never owned a copy?"

"Well, I can't say that I *never* owned a copy. I believe I had the yearbook at one time but lost it somewhere along the way."

"Then please explain how you saw a copy of the yearbook recently."

"My attorneys showed it to me."

Choudhary looked at Evan and Mineko in turn. Evan only smiled and shrugged his shoulders with an expression on his face that said, *so what?*

The pause was felt, and then it was gone. Choudhary had no reason to fault them for showing the yearbook to their client. She continued. "When was that? Do you remember the date?"

"I think it was last Thursday."

"Did your attorneys open the book to a particular page or say anything as you looked at it?"

"I'm going to have to interrupt here, counselor," said Evan. "Our conversations with our client are subject to attorney-client privilege."

"I'd say this doesn't fall under the privilege," said Choudhary. "Anything you said or did at the time you showed her the yearbook could have influenced her memory or her identification of the photograph."

Evan smiled. "An interesting theory. Sounds like we're in criminal court." He remembered his days as a prosecutor, arguing to the judge that the police had done nothing suggestive to influence a witness's identification of a particular mug shot in a photo array. "But this isn't an eyewitness identification procedure subject to constitutional rights," he said to his adversary.

"All right, Mr. Goodhue. For now, I'll withdraw the question and move on to another topic. But I reserve the right to ask the judge for a ruling."

During this conversation, Tina Delmonico's eyes ping-ponged between the two attorneys, her face a picture of befuddlement. Choudhary turned to the witness now, but before she could ask the next question, Delmonico blurted out, "They didn't say a thing to me. I just leafed through the book."

The lead attorneys briefly exchanged resigned looks and said nothing further on the subject. Evan briefly instructed his client, "Please wait for the next question, Ms. Delmonico."

"Okay, all right." She took the last sip of her coffee, which was surely cold by now, and awkwardly lowered the cup to its saucer with a clatter. "Okay."

"When you looked at the yearbook," continued Choudhary, "did you see the senior portrait of June Tinker?"

"Yes, I did."

"When you saw the photograph, as you said, you were 'made aware' that June Tinker was in your graduating class, is that correct?"

"Right, yes, I saw she was there, of course."

"And, is it your testimony that you did *not* remember June Tinker before you saw that photograph in the yearbook last Thursday?"

Delmonico squirmed slightly in her chair. The pinch between her brows grew more pinched, and her sharp nose pointed ever more upward. "Last Thursday, when I saw that picture I remembered her. Yes, I did remember her then."

The inquisitor sat up straighter and leaned into the table, toward the witness. "Please listen carefully to the question, Ms. Delmonico. Is it your testimony that you *did not remember* June Tinker *before* you saw that photograph last Thursday?"

The witness gave a wry smile. Barely visible under the opalescent gray lenses, a twinkle in her eyes conveyed the haughty belief that she was about to gain the upper hand. "How can I say one way or another? It was a big high school. I saw *hundreds* of people walking through the hallways *every* day. This Tinker person was probably one of them…"

The floodgates had opened. Evan debated whether to interrupt.

"…and you're asking do I remember her? Do *you* remember someone you've seen in a hallway, maybe a hundred times? Twenty-five years ago? Someone you've *never* spoken to *in your life*?"

"Objection," interjected Evan. "This is nonresponsive. Ms. Delmonico please—"

"Do you know how many people were in *my* class *alone*?"

"—just answer the question."

She looked at Evan as if he wanted her to go on. "There were *six hundred and twenty-nine* people in my graduating class. And I'm supposed to remember *one* of them?" At last, she stopped for air.

"So, there were six hundred and twenty-nine?" asked Choudhary, her eyebrows raised.

"Yes. You can check."

"I will. Indeed, I will," said Choudhary, nodding her head thoughtfully.

Delmonico reached for her cup again but saw that it was empty.

Mineko jumped up. "Let me get you some more coffee. Or maybe you'd like some water?" She walked to the witness and picked up the cup. Delmonico fell into a slump, looking deflated.

"Let's take five minutes," said Evan.

"Certainly. By all means," agreed opposing counsel. Choudhary was a civil, accommodating person, who discerned no benefit in fighting her adversary's need to remind his client of the rules and to give her a little time to decompress.

To Evan, however, this accommodation only enhanced his suspicion that something big was coming. Every instinct screamed it. Rajani Choudhary was leading up to a significant, possibly devastating revelation.

Evan asked his client to stand up and stretch a bit and take a brief walk out of the conference room. Meanwhile, Mineko poured a glass of water from a pitcher at the side table and followed them out into the hallway. They closed the door behind them.

"Here," said Mineko, handing the glass.

Delmonico waved it away, shaking her head. She huffed and paced a few feet away and back again.

"Take it," Mineko urged. "Take a deep breath and drink the water. It'll help."

"Oh…all right." Delmonico took the glass and swiftly drank

it halfway down.

"How're you doing, Tina?" asked Evan.

"This is ridiculous. That woman has it in for me."

"Just try to keep your cool and we'll get through it."

"But she thinks I *know* this person. She thinks I wrote a *book* about this person. It's insulting."

"Well," Evan began. He hesitated, remembering their fruitless conversation of last week. What the hell? He'd take the chance. "Is it possible you're beginning to remember something about June Tinker?"

"Bah," spat the author. She started to pace again, walking in a little circle and coming back to stand in front of her attorneys. "And what if I *did* remember something? That doesn't mean I wrote a book about her." She crossed her arms, turned her head, and looked into the distance as her foot tapped furiously on the carpet, allowing Evan and Mineko the chance to exchange a look in the air alongside. Their suspicion was now palpable. They were going to get cooked when they walked back inside and the deposition resumed.

"What did you remember?" asked Mineko gently.

Delmonico shook her head. "Nothing. It's nothing at all. A girl with Twiggy lashes. So, what if I remember her, right? That doesn't prove a thing. Let's just go back in and get it over with."

Evan considered whether to press further, but this was not the time to extract the details that Tina should have disclosed well in advance of the deposition, in the privacy of his office. They were in the middle of it now. Maybe this was the best way to get it out, to see where they stood.

"Okay. Just keep the answers short. And please remain quiet when Ms. Choudhary and I are discussing legal points. When we interrupt you, wait for the next question. Let's go."

Back in the conference room, the young Mr. Teague was looking very pleased with himself, likely because he'd just had a private strategy session with his mentor.

"Are you ready to continue?" asked Choudhary.

"Yes," said the witness, taking her seat.

"I remind you that you're still under oath."

"Of course."

"When we left off, I had just asked you if you remembered my client June Tinker before seeing her picture in the yearbook last Thursday. Would you like to add anything to your answer?"

"Yes. I was trying to say that she looked familiar, like someone I'd seen before. That's about all I remember."

"Were you aware that she dropped out of high school in May of her senior year?"

"May? I don't know anything about that."

"Were you aware that she dropped out before graduation?"

"I don't know. Maybe I didn't see her in the hallway any-more. I never spoke to this girl."

"What, if anything, do you recall about the circumstances of her leaving high school in her senior year?"

"What do you mean, 'circumstances'?"

"The reasons she left. Do you recall the reasons?"

"Objection."

"All right, I'll rephrase," said Choudhary, understanding why Evan was objecting. "Did you learn anything about the reasons she left?"

"There were rumors." Delmonico turned to look at Mineko, the person she should have confided in before all of this came down on her. "You know. Rumors are always circulating in high school."

Rumors were not evidence, Evan knew, but he had no basis to object. Anything within the author's knowledge, rumor or not, was relevant to whether her fictional character, April Taylor, was really meant to depict June Tinker, and whether the author really meant to defame her.

"What were the rumors you heard?" asked Choudhary.

"I think you should know. You alleged it in your complaint."

"What were the rumors, Ms. Delmonico? The rumors *you* heard in the spring of 1968?"

"Humph," the witness uttered, playing as if the answer was obvious. "That she was pregnant, of course."

"Of course. What other rumors did you hear about her pregnancy?"

Delmonico averted her eyes. "Just that she was pregnant. That's all. Nothing else."

"Do you remember a boy at your high school named Michael, or Mike, Ferrone?"

Delmonico wiggled and blanched. "Ferrone?"

"Yes. Do you remember him?"

"Sure, everybody knew him."

"Michael Ferrone?"

"Yes, Mike...Michael Ferrone."

"And what do you remember about the relationship, if any, between June Tinker and Mike Ferrone?"

The witness emitted a choked gasp, as if Choudhary's hands were squeezing her neck.

"Ms. Delmonico?"

"What do you mean, 'if any'?"

"Did you ever observe June Tinker in the company of Mike Ferrone?"

"I don't recall."

"In 1968, did you hear any rumors about June Tinker and Mike Ferrone?"

"No."

"Well, let me ask if you remember this." Choudhary extended her hand toward her associate, who'd already extracted from his special manila folder an aging piece of three-hole punched, wide-ruled paper. With a barely contained bubble of energy, he handed it to his boss. Choudhary pulled her half-frame glasses down from their perch atop her head and positioned them on the bridge of her nose. She held the wrinkled, fold-marked paper in both hands, peered down at it, and began reading. "June…"

"Objection," said Evan. "We're entitled to see what you're reading from."

Choudhary looked up from the paper and met his eyes over the top rim of her glasses. "Well, no, I don't agree. I'm not introducing this into evidence but merely asking the witness if she remembers something…"

"Anyone could have written anything on that piece of paper, and you've made no showing of relevance."

"You know as well as I that a witness's recollection can be refreshed with anything at all. Even a ham sandwich."

"If that's what you're doing, refreshing recollection, then the correct procedure is to show it to the witness…"

"I have the Civil Procedure Law here if you want to see the rules on this," added Mineko, entering the fray with a black book in hand.

"I haven't even *gotten* to the point of refreshing recollection. The witness hasn't said whether she remembers what I'm asking. We were interrupted." Choudhary was sitting tall when she said this, but then her shoulders curled slightly inward and she sighed, as if surrendering. To Evan's eye, it appeared that she'd just realized her mistake. She'd confused the rules. "Okay," she said. "I'm not fighting this. Doug, hand over the copies." The assistant complied with a flourish. Two photocopies, one to each opposing counsel.

Evan took one glance at the paper, felt his gut wrench, and fought for a poker face. Mineko did the same. Meanwhile, the witness had been ping-ponging and fidgeting. "One for me too?" she asked.

"Just listen to the question, Ms. Delmonico," Choudhary

admonished.

"But this is ridiculous. You can't just gang up on me—"

"Please. Am I going to have to…"

"—and ask about some mystery thing."

"…move for an order of contempt?"

"But you're making something up and I can't even see it!"

Evan reached over the table and grasped Tina's forearm. "You'll have to answer the question," he said in a low, calm voice.

With the paper in hand, Choudhary stood up. Delmonico quieted down. Her skin was pasty white, with two red clown circles high up in the cheeks.

"Ms. Delmonico, do you recognize these words? 'June, I told you before, bitch, stay away from Mike. He's mine…'"

"What kind of scandalous trash…," muttered the witness under her breath.

"'…and he's going to dump you anyway when he sees what a tramp and a slut you are, Twiggy eyes.' Do you remember these words?"

Delmonico's eyes were wide and impossibly dark under her fake contact lenses.

Evan looked again at his copy of the letter, its salutation, "June," the signature, "Tina," the lines of the school binder paper faintly photocopied, the handwriting juvenile and feminine. Each "i" was dotted with a small, neat circle.

Things were working out just as he'd feared. They were getting cooked. To well-done.

12 »   *LETTER*

THE LETTER HAD been saved for a long time, and now, it was almost in tatters. She was straightening up their home office when she found it sticking out of some papers on the desk. It caught her eye, something that didn't match the crisp white paper of new bills and statements. An old letter, the paper worn, the ink faded. He'd left it there for her to find. Carelessly or deliberately? It was all the same. Why else would it be there, if not for her to find it?

Two years ago, in the eleventh year of their marriage, Kaatje came into their lives. Renske had been hoping for a child for such a long time. She was barren, or possibly Niels was to blame. They didn't know. He wasn't hostile to the idea of children but indifferent and evasive whenever the subject came up. Every time she suggested fertility testing, he dodged the question.

"Afraid that it's you?" she teased him. "A threat to your manhood?"

He looked at her with mock sympathy and said with a straight face, "Not worried, *liefje*. You forget. I have ten bastards scattered across Europe."

"If there were ten bastards, there'd be ten women knocking at the door."

He shook his head. "Wrong again, my dear. I'm just very

good at covering my tracks."

There was a kernel of truth in this. Before they married, he'd been with many women. He didn't hide it and was almost proud of his exploits. As much as she disliked his self-satisfied air, she found that his teasing about other women could be stirring. It often led to passionate, renewed efforts at conception.

The efforts were fine enough for a while, but the failure was not. Renske was thirty-eight, and time was marching on. They still had a window of opportunity, but they'd begun to tire of their failure, and perhaps, they'd begun to tire of each other. Niels more than Renske.

He was a busy man, constantly distracted, leaving home at dawn and returning at dusk or later, no complaints about their quiet, echoing household with its finite life forms, a wife and some houseplants. A glass of wine and dinner at eight o'clock, followed by an hour of reading before bed, put the finishing touches on the main part of his day, the important part already spent away from her.

She didn't push him very hard to undergo fertility testing because she suspected that she was the one. Her annual checkups at the gynecologist were normal, but there was a time during her teen years and into her mid-twenties, at the height of her training, when she'd lost her period. Long distance speed skating had been her passion, and she'd been good at it—just not quite good enough to make international standing. The Olympics was beyond her grasp by no more than a tick of a second. Back then, she'd trained six to eight hours a day. Although it was more than a decade ago, she still dreamed of the race, the homestretch, the ice just inches from her left thigh as she took the last bend tilted low to the course, slicing right, left, right with her blades.

She'd given it up for Niels and a family. This was her ostensible explanation. But if she'd been true to herself, she would have admitted the real reason. She gave it up out of heartbreak. The single second she needed to shave from her best time became two seconds and then three. As the effort increased, the goal drifted farther away. The body matured, time irreversible. The human body was capable of only so much.

The new heartbreak about childlessness was reminiscent of the old: the repeated efforts, the maddening elusiveness of the goal, and the creeping certainty of physical impossibility.

In the midst of her misery, on the eve of their eleventh wedding anniversary, Renske considered ending their marriage and moving on…to what? Another unattainable goal? For more than ten years now she'd worked as a trainer on the ice. Even in her profession, she'd only succeeded in coaching second-rate speed skaters, teenagers she grew fond of, none of them Olympic hopefuls. It was enjoyable work, but not enough to fulfill her. Why wasn't she fulfilled? A child, she thought. If only she had a child. There was still a chance, and she clung to that. Niels remained indifferent to the issue. "We're trying, right? Whatever you want."

Renske and Niels were at opposite poles. The differences between them accounted for their initial attraction, love, and marriage. She was athletic, disciplined, practical, and some said, severe. Niels was artistic, a dreamer, an intellectual with a passionate side. He had a free, independent spirit and fiercely spurned the hand of authority and any restraint placed on his freedom. Their differences were causing them to drift apart.

In the year before Kaatje came into their lives, Niels became more distant than usual, absent and uncommunicative. She suspected he was seeing someone, but by the time she was angry enough to care, the behavior stopped. He started coming home earlier every night, they had dinner at seven, and their love-making resumed.

And then, he did something to prove the depth of his love and commitment to her. He surprised her with a question.

"Renske, what would you say to the idea of adopting a baby?"

They'd never spoken of adoption. She'd never even thought to raise the subject. The minute he mentioned it, she discovered why. Her immediate reaction was a visceral aversion. She stepped outside herself and discovered, with surprise, that she'd never been attracted to babies in a general way. She was not one to go up to a woman on the street and admire her baby, to coo at it, ask to hold it, or tickle it under the chin. She had no desire to adopt and raise the baby of a stranger.

As if he understood her thoughts, he explained that he had a particular baby in mind, and that the mother of this baby was not a stranger but a student of his, and a very special one at that. "This girl is exceptionally gifted, a person of very good upbringing, and she's in a bad situation. She had doubts about abortion, waited too long, and now she's about to have a child she can't care for. She's looking for adoptive parents."

"What about the boy?"

"The boy?"

"The boy she's with. The father of the child. What does he have to say?"

"As far as I know, the boy isn't really in the picture. I have the impression it was a very brief affair. I don't know the details. Maybe she hasn't told him, or maybe he just wants to cut and run. The girl—her name is Anneke Zonneveld—has left school and gone out of town to have the baby."

Renske was stupefied. Something didn't seem quite right. "How do you know all of this?"

"Well, when Anneke dropped out of school, naturally I was concerned, and I called the parents. We were speaking about the pregnancy and—"

"You raised this subject with strangers? Over the phone?"

"Well, actually, I hinted that I knew why she dropped out. Anneke confided in me before she left school. She knocked on my door during office hours one day, and before she could say a word, immediately she burst into tears. I think she needed to tell someone, and I'm…well, I was one of her favorite teachers, you could tell. She was so enthusiastic when she participated in class. I'd been noticing some changes in her behavior and in her body, although you couldn't say, really that she was, you know…" He gestured.

"Showing?"

"Not showing exactly but putting on some weight. When she stopped crying long enough to speak, she said, 'Mr. Van Leeuwen, I love your class so much, but I have to drop out of school. I won't be able to graduate. I'm pregnant.'"

"Just like that?"

"Just like that. The girl was very upset. She'd told her parents but no one else. She swore me to secrecy because she wasn't going to tell anyone at school why she was leaving. The next week she dropped out, and that's when I called the parents, to make sure that Anneke would come back and finish her degree. She's very intelligent, a bright scholar. They said she might return to the Lyceum, and when I asked when she might, they let it slip that the plan was to find adoptive parents. The two of them—Anneke's parents—have no interest in taking the baby themselves. It's just too much for them."

Renske was not looking at Niels but felt the heat of his gaze on her profile and the animation in his voice. He was testing her, fishing for a response. She said nothing. He continued.

"As I was speaking to Mr. and Mrs. Zonneveld, the connection jumped into my head. It was irresistible. Here we are, struggling to have a child, and there she is, a young girl caught in a predicament. And what better opportunity could this be? A perfect child. The baby of healthy young people, and the mother so very intelligent and good-natured and lovely."

Renske remained speechless. He was completely serious.

This idea, which was already in the planning stages for him, was an utter shock to her. She hardly knew how to react. But she'd been taken by the dream in his voice, and it was smoothing down the sharp edge of her aversion.

Finally, he asked her directly. "Oh, Renske, why not? Let's do it."

She dared to look at him then. His normally dark, deep, and brooding eyes beamed with a religious light. The idea of this child was transforming him. Could it be that Niels, in his own way, had been longing to fill their empty arms?

"I...my goodness, this is so unexpected. I'll have to think about it. I just don't know yet."

She couldn't hide her hesitation, yet she didn't give him a flat "no." In the days that followed, he worked on her, building on her hopes and dreams. Sooner than she would have thought, the day arrived when, click, the plan was locked into place in her mind as well as his, and there was no turning back.

A few months later, Renske held a newborn in her arms.

She never met the birth mother, the girl named Anneke. She didn't even ask to see a picture, although she chanced to see a photograph inside a file folder when the social worker opened it. A flash of strawberry-blonde curls.

Renske was afraid to put a countenance on the person who would be giving up something so precious. There was no need for a face-to-face meeting, and actually, it was not encouraged. The adoption agency acted as intermediary between the mother and the prospective parents.

But because Renske had a practical side, she was compelled to investigate a few things before the baby was born and the process of adoption finalized. She insisted on learning the mother's social and medical history. A good family and spotless health were reported by the agency. Renske also insisted on learning the father's social and medical history. On that account, there was a bit of trouble. Anneke refused to name the father.

Renske asked Niels to intervene, to find out whatever he could. She believed her husband could charm this information out of the teen mother because of his status as a favorite teacher. Hadn't she gone to his office and blurted out the news? She'd already shown a willingness to confide in him.

Renske became obsessed with her mission. She sensed that her driving need to know every detail about the father was inappropriate, but she ignored that little voice. On this issue, she was unable to step outside of herself. If she had, she might have been puzzled to discover the extent of her zeal, especially since the expectant teen mother seemed to regard the mystery boy as no more than a mere sperm donor.

Renske urged Niels to find out where Anneke was staying and arrange a meeting. He was to lend a compassionate ear and get her to talk, to reveal the identity of the father. Renske suggested the script for this encounter. Niels would assure complete confidentiality and promise to tell no one but his wife. If he wanted, if it advanced his goals, he could blame everything on the nervous adoptive mother-to-be. He could say that Renske suffered from outlandish fears about the boy's gene pool, that he might be psychotic or a hoodlum, a drug addict or a close blood relative of the birth mother.

These were exaggerations of course, but still, Renske needed to know.

"Success," he told Renske when he returned. "She was very emotional, and eventually she broke down again. It was a guessing game at first. She really didn't want to say, but then she gave me the name. She hasn't told anyone about him, not even her family. He's a student at the Lyceum."

"Well, the other students are bound to have seen them

together at school. They'll speculate."

"Sure, she's worried about rumors, but she made up a credible reason for leaving school. She's gone to study abroad. Anyway, even if people guess at the real reason she left, no one could know he's the father. She's told no one, not even the boy."

"So, you're saying she had more than one boyfriend?"

"No, I'm not saying that."

"But if there's only *one* boy, and rumors are circulating about the reason she left, he'll know he's the one. What's his name?"

"Joost Eerland. I know him. He's in my art history class, the same one Anneke was taking. It makes complete sense to me now."

"In the same class? Then they could have been seeing each other all year."

"She said it lasted only a month or so. Very brief. They were never really a 'couple,' and then they broke it off completely. I remember seeing them talking outside the classroom, and a week later, it was the cold shoulder. We don't have to worry. She refuses to have anything to do with him. Even if he suspects what's going on, she says he isn't the kind of boy to make a claim."

"He could, you know. He has the legal right, doesn't he? He could have a paternity test."

"That's not going to happen. He's out of the picture. Look. I'll try to find out more about him. He's a good kid, but immature. Not the type to be all responsible at age seventeen."

There were still a few weeks to go in the school year, and Joost was still coming to art history class. Niels "investigated" and came home with more information about the boy, his personality, his temperament, his grades, his family, and school health records. It was all just as Anneke had said. Joost was a good boy, an average student, handsome, healthy, strong, and popular, more interested in living his life as it was, without the premature imposition of paternal responsibility.

Renske asked to see his photograph. Niels produced it, a school photo from the previous year. A sexually attractive boy with a narrow, aristocratic face, fine, black hair in a short cut, and dark, deep-set, probing eyes.

She stared at the boy's photograph for a very long time. She'd asked to see it, and she took full advantage of the opportunity, imagining what the boy must be like in real life.

But she didn't ask to see Anneke's photograph. She didn't imagine what Anneke must be like in real life and didn't think to ask herself why. Slowly, with the passage of time, she was awakened to her doubt. The reason for her behavior gradually took shape, coming into clear relief.

Niels was often critical of her, increasingly so as Kaatje grew into a toddler. His criticisms veered irrationally left and right. He would say that Renske was not gentle enough, and the next day, she was too forgiving. Or, he would say she was not playful enough, and much too serious. Why would a child prefer to practice numbers and letters when she could be playing with her dolls, lost in a world of make believe? Why not give her ice cream every once in a while instead of sliced apples?

One thing was clear to Niels, a fact he could never criticize. Renske loved her little girl. Loved, loved, loved her. Kaatje was a unique individual, a rosy-cheeked giggler with dancing green eyes and unruly strawberry-blonde curls. That she inherited her features and temperament from strangers was no longer of concern to Renske.

But, about a year into parenthood, the momentary glimpses began, those sudden little impacts of recognition. She would be playing with her baby, this unique being, when she'd look into Kaatje's eyes and find, staring back at her, the hidden intensity of her husband's deep-set, cobalt irises. The moment would ambush her with a shock like impending death, draining the blood from her face and rushing it to the rescue of vital organs at her core, her heart. A snap, a shake, a laugh, or a blink—and the feeling would pass. With a surge of renewed, pumping life, she would explain it all away as a fantasy arising from maternal instinct. Her husband, not Joost Eerland, was the day-to-day father, the one who'd taken responsibility for the child. As her protector and provider, he was the person whose light *should* be shining from their daughter's eyes.

When these moments occurred, she would remember the photograph. Didn't the boy-father bear a slight resemblance to Niels?

At twenty months, as the child's motor skills developed, Renske noticed a stunning similarity that delivered the biggest jolt yet. Kaatje's walk was slightly pigeon-toed, and when she halted on a spot for an appreciable time, she would stand with her feet slightly apart, a gently swayed back, the little arm bent at the elbow and a balled-up fist placed in the small of her back. Could a toddler learn these movements and postures from watching her father? Or was she born with her body shaped in such a way that...

Renske's examination of her child intensified. She uncovered one doubtful trait after another. Each discovery brought up that funny feeling in the pit of her stomach, just like the day when Niels first told her of his conversation with Anneke's parents and she asked him, "How do you know all of this?"

The truth exploded on the day she found the letter. How convenient that a corner was sticking out from the middle of a stack of bills on the desk. How convenient that he'd left it there— and how convenient that she'd had her eyes open, ready to pick up the clue. Truth be told, perhaps she'd been looking more closely for confirmation during these last few months, when her dread-filled curiosity had been piqued by the living evidence of his sin, incarnate before her.

Underneath the letter was the original envelope, no return address, sent to Niels at the Lyceum, marked "PERSONAL AND CONFIDENTIAL." Gingerly, she laid the envelope on the desk and held the single, thin sheet in her hand. Here is what she read:

"Dear Niels,

"Yesterday, when you broke your promise to me, you backed me into a corner. How could I possibly say 'no' to your new plan? I'm six months pregnant and have to think of the helpless baby.

"You still have a chance to reconsider, even though, by now, you've told your wife this story about helping a poor unwed teen mother. When you broke your promise to me, you said you had to honor your commitment to your wife of eleven years. But you forget that you stepped away from that commitment the first time we were together.

"The worst part is that I know you're making a mistake. Every time you speak of her, I hear dissatisfaction in your voice. It's clear that you two are not compatible. You say that the baby will make her happy and will turn you into a normal family. Maybe I'm only seventeen (almost eighteen), but even I can see that your justification is going to fall apart.

"Where is the real family here? Think about what we have together, especially now that we've created a baby. We are the family, or should be a family.

"Since the first day we met, you told me over and over again how mature I am. Yesterday, all of a sudden, I'm too young and shouldn't give up my life for this. I shouldn't give up my studies and my ambitions. But I want you to remember what you said to me in the studio on the afternoon before I left. Remember those words of love and ask yourself if you're doing the right thing, giving our baby to her."

As Renske absorbed this message, a quake rumbled deep inside her womb and worked its way upward, into her lungs and heart and through her extremities. She began to shudder. The involuntary movements intensified and became convulsive. Moisture streamed from her eyes and nose, hiccups choked her throat. *Ik hou zo verschrikkelijk veel van je* were the final words written on the page. I love you so terribly much.

It was three thirty, and Kaatje was in her bedroom taking her afternoon nap. On Renske's second reading of the letter, Niels walked in the front door of their house and made his way to the office. His classes at the Lyceum were finished for the day, but he rarely came home this early.

He knew she would find it. He wanted her to find it.

The room was spinning, framed in a black, tar-like oval, when his face appeared in the center of her constricted vision. He stood in the doorway to the office, looking at her as she held the limp piece of paper.

For several seconds they regarded each other in silence. Finally, he asked, "So…you see everything now?"

There was no air to breath. The skin on her face and chest burned. She couldn't speak.

"Well then," he said calmly, "I'm leaving. I'm going to her." He retreated and closed the office door behind him, shutting her in. She dropped to her knees. Air rushed into her lungs, fuel for sound. She began to howl and ripped the letter to pieces, destroying it. "Just go then. Get out. Get out!"

Rage and despair shook her for minutes or hours. She was unaware of the passage of time. Finally spent, she retreated inward and collapsed onto the floor in a fetal position, the letter in shreds around her. The room had grown dark. Like a gentle snowfall, the cold mantle of an unbearable silence descended.

Kaatje.

Renske got to her feet, opened the door, and staggered down the hall to the child's bedroom. The sleeping tot was gone.

13 »   *TRUTH*

WEDNESDAY MORNING EARLY, on her way to work, Dana
should have been mentally preparing for the hearing in *People
versus Marshall*, but her mind was on Evan's case. Last night over
dinner, Tina Delmonico dominated their conversation while, on
the periphery, Anneke skulked around the apartment in a
strangely sour mood.

Squeezed on a bench in a crowded subway car, Dana felt the
press of hips, thighs and shoulders on both sides. Her thoughts
centered on Evan and the law of defamation. The express train
hurtled past one local stop after another, the windows momentarily filling with bright station light before shooting into the black
tunnel. Against the dark windowpanes appeared the fleeting
images of her au pair's distressed features and Evan's sunny
smile.

Evan didn't like it when people lied to him, and he didn't like
to lose. Who did? But his upbeat, optimistic personality kept a
smile on his face. For him, the stress of dealing with dishonesty
and the fear of losing a case usually translated into an excited,
nonstop loquaciousness, a need to discuss everything with Dana.
She loved this about him and about their relationship. Their
favorite topic was the law, and they shared a profound mutual
respect. Dana was the best lawyer Evan knew, and Evan was the
best lawyer Dana knew.

Last night, as a result of Evan's need to talk, Dana's murder case had taken the back seat. She didn't mind. In recent days, they'd discussed *People versus Marshall* many times. Her strategy and arguments were solidified, ready for articulate presentation when she arrived in Jack's courtroom. As a fun diversion, Evan's story about the players in *Tinker versus Delmonico* offered a respite from her worries about gang murderers.

Many times in her seven years as a prosecutor, Dana had been caught unawares by little tidbits not unlike the one that surprised Evan, the letter that Delmonico had somehow "forgotten" to mention. Where guilty minds were at work, memories invariably failed. The prevarication could be intentional or the product of a subconscious defense. An attorney had to know the difference and either outsmart the deliberate dissembler or psychoanalyze the unwitting fibber.

"You should've seen her, Dana. That fake eye color and the op-art suit. I felt dizzy just looking at her. Those cloudy gray eyes turned shifty after Rajani's first question. It was obvious Tina was lying. I saw it last week when we interviewed her, but I couldn't get her to open up. What *is* it about me?"

"It's not *you*. I can't tell you how many times I failed to get the truth out of someone."

"Yeah, but your witnesses have better reasons for lying. They're afraid the bad guy will retaliate, or else they're *in* with the bad guy and don't want to be caught on a criminal charge. In a civil case, the lies are also about self-preservation, but the only thing at stake is money."

"And reputation."

"In this case, true. Tina doesn't want to admit the defamation. But her lying backfired on her. It always does. I depend on my clients to give me the truth so I can come up with the best defense."

"Sometimes a lawyer doesn't need to know the truth,"

suggested Dana. "Or *want* to know it."

"Maybe in your business, not mine. And maybe not you, but..."

"My adversaries." They exchanged a knowing look. As a prosecutor, Dana was ethically bound to uncover the truth. Her goal was not necessarily to convict but to achieve justice, even if that meant dismissing a case for lack of evidence. But a criminal defense lawyer walked the difficult line between two competing rules of professional conduct. An attorney must not suborn perjury while, at the same time, must zealously advocate in the client's interest. A criminal defendant's interest was always to beat the rap. Sometimes, when a client insisted on testifying, it was easier for his attorney to "believe" an unlikely alibi instead of looking behind it for the truth.

"I suppose there are times when I don't need to know everything," said Evan. "But something this big—it's absolutely crucial. This was the bombshell that destroyed us."

"They haven't won yet. They still face a risk taking it to trial. Juries are capable of anything. They could find Delmonico liable but still award the plaintiff only two cents in damages."

"I'm thinking more like two million. Tina looked worse by the minute. She was still trying to spin stories when Rajani showed her that letter. You should have seen her." Evan tapped his chin with an imaginary feminine fingernail, "'Hmm...I just *don't* remember writing that.'"

"An honest answer," said Dana, tongue-in-cheek. "Who can remember anything twenty-five years later?"

Evan laughed. "Afterward she was trying to convince me how clever she was with her airtight defense strategy. 'I wasn't the *only* Tina at Ellsworth High School, you know. How are they going to prove it's my handwriting? I haven't made little round circles for dots since I was eighteen.'" Evan's "Tina" screeched like a seagull. Dana winced.

He shook his head. "I've been a lawyer for twelve years and still don't know how to break down a liar. I'm too damn nice, that's the problem."

"But 'nice' is a good tactic. You didn't have much choice. She's a bestselling author for Mysterion. You can't alienate a big client like that. Diplomacy is usually better than hardball tactics anyway."

"Well, it didn't work here. I told her a hundred times, in a nice and diplomatic way, that we couldn't help her in this lawsuit unless she told us everything she knew about June Tinker. Minnie even confronted her with the yearbook. We thought that would get to her, but she said she didn't remember a thing."

"How *is* Mineko? I miss her." The two women had worked closely in 1988, when they were both investigating Colombian cartel money laundering in the Financial Crimes Bureau of the DA's office.

"She's doing well. She's been a huge help on this case, that's for sure."

"Let's invite Mineko and her boyfriend over for dinner. I want to meet him."

"Yes, let's do that."

Dana brought her focus back to the present. "So, anyway. The liar. Tina lied about the letter, and she lied about her jealousy of June Tinker. But here's the question. Is *truth* still an available defense in your defamation case?" Dana pursed her lips in an effort to keep a straight face, while her joke succeeded in pushing Evan's grin into a huge smile.

"Ha ha. Yes, ladies and gentlemen of the jury, you heard the testimony. Junie actually did give birth in a heroin den. And because the baby's father deserted her, out of spite and anger against him, she did those unspeakable things, limped out of that den of junkies into the dark, dirty alleyway, and made her way over to the dumpster—"

"What a lovely tale."

"A true story of a heinous murder. And truth is a complete defense to defamation, ladies and gentlemen."

"Okay, I'm on the jury and I don't buy it. What else do you have up your sleeve?"

"Mineko's 'ridiculous' defense."

"She's too brilliant to come up with ridiculous theories."

"I'm talking about her *brilliant* 'ridiculous' defense."

"How's that one go?"

"The story in *Dumpster Grave* is so fake and ridiculous that it isn't defamatory. Everyone who reads it thinks it's a joke."

"Hmm." With a smile on her lips, Dana gave that one some thought. "A novel defense. This is going to be a case of first impression."

He gave her a sheepish look. She reached across the table over their empty dinner dishes and touched his cheek. "Sorry, darling. I still don't buy the defense. Is there anything about June you can impeach? What was she like at her deposition?"

"She's a decent, straightforward, respectable, *nice* person. She testified that she never had a desire to read any of Delmonico's books, not after what happened in high school. But she came upon an advertisement for this one in the newspaper, and it had a blurb about the plot that sounded all too familiar. So, she picked up a copy and was shocked to read about a character resembling herself. Her testimony at the deposition was very genuine. You could see it in those unadorned, baby blue eyes. She testified that she was, indeed, a Twiggy look-alike in 1968, just like the character in Tina's novel, April Taylor."

Dana understood the allusion, but only because Evan had explained it when he first took on this case. Her knowledge of Twiggy was limited. After all, Dana was still only in preschool in the mid-sixties when the supermodel achieved fame.

"June went all the way with that look," Evan continued. "She wore miniskirts and white go-go boots and painted on those Twiggy lashes under her eyes."

"All the more reason for Tina to be jealous."

"You bet. Junie was cute enough to attract Tina's heartthrob, that rugged linebacker Michael Ferrone. Tina started up with the hate mail, stuffing letters through the gap under the door of June's locker. There were many of them. But, after all these years, June had only that single page of Tina's early prose."

"Doesn't that seem a bit weird? Wouldn't you either throw everything out or keep it all? Maybe it's a weakness in their case, something that doesn't make sense."

"Maybe. But if you're getting hate mail, you wouldn't necessarily bundle it all up neatly and keep it in one place."

"True," Dana agreed.

"You might be so distressed you wouldn't remember where you left them. Or you'd throw each one away as you received it, and maybe overlook one. Anyway, June testified that she didn't intend to keep any of the letters, but when she read *Dumpster Grave*, she became so incensed that she started searching through the attic in her family home. The letter was in a box of high school stuff, like her old band uniform, school papers, and yearbooks. Her explanation seemed credible. She has an honest face, and without a doubt, the letter is Tina's work."

"Those telltale little circles for dots."

Evan smiled merrily. "And don't forget the distinctive literary style."

"So, what's the story about the baby?" Dana asked.

"A sad story. June found herself pregnant with Michael Ferrone's baby and didn't tell him. She dropped out of school when she started to show near the end of her senior year, and she stayed home with mom and dad. They were ashamed of the situation and ordered her to keep the curtains closed and the front door shut. They made plans for a quiet adoption by a couple in a distant state. Mr. Tinker rejected the other possibilities: a shotgun wedding or a lawsuit or a simple negotiation with the boy's parents. Michael Ferrone's father was a blue-collar worker in Mr. Tinker's employ at a manufacturing firm. The Ferrones were penny poor, and Tinker had enough decency not to impoverish them further. He also wanted to keep it quiet because he was embarrassed that his daughter crossed to the wrong side of the tracks for sex. So, dad made her a prisoner in their own home until the baby was born."

"Poor girl."

"Poor girl is right. It only gets worse. She was six months pregnant when she was home alone and started bleeding. She was terrified. By the time she called for help, it was too late. She was all alone when she delivered the three-pound baby girl on the pink ruffled coverlet of her teenage bed. Cut the cord with her scrapbook scissors. The baby was blue, not breathing, and so tiny. June tried to administer CPR, but the baby was gone before help arrived."

Evan paused. Dana's head filled with images of the terrified teenager covered in blood, frantically trying to resuscitate the tiny blue baby. They fell quiet for several seconds.

A shrieking voice shattered the silence. "But how can they prove it was a pink, ruffled coverlet and not a heroin den?" Evan's nose and mouth were scrunched into a Tina-like pinch.

"Oh please, Evan!" Despite the grim topic, Dana burst out laughing. She knew nothing of Tina Delmonico other than the airbrushed author photo on a paperback novel, but she could almost see and hear the woman, like she was there with them at their small dining room table. "How indeed?" asked Dana when she stopped laughing. "Where's the proof this wasn't a garbage bag dumpster murder? Did she keep the bloody pink coverlet in that box with the band uniform?"

"No, madam prosecutor. Better proof than that. Emergency

services records. Medical records. Date, time, and location. Death certificate. The decedent's weight of three pounds, two ounces, and cause of death."

"They brought all of that to the deposition?"

"You bet."

"Rajani did her homework."

"A damn good lawyer."

"Up against another damn good lawyer."

"Well, this lawyer can only be as good as his case. And this case stinks. This one ain't gonna make your hubbie the next partner of Belknap & Rose."

"Sounds like it's time for conciliation," suggested Dana. "I'd get the 'nice' out on the table—and the diplomacy."

"You're saying that hardball tactics aren't going to work here?"

"Not when you haven't got a leg to stand on."

"Maybe I could get down on my knees and beg."

"Worse. I'd stick with nice." With her fingertips, she stroked the top of his warm hand where it rested on the tabletop. "You do that exceptionally well. Put it together with the voice of reason and a little psychoanalysis, and you'll come out okay. What do you think June Tinker really wants out of this?"

"Gobs of money."

"I think there's something more important."

"I've thought of that," said Evan. "She wants her good name back."

"That's what *I* would want."

"A retraction and a big fat apology."

"For starters."

"But money would be very nice too. Enough to be set for life."

"You can talk her down with your very nicely worded retraction and the big fat apology. I'm sure she wants the apology to be published."

"I'd agree to that in a minute, but Tina isn't gonna like it. I can predict her reaction. I just can't predict her next choice of eye color." Evan sighed deeply and hung his head.

"Violet, jade, or butterscotch?"

Evan lifted his eyes in supplication. "I can't wait to see. Will you do me a favor?"

Dana evaluated his expression and asked, "Why am I afraid to say 'yes' to that?"

"I don't know why you should be. You'd do anything for me, wouldn't you?"

"Just about."

"Then I want you to forget your gang murderers tomorrow and come with me to the office. I need you to teach Tina how to say, 'I'm sorry.'"

Dana smiled and squeezed his hand. "I'm sure you'll do just fine without me, darling."

"So that would be a 'no'?"

She nodded.

"All right. I guess I'll have to go it alone. But, at least, help me find my sunglasses."

"I can do that much."

14 » BOUNCE

JAN TIMMERS WAS evaluating his luck, the good and the bad of it. All weekend and into Monday, he'd paced the corner religiously, leaving his post only briefly to take care of his needs. But he kept missing the au pair. Hell, he was only one person. Sunday, he saw her returning to the building alone, and Monday, she came back with the little boy. No sign of Van Leeuwen. Had she been with him? Both days, in the space of two minutes, he'd missed his chance to follow her.

All Monday afternoon, Timmers was down on himself. He'd been in New York since Friday, and still hadn't a clue where his target was holed up with the kidnapped toddler. Early mornings and late nights, before and after manning his post on the corner, Timmers made dozens of calls to hotels and rooming houses that might fit Van Leeuwen's budget, all without luck.

The P.I.'s client, the wife, hadn't been much help. At times, he doubted her. The idea that Van Leeuwen had flown to New York was based on no more than a love letter and a few words spoken in the heat of argument. Timmers was depending on the wife's continued cooperation, which hadn't yielded any new information. Even when she had something to report, he usually didn't find out until he got back to his hotel room and called her on the landline. The connection on his mobile phone kept breaking up.

The biggest lead was the one he'd gotten at the start, without any effort. The wife had found cryptic notes left behind by the love-sick kidnapper, with the name of the au pair agency and the address of Anneke's employers. Typical behavior. Timmers had seen it before. The sucker wanted to get caught. He was letting his wife know just what he was planning, without giving her every little detail. Why, then, was it taking so long to find him? Bad luck was all.

At the start, when the wife hired him, Timmers asked her why she hadn't called the police instead.

"Because I know what he's up to, and I know where he's gone. He wants that girl, Anneke. Well, let him have her! I just want my baby. Kaatje's mine, and the bigger girl is his. If he knows I called the police, he'll never return my daughter."

"I'll do my best to track him down. But if you can get the New York City police involved, you'll have two forces on your side."

She looked like she would spit in his face. "You don't know him. The man never liked anyone in authority. If he found out I called the police, everything would be over. Even if I did call the police, why would they believe me instead of him? He's the father. He has the right to take his daughter on a trip. Why would they believe me?"

"It happens all the time. One parent taking a child away from another parent."

"I can't risk it. We'll try this first. I know where that girl Anneke is living, and you'll find him close to her, you can bet on it. And when you do find him, you can't let him see you. You can't let him know I hired you. Contact me immediately and let me know where he is."

"And then what?"

"I'll catch the next flight to New York. I'll confront him myself. That's not your worry. Just find him."

He promised her results. It didn't seem difficult. But he'd been working the case night and day, without success. He would keep trying until the money ran out. Luckily, Mrs. Van Leeuwen had paid in advance for seven days of his services, plus expenses. By Thursday, one way or another, Timmers would be out of here, on a plane back to Schiphol. He hoped he would be leaving on a high note. It wouldn't do his reputation any good if he came back empty-handed.

Mrs. Van Leeuwen was checking the couple's joint bank accounts by the hour, looking for signs of where her husband was spending his money. So far, no checks written, no ATM withdrawals, no credit card purchases. She'd found, however, that over the course of the previous year, some of his paychecks weren't deposited into their joint account. Clearly, he'd been saving money for his getaway, either keeping it in cash or setting up a secret account, using an unknown address. Nothing about an extra account showed up in the postal mail or by e-mail, either at home or at the Lyceum. He'd kept no financial records on their home computer.

Timmers debated whether to approach Anneke again, but thought it best to hang back and continue to tail her. She was leery of him, that much was clear from the look she'd given him during their short meeting in the lobby of her employers' apartment building. Quite likely, she hadn't been truthful. He didn't expect her to react any differently now. And if she was seeing Van Leeuwen, she might warn him that a private investigator was still out there looking for him. The wife wouldn't like that.

On Tuesday, his luck changed.

As usual, Mr. and Mrs. Goodhue left the apartment early in the morning, at different times. They were professionals with important jobs, strutting off with their briefcases to higher callings. Career people with no thought for their son, that's how it looked to him. Timmers never would have left his own children in the care of a foreigner from an agency.

He had a wife and two kids, a boy and girl, six and nine years old. He felt secure in the knowledge that his wife was home with them right now in Zaandijk. She'd stayed home since the day she learned of her first pregnancy. That was just how it ought to be. He would not allow the sanctity of his home to be soiled by the depraved values and secret shame of strange babysitters.

When Timmers was away, he liked to think of his family just so, enclosed safely in their little brick tract home in Zaandijk. He was out of town a lot, but usually not so far away. His travels for the job had never sent him on an international wild goose chase like this one. He was being challenged, and he wanted to make good on it. Tuesday gave him his first break.

He was at his post that afternoon when Anneke left the apartment, holding the little boy's hand, with the umbrella stroller folded up and hooked over the other forearm. Timmers pulled his cap low over his forehead and followed them at a safe distance. They walked very slowly, and then she put the boy in the stroller.

After so many disappointing days, the P.I.'s heart was thudding with the thrill of it. Finally, he was in his element, enjoying the art of the tail. It came easily to him, especially in this city with so much going on, people on the sidewalks, newsstands, awnings, niches between buildings. Busy, but not so busy that he feared losing sight of them. It wasn't the financial district at rush hour, but a weekday, early afternoon in a residential district.

He followed Anneke and Travis to the playground in Central Park. Ten minutes later, Van Leeuwen and the little girl arrived. From a perfect vantage point behind a cluster of bushes, Timmers watched them. They hadn't seen him, he was sure of it. No problem. Why had it taken him so long to get to this point?

Their body language was easy enough to read. Anneke hugged the little girl a bit longer than she should have, but when the children went off to play, she wanted nothing to do with Van Leeuwen. The words were cold and cutting, Timmers could see, even from a distance. He reminded himself that Anneke had been a victim. Now, she seemed anything but. The rapist/kidnapper stared at her profile incessantly with uncomfortable intimacy while her eyes darted furiously sideways at him, the words delivered out of a corner of her stern mouth. She was telling him to get lost, to go home, to realize that the ideas in his head, whatever they were, couldn't possibly work.

It was not a good day for the park, and the children started to complain of the cold. They stayed only half an hour, and the foursome walked out together. At the exit on Central Park West, the two couples parted company. Van Leeuwen kept looking back until Anneke had wheeled Travis out of sight around a corner. After that, he held the little orange-haired girl tightly in his arms all the way back to where he was staying.

Timmers followed the target, angry at how easy it was, regretting all the near misses he'd had in the past few days. The building was just a few blocks from the park, and not many more blocks from the Goodhues' apartment. He watched Van Leeuwen walk up the stairs, insert a key into the front door lock, and push his way in, carrying Kaatje.

At last, an address. But he didn't have an apartment number, and it wasn't a doorman building. No one to ask, no one to bribe. Timmers waited a few minutes to make sure they were well inside, went up to the front door, and examined the intercom with the ten door buzzers. Only some had names next to them. Of course, the kidnapper's name wasn't there; he had to be subletting from someone.

Timmers considered ringing the bells one at a time until he found a neighbor to pump for information. Much too risky. He didn't know Van Leeuwen's voice and might give himself away, unwittingly starting up a conversation with the target over the intercom. Anneke might have said something. If he suspected that a private investigator was looking for him, he might run, and the wife wouldn't like it. She'd hired him for the specific purpose of finding them. Beyond that, he shouldn't get involved. He decided to go back to the hotel and give her a call.

It was four o'clock before he got hold of her, only to find that she'd been the better sleuth.

"I've seen them," he told her proudly. "Your husband and the little girl."

"Is she all right?"

"She looks fine. Well taken care of."

"Thank God!"

"And I have the address. The building where your husband is staying."

"The building on West 73rd Street?"

His jaw dropped. "Yes. You have it?"

"I've been trying to reach you all evening," she said. Reproach overlay the deep sadness in her voice. It was 10:00 p.m. in Amsterdam. "This afternoon, I picked up his mail at the Lyceum, and there was a letter from the apartment owner. Niels sent him a bad check for the balance due on the rent. The check bounced. There's a copy here. I've never seen this checking account before. It's blank where the address of the account holder should be."

"What's the owner's name and the apartment number?"

"Hans Visser. Number 7. He's a Dutchman who works and lives in New York. Apparently, it's a two-month sublet while Visser is in Holland. He mentioned a family emergency and his need for the money. He's absolutely irate and sent copies of this letter to both the Lyceum and the New York apartment."

"You want me to continue the tail on your husband? Or should I get the police involved?"

"No police! I told you, if he knows I called the police I'm lost.

I'll never get my daughter back! Just watch them, make sure you don't lose them. I'm flying to New York tomorrow. I'm coming to get her and bring her back."

"All right. Come ahead." Timmers had little faith in this plan.

"I'll be there tomorrow night. My plane gets into JFK at eight. Don't lose them!"

"I won't."

"Make sure, please…" Her voice cracked. "Make sure she stays safe."

Brendon Hayes looked far too young to be a murderer. That was Dana's first impression, although she was well aware that eighteen wasn't too young to commit the ultimate crime. She'd prosecuted a few murderers of that age, and Tyrone Marshall was only a year older.

Perhaps Larry Kleeger's description of the "body builder" had led her to expect something else. If she'd seen Brendon, a.k.a. Bounce, in person before the trial, she might not have repeated that phrase quite so many times during her summation to the jury. He certainly had a box-truck build, square, sturdy and muscular, strikingly broader in form than Tyrone, a.k.a. Stain. But his build appeared to be natural, not manufactured in a gym, and his face was childlike, round and innocent, with smooth brown skin as soft as a baby's bottom, dimples in his cheeks. He wasn't smiling, but even a slight grimace revealed those dimples.

By contrast, the nineteen-year-old defendant had a steely toughness that matched his reputed status as Bounce's superior in the hierarchy of Bred Nation. Stain fully embodied the gangsta attitude of the street, which, out of habit, he projected in the courtroom while his lawyer whispered instructions to sit up straight and act sincere—a pose he occasionally achieved. His vulnerability and true age were glimpsed only during interactions with his mother and at his lowest moments, when he seemed to accept defeat.

This morning, however, the defendant was back on top. His mom, as usual, was in the audience. Her eyes shone brightly when the court officers first escorted her son into the courtroom from a side door. He gave her a smart look of confidence. The tables were about to turn, his eyes seemed to suggest. The first long shot had failed—his attempt to prove that Seth Kaplan had botched his defense. But today, his loyal soldier was in court, ready to take the witness stand and exonerate him.

Bounce had no legal armor to hide behind. He'd already been prosecuted in federal court for racketeering, a charge encompassing all his activities with the gang, including the murder of Dwayne Little. He couldn't be prosecuted again in state court for that crime. Double jeopardy. So, he was free to testify fully about the murder without any worry of additional consequence to himself. He had no right to "plead the Fifth"—his constitutional Fifth Amendment privilege against self-incrimination. But would he be telling the truth? Dana sincerely doubted it.

His guilty plea was part of a deal he'd swung with Assistant U.S. Attorney Alan Prendergast. Perhaps his tender years and dimpled cheeks had convinced Prendergast to give him a break. Technically, Bounce hadn't pled guilty to murder. He admitted the killing in order to establish one of the "pattern acts" linking him to the criminal enterprise of Bred Nation. The seriousness of this pattern act increased the authorized sentence for his conviction of racketeering, but the federal judge had enormous discretion. If Bounce kept his end of the deal and informed on a lot of bad guys, he could end up spending no more than a few years in the federal pen.

There were plenty of gang members Bounce could rat on. Apparently, however, the defendant was not one of them. Something was going on here—a favor was owed, or a debt had to be paid.

The transcript of the federal proceedings quoted Bounce as stating under oath: "I got a gun from Tyrone Marshall. I used it to shoot Dwayne Little." This meager explanation was not enough to implicate the defendant in the murder. At most, it proved that he possessed a gun illegally.

And Dana wasn't convinced that the story was true. She found it hard to believe that Larry Kleeger's eyes had fooled him, even considering the stress he was under, witnessing a murder. The two gang members were so physically different, and the mark of Stain's vitiligo so apparent, that a mix up was unlikely. Bounce had to be lying. Why was he protecting Stain, and what did he owe him? That was the key.

This theory, like any other, had to be tested. Overconfidence in any scenario was never a good plan. In criminal court, anything was possible. Where human perception was concerned, surprising mistakes were not out of the question. According to Kleeger, the entire encounter spanned mere seconds. There was an argument between three men, the flash of a weapon, and the immediate burst of gunfire. Could it have been Bounce with the gun instead of Stain? This possibility, no matter how slight, was the reason Judge DuBois had ordered the hearing.

Vesma Krumins was conducting the direct examination, keeping it to the point. It wouldn't help her client to elicit the gangland association and criminal activities of these two men. The DA might get ideas for starting new investigations. Tyrone had already enjoyed a gang-free murder trial, thanks to a ruling by Judge DuBois. Dana was precluded from mentioning Bred Nation because there was no solid evidence of a gang-related motive for the murder.

Now, Vesma tried her best to steer clear of that subject. She must have realized, however, that the gang connection was bound to slip out at some point. She focused her questions on the basics:

who provided the gun and who pulled the trigger.

"Mr. Hayes, did you see my client, Mr. Marshall, on the date in question, March 19 of this year?"

"Yes."

"About what time?"

"Afternoon. I don't know. Right before, you know, I went next door and wasted him."

"Right before you killed someone?"

"Yeah."

"Killed who?"

"Dwayne."

"Where did you see Tyrone before you killed Dwayne?"

"Midnight's place."

"What happened at Midnight's place?"

"I just, you know, picked up the gun. I asked for a gun and Stain gave me one."

"Did you use that gun to kill Little?"

"Yeah. But we were just gonna… It was just a scare. I did like that and told him to back off." Bounce stuck out a finger to demonstrate. "He disrespected me bad and I shot him."

"Why did you want to scare him?"

"He been makin' threats, you know, to the Nation."

There it was, a reference to the gang. Vesma couldn't ignore it now. "Was Dwayne Little in a rival gang?" she asked.

"Yeah."

"And that's why you shot him?"

"Yeah, but it was supposed to be a scare. But I shot him."

"Are you saying that you didn't intend to kill him?"

"No, I didn't intend it. Not before anyway. But he dissed me, so, you know…"

"You decided on the spot to kill him?"

"Yeah."

"He disrespected you? What was the dis?"

"Said like, stick that piece up my ass where I wanted it. Like I wasn't man enough to use it."

"So, you shot him?"

"Yeah."

"Was Tyrone with you when you shot Dwayne?"

"No."

"Was Tyrone in front of Dwayne's building when you shot him?"

"No. He was still at Midnight's."

"So, you're the only one responsible for killing Dwayne Little?"

The question was improper, calling for a legal conclusion, but Dana let it go without objection. Judge DuBois would see right through it, and Dana had plenty to come back with.

"Yes," was the final answer on direct examination.

Vesma turned to the bench. "Nothing further, Your Honor."

As the defense attorney swiveled on her three-inch heels and returned to her seat, Dana remarked the cool smirk on Marshall's face. His eyes were trained on the witness, who didn't return the look. Throughout his testimony, Bounce had avoided any direct eye contact with the defendant. He seemed wary of his former gang associate, even as he nonchalantly admitted to murder in open court. He'd just accepted full responsibility for the shooting, yet his face expressed…what? Self-doubt. He was wondering if his testimony had been enough.

"Your witness, Ms. Hargrove."

Dana stood and approached the witness box. "Mr. Hayes, on direct examination, you referred to 'the Nation.' Would that be the street gang known as Bred Nation?"

He nodded.

"You'll have to speak up. Answer yes or no," instructed Judge DuBois.

"Yes."

"You're a member of Bred Nation, is that right?"

"Yeah." He glanced at the judge. "Yes."

"For your activities in that gang, did you plead guilty to racketeering in federal court?"

"Yes."

She turned back and picked up the transcript from her table. "During that plea, did you state under oath, quote, 'I got a gun from Tyrone Marshall. I used it to shoot Dwayne Little'?"

"I guess. Sound about right."

"But isn't it true that you didn't plead guilty until you had an agreement with the U.S. Attorney?"

"The deal, you mean?"

"Correct." She placed the transcript back on her table. "You made a deal to give up other members of Bred Nation so you could receive a lighter sentence. Sound about right?"

"Yeah. About."

"Tell us your understanding of that agreement."

"I have to tell them the people I know in the Nation and about any crimes I know about, and they might knock down my sentence."

"So, one of the crimes you told them about is that Tyrone Marshall gave you the murder weapon, isn't that right?"

"Yeah, but I have to tell the truth, or the deal is off. He didn't commit no murder." The witness sent a darting glance toward his cohort, as if seeking approval.

"But you used the defendant's gun to kill Dwayne Little, isn't that your testimony?"

"Not exactly."

"Who owned the gun?"

"It was the Nation's."

"So, it was communal property?" The witness gave her a puzzled look. "You shared the gun?" Dana explained.

"Yeah. It was for whoever, for the Nation's work."

"For the Nation's work. Part of the Nation's work was to get Dwayne Little, wasn't it?"

"Objection," said Vesma.

"Grounds?" asked the judge.

"Relevance. The issue here is who did the shooting. That question has already been answered. It was Mr. Hayes, not my client. Why he did it isn't relevant."

Dana had anticipated this objection. "It's relevant to his credibility, Your Honor. Relevant to whether we believe he would shoot the victim. Also, since Mr. Hayes testified that the defendant possessed the Nation's gun which was used for the Nation's work, it's relevant to whether the defendant shared that motive, like he shared the gun."

"Objection overruled. You may answer." The judge asked the stenographer to read the question to the witness.

"Get Dwayne?" mused Hayes. "We had to deal with it. He was a threat."

"Give us some details here. What was the threat?" Dana was fishing, but the answer, whatever it might be, had to help her. Ballistics evidence linked the gun to a previous shooting, and Little had told his sister, Darlene, that the defendant was the shooter in that incident. The motive was supposedly a personal grudge for Little's humiliating disparagement of Stain's physical appearance, the white splotches caused by his vitiligo. Dana had prosecuted cases where verbal taunts provoked a person to kill, but that explanation was too simplistic for these circumstances. She didn't believe that "disrespecting" was reason enough for the defendant to kill Little, just as she didn't believe that Hayes would kill Little only because he told him where to "stick" the gun. Something more was going on here.

"There was a fight," Hayes admitted. "He cut someone."

"Dwayne Little cut a member of Bred Nation?"

"Mm-hmm."

"Is that 'yes'?"

"Yes."

"Who did he cut?"

The witness nodded toward the defense table, without looking the defendant in the eye.

"Let the record reflect that the witness indicated the defendant."

"So reflected," said Judge DuBois.

"Just to clarify, is it your testimony that the defendant, Tyrone Marshall, is a member of Bred Nation?"

"Yeah." Hayes sat up taller. "But it's my testimony that he didn't shoot nobody."

"Well, when he gave you the gun, he knew what you were going to do with it, didn't he?"

Vesma stood and objected.

"Sustained."

"I'll rephrase that. What, if anything, did the defendant say to you when he gave you the gun?"

"Not much. You know."

"No, I don't know. What did he say?"

"He didn't say too much. Just like, 'You know what you gotta do,' like that."

"He said, 'You know what you gotta do'?"

"Something, maybe."

"Something like that?"

"Yeah."

Dana paced back to her table, head down, thinking. She turned. "The defendant ranked higher than you in Bred Nation, isn't that right?"

"Objection, relevance."

Judge DuBois hesitated a second and said, "Overruled. You may answer."

"Yeah."

"Tell us what a member of Bred Nation has to do to earn a higher rank."

"Objection," said Vesma more forcefully. "This goes way beyond the scope."

"It's relevant to motive, relevant to credibility, and relevant to whether this defendant," Dana pointed, "ordered the murder."

"The objection is sustained," said the judge. "I'm afraid, Ms. Hargrove, that we can't conduct a mini-trial on the internal workings of the gang. That's too far off the mark."

"All right, Your Honor." She turned to the witness. "Mr. Hayes, since the defendant held a higher rank than you, were there times when he gave you orders?"

"Sometimes, maybe."

"And sometimes, it was an order when he said, 'you know what you gotta do,' isn't that right?"

"Could be, maybe. It depends. It could be just like we know what we gotta do. We always know, you know…"

"And you're saying that he stayed there in Midnight's apartment while you went out and did what you were supposed to do?"

"Sure, yeah."

"You're saying he didn't come along to help?"

"I'm saying he was at Midnight's."

"He didn't want to watch you shoot the man who cut him?"

"Objection!"

"Withdrawn. You're saying he didn't come along to watch you shoot the man who cut him?"

"No, I mean yes. You're saying, did he?"

"I'm asking, was he there or wasn't he there?"

"He wasn't. I'm saying he wasn't."

"You're saying. Okay." Dana paused, crossed her arms, and looked at the witness with raised eyebrows. She turned to the bench and said, "No further questions."

The voices had been pitched high, and when the questioning stopped, a surprising silence fell. Dana's heels clicked and echoed. She took her seat.

The judge turned to the defense attorney. "Any redirect?"

Vesma stood and cleared her throat. "Just one or two, Your Honor. Mr. Hayes, did the defendant ever say to you, in so many words, 'go kill Dwayne Little'?"

"No."

"Why did you shoot him?"

Dana smiled to herself. All of a sudden, Vesma agreed that Bounce's motive was relevant.

"He was a threat to the Nation. Like I said, he also dissed me bad."

"Okay."

"It went down that way," he added before Vesma could stop him. "Stain didn't kill nobody. He didn't order no killing." Bounce sent another furtive glance toward the defendant, who wasn't looking very pleased.

"Thank you. Nothing further." Vesma resumed her seat.

Judge DuBois gestured and caught the eye of the senior court officer. "Take charge please," she said, and turned to the witness. "Mr. Hayes, that concludes your testimony. You'll be taken back into federal custody now." Three court officers, rather than the usual two, were deemed necessary for the task. The size of the "body builder" was daunting and seemed to call for extra protection. From the look on his face, however, the young Brendon Hayes was anything but a danger. The dimples were gone and the eyes were cast downward, indicating his fear that he hadn't done enough to help Stain beat the rap.

"Ms. Krumins, do you have any other witnesses?"

"No, Your Honor."

"Does the defendant wish to testify? I'll give you a moment."

Vesma leaned toward her client, and they conferred while

sitting at the defense table. Stain's voice rose above the reasonable drone of his attorney's measured advice. "…that's bullshit," Dana heard. Clearly, he wasn't impressed with his soldier's performance, but Vesma seemed to be advising him against taking the witness stand. He'd only dig himself in deeper. Reason prevailed, and Vesma announced that "Mr. Marshall has decided not to testify. The defendant rests."

"Any witnesses for the People?"

"No, Your Honor."

"I'll hear argument."

Vesma rose from her chair to address the court. As always, she made a fashionable picture, just short of flamboyant. Her mahogany brown ensemble was well put together, providing a good contrast to her light hair falling to mid-back with its incongruous, ragged edges. Her less-than pretty face was helped with the color on her lips and the earnestness in her voice. She was an effective lawyer, but not as persuasive or charismatic as Seth.

"Last week, ADA Hargrove repeatedly told the jury that my client was the trigger man." Vesma turned and shot a look at Dana before going on. "A minute before the jury said 'guilty,' she learned that Brendon Hayes was the real gunman. Even though this evidence proved Tyrone's innocence, she deliberately withheld it! She committed the most egregious violation of my client's rights!"

Okay, thought Dana. Let's make this personal. How about your attempt to mislead the court with that bogus witness, Jeremy Grant?

"This is the classic 'newly discovered evidence' situation," continued Vesma. "Hayes wasn't available to the defense during the trial. He would have taken the Fifth and refused to testify. His federal case hadn't been resolved, and any testimony in this court could have been used against him. We didn't learn of his guilty plea until it was too late to use it here.

"If Tyrone's jury had been able to hear what we heard today, he would have been acquitted. We now know that the prosecutor's star witness, Lawrence Kleeger, was mistaken. He was so traumatized by the events that he picked the wrong man. His eyes played tricks on him when he saw Tyrone in front of the building almost at the very moment of the shooting.

"Brendon Hayes is believable. He had a credible motive. Dwayne Little was a threat to the Nation and had to be scared off. The murder was a last-minute spontaneous reaction to Little's offensive taunts. The motive belonged to Hayes alone.

"Your Honor," Vesma concluded, "my client did *not* have a fair trial. The jury did *not* learn the truth. We ask the court to set aside the verdict and dismiss the indictment on the ground of actual innocence. Thank you."

"One moment, counselor," said the judge.

Vesma halted her descent to the chair and straightened up again.

"I'm not sure what you're calling 'newly discovered evidence' here. I see three possibilities. One," the judge hooked the index finger of her left hand with her right hand, "the alleged fact that Hayes shot the victim, two," a second finger, "the actual guilty plea when Hayes admitted the shooting, and three," a third finger, "the new availability of his testimony now that Hayes no longer has grounds to assert the Fifth. What is it? What's the theory?"

Vesma's eyelids fluttered and her weight shifted from one tall heel to the other in a moment of indecision. "It's really a combination of two and three, Your Honor. His guilty plea and the new availability of his testimony. We discovered both for the first time after the trial."

"I see," said the judge. "All right. Thank you, Ms. Krumins." The defense attorney sat down. "What do you say Ms. Hargrove? Is it one, two or three?"

Dana stood. "It's number one. And number one is *not* newly discovered evidence. If the crime really went down the way Hayes described it, the defendant knew this on the day it happened. If he really handed Hayes a gun with the instruction, 'you know what you gotta do,' he could have included that in his testimony at this trial.

"This isn't a new discovery. Counsel is trying," Dana shot her own look at Vesma, "to redefine the term to mean 'newly available.' Evidence isn't newly discovered just because a witness was unavailable to testify at trial.

"But even if we buy this argument, the defendant still hasn't shown that the jury probably would have acquitted him. Hayes isn't credible. He had two reasons for making up a story about shooting Little: to help himself, and to help the defendant, his superior in Bred Nation. He's trying to get a break on his own sentence in federal court by giving up a fellow gang member, and he's also trying to get the defendant off the hook for this murder rap.

"Let's suppose, however, that a jury would actually believe what Hayes said here today. That testimony still doesn't exonerate Tyrone Marshall or even raise a reasonable doubt as to his guilt. Tyrone supposedly gave Brendon the gun and told him to do what he had to do. This was a direct order from a superior in the Nation. The defendant wanted to exact revenge for being cut by Little during a fight. 'Here's the gun. Do what you gotta do.' Under the law, as Your Honor knows, this is the same as if the defendant pulled the trigger himself. He's fully responsible as an accomplice.

"For these reasons, Your Honor, the verdict must stand. We ask the court to set a date for the defendant's sentencing on his conviction of murder."

"Okay. I have a question for you as well, counselor," said the judge. "Don't you think that a jury might be troubled to hear two completely different versions of the crime? Wouldn't they find a reasonable doubt under those circumstances?"

"Not if they apply the law as instructed by the court. In the case of conflicting testimony, the jury has to decide which witness to believe. If they credit Larry Kleeger, the verdict is guilty. If they credit Hayes, the verdict is also guilty."

The judge paused to consider this. After a moment, she said, "Thank you," and Dana resumed her seat.

Judge DuBois clasped her hands and made a steeple with index fingers, raising the tip to her forehead in a moment of thought. They all waited. The two attorneys, the defendant, Mrs. Marshall, the judge's clerk, the stenographer, and the court officers.

The judge lowered her hands and focused on each of the participants in turn as she spoke. "This case presents a unique set of facts and a novel legal issue on the definition of newly discovered evidence. I'll reserve decision until tomorrow afternoon and give both sides the opportunity to submit written arguments. I doubt there's any case law in the books directly on point, but if counsel can find anything relevant, please let me know by delivering your written submissions to Robert before ten o'clock tomorrow morning. We stand adjourned and will convene at noon tomorrow." The judge banged the gavel and stood.

They all stood. As soon as the judge left through the side door, Dana was the first to make her way out of the courtroom, avoiding eye contact with anyone along the way. Written submissions? These proceedings were seriously screwing with her schedule.

Tonight she was on homicide chart. That meant little or no sleep and a new murder case—or two, possibly three. The odds were against her. Fifteen hundred murders in New York City last year, about five hundred of those in Manhattan, and most of them committed at night. Dana had never been on the chart without picking up a case. The crack epidemic of the eighties had sent the murder rate skyrocketing to a peak that had been steadily declining since 1990, but not fast enough to help her out tonight.

It was one o'clock, and a hundred little emergencies awaited her back at the office. She didn't have the time to do the proper research and writing. It simply wouldn't get done, unless…

On her way to the elevator, she stopped in an area of the corridor known for its adequate signal strength and pulled out her mobile phone. She would call Anneke in a minute, but first, she punched the number "6" in speed dialing. He answered.

"Eric. How's the burglary trial going?" Today would be the fourth day, if it was still on.

"The jury came in with guilty yesterday."

"Congratulations!" Those were the days. Short and sweet trials. Property crimes and other low-level felonies. "Now that your trial is over, do you have a little time this afternoon and tomorrow morning?"

"Sure, I mean, I'm swamped, but what's up?" There were always other responsibilities, but this was Dana calling.

She explained the problem and her need for help, feeling only slightly ashamed of herself. Eric knew this case inside and out. But did he really have the time for this unexpected project? No one in the DA's office had any time, but some of them felt the lack of time less than others.

15 »   *NEIGHBORS*

NOTHING HAD CHANGED, and something had to be done. Anneke was sick over it, dizzy, distracted, unable to sleep or eat.

Monday in the park, Niels hadn't listened. Tuesday in the park, he was deaf to her, scarily insistent. He plied her with his irrational beliefs and demands. She held him off, silently calculating her next step. Outside in the playground wasn't the place; she needed to confront him within the privacy of four walls. She proposed that they meet the next morning at his apartment. He greedily assented.

After a restless night, Anneke walked through her usual morning routine in a haze. At about ten thirty, she could delay no longer. She asked Travis to pick out a few toys, and she gathered their coats and hats, preparing to go. Downstairs, on their way through the lobby, one of the "twins" gave her a pleasant "good morning." She replied without meeting his eyes, failing to notice if she spoke to Endrit or Bashkim.

The morning was a gray one, even chillier than yesterday. With tender thoughts of Kaatje, she pulled the hat down tighter over Travis's ears and took his hand. In her other hand, she held the curved handles of the collapsed umbrella stroller, and they made their way haltingly east on 75th Street. Strangely unlike Travis, a whimper escaped his lips. The sound grated on her, filling her with annoyance at this little boy who wouldn't disappear long enough to let her take care of her problem.

As they walked, her anger and frustration burned through the haze, sharpening her wits. Niels would not go away. She saw his fierce eyes, heard his intractable demands, and felt crushed by her unbearable burden. Under her breath, she rehearsed the lines she would speak, moving her lips with emphatic precision.

Travis complained. She was squeezing his hand, pulling on his little arm. She released him, opened the stroller and placed him in the seat. "Careful now," she muttered. A warning to herself. The internal controls and tacit commands were ever increasing and more deliberate. She must take caution.

On 73rd, the brownstones were drab and morose like the morning sky. At the foot of the ten stairs, she took the boy out of the stroller and collapsed it again. They climbed to the top, where she applied the brunt of her anger with a fingertip pressed hard into the round plastic circle next to the number 7. A scratchy voice came over the intercom with a Dutch greeting. "*Dag*," Niels said. He was expecting her. She replied with the same, single word. The buzzer sounded, disengaging the lock on the heavy front door.

She gripped the handles of the stroller and let the boy run free as they took the three flights up. He traipsed merrily along-side, showing a dramatic shift in mood, unaware of anything except his own innocent glee. "Caught—ya—caught—ya..." marked his steps. His little friend would be waiting for him.

With every step, Anneke's temperature rose, heating her blood to a rolling boil. By the time they stood on the top landing, she was about to explode. There were so many things to say, things she'd already said and still needed to hammer into him. The man was obtuse, unaware of anything except his own dis-torted vision. He must see, he must.

But then she knocked, and then he opened the door. Their eyes met and held. He was calmer than before, and it threw her off. His face was misty, the lips and eyes moist, the cheeks pinked from the overwarm apartment. Somewhere behind him, inside, a radiator clunked and hissed. In a whoosh, the unbearable pressure was expelled, deflating her into a limp, warm, used balloon.

This wasn't a cold playground in the park. Before Anneke knew what had happened, he kissed her on the cheek. His lips were soft and warm, but there was also a bit of bristly, unshaven cheek brushing against her skin.

He asked her to come inside. "You must be cold," he said. She hesitated, feeling Travis's hand in hers. Beyond the open door, she saw the slanted ceiling of his attic studio in Amsterdam with his portrait of her propped on the easel. In a blink, his studio became the foyer of this apartment in a pre-war brownstone in Manhattan. Somewhere inside, Kaatje was waiting for Anneke's gift of love and protection.

"This place will warm you up in a minute," he said. "The Americans keep their apartments too hot, don't you think? And I can't adjust it. Come in, please." He'd become one of his former selves, the one she hadn't seen since his arrival in New York. His speech was lilting, smoothing the edges of the guttural Dutch language. His manner was fatherly, kind, attentive, and hypnotic.

Anneke put down the stroller, pulled off her hat, and stuffed it in a pocket. She unbuttoned her pea coat but did not remove it. Kneeling as she took off Travis's hat and coat, she looked over his shoulder to the left and spied the little girl. Kaatje was sitting on the floor in a corner of the living room, alternately hugging a soft dolly and holding it away from her, chattering. Anneke gazed at the child for a moment and spoke to Niels. "How is Kaatje today?" she asked, letting this soft noise fill her dream.

"Very fine," he said.

"She looks happy." Anneke was lulled into a pleasant passivity, the words gently tumbling from her mouth, polite and civil. She liked this better than the way she'd been before. Better than Monday and Tuesday in the park, her voice and manner severe. Better than how she felt this morning, obsessing over the pent-up rage. It was so much nicer like this, floating on a whipped cream cloud, soothed and transported.

Travis ran over to Kaatje. Anneke glided. The two little ones performed their miniature hug. Anneke did not receive a hug; the tots were more interested in each other. But she touched Kaatje's hair and felt its silky texture before the little girl plopped down on the carpeted floor again.

"Chockit?" asked Travis. He followed Anneke back to the stroller in the foyer. She bent down and pulled some toys out of the pouch. It was difficult to wedge her fingers inside with the stroller folded up. She extracted two Beanies, Chocolate the Moose and Flash the Dolphin. Flash was not a favorite with Travis, but he'd picked it out of his toys to bring along for Kaatje. He took both of them from Anneke, and like a little man, walked over with a dignified air and presented the gift of a dolphin to his girlfriend. From her spot on the floor, she looked up and accepted.

"He's a gentleman," said Niels. "Would you like some coffee? I just made it."

"Yes, please," she said. If they could only remain like this, sweet and respectful, a certain emotional distance would be maintained. But he'd kissed her, and she still felt the warmth of his bristly cheek.

While Niels was in the kitchen, Anneke began to notice a few things about the apartment. This was the second time she'd been here, but the first time she'd opened her eyes to see it.

The apartment was spacious. On the wall facing the street, the living room had a large window with only two panes, upper and lower, and a window seat underneath. The moldings around the window were thick with rounded corners, painted many times over in standard white. Of the same white, the walls appeared to be more solid than plaster, too hard for a hammer and nail because no pictures were hung, yet there was an attempt at decoration. A few framed photos were propped upright on a tall, decorative bookcase on the outer wall.

Suspended in the middle of the high ceiling was a brass chandelier-type fixture, the metal darkened with age, the candle-shaped bulbs yellow and cloudy. The dim lighting in the room lent an aura of dust and age. The inner wall of the living room ended at the foyer where the door opened onto the landing. A brown, nondescript couch was set against that wall, and across from it was an easy chair of a matching fabric. A low coffee table was placed between the two.

Anneke sat down on the couch, took off her coat, and looked to her right, into the open, adjoining dining room with its formal table, seating for six. There were some toys underneath the table, a set of soft, squishy building blocks, a storybook made of fabric, and another doll. On the far side of that room to the left was a closed door suggesting the kitchen, and to the right, an open doorway into a hallway, which she imagined would lead into the bedroom area. She heard the clinking of china and silver behind the kitchen door.

The children sat and giggled on the carpet in the unfurnished corner. Travis was speaking for Chocolate, dancing the moose around in the air in front of Kaatje, who dodged his movements and rolled onto her side. Travis leaned over and ruffled her curls with the moose. "Hair!" he exclaimed. He jumped up, ran to Anneke, and attempted to ruffle her hair in the same way, but was unable to reach. "Now, now," she said. "Settle down." He returned to his friend.

Niels walked in with a tray holding two cups of coffee, spoons, cream and sugar. He placed it on the coffee table. "*Alstublieft,*" he said, a very formal "if you please," and sat on the couch at a comfortable distance.

"*Dank u wel,*" she responded, equally formal. A silly game.

It was too late in the morning for the usual coffee hour, but the ritual was soothing. She stirred some cream and sugar into one of the cups and brought it to her lips. Warm and good.

"Look at us here, mama and papa, watching our children," he said. "When do we ever have any time for ourselves?" He smiled gently at his own joke, a farcical women's magazine lament. He drank his coffee black and set the cup down again after two generous sips. He turned to her.

"How is your job going?" His tone was conversational, real interest in his voice. He looked at her intently. Anneke liked the feel of his attention, but she focused on Kaatje, her little girl, so delightful and lovely. That child had grown inside her womb, which now felt like a heavy, swollen cavity. Maybe her period was coming on.

"Very well," she answered. "My bosses are quite nice, and Travis is good most of the time."

"A fortunate match for you, isn't it?"

"Yes, very fortunate." Anneke held her coffee cup with both hands, feeling the warmth. Removed from the frenzy of recent days, she was untroubled and relaxed, bathed in the surreal quality of their interaction.

"My girl at the open window found her ticket to the outside world." There was pride in his voice.

Over the top of her coffee cup, she smiled at his words, remembering.

"No longer on the inside, gazing out," he added.

She took another swallow of the rich liquid and placed the cup on the tray. Travis threw his arms around Kaatje, and the children started to roll around on the floor in a hug, laughing. They were so good together. It was just as Niels had said. The four of them were like a little family today, and at the center was the baby they had created.

She turned to Niels, startled to find that he'd scooted closer to her on the couch. Their eyes met, but she didn't shy away. Her boldness had returned, the old false confidence she'd felt at the age of seventeen. She had the power to make anything out of this chance to impress the man who wanted her.

He continued to hold her gaze as he spoke in his lulling voice, asking a humble question. "Anneke. Have you thought of me, even a little?" He placed his hand on top of hers where it rested on her knee. In the periphery, she sensed tumultuous movement. Kaatje got up and hurtled toward the dining room; Travis followed her. The adults ignored the children, who took up residence under the dining room table, making it into a private little home. Niels was waiting for Anneke's answer.

His hand burned in the way she used to crave, perhaps still craved. She didn't want him to remove it, and he knew this. The skin on his palm and fingers was hot and scratchy from frequent washing to remove the traces of artist's materials. Everything that was Niels could be felt in his hand.

She didn't speak, didn't need to answer his question. He assumed the answer. The children grew louder. Kaatje squealed, a sound that was half-happy, half-indignant. Travis was getting rough. Niels wrapped his fingers under her palm and squeezed tightly, the fingers digging deep, entering her. He lurched forward and his mouth was on hers, open, wet, entitled, expecting her complicity in his crime. She returned the kiss, willing to aid and abet, to take him back, to parent a stolen child.

Niels grabbed the nape of Anneke's neck, pushing harder and deeper into her. "*Niet doen!*" cried Kaatje. "Mine! Chockit, mine," insisted Travis. The little girl wailed. The kiss started to hurt in a bad way, teeth bruising lips, a powerful grip injuring her neck. Anneke panicked. She couldn't breathe. *What is this? What am I doing?* In a burst of strength, she broke his grip and pushed away. She jumped up from the couch, stumbled backward and righted herself.

"Watch the children," she blurted. Heading for the dining room, she ran past the children and into the hallway. A short way in, she found the bathroom and closed the door behind her. Sobbing, fighting for air, she choked on tears and the spasms in her throat. In the background, muffled, she heard Niels pulling the children apart.

She braced herself against the sink, leaned forward and dared to look at her face in the mirror. Downfall and despair were written there. The green eyes were red-rimmed, the mouth swollen, the nose dripping mucus. Who was she? What had she become? Travis was the one she had pledged to protect. She heard him cry out for her now. "Where's Anneke?"

Quickly, she blew her nose and drew in a deep breath. She splashed cold water on her face and dried it with a towel. She had to get back to Travis.

The scene in the dining room was pure chaos. The two children were wailing. Niels was a different man, changed from light to dark. He held Kaatje tightly and bounced her violently up and down. Travis was clinging to his leg. Niels looked down at him and barked, "*Hou je bek!*" Shut up. To a baby.

Anneke pulled Travis away and scooped him up. They had to get out. Get out now. She lurched toward the foyer.

"Don't go," Niels ordered. "Wait. I'll stop it. I won't anymore. Stay here."

With shaking hands, Anneke stuffed Travis into his coat and hat. The children were screaming at the top of their lungs.

"You'll regret this," Niels threatened over the din. He jiggled Kaatje impatiently. "I'll tell those people about you, the parents of that little brat."

Travis couldn't understand the Dutch words, but he clearly understood the tone. The boy was hysterical, reaching up to Anneke, wanting to be lifted into her arms as she struggled to put on her own coat and hat. She found Chocolate and gave Travis the toy. He clutched it tightly in his fist.

Reflexively, Anneke organized their escape. She propped the stroller next to the door, put Travis in a football hold under one arm, opened the door, held it with a foot, and grabbed the handles of the stroller. Niels was pacing, bouncing Kaatje roughly. He yelled demands at Anneke. She managed to get out the door and it slammed shut behind her. He couldn't possibly follow them out into the cold, not with a little girl in his arms.

Travis screamed and kicked at her as she raced down the stairs. *A mistake, a mistake, a mistake, dear God a mistake...* Her head rang with self-rebuke all the way down. A mistake to lose her resolve. To yield like this. To involve Travis.

On the sidewalk, she hurried along as far as the next building but could no longer manage her load. She lowered the squirming boy and told him sternly to stay put while she struggled with the stroller. It seemed to be stuck, and her hands were shaking. With a steady pull, it jerked open and locked into place, but when she turned around, Travis was gone. He'd started back to the building, still clutching his favorite moose and calling out to Kaatje.

The sight of him toddling away alarmed her. "Tug!" she screamed. Leaving the stroller behind, she ran back and grabbed his arm. He protested and dragged against her as she pulled him along the sidewalk. He gave her no choice. She forcefully picked him up, dropped him into the seat, and strapped him in.

No, Travis, you won't be coming back. A mistake, such a mistake.

Pushing the stroller at a desperate pace, she felt the sting of tears in her eyes. What next? Call Timmers? Tell Dana? Call the police? She was boxed in, nowhere to go. Any of these things would give her away, would ruin everything. Niels had ruined everything.

Tears blurred her vision. She felt the eyes of the people walking by, staring at her or pretending not to look. A crying nanny, a crying baby. *Hold it in, try to think!*

She pulled a tissue from her pocket and wiped her face with one hand, guiding the stroller with the other. She was responsible for Travis. She'd ignored him too long and had to get him home.

Her one-handed steering was making the stroller veer to the right. She stopped it, put the tissue into her pocket, and came around to the front. Travis was still crying but more quietly now, avoiding her eyes. She dropped to her knees on the pavement before him and stroked his cheek. "Tug, my sweet little boy. Quiet now." The gesture comforted the child, and his crying subsided to a whimper. He looked up and let out a final hiccup of a sob. At that moment, his focus changed distinctly, moving away from himself and outward to her. "Anneke crying?" he asked.

The concern in his eyes filled her with infinite tenderness. "Travis, are you my friend? I love you." She bent forward, kissed his cheek, and hugged him, lingering there.

"I love you," he said in return, offering his little child's heart of pure feeling. She felt his pudgy, warm cheek, so soft and smooth, next to hers.

How different it felt compared to that scratchy, masculine cheek. Only minutes ago, those familiar, warm lips had been pressed to hers.

Enlightenment rushed in. But it gave her no relief, only despair. She understood now what this was all about, and the truth slipped out into the open. "*Ik ben eenzaam,*" she told Travis, her cheek still next to his. She hugged him tighter, not wanting to let this little one go.

The tears came flooding back into her eyes. She wouldn't tell him the meaning of her words. She didn't want to admit to Travis, or to the rest of the world, just how lonely she was.

Shortly after twelve noon, Gerald and Eleanor Bishop were heading home from their favorite lunch spot on Columbus

Avenue. They were in the habit of lunching earlier than most people, at about eleven thirty. They'd taken up many of their habits almost five years ago, when they both turned sixty-five and retired from the New York City public school system.

The Bishops enjoyed their retirement. They were inquisitive people with much to talk about, she, a former principal of an elementary school, he, a former high school history teacher. Now, occasionally, they put in a few volunteer hours tutoring kids who were academically challenged. The rest of their days followed a predictable pattern.

Up at about seven. A cup of coffee and a small bite to eat. The newspapers, conversation about current events and politics. Perhaps a phone call from their daughter in Brooklyn or their son in Chelsea. A novel for Eleanor, a biography or historical treatise for Gerald.

As the morning progressed, their appetites grew. Before eating, they liked to get some exercise, weather permitting. At about eleven, they took the three flights of stairs down to the front door, the ten steps to the street, and a good long walk in the neighborhood. It took a while to get downstairs and even longer to get back upstairs, but the exercise was keeping them young. They reminded their adult children of this, whenever the subject came up.

Just yesterday, their daughter Stephanie called Eleanor to suggest, yet again, that they should move to a more accessible apartment. She'd taken a look in their neighborhood and found a few great possibilities in doormen buildings with elevators. In one of them, she knew the tenant and could finagle a loophole to get Mom and Dad the rent stabilized rate.

"But we've been here forty years, Steffi," said Eleanor. "You grew up here."

"Those stairs are getting to be too much for you, Mom."

Eleanor was slightly miffed. Kids in their thirties had no idea how fit a person could be at the age of seventy. But she responded with a good-natured comeback. "Why do you think we still look so good?" she said into the phone while glancing over at Gerald. He raised his eyes over the top of *FDR, a New Deal,* winked at his young bride, and fisted one hand to show off his flexed bicep. "Running up and down the stairs, that's what. No broken bones. Density galore."

"It's not just that. There's no protection for you at night, fiddling with your keys to get in the front door. Anyone could…"

"In forty years, tell me what's happened. Tell me. Nothing ever happens in this building."

Stephanie had no answer to that one. Either they'd been lucky, or they fully had their wits about them and a special facility for erecting that invisible self-protective shield every New Yorker strives for.

"Don't worry about us," said Eleanor. "Just like I don't worry about you, all grown up now and making your own decisions, even if that leaves us without any grandchildren." It was Eleanor's turn to grin and wink at Gerald, to show him she was joking.

"Oh, Mom. Children aren't completely out of the question for me *or* Tommy." Stephanie, at thirty-four, was living with a man who didn't want to commit. Stephanie's brother Thomas was gay and not seriously attached to anyone.

"Just making a point, dear. You know I'm not the kind of mother to tell you what to do. So please trust us. We'll know when the time comes to move out. Check back when we're eighty-five."

The elder Bishops were staying put for now, enjoying their usual routine. A favorite part of that routine was the daily walk. If they were out, at about eleven thirty their appetites would be upon them. A decision would be made where to lunch. Usually it was the diner on Columbus Avenue. Their chosen hour had the advantage of allowing them to beat the lunch crowd.

That day, the Bishops ordered standard fare, a tuna diet plate for Eleanor, cup of minestrone soup and turkey sandwich for Gerald. Coffee for each, their second cup of the day. As so often happened to them, a thread was picked up out of the blue, out of context, and the storyline continued.

"Can't fool me, Nel," her husband said. "All this joking around about it."

She thought back to the only joke she'd made recently, yesterday, on the phone with Stephanie. "I made a good point though, didn't I?"

"It's not the point, it's what's under it."

Eleanor slipped a slice of cucumber into her mouth and chewed. "I think I've had more than my share of young children. If we want more, we can tutor anytime we want. It's a blessing to have this peace and quiet, don't you think? The golden years and all that."

"Right on. Who wants the screaming rug rats?" His eyes smiled, but she saw the disappointment in them, hidden under the layers of his everyday occupations.

"Gerry."

"What?"

"*You* tell me what. Stop pretending you aren't depressed."

"I've told you this before."

"Yes, you have." He'd hinted how nice it would be to have a grandchild. He'd admitted how often he'd bitten his tongue not to pressure Stephanie and, yes, even Tommy. Anything was possible. Eleanor knew his sensitivity and kept her own expectations and desires largely to herself, not wanting to heap her disappointment onto his.

"You didn't hear what Steffi said. She said it isn't out of the question."

"With that moron she's with?"

"Maybe we can find her a reason to replace him. I have some

ideas. How about the Pendeckers' son? He's about the right age."

"So, the non-meddling Mom is going to meddle?"

"It'll be a sneak attack. The holidays are coming up. We'll throw a family party, multi-generational. The moron won't be invited. He doesn't like us anyway."

"Eat your tuna and dream on."

They finished their lunches, although the food had become as unappetizing as the subject of their conversation. With a slight damper on their moods, they paid the bill and made their way back home. After turning the corner onto 73rd, about halfway into the block, a rush of movement grabbed their attention. Someone was running down their front steps, arms laden down with a small child and a bulky item.

"What's going on over there, Gerry? Is that our house?" Eleanor, as usual, was not wearing her glasses. They both wore progressive lenses, correcting for vision both near and far, but Eleanor always took them off before going outside. They distorted her depth perception while walking.

"A young woman," Gerald said. "She's carrying a little kid. Why is she in such a hurry?"

"On our steps?"

"Yes. Maybe that's the child from next door? And her mother?" They were getting closer, and Eleanor saw clearly enough.

Simultaneously, they halted in their tracks and exclaimed, "Oh, no!" and "God in heaven!"

"Pulling on a baby that way," Eleanor said. "Now, look at that! She threw the little girl into the stroller."

"So rough. That kid isn't going to stop crying now." Gerald shook his head. They remained standing, watching the woman push the stroller away, increasing the distance between them.

"We should report it."

"Where?"

"Children's Services."

"Without telling the father?"

"Maybe we should tell the father."

They thought about this for a moment. "We shouldn't get involved, Nel. You remember how difficult our kids could get at that age."

"But we never did anything like that."

"Maybe not, but I remember giving them a good healthy spanking on the behind every once in a while."

"What that woman did was no spanking, Gerry. That was out of control. Child abuse, that's what I'd call it."

16 »   *HOMICIDE CHART*

ACROSS THE STREET from the brownstone, another witness skulked behind a parked van. *Au pair my ass*, Timmers was thinking. If the Goodhues had hired him, he'd be on his phone this instant, reporting their babysitter. But people of that ilk had no problem entrusting their children to strangers. They just didn't care. Anything to get rid of the kids, to get on with their important careers.

His own kids were waiting for him to come home. He'd been gone a week, the full extent of his contract. No way was this going past today. His ticket was ready, a 7:00 a.m. flight out of JFK tomorrow. He couldn't be concerned with Renske Van Leeuwen's travel problems.

In a miracle of mobile phone connectivity, he'd received her call about an hour ago, right here on the street, fifteen minutes before Anneke and the boy showed up for their short visit. His cell rang, he answered, and Renske's voice came over clearly. "My flight's been cancelled," she said. Her voice had a twitching breathlessness that reminded him of her desperation on the day she hired him. "Mechanical problems with the plane. I'm looking for another flight now."

He promised to watch the building for the rest of the day but avoided giving a direct answer when she asked about tomorrow. "Let me know when you get a flight," he said simply.

Miserable and cold, he remained at his post through the afternoon. After Anneke's dramatic exit, Van Leeuwen emerged only once, three hours later, carrying his baby the way he always did. Timmers followed him to a corner deli, waited while he bought a few items, and tailed him back to the apartment. That was it. The man wasn't going anywhere, that much he could assure the wife.

He quit the surveillance in the evening and went back to his hotel room. Renske called to say she'd found a flight and would arrive tomorrow afternoon. He gave her a full update on his observations of Anneke.

"Please, just stay one more day. Make sure you don't lose my baby."

"Sorry. I have a flight out in the morning. I have other obligations to get back to."

"I'll pay you extra when I get there."

"Look. He isn't going anywhere. He wants to be with Anneke, and she's here, and she's not going anywhere." Timmers wasn't going to rub it in by giving his opinion that the man was obsessed with his teenage girlfriend. It was obvious. It was sick. A statutory rapist and a baby kidnapper.

"He could pick up and leave in a minute. You have to watch him! He could go anywhere with my child."

"But it's been a week and he hasn't made a move. I'm telling you, he's not leaving until he plays his last card with Anneke. It's only a few more hours. Believe me. He'll be in that apartment with the little girl when you get here." He was referring to Kaatje, the two-year-old little girl. He hoped, for the wife's sake, that the big little girl wouldn't be in that apartment too.

Timmers wished her luck, extracted himself from the conversation, and hung up. Off his plate.

* * *

At about ten, Dana kissed Evan goodnight in their bedroom and returned to the living room. As she usually did on chart nights, she remained fully dressed in casual clothes and stretched out in the easy chair to doze while she waited for the call. On the side table, within reach, she'd placed the cordless phone, a notepad and a pen.

In her mind, she heard her son's voice squealing "caught ya." Tonight, the game had been more frantic than last time, and Travis quickly disintegrated into crankiness and fatigue. By eight o'clock, he was fast asleep in his crib. The baby monitor was on, with a receiver next to Evan on his bedside table, delivering the sound of their child's breathing to his ear. Soothing and regular, with little hiccups and gurgles. It was better than relaxation therapy, the cassette tape of ocean surf and chirping birds that Cheryl had given them last Christmas. If anything out of the ordinary came over the monitor—a word or a cough or a cry—Evan would pop up like toast and be swiftly on his way to Travis's room to check on him.

Anneke had been strangely uncommunicative this evening, saying little about her day with Tug. Her face looked puffy, as if she'd been crying. She stayed in her room behind a closed door while they had their dinner and got Travis into bed. At about nine, when Evan and Dana were in the living room, Anneke emerged from her bedroom, turned out the light, and closed the door hastily behind her. Perhaps she didn't notice that the latch slipped, leaving the door open a crack. Her room was her sanc-tuary, and she liked to keep it hidden from view. She mumbled that she was going to visit her friend Marije, grabbed her pea jacket, and slinked out the front door. A bit unusual, a bit unsettling. Dana tried to put it out of her mind.

With Anneke gone, Evan and Travis asleep, a hush fell over the house. Dana stretched out in the easy chair, its footrest extended, and sunk into the comfortable cushions. A single light burned in the foyer, faintly illuminating the living room, enough to suggest the contours of the furnishings. In the kitchen, the refrigerator cycled on. From the common hallway, the elevator hummed, bringing someone up. A timid knock came at the front door, and Mrs. Marshall tiptoed in, wearing her single taupe-colored conservative suit for the courtroom and a funny little pillbox hat from the sixties. She came all the way in and stood next to the easy chair, posture erect, hands clasped in supplication, gazing down with doleful eyes. "My son," she said. "Can't you see he's my son, my only son?" Her voice droned on until it became a shrill siren. Dana wanted to say that everything would be all right, but she choked and sputtered, unable to find her voice. Behind Mrs. Marshall at the dining room table, the court clerk sat with his hand poised over a black phone…

Dana lurched forward, fumbling for the ringing phone. "Hello?"

"Dana, you've got a case."

"Where?"

The dispatcher gave the address of the location and said that a patrol car would be there in five minutes to pick her up. She asked Dana to repeat the address and write it down. Attorneys on homicide call in the middle of the night had been known to credibly mimic coherent speech in the depths of sleep and fail to wake up for the ride to the scene. When Dana hung up, she looked at the time. Eleven thirty. Up and to the foyer, she grabbed her coat and briefcase, but stopped. She would take a quick look before going.

Through the open door of the nursery, in the glow of the nightlight, she saw Travis's covered form. She stepped in just far enough to confirm his steady, deep breathing and stepped out again. The door to the master bedroom was closed, and she would not interrupt Evan's sleep to tell him she was leaving. Nor would she bother Anneke. She wondered—could that have been Anneke creeping in, returning from her walk in the midst of Dana's dream? But, no, the door to her dark room was still open a crack, just as she'd left it. Odd for Anneke to remain out so late at night, but there was no time to contemplate the girl's nocturnal wanderings. A dead body awaited.

A uniformed officer, Aurelina Vargas, drove up and stopped in front of the building. Dana hopped into the front passenger seat, like a partner riding radio. The women recognized each other from a previous case, and they exchanged small talk for the first few blocks of the drive.

Dana was now wide awake, her brain primed for catching legal problems. The crucial minutes and hours immediately after the discovery of a murder often shaped the course of the investigation and the success of any resulting prosecution. At this point, she knew only that a body or bodies had been found in a private apartment. Her immediate concern was to guard against violations of the constitutional sanctity of a private home. A court could throw out any evidence they collected—or even the entire case—if the police or prosecutor violated the personal rights of a tenant or homeowner.

Officer Vargas told Dana that she and her partner, Ted Forrester, were the first to respond to the crime scene. When their lieutenant arrived, he put in a call for the ADA on homicide chart, and Vargas offered to chauffeur.

"I was just as happy to get out of there," she said. But her escape was short-lived. The drive from Dana's apartment to the crime scene took only five minutes. As Officer Vargas spoke, she was pulling into a row of double-parked official cars, immediately behind a detective's unmarked vehicle. Dana recognized it by the dent in the rear fender. Detective Paul Donegan was here.

Judging from the officer's mood, Dana wondered what she

was in for. "That bad?" she asked, steeling herself for the worst. She'd pretty much seen it all: murder by knife, gun, rope, machete, baseball bat, and blunt objects of every kind, including fists and walls. There'd been times when her vision threatened to go black and she had to step away to compose herself. The sight and smell of blood, the stench of bodily odors and decomposition, the heartbreak of decrepit surroundings and poverty. It never got any easier.

"This is a new one for me," Officer Vargas replied. "It's just so damn sad." Without saying more, she jumped out of the patrol car.

Dana already suspected that this case would be different. She'd felt a pinprick of shock when the dispatcher told her the address. It wasn't a tenement far uptown or in Hell's Kitchen or the Bowery. This was a building very close to home. Too close.

She followed the officer up the front steps of a brownstone. The entry door had been propped open to allow for the free flow of law enforcement traffic. For someone who'd been happy to get out of there, Aurelina Vargas seemed anxious to return. Inside the building, she started to take the stairs two at a time in her thick-soled shoes. She was young and strong, petite, in her late twenties, and she nimbly bore the extra weight hanging from her utility belt, the gun, memo pad, handcuffs, flashlight, and a dozen other items. Maybe this was a "new one" for Officer Vargas because she hadn't investigated many homicides. This precinct was not known to have a high murder rate.

Each floor of the building had two apartments. On the top landing, the doors to both apartments were open. Officer Vargas greeted her partner Ted Forrester, who stood military style, guarding the hallway. Dana introduced herself to the tall, square-shouldered young man. He nodded in the direction of number 7, and Officer Vargas accompanied Dana inside.

The large apartment was humming with activity, giving the

space a cramped feel. Besides the swarm of officials, nothing out of the ordinary was immediately apparent, by sight or smell. With a quick visual scan, Dana identified an investigator from the Office of the Chief Medical Examiner, two crime scene investigators, and a detective and lieutenant from the precinct. Off to the right in the dining room, she spotted her longtime pal from the DA's squad, Detective Paul Donegan, affectionately known as the Don. He was standing next to the table, an overturned chair at his feet. She walked over to him first. "Paul."

"Sleepwalking again, Dorothy?" he asked.

"My dreams have been too sweet. I needed a new case." She conveniently omitted telling him about her nocturnal vision of Mrs. Marshall.

"You came to the right place. This ain't the Land of Oz." The seasoned detective emitted a short laugh and broke into a dry cough, sending a spurt of venous color into his cheeks. He held a fist to his mouth, and when the coughing subsided, opened his hand and briefly massaged the grizzled stubble on his cheeks.

"I thought you weren't working nights anymore," Dana said, looking into his sunken, blue eyes, pink in the whites. She stopped herself before making a less oblique allusion to rumors of his declining health. The cough and nicotine stains on his fingers seemed to say it all, but the Don was in persistent denial.

"This is still swing, not graveyard," he said.

Dana looked at her watch. True. Seven minutes remained before the stroke of midnight.

"Besides, I heard you were on the chart."

She smiled at this reminder that he liked to work her cases. "So, tell me what's what," she said. "I'm still in the dark."

"The body's over there." He nodded toward the living room, where most of the officials seemed to be clustered around the couch.

Dana's eyes focused on the area indicated. A crime scene

investigator with a camera clicked a couple of final shots before moving aside to let the OCME investigator in. As the activity shifted, Dana was afforded a direct view of the couch, where a small, oblong object lay bundled in a blanket. Her throat tightened. "A child?"

The Don confirmed with a nod.

"How old?"

"About eighteen months."

"Any other bodies?"

He shook his head.

"Anyone in the apartment when the officers responded?"

"No. The next-door neighbors discovered the body and called 911."

"You questioned them? Are they credible?"

"Yes and yes. They say the tenant is out of town. He sublet the apartment to a couple and their child, but the neighbors don't seem to know how to reach any of these people. They only have a phone number for the management company. I called and left a message. Middle of the night, answering machine." Dana went through her mental checklist: *No consent, emergency abated, search warrant needed.* "They heard a lot of noise," continued the Don, "and when it got too quiet, they came over for a look. I don't have all the details. I was waiting for you." He coughed again.

"Okay," Dana said, trying to ignore the distressing sound he was making. Most likely, his lungs had interrupted his interview with the neighbors, making it impossible to continue. "We'll go next door in a bit and finish up with the witnesses. But first..." She tipped her head toward the living room to indicate her next destination.

Approaching the crowd, she said, "Good evening," and introduced herself. She stopped just inside the living room, close to the foyer, and turned to the highest-ranking officer, a man of about forty with a name plate that read *D. Amundsen.* "You're in charge here, Lieutenant?"

He dipped his head in acknowledgment and eyed her obliquely, unwilling to bestow a direct look.

"What time did the 911 come in?"

"Twenty-two forty-five hours or thereabouts."

"Vargas and Forrester were the first on the scene?" she asked.

"Right. Five or ten minutes after the call. Another unit and the EMTs also responded, but the medics took one look and declared her dead. When I got here about twenty-three ten hours, I made the calls to crime scene, our detective unit, OCME, and the DA homicide number. I let the other unit go when Detective Greeley and crime scene showed up. Didn't need 'em."

"So far everything's left the way you found it?"

"Haven't touched a thing." He flicked an indignant look that told her she shouldn't have asked the question. "Chair overturned in the dining room, framed photograph on the floor, broken." He pointed to it, next to the bookcase in the living room. "The child was wrapped up like that on the couch, and there was a puddle here on the ground. Looks like vomit." He pointed downward to a spot next to the end of the short wall that separated the foyer from the living room. A plastic number had been placed next to it by crime scene. Everyone knew not to step in it, and the Lieutenant's comment had prevented Dana from making that mistake.

He continued. "We found some blood on the edge of the wall there. Looks like it anyway. Samples were taken." He pointed behind her. She turned to look. The spot was very small, at about shoulder level to her, and located on the thin edge where the side of the wall came to an end. "A few spots of blood on the floor on the way to the kitchen." He pointed again. Plastic evidence markers were laid out in the dining room on a path around the table to the kitchen. This was the first time Dana noticed them. She'd been talking to Detective Donegan on the other side of the table in the dining room. "Found some crumpled paper towels on the floor in the kitchen. Blood on them. Samples taken. Crime scene photographed everything. The OCME is about to start the exam."

The two crime scene investigators were wandering around the perimeter of the living room, one of them taking pictures, the other dusting for fingerprints. They were trained not to disturb anything, and it wasn't in their job description to seize physical evidence, but Dana was still nervous. "We haven't ID'd the tenant and subtenants, so we'll have to search for evidence of their identities and anything else that's relevant to this murder, if that's what it is." She nodded toward the OCME investigator. "But we can't search without a warrant."

Lieutenant Amundsen frowned and squared his shoulders. "We can grab anything in plain view, counselor. There's some mail and papers on the desk in the bedroom. It's a start on making the IDs."

"You've been in the bedroom?"

"Checking for occupants. This was an emergency."

"That's fine, but now the emergency is over. There aren't any perps here destroying evidence. The child couldn't be saved, and no one's in any danger. If we take anything now, the court will throw it out. I'll contact the night judge, and we can apply for the warrant over the phone. Officer Vargas is the logical witness." Dana glanced at her watch again. Swing shift had just ended. "Can you arrange for overtime?"

"Sure." His voice was mildly flippant. He turned and called out: "Vargas! You and Forrester are staying." Aurelina tipped her head and raised a hand in response.

"Thanks," said Dana. "It shouldn't take long. I'll prepare Officer Vargas. We'll have the phone call, and the judge will sign the warrant. You can start the search right away without getting a copy of the warrant because it will be on file in court. But let me talk to the OCME first. We need his impression of the likely cause of death before we call the judge."

Dana dared to move closer to the couch and spoke to the investigator kneeling alongside. "How's it going?" He looked up at Dana and introduced himself. "Pradeep Kumar, OCME. I've only had a brief look at the face. Haven't moved anything. Crime scene just finished taking photographs, so now I can make my examination."

The child was lying face up, carefully wrapped in a pink blanket, the entire body swaddled up to the chin, with part of the blanket wrapped around the top of the head, covering most of the hair. Strawberry-blonde curls framed the tiny, pale face. A lovely, delicate face. There were no visible injuries and the eyes were closed. She could have been sleeping, if it weren't for the color of the skin and the absolute stillness of the body.

"Are we sure this was homicide? Could it be natural causes?" Even as Dana asked these questions, she doubted an innocent explanation. What was under that blanket? If a parent had gone for help, he or she would have returned by now. Flight usually meant guilt. Dana gazed down at the child's face for a moment, mesmerized by the china stillness. The more details she perceived, the clearer the picture became.

"I have a good guess what it is, but I'll know more in a few minutes," said Kumar.

By now, Dana also had a good guess, something almost too painful to think about. "Please check the blanket and collect any strands of hair that look different from the baby's. Scrape under her fingernails. I don't know if I'll get the authorization, but I'm ordering DNA on this one." Two parents, two suspects. At least. One might point the finger at the other, and DNA would help. The use of DNA evidence in court was a relatively recent phenomenon, still unusual, and testing was not routinely ordered. The city was stingy about allocating resources for this expense, but Dana would ask for it in this case. Her emotions were running high, and she struggled to maintain composure.

Kumar opened a leather bag at his feet and removed an instrument that reminded Dana of the one that Tug's pediatrician placed in his ear. A tympanic membrane thermometer. As Kumar gently pushed the blanket off the child's head, Dana turned away.

"Aurelina." Dana motioned. "We need to call the night judge for a search warrant. Let's go over some things while the OCME is working." She directed Officer Vargas to the dining room table, where they could sit down and talk. On the way over, she noticed a clutter of objects under the table. "Look at that," she whispered to herself. A set of foam blocks, a fabric storybook, a doll, and a Beanie Baby that looked like one they had at home. A dolphin.

The officer's eyes went to the point of Dana's focus and turned away. "I can't look at that," she said. "Poor little girl."

The two women sat and discussed the sequence of events. Dana explained what to expect when they made the phone call. Officer Vargas would be put under oath and her testimony recorded over the phone. She would have to relate the information she received from the 911 call, her observations in the apartment, and the preliminary opinion of the OCME investigator as to the cause of death.

As they spoke, Dana glanced over at Kumar. He was lifting an eyelid and peering into the eye with an instrument. What color could those eyes be? Green came to mind. Strawberry-blonde hair went very well with green eyes.

After Dana got a complete report from Officer Vargas she said, "Okay. Let's see if the OCME is almost done." They stood up from the table. Over by the kitchen doorway, the Don was finishing his conversation with the precinct detective Greeley. Dana caught his eye, and he followed the women over to the living room couch.

Kumar was still on his knees by the couch. He'd removed the blanket, revealing the child's cotton pajamas, white, with pink outlines of leaping baby lambs. The pant legs were pushed up nearly to the knees. Ten toes, thin ankles, the calves turned inward from the knee, slightly pigeon-toed. What a perfect child, Dana thought. A beautiful child. The pajama top was stained with a light-colored substance, perhaps milk or cereal. There were no visible injuries, no blood.

Kumar pulled up the shirt and palpated the rib cage. "Posterior rib fracture?" he mused and pulled down the shirt. "All right," he said, and stood up. "This is what I think. SBS. Shaken baby syndrome."

"Someone shook this baby to death?" blurted Officer Vargas.

Kumar nodded.

"How sick can you get?" The officer shook her head in disgust.

"There's also blunt force trauma to the back of the head." Kumar started to lift the head, as if to show them the injury, but he seemed to think better of it and removed his hands. "The baby was not only shaken, but the back of the head came into contact with a hard object. The shape of the contusion is long and thin, consistent with the edge of the wall where the blood was found. Quite likely, the child's head snapped back during the shaking and hit the wall. The cause of death could have been the shaking alone, or the impact to the back of the head, or a combination of the two. We'll confirm this on autopsy."

"What's your estimate of the time of death?" asked Dana.

"I'd say less than two hours ago, maybe an hour and a half, just before the 911 call. The body temperature is down only a couple of degrees and rigor has just started in the smaller muscles, the face and neck. Now that I've had a closer look, I would say she's about two years old, but she's tiny for her age. With a young child in a warm room, rigor can set in quickly, in less than two hours. She didn't die neatly bundled in that blanket either. If it's SBS and head trauma, as I suspect, then she vomited before she died. The killer tried to clean her up and wrapped her neatly, maybe even closed her eyes. I felt a fractured rib where it meets the spinal column. This can happen when a baby is held tightly on the chest and shaken violently. I also saw retinal hemorrhage in her eyes. That's another sign of SBS."

Dana was momentarily at a loss for words, imagining the horror and helplessness of the little victim. Earlier today, the child was playing with the toys under the table. This evening, a parent fed her and dressed her in the pajamas with the little lambs. "What...I guess I'm wondering what other findings you need to confirm this?"

"On autopsy, I'll be looking for subdural hematoma—bleeding around the brain—and cerebral edema—swelling in the brain. These are the best indicators of SBS. We'll also look for internal bleeding originating from the impact to the back of the skull. But for right now, I'm telling you, there's no other logical explanation. No other visible sign of injury or illness. The vomitus is from recently ingested food brought up by the trauma. She doesn't show any signs of, for example, poisoning. But of course, a full toxicology will be done."

"Thank you," said Dana. She pulled a card out of her jacket pocket. "Call me as soon as the autopsy is complete." She turned away and said to Officer Vargas, "Let's go make that phone call to the judge."

Before Dana walked away, the Don leaned in and directed a raspy whisper into her ear: "I'll just go next door and see how Fred and Ethel are holding up."

Dana smiled. "Okay. I'll be over in a few minutes."

"Loud voices and banging furniture," said Eleanor Bishop. She was still visibly shaken, two hours after her tragic discovery. "They were so loud I could have told you what they said, except it was a foreign language. Probably the same language as the man who lives there, wouldn't you think?"

"What makes you say that?" asked Dana. She glanced at the Don. They sat in matching chairs across from the Bishops, who sat very close to each other, nearly touching, on the living room couch. Their apartment, number 8, was the mirror replica of number 7. The Don seemed happy to let Dana do the talking, to give his unreliable voice a rest. Later, she would get his impression of the interview. With forty years of experience, Paul Donegan had insights and instincts she could count on.

"Well, you'd think he might sublet his apartment to his own countrymen," said Eleanor. "It's just a hunch. I've heard him speak in his native tongue a few times over the years, and…"

"How long has he been your neighbor?"

"About five or six years."

"What's his name?"

"Hans Visser. A Dutchman from Amsterdam. A very pleasant fellow."

"A Dutchman," echoed Dana.

"Yes. He's in Holland right now. I wish he'd said something about subletting his apartment, but I don't really blame him. It seems there was a family emergency. I saw him about ten days ago on the landing, coming out the door with a suitcase. I asked if he was going on a trip. He said his mother was very sick and he was going to Amsterdam for a while. He was in quite a hurry to catch his flight, and he didn't say anything else. Next thing we knew, a couple and their little toddler were staying there."

"I saw the mother and the girl," said Gerald. "We both saw them. But Eleanor also saw the man."

"Tell me about the man," said Dana. "When did you see him?"

"About a week ago. But before we saw anyone, we heard voices in the apartment, didn't we, Gerry?"

"Right. The walls are pretty solid here, but the voices came through faintly. We were surprised to hear anything at all after Hans left. We thought the apartment would be empty."

"Did you consider telling the landlord or asking the management company to contact the landlord?"

"Sure we did," said Eleanor. "But then I saw the man, and he explained everything, so we didn't call. I was downstairs at the mailbox, and he was there, holding his little girl. She was such a lovely little girl, you should have seen her. Alive, that is." Eleanor caught Gerald's eye, communicating her distress. "The man was letting himself in with a key, and so I said, 'Hello, I don't think we've met. I'm Eleanor Bishop, in number 8.' He was very polite and said he was just visiting and sightseeing in New York and would be renting number 7 for a while. Very good English, but he had a slight accent that sounded like Hans."

"What did he look like?"

"Oh, he was quite tall and broad shouldered and had short dark hair, nearly black. His eyes were dark, I don't know the color. But the baby didn't look very much like him. She had a different complexion and light orange hair."

"Was the mother with him then?"

"No, we didn't see her until this afternoon. I guess you'd say yesterday afternoon, since it's after midnight now."

"And I saw her again tonight," said Gerald.

"Let's take this in order," said Dana. "What happened in the afternoon?"

"At about twelve fifteen," said Eleanor, "we were walking home after lunch. We just turned the corner from Columbus when she came running down our front steps, carrying the little girl under her arm. She was also carrying one of those light collapsible strollers. She was in a big hurry, and the baby was crying. She put the child down on the sidewalk while she opened the stroller, but the little girl ran back to the front steps, like she wanted to go inside. After that…well, it was just awful what that woman did." Eleanor sighed and shook her head.

Gerald picked up the story. "She jerked that kid by the arm and yelled 'tug' at the same time."

Dana frowned in puzzlement. "She actually *said* what she was doing?"

"I know it's odd, but that's what it sounded like. She yelled like that, and then she dragged the little girl by the arm over to the stroller, picked her up, and dropped her hard into the seat. The kid was howling."

"It looked like it hurt if you ask me," added Eleanor. "She yanked her around and almost threw her down."

"What did the woman look like?"

"She was very young," said Gerald. "That was my impression. I couldn't tell you much more. She must have been strong, the way she was holding that screaming toddler and a stroller while she was running."

"You don't remember anything else? Height or weight or skin and hair color?"

"Maybe average height," said Eleanor. "Actually, a little on the short side. Not thin but not big either. Her skin was white. Hair color, I don't know. I don't remember. Why don't I remember, Gerry? I'm losing my mind."

Gerald patted his wife's knee. "You're not losing your mind, dear. She was wearing a hat. They were both wearing hats and coats, dark clothing. We couldn't see anyone's hair."

"Yes, it was cold out, wasn't it? And I wasn't wearing my glasses."

"You normally wear glasses?" asked Dana.

"Yes," admitted Eleanor. "But I mostly need them for reading, and Gerry…"

"I had my glasses on," he said. "The young woman was wearing a hat, and it was the same hat she wore tonight. This time she was alone, without the child."

"Because she left that little girl in the apartment," blurted Eleanor, "just where we found her."

"Where were you when you saw her?" Dana asked Mr. Bishop.

"I was coming home from a trip to the deli on Amsterdam Avenue. I was walking up the front steps of the building when she flew out the front door like she'd been shot from a cannon. Ran right past me. I turned around to see where she was going. At the bottom of the stairs she turned right."

"So, she ran west?" asked Dana.

"Yes. It was the same direction she ran yesterday."

"Gerry wouldn't have been out there if it weren't for my sweet tooth," Eleanor explained. Her tone was apologetic. "At about ten o'clock I asked Gerry to go out and buy something for a late snack. I gave him some choices of sweets that the deli might have. He found my favorite, the coffee cake with cinnamon and white frosting. We also needed some milk for our cereal in the morning."

"I was carrying the coffee cake and a carton of milk in a plastic bag. About halfway up the front steps, the front door burst open. Frankly, I was a little startled, maybe even scared," Gerald admitted. "I don't know why. She was just a young woman, but she was very upset in a really desperate way. Her face was raw and wet, like she'd been crying. I could tell because it glistened in the light. We have pretty good lighting on the front steps. I don't remember much else. Just that expression on her face."

"You'd be able to recognize her if you saw her again?" asked Dana.

"Probably. I have an image in my mind—her look of anguish."

Eleanor was gazing at her husband as he spoke, and now she turned to Dana. "He must have sensed that something awful had just happened." She turned to him again. "That's why you were afraid, Gerry. You sensed it. Right before you saw her, I was up here listening to the most horrible argument you can imagine. You were gone fifteen minutes or so when those people started screaming at the top of their lungs. And the whole time, you know what was worse?"

Dana and Gerald and the Don looked at her intently.

"The sound of that little girl crying. It carried over those two voices. And then—it was so abrupt—the arguing stopped, and the child's crying cut off just like that." She snapped her fingers. "Like a switch had been thrown. Then the door slammed, and I heard footsteps on the landing and running down the stairs. You can always hear someone going down because the stairwell echoes. This time it was very loud because the woman, the mother of that child, was running away! I'm sure of it."

"What about the man?" asked Dana.

"What about him?" asked Eleanor.

"You heard two adults arguing, isn't that right?"

"Yes. The couple. The man and the woman. They were arguing in that foreign language. It must have been Dutch. If I heard it again, I'm sure I could identify it. Maybe you could play one of those language study tapes for me."

Dana considered this. "All right. Maybe. So, they were arguing, possibly in Dutch, and you heard the door slam and footsteps." Her eyes locked on the Don's. Subtly, he fiddled with his wristwatch, rotating the band on his wrist. Timing was important here. "Did the child's crying stop before or after the door slammed?" she asked.

Eleanor's eyes were moist as she remembered. "Before. I would say before. But...now wait just a minute..." She seemed to be listening again. "This was all so upsetting..."

"Of course," said Dana.

"The toddler was crying, and I felt so afraid for that little one.

Then everything seemed to happen at once. The arguing stopped, the crying stopped, and the door slammed. Yes, that must have been it, because Gerry saw her running away."

"She was in a big hurry," he agreed.

"You heard only one set of footsteps in the hallway?" asked Dana.

"Yes. I see what you're saying now. What about the man? The woman ran down, but what about the man? I don't know."

"I didn't see him," said Gerald.

"The next thing I remember is Gerry opening the door, coming inside, holding the bag with the cake and the milk. He was out of breath and almost purple from the exertion."

"I'm never purple, Nel."

"You had those bright circles in your cheeks like Santa Claus. I've warned him," she told Dana, "not to take the stairs so fast, to take his time. It was my fault for sending him out in the first place. He started telling me about the woman running out of the building but could hardly get a word out, he was panting so hard…"

"I took one look at Nel and was worried about *her*. She was white as a ghost. When she told me what she heard, we debated whether we should do anything or call the police. We were concerned about the kid, especially after we saw the mother throwing her around yesterday. But I thought we shouldn't get involved. The argument was over and the mother was gone, so the kid was safe, right?"

"Gerry wanted to know what I thought of the father. I remembered the time I met him down at the mailbox. He smiled at his little girl and stroked her hair so lovingly while we were talking."

"So, it must have been the mother," said Gerald. "She was the main threat. That's what we thought."

"While you were talking, could you hear anything else coming from the apartment?" asked Dana.

"No," said Gerald. The Bishops exchanged looks. "But when we stopped talking, everything seemed so still. We listened, and then we said the same thing at the same time. Sometimes that happens to us, doesn't it, Nel?"

"An identical thought will pop into our heads simultaneously. I suppose it's because we're together so much." Eleanor gave a tepid laugh but didn't look much amused.

"What was that thought?" asked Dana.

Eleanor spoke. "That it was unusual how the child stopped crying so abruptly. Screaming, and then silent."

"I asked Nel if it was possible that the kid just settled down a bit. We can't hear everything that goes on next door, not if it's a soft voice. Maybe she calmed down and was less vocal as soon as the mother left."

"But that wasn't what I heard. It was almost like…" Eleanor searched her thoughts. "You know how it is when all the breath is pushed out of you? All of a sudden. I thought that's what I heard."

"We didn't know what to think. I told Nel I'd just go next door and check on it. If the mother had hurt the kid, maybe the father needed help. After all, he was in a foreign country. I went out on the landing…"

"I was right behind him…"

"And it was strange…the door was open. Not all the way, but a couple of inches. It looked wrong, everything so quiet and the door open. I knocked on it and yelled, 'Hello, is everything all right?' There was no answer, so I walked in."

"I was thinking maybe he'd taken the child to the hospital."

"But then we saw that pink bundle, all wrapped up on the couch. The child was so still. I called out, and the man was gone."

A tear rolled down Eleanor's cheek. "How did we let him get away, Gerry? What were we thinking? Dear God, why were we wasting all that time talking when a little girl was dying? Why?"

17 »   ARREST

THE CLOCK RADIO was set at high volume to an oldies station. At six thirty, the Four Seasons shrilled Dana awake on a high note. From inside her soft, warm cave under the covers, she extended a determined fist and punched the "off" button. Her body ached for more sleep.

Eyes full of grit. Incipient headache. Subliminal dread. Willpower. She sat up and swung her feet to the floor.

As she showered, the Don's voice came to her: "This one's easy. Only two suspects, and they're gonna leave tracks. We'll haul 'em in—if they're not on a plane back to Dutchland." Coughing and more coughing. Paul, dear friend, please be well. This was a black morning indeed.

Dana's head was in a lather. Was it the mother? The Bishops were convinced of it. They thought she was abusive and physically strong. During the argument, her rage at the father must have been misdirected against the child. While the Bishops were in their apartment debating what to do, the father was trying to revive the dying child, but it was futile. He cleaned and bundled her, then dashed down the stairs. Where was he now? Wandering the streets in grief, searching for the mother? What would he do if he found her?

Dana tilted her head back under the jet of water, rinsing the shampoo down her body in foamy sheets. "But the missus isn't too clear on the timing." The Don wasn't impressed with Eleanor Bishop's hypothesis. His own instincts told him it was the father. The child didn't die immediately, and the mother wouldn't run at the very moment of unconsciousness. No mother would do that. It was the Don's theory that, before anything happened to the child, the mother ran from the father. She was angry at him, maybe scared of him. Her flight sent him into a rage, and he reacted with deadly force against the screaming little girl.

Occupied with these thoughts, Dana robotically completed her morning routine and was dressed for the office by seven. Evan had not returned from his morning run. In the bedroom, while checking her outfit in the full-length mirror, she heard Travis on the baby monitor. He often woke in a good mood and would sit in his crib for several minutes babbling playfully, experimenting with his morning voice.

She headed straight for his room, despite her concern about Anneke. By this time of the morning, the au pair was usually stirring in her bedroom or in the half bathroom. But all was quiet down at that end of the hall near the kitchen.

Last night, Dana returned home shortly after one o'clock and was surprised to see Anneke's door still open a crack and the room dark, unchanged since eleven thirty. Alarmed, she considered calling Anneke's mobile phone. First, she checked its usual resting place on the table in the foyer and found the phone there, left behind. A flash of anger unsettled her. She was so exhausted, and now she had this new reason to be uneasy. Well, she wouldn't worry. She didn't have time to worry. Only a few hours remained for sleep—as long as she wasn't called out again. Although she was allowed a day off from work to recuperate, she wouldn't take it. The new murder investigation, the Marshall hearing, and other looming deadlines awaited her at the office.

She didn't return to the easy chair in the living room but spent the rest of the night in bed next to Evan. After taking off her coat and shoes, she slid in beside him still wearing her jeans and T-shirt. A phone extension was on her nightstand, just in case. She willed it to remain silent. The city cooperated and was murder-free in the pre-dawn hours. Swiftly, she dropped into a fitful sleep infused with her anxiety about Anneke.

Now, as she headed into the nursery, she wanted to forget last night, but couldn't. She hesitated at the door and glanced in the direction of Anneke's room. It could wait. The mix of anger and worry had boiled down to a fine point of resentment. Surely, Anneke was in that room, still in bed, tired out from a late-night jaunt with her friend. Her irresponsibility was uncharacteristic, making it that much more noticeable. Late nights were fine on the weekend, but not during the workweek.

The only person Dana longed to see at this moment was Travis, full of life and exuberance for living. She walked in and greeted him, "Hi, big boy." He clambered to his feet and grabbed the railing of his crib. "Mommy, up!" He reached out to her. She pulled him into her arms, feeling the warmth of his flannel pajamas and the softness of his plump cheek against hers. So precious was this life.

She kissed the silken head and laid him on the changing table. Pajamas and wet diaper off, fresh diaper taped into place. Dana wondered how her own mother had ever put up with cloth diapers and safety pins.

Like every phase in a young child's life, this one would soon be over. Christmas was next month, and Dana would be taking a week-long vacation, the perfect time to start a toilet training regime. She and Evan didn't want to rely completely on Anneke for this. It was their responsibility. They'd already started the psychological preparation, the little daily reminders like the one she gave him now: "Very soon, no more diapers. You're growing up."

"I'm a big boy!"

"That's right, Tug."

What did Eleanor say? "The woman jerked that kid by the arm and yelled 'tug' at the same time."

"Good morning. Can I help?"

Dana swung around. Anneke was standing in the doorway, looking unprepared for the day. She pulled her robe tight, holding it closed at the waist with one hand while she raked back her unruly curls with the other hand. "I'm sorry," she said.

"It's okay, Anneke," said Dana. Her heart slowed to a comfortable rhythm. "I didn't hear you. We're fine here. You can go ahead and get ready."

"Sorry," she said again in a low voice.

On the changing table, half-clothed under Dana's hand, Travis rolled to his side and called Anneke's name.

"Hi, Travis," she answered. There wasn't a trace of the usual sparkle in her green eyes, and the purplish circles underneath were dark against her pasty skin.

"Keep still, Travis." Dana turned her back on Anneke and looked down at her son. Holding him firmly on the shoulder and chest, she jiggled him playfully. "Tickles!" he squealed. Anneke was still standing in the doorway, Dana could feel it. "There *is* one thing you could do," she said, turning her head slightly over her shoulder. "It would be a big help if you could make a pot of coffee."

"Sure," said Anneke, and she stepped away, the tension between them avoided.

When Travis was fully dressed, Dana picked him up and held him close again, not wanting to let him go. She heard the front door open and bang shut. "Everyone up?" Evan sounded well-exercised, his voice cheerful. She needed some of that cheer to rub off on her.

"In the nursery," she called out. She heard Evan saying "good morning" to Anneke, who gave a lackluster greeting in return. "Coffee's almost ready," she said. "I'll just go get dressed."

Evan came into the nursery, sweat-soaked and gleeful. Travis reached out to his father, who cupped the boy's head in his hands and kissed his forehead. "How'd it go last night?" he asked Dana.

"Only one case."

"You okay?"

"Just great," she said, trying to sound as if it were so. Travis was squirming in her arms, and nothing could be said in front of him. "I'm just going to fill my travel mug with coffee and get going. Maybe Anneke can help with Travis this morning." She put the boy down and took his hand.

"Sure. While I'm in the shower."

"Come on, Tug." The family left the nursery and walked to the kitchen, where Dana took her travel mug and Travis's sippy cup from the cabinet. While she filled the mug with coffee, Evan filled the sippy cup with orange juice and took Travis into the dining area.

Anneke emerged from her room dressed in slacks, a sweatshirt, and socks, no shoes. "You need some help?"

"Yes, please, Anneke," said Evan. "Dana's about ready to leave, and I need fifteen minutes to get ready." He ruffled Travis's hair. "Then we'll eat breakfast together, okay Tug?"

Dana came out of the kitchen and saw Travis sitting on Anneke's lap at the table. They were fully engaged, oblivious to their surroundings. Anneke whispered in his ear, and Travis giggled. Dana's anger instantly vanished, replaced with gratitude and warmth for this capable caregiver, a loving young woman who was clearly fond of their little boy. What would they do without her?

Evan caught Dana's eye in a silent plea for a private word. She picked up the cue and said, "I forgot something in the bedroom." He followed her down to the end of the hall and closed the bedroom door behind them.

"Was it a bad case?" he asked.

"Bad, yes. But no B.A.G. Really heartbreaking. A little child."

"Murdered? How?"

"Shaken baby syndrome. One of the parents did it; we're not sure which one. A charge of intentional murder won't stick, but it's at least reckless manslaughter."

"Make an arrest?"

"No. The parents are on the run. I have to call the Don and see if he has an update. I'll tell you more about it later. Thanks for following up with Anneke this morning." She met his eyes briefly and looked down at the travel mug in her hand, adjusting the top, testing it for tightness.

"No problem. I don't have to be in until nine. Tina and the CEO of Mysterion are coming in at nine thirty." He touched her shoulder with one hand and gently lifted her chin with the other. "Sure you're okay?"

"Tired, that's all. And I was kind of mad at Anneke but didn't say anything to her. I got home after one this morning and she still wasn't back."

"Really? What's she up to? Becoming a party girl?"

"I have no idea. I'm afraid to ask. Evan…" She lifted her eyes to his, and their gaze held as they found the same thought. Eleanor's voice spoke again. *Sometimes that happens to us…*

"She won't let us down," he said.

"We can't go back to those days. I can't work if I'm worried about Travis."

"She's better than that. I'll talk to her."

"Okay. Thank you."

"Listen, maybe I have something to cheer you up." He pulled Chocolate out of the pocket of his sweatpants, looked at it, and said, "Then again, maybe not."

Her face lit up. "Where did you find it?" She took the toy

from him.

"It was on the sidewalk, on the way to the park. I didn't want to take it out in front of Travis. I don't know if it's salvageable. You be the judge."

"Well, maybe it isn't, now that your sweat is all over it."

"Very funny. But there's more on it than just sweat."

She scrunched her nose and handed it back to him. "How close to the curb was it?"

"Not in the dog zone, I don't think."

"Are Beanie Babies dry cleanable?"

He shrugged.

"I'll try to wash it this weekend. Don't show Travis yet."

"Right, boss."

She craned her neck and planted a kiss on his mouth.

"Anything?" she asked Paul. With her elbows on the desk, forehead propped in her right palm, she held the phone receiver to her left ear. The coffee had done little to remove the fog.

"No other witnesses in the building. Talked to all the neighbors except the person in the apartment immediately below. We're working on finding him."

"What's the landlord say about the sublease?"

"The management company has no record. It's an illegal sublet."

"What about the tenant, Hans Visser? Any leads on where he might be?" She spoke over the sound of coughing on the other end of the line and had to wait for his answer. Perhaps she should have called the precinct and talked to Detective Greeley. But she knew that the Don would be on top of the investigation. He hadn't surrendered to his condition, and she wouldn't abandon him. Professional avoidance would be more painful to him than his chronic cough and secret diagnosis.

"The search gave us an address and phone number in the Netherlands. Greeley called and spoke to Visser. He gave us a name, Niels Van Leeuwen. A high school teacher in Amsterdam."

"Did Visser mention the wife?"

"He doesn't know anything about a wife or a child. Thought he was renting to a single man. Van Leeuwen stiffed him on a month's rent."

"What's the high school say?" Given the time difference, six hours ahead in Holland, Dana assumed that one of the detectives had called in the pre-dawn hours and got through to someone in Amsterdam during their regular school day.

"They gave us the home address and phone number, and they're sending us a photo. The school had no idea he was here; he gave them a bogus excuse for taking leave. We also got the wife's name, Renske, but they just saw her on Tuesday. She came to the school to pick up his mail."

"What...?" Before the detective could answer, he started coughing again. Dana filled in, to give him time. "So that wasn't his wife here in New York? Maybe he was making excuses so he could meet a girlfriend."

"We called their home number. No answer. No Renske so far. We'll keep trying."

"Better check the airlines to see if Niels is leaving the country under his own name."

"Checking."

"Okay. Thanks, Paul. Keep me updated."

A knock sounded on her open door. She replaced the receiver in its cradle and looked up to see Eric standing there, holding the product of his research. "Finished the memo. No case law exactly on point—our facts are too weird."

"It's a case of first impression."

"Right about that. But I found enough to support our position. There's no way that Bounce's guilty plea is 'newly discovered evidence' under the definition in the statute."

She took the papers from him and looked into his eyes. It seemed that everyone was wearing dark circles today. "You worked late last night?"

"Not as late as you."

"You're a lifesaver, Eric. Thank you. I owe you one."

He gestured "forget it" with a shrug. "That copy is for you. Another was delivered to Krumins, and I'm taking the original to Jack's courtroom now."

"Try not to say you have a delivery for 'Jack' when you hand the memo to Robert."

"Okay." He laughed. "And if the judge is there, I'll remember to say, 'Your Honor.'"

"She'll like that."

He started to go, but hesitated. "How many cases did you pick up last night?"

"Just one."

"Just."

"I'll survive."

"Okay, but my calendar's clear this afternoon if you want me to cover the hearing. I'm up to speed on this case if Jack—Judge DuBois—wants more argument."

"I appreciate the offer, but you've done so much already. I'm here the rest of the day and I'll cover it."

"All right, but—"

"I know. I look like something the cat dragged in. Don't sweat it. I'll catch up on my sleep tonight."

Travis was cranky and erratic this morning, but his moodiness only brought Anneke closer to him. She felt a desperate tenderness, stronger than ever before. She wanted to keep this connection, nurture it, and forget the other. The depth of her sadness was eased with every touch. He smelled so good. She loved his energy and smile and tears and fussing. His hair was messy and she tried to comb it. "You need a haircut, Travis. Should we tell Mommy?"

Aimlessly, they meandered from one activity to the next, moving from one room of the apartment to another. Their routine had slipped away, and the boy was reacting. The rhythm and certainty of a daily schedule was gone. The rooms were cast in a surreal blur, the air thick, her eyes clouded. Nothing was back to the way it had been or should be. She needed certainty.

Her employers were good people and she'd lied to them. Her latest lie was to Evan this morning. "Dana says you were out very late last night. Everything okay?" he asked. She apologized and said that her friend Marije was having personal problems. They'd stayed out very late, just talking. When she realized the hour, she thought of calling, but didn't want to disturb their sleep.

A real apology was due. The truth. Why was it impossible? She hoped that intelligent people like Dana and Evan wouldn't completely blame her. She understood the viewpoint that a man of a certain age, a married man, was the one to blame, not the underage girl. But that wasn't how it felt. And the parents of the young boy she was caring for might not feel that way either.

A true apology would span almost three years and would have to be made to herself more than anyone else. She would have to apologize for having an affair with a married man, carelessly becoming pregnant, allowing Niels to "adopt" his own baby, and two years later, failing to get the child back home. She would have to confess that she'd fallen in love with her own little girl and had nearly surrendered to the fantasy that Niels had suggested.

A real apology to the Goodhues for her disappearance last night would have to include an explanation that she was only trying to erase this history. Last night, when she finally took action, she was trying to remake herself into the person they believed her to be.

The first idea led to nothing. She filled her pocket with quarters before leaving the apartment. She didn't want to make the call with the mobile phone that Dana had given her. Didn't want to use it for dirty business. Out on the street, shivering in a telephone booth, she pulled out the business card and dialed the number of the hotel where Timmers was staying. He was in his room and answered after several rings, sounding as if he'd been asleep.

She told him she could lead him to Niels and Kaatje. He said thank you very much, but he'd already found them. He refused to say when it was, or what he would do with that information. He didn't want to breach client confidentiality.

Anneke supposed that he must have given the address to Renske. Of course he had. But what would they do? Was Renske coming for her child? Had they contacted the police?

This wasn't the outcome Anneke had hoped for. This wasn't the assurance she needed.

She went to a diner, nursed a cup of coffee, and thought long and hard about it. Either Timmers had driven Niels away, or he was still here. She would go and see for herself. And if she found him, she would deliver an ultimatum. She now had the ammunition to make a credible threat.

It took some time to build the courage and to compose the words in her head. Procrastination worked to her advantage this time. The later it got, the more likely they would be gone, or if they were still here, Kaatje would be asleep. She didn't want her little girl to be a witness to this. She didn't want to see her again, to feel that pain again.

As much as Anneke wanted him gone, the sound of his voice over the intercom was a relief. She was glad to have this final chance to take action, to prove something to herself. She worried about disturbing the baby with the jarring sound of the door buzzer and the static of the intercom. As she climbed the stairs, she heard passionate orchestral music coming from a stereo in the apartment directly below his. Perhaps her baby would be awake. But when she got to the top of the stairs, Niels was alone, Kaatje out of sight.

"You've come back. I knew you would." He was unkempt and exuded the tang of nervous energy. She was struck with a visceral distaste for him, for their past, for their current predicament. Had she really fooled herself into loving this man? The shame of her disillusionment smacked her in the gut. The taste of coffee and stomach acid bubbled up.

She stepped into the foyer. Hastily, he closed the door behind her, letting it fall shut with a shuddering slam.

"This is the last time, Niels." She spoke in a hoarse whisper. "I've just come to say goodbye, without the children to interfere. Kaatje is asleep?"

"In the other room."

"Let's speak quietly. I don't want her to know I'm here. I don't want to see her again. I...I can't..." Against her will, a fist of emotion choked her throat.

"You love her, Anneke. You love your little girl. She's you all over again." His voice was a facsimile of the lulling, cooing sounds he'd used that morning to draw her in. He touched her shoulder, pushing her into the apartment with a tremulous hand.

Anneke jerked away, taking a couple of steps into the living room. "She's not my little girl. I gave birth to her, but she belongs to Renske. You have to take her back to her mother."

"But she's ours."

"I spoke to that investigator, Jan Timmers. He told me he found you. He knows where you are."

"That little mouse? He couldn't find the nose on his face. I suppose you led him to this apartment."

"No, I didn't. He found you all on his own."

"Then let him do what he wants. Let him come here. Let him

tell Renske. They can't run me out of this city without you."

She took her chance and spoke the lie she'd practiced. "He's going to the police, Niels. He told me."

"Hah! A good story. But Renske wouldn't allow it. She knows I don't like the police." His eyes gleamed with a sense of power.

"They could arrest you. Is that what you want Kaatje to see? You should take her home before it's too late."

"Sure, we'll go home. But you're coming with us." He took her arm in a pincer-like grasp and she broke away, blindly careening into the bookcase. A framed picture fell, shattering the glass.

"Now look what you've done!" She stared at the damage as she rubbed her arm, startled by the pain.

"Papa." Anneke turned and saw the sleepy-eyed little girl shuffling out of the hallway into the dining room. A pink blanket trailed behind her. Anneke was startled by the sight. Travis would never escape from the nursery after being put to bed. But then she remembered. This apartment belonged to a single man—there was no crib to confine a wandering toddler.

Niels rushed over and swept up the child. His action was too abrupt, and she started to cry. "Anneke!" She reached out past her father's shoulder and wailed.

"You're going back to bed," he snarled. "Stay in the bedroom." He carried her into the hallway.

"*Nee, Papa, niet doen!*" She screamed in full voice, reacting to his manic jerkiness. Everything was wrong. He was too rough. Anneke yearned to take the child in her arms.

She followed them as far as the dining room and stopped there with her hand on the table. Horrified, she listened to his harsh words while the baby protested. He came striding out of the hallway.

"Every day I have to hear all that crying for you!" He turned and gestured to indicate the noise they couldn't ignore. The girl was inconsolable.

"She needs her mother."

"*You* are her mother." He grabbed her by the elbows. "Come with us. We'll pack our bags and leave. Right now."

"You're crazy." She shook him off, stumbled backward and tripped, grabbing the back of a chair. She fell to the floor, onto her hip. The chair came crashing down. "Don't you understand? The police will be after you!"

He grabbed her forearm and yanked her up. "Timmers doesn't have the balls to do anything."

Kaatje emerged from the hallway and ran into the dining room. They both went for her, but Niels was faster and snatched her up. She screamed and struggled against his hold, pushing at his chest as he bounced her furiously up and down like a toy that needed fixing.

Anneke yelled over the crying. "It doesn't matter about Timmers. *I'm* calling the police."

"You wouldn't do that. Those people will find out."

Kaatje shrieked and hiccupped, jostled by her father's jerky movements.

Anneke could stand it no longer. Tears stung her eyes. She threw her hands over her ears and backed away. "I'm waiting an hour. That's it. One hour. Pack up and get out before it's too late!"

Niels came at her. Holding the child with one arm, he swiped at her and missed.

She ran, screaming as she went. "I'm calling the police!" She was at the door. "I swear it! One hour!"

She pulled the door open, slid out, and slammed it in his face. Down the stairs, fast, fast, heart beating. Down three flights, through the lobby, and out the door. On the front steps she rushed past a man who was walking up, returning home. He looked at her curiously. *Let him look. Let him think what he wants.*

Turning right onto the sidewalk, a blast of chilly wind on her face gave welcome relief. She was free of Niels. She would never see him again.

After wandering the streets for many blocks, she finally took refuge from the cold, entering a diner she'd never seen before. This time she ordered hot soup and spent several minutes gazing down at it, alternately breathing the steam and using a napkin to dam up her dripping eyes and nose.

She'd been serious. Her threat was real. She would make good on it. A call to the police. He'd seen she was serious. He would pack up and go.

Kaatje's face floated on the yellow surface of her chicken noodle soup. Her little girl was smiling and then she was crying, calling her name. *What will your life be, my little one? What have I done?*

The minutes ticked, her stomach rumbled and clenched. She ventured a spoonful of soup, hoping for comfort. The place was quiet but not empty. Two seats at the counter and a couple of booths were occupied. Voices wafted, thick coffee cups clinked on thick saucers, tinny silverware clattered. The fluorescent lamps cast a sickening gray light. She sat in a booth by a window, where anyone on the sidewalk could see her. At this hour on a weekday night, the city moved slower but never came to a halt. Every few minutes a pedestrian walked by. She didn't know these people, all of them strangers.

Seconds bled, one into the next. Without knowing it, she'd been sipping at her soup. At the bottom of the large bowl, five noodles floated in the cold broth. She counted them. The waitress came by to ask if she wanted something else. "What time is it?" she asked. The waitress pointed to a clock over the counter. She hadn't seen it when she first came in, and now it was past midnight. An hour might have come and gone. Surely an hour had passed. It was time to carry out her threat. She paid the tab, pulled on her hat, wrapped her scarf around her neck, and buttoned her pea coat.

The nearest police precinct was north of here. She'd seen it before on one of her longer evening walks. Eight or ten blocks away, she wasn't sure. She stepped out of the diner and went looking for it, taking an indeterminate path. Soon her nose was cold and her toes painful, like little hard rocks inside her shoes. She zigzagged, checking each block. The upper seventies, the lower eighties, and then she came to it, a solid edifice. On the first floor, the exterior was neatly sheathed in bricks, and the upper floors were encased in a dense, gray concrete. "20th Precinct." The large, double door was illuminated on either side by a rectangular fixture of frosty glass, emitting light of a greenish hue. A half dozen blue and white police vehicles were parked in angled slots out front.

She stood across the street and examined the building, taking in its details. The double door was made of large glass panes. From inside, a white brilliance emanated. With little effort, she could walk out of the dark, into that unforgiving light. A man in a uniform, or maybe a woman, would see her face in sharp contrast. The officer would inquire about her business, listen to her excuses, guess her secrets.

A patrol car pulled up front. Two uniformed officers got out and walked into the precinct. Anneke turned and strolled away, jiggling the quarters in her coat pocket.

On the avenue, she came to a pay phone. A chance to call the precinct, cloaked in anonymity. She passed it by. Several blocks on, she passed another phone booth.

Walking the neighborhood, faster this time, her toes became warm. It felt better to move. She quickened her pace until she was nearly jogging, maintaining perpetual motion. She crossed streets at every green light and turned corners at the red lights when traffic prevented her from crossing. Blocks and blocks of this, until she built up a sweat. It felt good. She felt good. She was rid of him.

He had gone.

Finally, she was exhausted, incapable of moving another inch. Her exhaustion hit full force just as she arrived at the familiar building with its welcoming, well-lit lobby. Endrit was at the door. He greeted her home. It was 2:00 a.m. by the time she got upstairs and fell into the twin bed in her little room. Dark. Sleep.

Never enough. The new day always dawned, and here it was.

"Caught ya!" said Travis out of the blue, waking her from shifting visions of her nocturnal visit and aimless wanderings of the night before.

"Silly boy," she said.

"Can we go? I want caught ya."

"It didn't go so well with your friend last time, did it?"

"I want to play."

"But Kaatje has gone home, didn't I tell you?"

"She's home? Let's go."

"But she's gone back to her real home, very far away. Her papa took her back to her mama."

"To where?"

"To Holland."

"Witte bloemen, rode bloemen, blauwe bloemen…"

How precious! Smart little Travis, speaking Dutch. She hugged him tight.

"I want caught ya!"

"Okay, okay. We'll go. I'll show you. She's not there anymore."

It was just as well to have this final confirmation. The buzzer would go unanswered, and Travis would understand.

Pushing him in the stroller, Anneke hummed a Dutch clogging song on the way to the brownstone on 73rd Street. Her sneakers were hardly *klompen*, but she skipped and brushed and heeled them against the sidewalk, pretending to make the distinct sound of wooden shoes. In gleeful play, she stopped the stroller in the middle of the sidewalk and toed and heeled all the way around it, making Travis giggle. "I'm going to get you some *klompen*, Tug. You'll like them." Small children always looked so cute in wooden shoes. She remembered her own baby shoes, the little *klompen* that her mother was still saving for her back home.

In front of the building, she helped Travis out of the stroller, folded it up, and held his hand as they ascended the ten concrete steps. At the top, she rang the bell to number 7. "I don't think there will be an answer, Travis." A second later, she was proved wrong.

"Yes," said a male voice.

Her heart sank. Terror rose, freezing her voice. Again, the man said "yes." But there was nothing familiar about that word or the way it was said. The inflection and tone sounded nothing like Niels.

She smiled in relief. Of course. It was the tenant, the man who lived here. He'd come back. "Hello," she said. "I was looking for the person staying here, but never mind."

"Come in," said the voice, and the door unlocked with a buzz.

"Caught ya!" Travis pushed on the door and pulled at her hand.

Well, what could it hurt? She'd speak to the tenant and confirm that Niels had gone back to Amsterdam. She'd show Travis that his little friend was no longer there.

She stepped into the lobby and started up the stairs, Travis pulling on her hand. An odd noise sounded behind her. A metallic screech was followed by a voice, scratchy with static: "…inside, over." Another voice, directly behind her, replied, "I'm in the lobby." She spun around to see a uniformed police officer following them, releasing the button on a hand-held walkie-talkie. She gasped and stubbed her toe on the next stair.

"Going up to number 7?" he asked, unsmiling. He was

young and had an open expression which, under different circumstances, might have seemed friendly. Anneke stared at him, momentarily unable to speak. He towered over her, this official with thick black hair and warm brown eyes. He looked strong enough to crush her like a twig underfoot.

"Y-yes," she stammered, finding the brass name tag on his chest. *E. Tiriac.* Her eyes moved to the holstered gun on his belt.

"You know someone up there?"

"No… I don't think…"

"You don't think you know anyone up there? Or you don't know?"

"I don't think he's there."

"Okay, let's go up and see."

She started up the stairs again with Travis, who was equally dumbfounded. Officer Tiriac walked close behind. All the joy had vanished, and Travis dragged his feet, whimpering. She put down the stroller, picked him up, and placed him on her hip with his arms wrapped around her neck. Before she could grab the stroller again, the officer said, "I'll get that."

What was this? He was leading her into something bad, she could feel it, but there was nowhere she could go. Nowhere to run.

They were coming to the second landing. "Did something happen?" she asked.

"You tell me," he said.

What kind of answer was that?

As they walked up the final flight, she became aware of activity on the third landing. Another male police officer, this one smaller than Tiriac, was talking to a petite woman with gray hair and large, buggy glasses. The woman turned away from the officer, glanced at Anneke, and exclaimed, "That's her! That's the one we saw!"

"What? What do you mean?" Anneke was stupefied.

"But who is that little boy?" asked the woman.

"What *is* this?" asked Anneke. She stepped up onto the landing and saw that the door to apartment number 7 was open, a yellow crime scene tape strung across. "What happened here?"

"That's the mother of the little girl!" the woman yelped. She was jumpy and excited as if she might collapse in fright. "But who is this? You have a little boy too?"

The other officer nodded at Tiriac and directed the woman back into the apartment across the landing, number 8.

"What's going on?" Anneke asked again.

"Where's caught ya?" asked Travis.

"You know the man who was staying here, right?" Officer Tiriac asked Anneke.

"But he's not here, is he?" she asked.

"I think we have to talk about this. You'll have to come with us."

"But…no. I have to take Travis home."

"Is this your little boy?"

"No, he's not. I have to take him home."

"You'll have to come with us."

Now the other officer had joined them, and they directed her back down the stairs. She was flanked by them, guided against her will. Travis was in her arms, swinging his head right and left with wondering, wide eyes. Officer Tiriac was on the left, holding the stroller in his left hand, touching Anneke's elbow with his right hand. The other officer was on her right.

She started to tremble, holding Travis close. Of all things, she remembered that he had to be changed. His diaper was heavy with moisture. She should get him home, change him, give him lunch, and wait for Dana's midday phone call. She had to do these things, but the police officers were getting in her way.

"Where are we going?"

"To the precinct."

"But, why? I have to get Travis home."

"Who are the boy's parents? We'll call them."

"No! You can't call them! I'll call them."

Travis started to cry, and she stroked his head. Her heart was beating fast, so hard that he must have felt it through the double layers of their coats.

"Look, you can tell us who the parents are, or we can call Social Services to pick up the boy. Your choice. He shouldn't stay with us at the precinct." They were at the bottom of the stairs now, in the small lobby at the front door.

"But I can't go with you! I…I'm late for home. Why are we going to the precinct?"

Over her head, the two officers exchanged a look. "You're under arrest," said Officer Tiriac.

"Arrest? I haven't done anything…arrest for what?"

"For murder."

Her knees buckled. Travis slid to the ground and wandered off to the side as the officers propped up his caregiver. He looked on, his little face white as a sheet.

"Niels? Someone killed Niels?" She swung around, frantically seeking out one pair of stern eyes and the other, growing steadily more erratic. "What happened here? Won't you tell me?" Tiriac removed the cuffs from his belt, pulled her hands to the small of her back and applied them to her wrists.

"We'll explain at the station," said the other officer. "First, let me read you your rights."

"Wait, wait, no! Where's my child? Where?"

"He's right here," said Tiriac. "He's fine." Travis, all alone in a corner of the lobby, started to wail.

"No, no, I don't mean Travis. My little girl! Where's my little girl? Where's Kaatje?"

18 » DUNGEON

Vesma was outside the courtroom at the designated hour. She stood in the corridor with her arms crossed, hands clutching opposite elbows, her briefcase dangling from a shoulder strap. High heels in cranberry red shaped her legs; the skirt of her slate-colored suit was form-fitting and ended at the knee.

"Hi," she greeted Dana. "Got your memo. Did you get ours?"

"Yes. I just finished reading it." She declined to add that she was not convinced by the arguments in the defense memo and expected that the judge would agree with her.

Hit by a wave of fatigue, Dana pulled up straighter and firmed her grasp on the handle of her briefcase. As she slipped her other hand into the pocket of her jacket, she wondered if she'd worn this black suit anytime in recent history, particularly during one of her three court dates with Vesma in the past several days. She might not win a fashion contest against her adversary, but she had full confidence in her legal arguments. "What's going on?"

"The judge is still sitting on another case." Vesma tipped her head toward the courtroom, letting her long hair sweep sideways off her shoulder. Dana went up and peeked through the small, rectangular window in the door.

The judge was on the bench, Robert was sitting at the clerk's desk, a defense attorney and his client were at their table, and an assistant district attorney was standing, questioning a police witness. The jury box was empty. Two court officers and a steno-grapher completed the assemblage behind the bar. The sole observer in the audience sat in the middle of the first left-hand pew, directly behind the defense table. Mrs. Marshall patiently listened to the proceedings, waiting for her son's arrival and his final chance to be acquitted of murder.

Dana looked back at Vesma. "Shall we?"

"Sure. Let's show our faces."

Dana opened the door, and the two women walked up the aisle together, Vesma on the left. While Dana gently padded on the balls of her feet to minimize noise, Vesma was more careless, allowing the heels of her shoes to click distinctly on the linoleum. When they reached the front of the audience section, Mrs. Marshall turned to look. Vesma nodded cordially at her before taking the aisle seat in the same row, keeping some distance between them. The chilliness was evident. Dana took a seat across the aisle.

Within minutes, the police officer finished his testimony. The attorneys made brief statements, arguing for and against the suppression of narcotics seized from the defendant's car. Judge DuBois didn't need to reserve decision on this one. "Motion to suppress denied," she said. "We'll start jury selection tomorrow at ten o'clock." With a bang of the gavel, the matter was con-cluded, and the participants left the courtroom.

Vesma and Dana replaced the departing attorneys at their respective counsel tables. "Well," said the judge, looking at her watch. "I timed this one pretty close." It was ten minutes after twelve. "I have a decision on your motion. Bring the defendant in." The court officers left through the side door and soon re-turned with Tyrone Marshall in tow. As usual, he caught his mother's eye and they communicated silently before he took a seat next to Vesma.

Mother and son were aware that, whichever way this went

today, immediate release from prison was not in the cards. Even if Judge DuBois vacated the jury verdict, Tyrone's legal troubles were not over. The feds had a hold on him for racketeering, and he would be released into their custody. Meanwhile, in this case, any ruling adverse to the People would be appealed, and if they won, the murder verdict would be reinstated.

Although Dana predicted that Judge DuBois would deny the defendant's motion, there was security in knowing that the federal authorities would take over if the unpredictable happened. Either way, she was already starting to feel relieved that this phase of the case was coming to an end.

When everyone was in place, the judge continued.

"Mr. Marshall, I'll be issuing a written decision, but here's the gist of it. Earlier in this proceeding, I denied the first part of your motion. You claimed that your right to effective counsel was violated because Mr. Kaplan failed to call Jeremy Grant as a witness for the defense. But Mr. Kaplan discovered that Mr. Grant wasn't anywhere near the scene of the shooting—he was attending a hearing in his own criminal case that day. Mr. Kaplan cannot be faulted for declining to call a witness who had nothing relevant to say and might commit perjury. Therefore, you failed to prove a violation of your constitutional right to effective counsel.

"Second, you claimed that the prosecutor improperly withheld exculpatory evidence. The jury had finished deliberating and was about to give the verdict when Ms. Hargrove learned for the first time that Brendon Hayes pled guilty in federal court. She delayed the disclosure for one minute, until the verdict was announced. This delay was not improper, and you suffered no ill consequences from it. If the disclosure had been made a minute earlier, it was still too late to reopen the trial. As it was, you were given a full opportunity to use this information in your post-trial motion. Therefore, you failed to prove the second ground for your motion.

"And so, we come to your third argument concerning 'newly discovered evidence.' I've considered the testimony of Brendon Hayes and the oral and written arguments of counsel. No further argument is necessary. I've come to a decision."

The judge paused and cast her intelligent brown eyes on the defendant, the attorney for the defense, and the attorney for the prosecution, in turn. A glint of gold from her hoop earrings enlivened her visage. The moment was tense. Everyone waited.

On the elevated bench, the judge sat erect and placed her hands, with interlaced fingers, in front of her. "Under the law, this court may set aside the jury verdict based on newly discovered evidence that might have led the jury to acquit. In your case, Mr. Marshall, you were not aware that Brendon Hayes had pled guilty in federal court until after your jury announced the verdict. In that sense, the revelation of the guilty plea was certainly 'new' to you."

Uh-oh. This was not starting out well, thought Dana.

"If you had known about the guilty plea earlier, your attorney, Mr. Kaplan, certainly would have offered it into evidence at your trial. Any defense counsel would have seized the opportunity to inform the jury that another person had confessed to shooting the victim."

Double uh-oh.

"Let's imagine this fictional trial in which Mr. Hayes is a witness for the defense. He testifies that he pled guilty to racketeering and admitted to shooting Dwayne Little. However, this evidence isn't going to get you very far. The door is open for the prosecutor to cross-examine Mr. Hayes. The jury is going to hear that you gave him the murder weapon and said, 'you know what you gotta do.' If the jury believes that testimony, it's enough to convict you of murder as an accessory. You had the intent to kill Little, and you gave material aid to the shooter. On top of that, the jury heard the evidence about the shooting that occurred two weeks earlier. The same weapon was used, and Little pointed the finger at you. Considering everything together, I cannot grant your motion to set aside the verdict. You haven't shown that this so-called 'new' evidence might have convinced a jury to acquit you."

Phew. Dana started to relax.

A muffled sob erupted from the sole member of the audience. Vesma started to stand up, but the judge held out a flat-palmed hand like a traffic cop. Vesma resumed her seat.

"You might say," continued the judge, "that I'm speculating about what a jury would do. Well, let me give you the full benefit of the doubt. Let's assume that the jury ignores my instructions on the law and wants to exercise mercy. Maybe they want to give you a break, and they're inclined to acquit you. If we assume this, then you've established only one of the requirements needed to set aside the verdict. You still haven't proven that you first discovered the evidence when it was too late to use it at your trial. If the crime really went down the way Mr. Hayes said it did, this was no surprise to you, Mr. Marshall. You would have known this on the day it happened.

"Further…," the judge continued, launching into the next topic. As she spoke, the red light flashed on Robert's phone — a silent signal that it was ringing. "…this court does not adopt the defense argument that the evidence is 'newly discovered' just because it's newly available."

Robert picked up the receiver and said "Part 52" in a low voice.

"Mr. Hayes was not an available witness during this trial because the federal prosecution was still open."

Robert huddled around the receiver as he listened to the caller.

"If he'd been summoned to this trial, he would have taken the Fifth and refused to testify, to avoid compromising his chances in the federal case. In that sense, his testimony was not available at the time of this trial."

Robert said, "All right, thank you," in a soft voice, and replaced the receiver. He got up, walked toward the side of the bench, and stood a few yards away from the judge.

Without a break in her speech, the judge glanced obliquely at him and held a single finger up to the side, telling him to wait. She was almost finished. "But the statute says, 'newly discovered,' not 'newly available.' I can't rewrite the law. Therefore, Mr. Marshall, you have not sustained your burden of establishing grounds for setting aside the verdict. You've had a fair trial, and the jury found you guilty of murder. Your motion is denied. Let's schedule a date for sentencing."

A clamor broke out in the courtroom. Mrs. Marshall protested that her son was innocent, Tyrone dropped his head into his hands, Vesma sprang to her feet and objected to the decision, and the judge beckoned Robert, who leaned in and whispered the message he'd just received. When Robert finished what he had to say, the judge banged the gavel. "Silence! Your objection is noted. I'm issuing a written decision and you have the right to appeal." She motioned to the senior court officer. "Take charge."

The two officers approached Tyrone, coaxing him up to his feet. He resisted, mumbling obstinately under his breath. "The defendant requests a courtroom visit with his mother," Vesma said. Mrs. Marshall jumped up and put her hands on the bar, leaning over it toward the defense table. Her eyes were wild and panicky. Dana stood, waiting for a break in the uproar, wanting to give her thanks to the court and be on her way out the door.

"Granted," said the judge, "but keep your voices down. You're in a court of law."

The judge fixed her keen attention on Dana. Her eyes had changed. They seemed to hold a secret, carefully wrapped in a soft cocoon of understanding, concern, and protection. Where had

Dana seen this look before? Instantly, she was transported back in time more than six years. She was a rookie again, stepping over the yellow police tape into a crime scene. On the other side, in the midst of buzzing police activity, was ADA Jacquelyn DuBois, Dana's revered mentor. Jack's eyes met hers. The look she gave her then was the look she gave her now.

Today, however, the voice that went with the look sounded far more formal. "Ms. Hargrove, please approach the bench. I have a message for you on something unrelated to this case."

The words meant nothing, but the tone struck a note of panic. Dana's heart was in her throat as she sidled around the table and walked up to the bench. Behind her, a noisy, emotional meeting was taking place between mother and son at the bar.

"Who called?" Dana asked.

"Patrick McBride. He'd like you to return at once."

"Did he say why?"

The judge paused before finding the words. "Not exactly. He did say you were to go immediately to the Dungeon. I suppose he didn't use that word, did he, Robert?"

"The DA's detective unit," said Robert. Automatically, the judge had reverted to a habit acquired in her days as an assistant district attorney, when she always used the descriptive nickname for the basement headquarters of the DA's detective squad.

"Right," the judge agreed with Robert. To Dana she said, "Your nanny and your son are there. They want you to pick up your son."

"In the *Dungeon?*"

"They'll explain when you get there. Talk to Detective Donegan. He'll explain everything."

In the corridor, shaken with disbelief, Dana pulled the Nokia from her jacket pocket and looked at the screen. A decent signal. She was on the tenth floor of the Criminal Court building, and the trip to the basement could take two minutes or five, depending. She wouldn't wait.

Oblivious to the attorneys milling around, she pressed "4" in speed dialing, held the mobile phone to her ear, and punched the down arrow for the elevator with a knuckle of the hand holding her briefcase. Nervously pacing the floor, head down, she listened.

Detective Donegan answered immediately. He'd been waiting for her.

"What's going on, Paul?" She hit the elevator button again.

"Just get down here."

"Is Travis there?"

"We took him to the nursery in SCU."

"*What?*" The sex crimes unit maintained a nursery for the children of witnesses and victims who were visiting the office or testifying in court. SCU was across the street, in the same building as Dana's trial bureau, TB90.

"Come down here first," Paul said. "The kid's fine, happy as a clam. No crack babies today. He's all alone over there, playing with Bethany." The Don was referring to a receptionist in SCU, who doubled as a babysitter when the volunteer caregivers weren't around.

The elevator dinged, signaling its arrival. "I'm coming down." She pressed "End."

On the first floor, Dana filed out with the rest of the passengers, walked through the lobby and out the front door, making her way around the corner to the side of the building and the private entrance for the DA's office. Access to the basement was allowed only on the secure elevator bank. She flashed her ID at the security guard and waited impatiently at the end of the line. There were three elevators. Everyone else caught an elevator going up, and she was the only one to board an elevator to the basement.

One floor down, the door opened on the gray environment of the Dungeon in the bowels of the Criminal Court building. She stepped out. Behind her, the heavy metal doors joined with a decisive, sucking clang, shutting her inside the vault. Why *this* place? It gave her a sense of desperate suffocation. An unknown something had happened, something bad, or at least serious. Travis had been along for this unknown thing, and maybe, he'd been affected by it. Why was Dana following Paul's instructions to come down here instead of running to her child across the street?

Anneke. That's why. The DA's squad had taken Travis away from this young woman—a girl really—entrusted with her child's care. Dana felt sick with mistake. Because of this unknown bad thing, Anneke was not to be trusted. Travis was safer with Bethany in SCU. That is what Paul was saying when he told her to "get down here."

Dana's heels clicked on the cold cement as she made her way through the maze of narrow passages. The walls and ceiling were covered with sweating, exposed pipes. Dank and dim, the basement hissed with the sound of distant machinery. She opened a steel door and entered an immense, low-ceilinged expanse, strewn with surveillance equipment and furnished with metal desks and wheeled chairs, the individual workstations divided by partitions. Several stations were empty, others were manned by detectives listening to wiretap evidence on headphones, preparing paperwork, or talking on the phone.

The hand that clutched her briefcase handle was cramped with tension. She shifted hands and quickened her pace to reach the far end of the room where the Don presided over his crew. Along the way, a few faces lifted to hers and smiled or raised a hand in greeting. She replied with a nod, hardly acknowledging them. At this moment, the only faces she sought were those of

Paul and Anneke. Her ire was stoked at the thought of how she would ream the girl out for whatever it was she'd done with her child.

But Anneke was nowhere to be seen. Dana heard Paul's cough echoing in the cavernous space even before she saw him sitting on the edge of his desk in the company of two men: ADA Jared Browne, and Senior Investigator Gilbert Herrera. As Dana approached, Gilbert was the first one to look up and say, "Hi Dane," using his own shorthand version of her name. His pock-marked skin, broken nose, and asymmetrical features gave him a dangerous appearance useful for undercover work. He was a man of few words with a true heart, a good friend from Dana's rookie days, when they'd worked together on the Colombian cartel investigation.

Gilbert flashed a timid smile with a mouthful of crooked teeth, transforming his gangster look into the innocence of a lamb. His expression conveyed embarrassment—for her.

Jared, however, didn't surrender his poker face, even to give her one of his movie-star smiles. He wasn't Denzel, and she wasn't Dorothy. Not today.

"Dana," he said grimly. "What did Patrick tell you?"

"Nothing. We haven't spoken. I was in Part 52. What's going on?"

"The 20th Precinct picked up your au pair."

"Picked her up? As in arrested?" She dropped her briefcase.

"Yeah."

"With my son?" Stupid. Of course with her son.

"Yes. But he's okay." Jared's black-brown irises sparkled for an instant with an unspoken thought: Yes, Travis was picked up by the police, but he wasn't placed under arrest. The joke might have worked under different circumstances—if it wasn't Dana's son, and if Jared didn't have two small children of his own.

Seeing the pain in Dana's eyes, Jared's look quickly turned

apologetic. He started to brief her. "They gave your nanny *Miranda* warnings. She waived her right to an attorney and made a statement. They transcribed it, five pages. Then they brought her here for a video. I'll be doing the questioning. Paul's going to second the interview, and Gilbert's going to work the camera."

Paul started to cough.

"Questioned for *what*?" demanded Dana. "Arrested for *what*?"

"Siddown," said Paul gruffly, still coughing. He pulled up a wheeled chair.

"I will *not* sit down. Come on now, this is unbelievable! Jared?"

The apologetic look deepened. "I'm sorry, Dana. They arrested her for murder. It's the case you picked up last night."

Dana felt the blood drain from her face. The next thing she felt was a hard surface beneath her—the chair that Paul had offered. She was sitting, but the room had taken flight. Above her, three men hovered grotesquely. Around her, the air swirled with Jared's legal explanations. The arresting officer had written it up as murder, but the facts would only support reckless manslaughter at the most. Dana recognized the words as her own. This morning, before leaving for work, she'd explained her new case to Evan in precisely these terms.

"Patrick reassigned the case to me," said Jared.

"Of course." Thoughts rushed in her head, mere blips of image and sound. The neighbors. Dutch. "Tug." A moose. A dolphin. Strawberry-blonde hair.

"Who's the child?"

"Kaatje Van Leeuwen."

Caught ya. The connection was clear, bringing the painful discovery of Anneke's deception. "Okay, but who *is* she?"

Jared didn't answer immediately. Gilbert crossed his arms and shifted his weight from one foot to the other. Paul's cough filled the silent seconds, his noise driven by nerves as much as his failing health.

"She says she's the mother of the child."

Confirmation. Dana nodded vaguely in agreement. The room hadn't yet settled into place. She fought for objectivity and a level head, the skills she possessed for gathering and processing the information she needed. "The man who was subletting—he's the father?"

"Yes. That's what she says. His name is Niels Van Leeuwen."

"From Holland?"

"Yes. And he's married. She gave the baby to the couple at birth."

Dana's thoughts circled for another moment, finally settling on an image of Anneke in custody, somewhere in this building. "You've got her in the video room?"

Jared nodded.

"Cuffed? Shackled?"

"No, but she's locked in. We're about to go in there now."

"Wait. I'm going in first—"

"Dana." Jared put a hand on her shoulder, halting her unsteady effort to get up.

Paul stopped coughing long enough to speak. "Come on, Dorothy." He used a fatherly tone. "You really can't get involved. You know that."

She remained seated. The tremor in her gut branched upward and outward. She began to shake.

"Don't worry, Dane," said Gilbert. "We're treating her good. She's a princess." Dana met his eyes and recognized a thought in them, the one she hoped for. He believed in Anneke. She looked at Jared and Paul but didn't see quite the same thing. They couldn't possibly think—

"Get a grip," said Paul. "Calm down. Take a deep breath. Whatever." He patted her shoulder awkwardly, an atypical gesture of comfort, brusque as it was.

"I'm fine, Paul."

"Then go get the boy. Take him home, Mom."

"But—"

"We'll fill you in later. Every detail."

"Okay. I'm leaving. For now." She rose into the nightmarish gloom of the Dungeon, absently taking her briefcase from Gilbert's hand. Her head pounded with an urgent message: *This is wrong. Anneke is innocent.* But she didn't say it out loud. Didn't fight for the girl. Didn't utter a word as she shifted her weight, testing her jelly legs, remembering.

Six years ago, she'd been too close to a case. With shameful certainty, she'd jumped to conclusions based on scanty clues, hunches, and assumptions. Now, just like that other time, she didn't have all the facts, and her self-interest was involved. She couldn't trust herself. She might be wrong.

Turning away from her colleagues, she started to retreat when, behind her, Paul spoke. "We're keeping this quiet. Don't think twice about it."

She froze in mid-step. The thought of public exposure hadn't crossed her mind—until now. This could reflect badly on Patrick McBride, the DA-elect. This was an item for scandalmongers.

Without turning around, she raised a hand in thanks to Paul. He meant well, but his attempt to allay her anxiety had done the opposite. She kept walking, retracing the steps she'd taken ten minutes ago, this time at a slower pace. She wanted to be fully composed by the time she greeted her little boy in the strange surroundings of the SCU nursery.

They'd assured her that Travis was fine. Her baby was healthy and happy. But she couldn't take these words at face value. It was clear now that Travis had seen a few things. He'd been with that little girl, maybe even played with her in that apartment on 73rd Street. And he was the one Anneke had been rough with, yanking his arm, dropping him physically into the stroller. He had to be the one. The Bishops were wrong in thinking it was the little girl. Otherwise, where would Travis have been? Left alone with that man in the apartment? Anneke would never do such a thing. No, never.

Maybe not that, but now, there were other possibilities. There were things that Dana didn't know about Anneke, things she might do, or was capable of doing.

A simmering rage surfaced. *How dare she.* Anneke had kept this big secret, going to visit her lover and her little girl, taking Travis along with her. How many days—or weeks—had this been going on? *Caught ya.* She'd concealed everything from them, while thinking nothing of involving a little boy in her messy past.

In the grip of anger, Dana fought to regain composure. *Keep walking. Think. Refocus.* This case wasn't about Anneke's past or her lapse in judgment as a babysitter. She was charged with violently shaking a little girl to death. Was she capable of such a complete loss of control? Dana had never seen any indication of it.

On her way out of the building, Dana reflected on everything her colleagues had implied. It was unethical for her to come anywhere near this case. She couldn't be involved in the investigation. She couldn't even visit the prisoner, at least not until Jared finished the videotaped Q & A. Anneke had to remain isolated from people with divided loyalties, people like Dana who might leak investigative secrets. During the questioning, Jared would be looking for those telling little slipups, any details that only the perpetrator would know.

Still, the voice in Dana's head refused to fade. *This is wrong.*

A wave of compassion cooled the anger. A vision arose of a young woman sitting alone in that tiny, windowless room, scared, shaken, grieving, accused of the ultimate crime. There was no lawyer by her side to explain the process. Sure, Anneke had been informed of her rights. Her decision to be questioned without a lawyer was valid in the eyes of the law. But under the surface, her decision was driven by emotion, not reason—the irresistible urge to explain, to rectify an injustice.

And Dana was powerless to advise or comfort her.

Across the street, she paused in the lobby and thought for a moment before taking the elevator up to SCU. If a prisoner's lawyer happened to show up and ask to see a client, the request must be honored. It was the law. And there was nothing to stop Dana from trying to arrange it. Except...maybe this was one of those gray areas of professional ethics. Despite this doubt, her instincts told her it was the right thing to do. She pulled out her Nokia.

She searched her mental directory of the defense bar. The attorney had to be good, better than good, a skillful, zealous advocate. The person she picked had to be articulate and brave, someone who wouldn't begrudge the fact that saving Anneke would also save the reputation of Dana and the DA's office.

Only one attorney came to mind, and he wasn't for hire. Still, it was possible. Anneke might qualify for free legal assistance. Her income consisted of room and board and a modest stipend. Dana pressed "5" on the number pad of her Nokia to speed dial the main number for the Legal Aid Society.

The switchboard operator came on the line, and Dana asked for Seth. The call went to voicemail, and his outgoing message included an "emergency" number. Dana recognized it. Seth was so dedicated to his clients that he made himself available day and night by mobile phone. She called that number now, and he answered. He was in the courthouse.

"Seth, I'm calling to ask a favor. Something urgent."

"What's up?"

"A young woman has just been arrested and needs a lawyer."

"She'll have to take the Legal Aid attorney picking up new cases in arraignments."

"I'm hoping you can bend the system for a special case."

"What's so special? She's a friend?"

"Before I say another thing, you've got to know that I'm not speaking as a prosecutor. I'm not giving you the DA's position. Nothing I say is conceded by the DA's office."

He laughed. "You never cease to surprise me, Hargrove."

"But, is it understood?"

"Sure. You bet. Understood." One thing Dana could count on. Seth always kept his word.

She took a deep breath and dived in, head first. "She's my au pair, she's been arrested for murdering her own child, and she's innocent." Seth wouldn't be able to walk away from this.

"Phew! In all these years, I don't think I've ever heard you say that word."

"I know I've said 'not guilty' many times."

"Not the same thing."

"Maybe not."

"Well, you must have a damn good reason for believing in her."

Dana didn't respond. She had a gut belief in Anneke's innocence. But she also had a healthy respect for the mind games that followed when her self-interest was involved. Evidence is what she needed. Hard, cold, objective evidence. With Seth on the case, he would assign a Legal Aid investigator. That would make two more people working to uncover the facts now, when the clues were still fresh.

In the silence, Seth picked up the thread. "Okay," he said. "Say no more. Tell me where to find her."

Dana gave him the details, knowing that he wouldn't be able to reach Anneke before the end of her video session with Jared, which was taking place as they spoke. But it was enough to know that Seth would be calling on his new client later today. He had the kind of optimism, charisma, and confidence to give Anneke comfort and a deeper understanding of what was to come. Just as important, he would deliver Dana's message of support.

Minutes later, feeling less helpless, Dana walked into the SCU nursery, as ready as she could possibly be under the circumstances to face her son. She scooped up Travis, hugged him close, and showered his plump, soft cheeks with kisses, bringing up the giggles.

In this whole mess, the person who mattered the most was right here in her arms. He was safe. He was hers. She would never let him go.

At twelve thirty, in the midtown offices of B & R, Mineko and Evan conferred with partner Steven Belknap in his grand corner office. Sitting behind his desk, Steve tilted back in his executive chair, hands interlaced behind his head as he considered the proposal his associates had crafted for the settlement of *Tinker versus Delmonico*.

Evan loved this office. One day, perhaps, an office like this would be his. The large, glass panes in the south and east walls opened onto a panorama stretching out for miles, lending the illusion of boundlessness. An inviting distraction. If he were to rise out of the leather chair right now and walk straight toward that horizon, he could pass through the invisible barrier to the other side and be suspended in air, just another silhouette in the Manhattan skyline.

Brilliant blue. The gray skies of recent days had given way to a bursting, late-autumn intense sunlight. To the south, Evan beheld the gargoyles and the silver art deco design of the Chrysler building glistening in the midday sun.

Steve's voice brought him back. "You think they'll go for two hundred grand? It's a good figure for us. Something Mysterion can live with. But do you have any wiggle room? What's the ceiling?"

"The CEO approved a cap of five hundred this morning," said Evan. "But we have high hopes that two hundred will do it. We're going to put that figure on the table."

"June Tinker is interested in salvaging her reputation," said Mineko. "She made it clear during her deposition. This woman is so lovely and gentle and sweet that no one could possibly think of her as a baby murderer, but that's really her main worry."

"All that whispering behind her back at the next high school reunion, eh?" Steve chuckled and rubbed his snowy-haired crown. "So, she's not a money grabber. It's the principle of the thing. Let's sue on principle."

"Mineko has an uncanny take on these things," said Evan. And it was true. She had the ability to size up a person with a single look and a handshake. They had faith that, when Rajani Choudhary conveyed their proposal to her client, June would take it.

"If Choudhary buys it, she isn't going to make much money bringing lawsuits like this one," said Steve. A typical lawyer's fee was one-third of the amount recovered by the plaintiff.

"She can afford it," said Evan.

"Plenty of corporate clients to make up for it."

"Right. I wouldn't worry about Rajani. She'll present the offer fairly, and she won't try to scuttle the deal. The harder sell was Tina Delmonico, but we persuaded her. As you know, the only reputation at stake is hers."

Steve chuckled again. Evan and Mineko had big smiles on their faces, remembering their meeting with Tina this morning. Her outrage. The screeching voice. *My reputation!* Today, the irises were lime green. "The biggest part of the proposal," continued Evan, "is to remove every remaining copy of *Dumpster Grave* from the shelves and publish a strongly worded retraction and apology. Tina wasn't too happy."

"I got her to calm down," said Mineko.

"You seem to have the magic touch with her." Evan was truly grateful. "I'm worried you're going to leave us for a job as her editorial assistant."

"Please." Mineko rolled her eyes.

"Is Mysterion worried about lost revenue on the book?" asked Steve.

"Not a concern. There was a spurt in sales when word of the lawsuit went public. Immediately after that, they voluntarily stopped filling new orders. They weren't going to fuel the fire."

"Besides," added Mineko, "they already recouped their initial investment."

"Okay. All good. Sounds like a plan." Steve hurtled forward and popped up straight in his chair, rubbing his hands together in front of him. "You're going to Rajani's office now?"

"Two o'clock."

"All right. Let's make a deal."

At this signal that their meeting was over, Evan and Mineko rose and took their final look through the glass into the outside world. Back they went to their modest digs: Mineko's four-walled, inside office, and Evan's somewhat larger office on the north side of the building. His small window offered a shadowy view of the gray cement wall next door.

At one thirty, as he was getting ready to leave for Rajani's law firm, the private line on his desk phone rang. Caller ID was a recent upgrade in the system, but Evan still wasn't used to it. He picked up in a hurry without looking at the display. Only a few people had his private number, and he assumed it was a lunchtime call from Dana. He wasn't surprised to hear her voice.

"Hi, Evan" she said. Her tone was subdued.

"Hi. You just caught me. I'm about to leave for the settlement meeting."

"Good luck."

"Thanks. I have a feeling we might hammer out a deal. This nightmare of a lawsuit is almost over." He paused, but she didn't respond. "Hey," he said. "Is that Travis?" He could swear he heard their child babbling in the background.

"Yes. I'm home with Travis."

"Home? Is everything okay?"

"Sure." She fell silent again for an instant too long. But before he could speak, she said, "I have to tell you something, but I don't want to make you late for your meeting."

"No, please tell me."

"Just…if you're able to, please come home early after you finish the meeting."

"Dana. Something's wrong. What is it?"

"It's too complicated to explain right now, but we're okay. Really. Travis and I are doing fine. Just go do your meeting and then come home, okay?"

"You're sure?"

"Yes."

"Okay. But I'm worried."

"Don't worry. I'm sorry I called. I'll tell you all about it later."

"All right."

"I love you. Bye-bye."

And she ended the call.

19 »   PRESS

AFTER A SLEEPLESS night, Dana gave up at five forty and went into the kitchen to make coffee. It was Friday morning, and in a few hours, Anneke Zonneveld, her sunny nineteen-year-old au pair, would be arraigned on the charge of manslaughter in the second degree.

Nothing had been decided last night, except that Dana and Evan would both be taking a day off from work. They'd been awake into the wee hours, talking along the edges of their disillusionment. The reality and what it meant was slowly dawning: the betrayal, deception, and omission. Clandestine meetings. Evasion under questioning. In hindsight, Dana and Evan picked out the clues they'd missed, reevaluated the moments they'd been led astray, and tiptoed over possible theories as to how they'd been duped. Self-delusion. They were uncomfortable to own it, but that's what it was. Their perfect nanny had arrived on their doorstep four months ago with her skeletons in tow, and they'd been blind to it.

After going to bed, Evan dropped off to sleep shortly after 2:00 a.m. Dana stretched out stiffly on her back, listening to both of her men breathing deeply, Travis over the baby monitor and Evan by her side. She stared into the black abyss, mentally reliving the events of the day, looking for a shining spark of hope in the meager list of new developments in the case.

Jared had called late in the afternoon with an update. The wife, Renske Van Leeuwen, had shown up at the apartment looking for her husband and child. The police tape was still up. Officers at the scene told her they were investigating a complaint at the apartment and needed to find Niels. They asked her to come to the 20th Precinct for a talk with Detective Greeley. As the questioning became steadily more personal, she began to suspect that something was up. But before she lost all trust, she revealed some surprising information. She and Niels had adopted the baby from Anneke under a ruse that the baby's father was a teenage boyfriend. Only recently did Renske start to suspect that Niels was the true father, and when she confronted him about it, he left her, taking the child with him. She believed he'd come here to find Anneke, and she hired a private investigator to track him down. Greeley got the P.I.'s contact information and was now trying to locate him in Holland, to see if he had anything to add to their investigation.

Renske said she had no clue where they might find Niels. Detective Greeley suspected that she was protecting him. To smoke out any hidden agenda, he told her about Kaatje's death. That marked the end of any intelligible information to be gotten from Renske. But it was clear from her grief-filled exclamations that she didn't know where Niels had gone.

Jared also related a full account of Anneke's videotaped statement. When he finished, Dana said, "She's telling the truth, Jared."

"We can't rule her out yet, Dana. You know that."

"It's the father…"

"I've gone over the evidence with everyone, the Don, Patrick, Gilbert, Detective Greeley. She was there. We can't drop the charges."

Dana knew exactly what evidence he meant. "They're wrong." She conjured an image of that well-meaning retired couple, the timid man who made deli runs late at night to satisfy his wife's sweet tooth, and the woman with the bug eyes behind thick glasses who was so sure that Anneke had abused Travis. They'd seen it wrong. They'd heard it wrong. The argument, the cry, the sudden silence, the door slamming, the guilt-ridden face, the escape. The nanny who yanked and jerked and dropped a helpless, screaming tot into a stroller on a public street.

"Step back for a minute and think about it, Dana. If you were me looking at this evidence, what would you do?"

What *would* she do? An impossible question to answer, because it was impossible for her to step back.

Shortly after Jared's call, Dana was reading a book to Travis when the phone rang again. Evan answered it. "For you, Dana." He covered the mouthpiece with his hand and whispered, "It's your boyfriend." She smiled. On another day, she might have laughed at the joke. Evan liked to tease his wife about her brief attraction to Seth Kaplan, which ended after a single date years ago.

Seth started out: "I'm not going into any details." He didn't owe her the details. Ethically, he couldn't say much without violating attorney-client privilege. "I'm calling just to say three things, Hargrove. Number one: we're scheduled for 11:00 a.m. in AR-3. Number two: she's hanging in there. And number three: thanks for the case."

Buried in these words, Seth's implied message blazoned to the surface. Dana had done the right thing in calling him. He believed in Anneke to the nth degree, and his visit with her this afternoon had helped to lift her spirits. He'd also managed to arrange a definite time for the arraignment.

Dana examined the roster for AR-3 and found to her dismay that Judge Morris Chomsky would be presiding. Chomsky was notoriously tough on bail issues, increasing the chance that Anneke would be remanded without bail pending trial. For now, she was in the court pens in the Criminal Court building. If she was remanded after the arraignment, she'd be transported to Rikers Island to await trial.

The last phone call Dana received was from the Don, at about ten o'clock. His delay in calling did not go unnoticed. She'd been itching to call him first but held back. He would do anything for her, but he was physically ill, and she didn't want to pressure him. In the Dungeon that afternoon, his eyes had revealed his thoughts. His instincts were almost in line with hers, but he wasn't quite there. Hoping for a break in the case, he waited before calling her. But the break hadn't come.

"The manhunt's still on for the scuzzball. No leads. And we're still looking for the downstairs neighbor. The OCME is putting a rush on the DNA, but you know how that goes. Nothing's fast."

"Thanks, Paul. Keep Detective Greeley on this and get some rest."

"Easy enough for you to say."

She read the buried message there as well: neither one of them would be getting any sleep.

And they didn't. She didn't. Two nights in a row, first homicide chart, and now this. She was wired, the sleep center in her brain rudely disrupted. While Evan slept, she stared wide-eyed into the dark, reviewing everything she knew about the case. It was useless. In the pre-dawn hour, there was nothing to do but give in to it, get out of bed, and begin the new day.

After getting up, she moved quietly through the apartment in the semidarkness. No sense in robbing Evan and Travis of their sleep. The coffee was almost brewed when she heard the slap of the newspaper against the front door of the apartment. A surprising sound. Was it always this loud? She couldn't recall ever being awake when the delivery boy made his rounds in the building. Beyond all reason, it felt like an assault, this hard slap on the threshold of her home.

The assailant could wait. She filled her mug and took a sip. It didn't satisfy. It burned her stomach with acid and reminded her that no amount of coffee could wake her up in a different time and place. She stepped out of the kitchen into the foyer and looked at her front door. The light in the foyer was switched off. At the bottom of the door, in the sliver of space between it and the floor, the light from the hallway shone through, except where the newspaper covered it. A darkness there.

She cradled the mug in both hands, feeling its warmth, letting her eyes glaze over. Everything was a dream. Alone, the apartment still. In this moment, she had no child, no husband, no Anneke. No job. She didn't know the law or the facts, didn't know right from wrong. Her heart was beating, her hands were warm. Her bare feet were cold, feeling the smooth wood floor underneath. Slippers would be nice. She should go now and put on her slippers.

A shrill sound broke the silence. She jumped and ran into the kitchen, set the mug on the countertop, and clicked the phone receiver on, interrupting the third ring. "Hello," she whispered into the mouthpiece.

It was Paul. "Dana, sorry. You were up, right?"

"Of course."

"Damn." She could feel him thinking. "I wasn't bullshitting you yesterday."

"You never do."

"So, you know it wasn't me. It wasn't Gilbert or Jared or Patrick or any of us."

"Okay. It wasn't. *What* wasn't?"

"It was someone at the 20th who talked. Had to be."

They both fell silent. She didn't like guessing games, but she knew Paul well enough that she didn't need to guess. In a blink, she understood. "Hold the line, Paul." She put the receiver down and went to the front door, opened it, and picked up the paper.

Nothing in the top right column or the top left, but no, wait, there it was. Boxed off in the middle of the front page was today's article on "Women Who Kill." The paper was running this featured series to indulge the current national fascination with Susan Smith, the young mother from South Carolina who murdered her two small children by seat-belting them into the family car and running it into a lake.

The bold headline for today's article read: "Prosecutor's Nanny Murders Toddler."

As early as seven, the phone started ringing. Cheryl. Mom and Dad. Melanie. Dana's mother-in-law, Brenda Goodhue. All of them wanting to know. All of them wanting to help.

No more Anneke. No more perfect, problem-solving au pair. "Where's Anneke?" Travis wanted to know, missing her already. Dana could only hug him tight and hide her face, the tears stinging her eyes.

Childcare issues, the question of what they would do beyond today, would have to wait. For now, Dana had to face the damage head on. She was not one to hide. She had to go to Patrick and talk it out.

Evan understood her need and was fully supportive. "You should go. We'll do something fun, right Tug? Maybe we'll go out to breakfast." He took the boy from Dana's grasp, held him in the crook of his arm, and ruffled his sleep-mussed hair.

"Boys?" asked Travis, mimicking one of Evan's expressions.

"Right! Just us boys." Over the child's head, he gave his wife a look of encouragement. *Go on. Face what you have to face.*

It was seven forty-five when Evan took Travis into the nursery to get him dressed. Dana pulled on a pair of slacks, a sweater, and a light overcoat before calling out a "goodbye" to the boys. No need for her briefcase. In a small shoulder bag she carried her DA identification, wallet, and keys. With hands shoved into her pockets, she set out for the subway.

Frazzled and on edge, she pushed onto a peak-hour train, people on all sides jamming her into the chest of a man wearing a paint-spattered sweatshirt and holding a metal lunch box. In her forced intimacy with this construction worker, she stared into a splotch of the white paint he must have applied to an unknown building in the city. With her eyes focused on white, she thought of what she would say to Patrick.

At the Franklin Street stop, she wiggled out of the car and ascended into the light. Above her, the sky was pale blue under the influence of a cold, early-morning sun hidden behind city buildings. The people on the street seemed far too happy. It was a workday, but it was a Friday, the day of the week that every nine-to-fiver looked forward to. She made her way to the Criminal Court building. This was her usual route. She was on her way to work, just another ordinary day.

The familiarity of the route jostled a thought to the surface of her mind. Under her breath she blurted an expletive and stopped short. Yesterday afternoon, all other responsibilities had gone completely out of her head. This morning she was scheduled to start pretrial hearings in the next murder case on her trial calendar, *People versus Sengara*. She'd have to find someone to cover her.

Approaching the Criminal Court building, she saw news vans from two television stations parked halfway down the block. A common sight. A newsworthy case could always be found in the courthouse. And today, in a few hours, the nanny murder case was scheduled for arraignment. She turned up the collar of her overcoat, looked the other way, and quickened her pace. There. They couldn't have seen her.

Entering her building next door to the courthouse, Dana

refolded her collar but kept her head low to avoid the prying eyes of people she passed. Their burning attention could be felt in the way they swung their arms or shuffled their feet or hesitated or strode past. She needed only to glance at their hands and feet and suit jackets to confirm their knowledge.

At eight thirty-five, she knocked on the doorjamb of Patrick's open office door. He'd just walked in and was setting his briefcase on the credenza. Looking over his shoulder, he calmly returned her glance, conveying his lack of surprise at her presence in his doorway. "Dana. Come in and close the door."

In a flood of memory, she relived that moment in her rookie year when she'd come to him with all her big, awful secrets and impossible dilemmas. In that dark hour, Patrick's counsel had saved her. He had guided her to the point of revealing her options, confirming the soundness of the decision she'd already made. But today, her problem was intractable, yielding no options within her control.

She sat down across from him at the desk. Suddenly out of breath, her throat tightened around the words she'd planned.

He spoke first. "Forget the press. I don't like it, of course. But people have short memories when it comes to scandalous newspaper stories."

"Until they want to dredge up the past and use it against you."

"That too. But I've lived through it. And so can you." During his campaign for DA, Patrick had weathered the smear tactics of his opponent, who exposed the single big failure of his career and played it up in the press. It was a prosecution for stalking and menacing. Patrick dismissed the charges because the complainant, who was the defendant's ex-girlfriend, refused to testify, and the remaining evidence wasn't enough to convict. The day after the defendant was released from jail, he brutally murdered her.

"Maybe we'll live through it," said Dana, "but it's happening right now, just a few weeks before you take office. I feel responsible for putting a stain on your new administration."

"Ultimately, any stain will be yours to bear. That is to say—"

"—you'll fire me."

He looked at her long and hard. "That is to say," he repeated slowly, "*not* that I'll fire you. Knowing you and your conscience, you'll resign from the office and bear the brunt of the scandal. That is, if this case pans out the way the press is portraying it. But I have every expectation that it will not."

"So, that means you're willing to drop the charges? We can set my nanny free so she can go murder another baby tomorrow." Dana heard the sarcasm in her voice and didn't like it.

"The way it stands now, we can't drop the charges. I've discussed this with Jared."

"Who, by the way, should be the next deputy bureau chief. I'm withdrawing my name from the list. That is to say, if you don't fire me first."

"Dana. Step back from this a minute."

"That's what Jared said. But I can't step back." She felt the trembling coming on again and fought to compose herself. There was something important she had to say. "Anneke has been living with us for almost four months. She spends long hours with my little boy, and he adores her. She's a loving, gentle caregiver. And there's no way I can prove it to you or to anyone else. The testimony of a two-year-old isn't admissible in court. *Or* the testimony of an interested prosecutor."

Patrick's eyes were full of compassion, but he was firm. "I trust your judgment on her character, Dana. But this is the type of crime involving a loss of control that isn't always visible on the surface."

"I've never known her to lose control. It had to be the father. It's clear he has an emotional screw loose, the way he chased his ex-girlfriend halfway around the world."

"It's likely that emotions were high on both sides."

"But he's taller and stronger, more physically able to kill."

"Almost any adult was capable of killing the child. I've been over this with the medical examiner. The girl was small and underweight for her age. The killer happened to be standing near a wall. The blow to the head, whether reckless or intentional, contributed to the death. Any adult is strong enough to kill under these circumstances, especially when acting in a rage or out of control."

"Sounds like you've made up your mind against Anneke."

"I haven't. No one has. But, at the moment, the evidence supports the arrest. Witnesses place her at the scene, and the circumstances suggest her involvement, even if she only witnessed the assault on the child and failed to report it."

"She wouldn't do that. Not even that."

"Dana. This case is like so many others you've handled. If you could look at this objectively, you'd agree that the grand jury should decide on the charge or whether to prosecute at all. Seth Kaplan has given notice that she intends to testify. The grand jury will be hearing both sides. Twenty-three impartial citizens are better judges than a prosecutor who's much too close to the defendant. And they're better than a handful of prosecutors who care very much about their colleague who can't be objective right now."

She was stunned into silence by this statement of his feeling.

He cleared his throat and continued. "Out of respect for you, the DA's squad is working around the clock on this case."

"And, out of respect for *you*, Patrick. You're being very nice about it, but we can't pretend that the story doesn't affect your reputation. Page one. An assistant district attorney hired a baby killer to take care of her son."

"It's only an accusation."

"Right. Presumed innocent until proven guilty. Let's remind

the entire press corps about our constitutional rights." She rolled her eyes heavenward. "Come on, Patrick."

"I'm not going to speculate about the headlines in tomorrow's newspaper. We can't operate like that. For now, we're moving forward as fast as we can. Investigators are trying to track down other witnesses and the father, Niels Van Leeuwen. A warrant was issued for his arrest with a full description. He *will* be found. He can't fall off the grid for long. He'll be caught at the airport, or if he's still in town, he'll give himself away somehow."

"And then you'll all have fun playing our two suspects against each other."

Patrick lifted his brow and said nothing to that.

Dana lowered her eyes and shook her head. "Sorry. I didn't mean it that way. Paul's leading this investigation, and it isn't any fun for him. He would never permit thumbscrews or scare tactics."

"*If* he's able to spend another day on this case."

She lifted inquiring eyes.

"The Don," said Patrick, and stopped, as if the familiar nickname was all he needed to say.

"His coughing is very bad, isn't it?" asked Dana.

"He hasn't told many people, but he's going to take a medical leave of absence. I just learned about it yesterday."

The news wasn't unexpected, but still, it delivered a jolt and a wave of panicky concern. It was just like Paul to keep his secret from Dana. Protecting her, as he always had. "When?"

"Today's his last day. He goes under the knife next week. They're taking part of a lung and following up with chemo after he heals from the surgery."

Again, a shock. She fought down her fluttery stomach and pulled her thoughts back to the investigation. Think. Without Paul, they needed second best. "Gilbert Herrera," she said. "He'll stay on the case, won't he?"

"Yes. He'll be the lead."

"We need him to light a fire under the 20th. Officer Vargas is the best one up there. She's relatively new, but she's good, and she really cares about the case."

"I know her. Detective Greeley is also sharp."

"I hope so. I've never worked with him. I can tell you, though, that the Lieutenant sure didn't impress me."

"The Don thinks he was the one who called the newspaper."

"Figures." Dana shook her head, remembering the surly look on Lieutenant Amundsen's face when she reminded him how to conduct a constitutionally proper search of the apartment.

They didn't speak for several seconds and didn't look at one another. Patrick broke the silence. "Go home, Dana. I'm asking other assistants to cover your cases. Everything will be adjourned unless we run up against speedy trial deadlines. If that happens, someone else will have to do the hearings and trials."

"You're acting like I'll be gone for weeks."

"It's understood that you need time…"

"To make other babysitting arrangements."

"Exactly." Their eyes locked. Dana wondered if Patrick could read her guilty conscience as she wrestled with her internal conflict between motherhood and career. Maybe, instead of thinking about babysitting arrangements, she should be thinking about giving up her career, at least temporarily, to stay home with Travis. Whose fault was it that her child had been placed in harm's way? Anneke's? Maybe in part. But she and Evan were the ones responsible for hiring their child's caregiver. These coming weeks would be the time for reexamining their lives and weighing their choices.

Certainly, Anneke was no longer a choice. She could not possibly return as their au pair, no matter which way this went. If she was guilty, well… But even if she was fully cleared of the charge, Anneke would still be grieving for the loss of her little girl.

She would be grappling with a guilty conscience and regret for the mistakes that couldn't be undone.

And, yes, the trust was gone. Anneke had hidden the truth, and that would always be between them.

"We'll keep you updated," said Patrick, "but we can't have you here right now. It's the right thing for everyone concerned."

Dana knew he was right. Still, she didn't make a move to go. There was another reason she'd come downtown this morning.

Patrick could see her mind working and ventured a guess. "If you're thinking of attending the arraignment, I wouldn't advise it." Sketch artists, reporters, cameras.

"I wasn't planning on it. But, before I leave, I'm going to visit Anneke in the pens. I'll take the alley behind the building and avoid the reporters."

The look on Patrick's face said it all. He was her conscience, and this was her test. Why else had she mentioned it? She knew now that she wouldn't be able to convince him, or herself, of this plan.

Still, the roiling emotion drove her to push ahead. Rage and compassion—such powerful, conflicting calls to action were provoked by that image of Anneke, sitting behind bars on a cold bench in a cement cell. On first sight of the prisoner, would Dana see red? *How dare you involve my son in this!* Would those be the first words out of her mouth? She wouldn't admit this possibility to herself, much less to Patrick. She told him, "I can't let her believe she's abandoned."

"She isn't abandoned. Don't push this, Dana. You've already come close to the line."

So. He knew she'd called Seth. For Patrick, it was as easy as putting two and two together.

"There's nothing wrong with arranging a lawyer," she defended herself.

"The police treated her properly, and the waiver was valid."

"From a procedural standpoint. Her statements were properly obtained and admissible in court. But the right to counsel goes beyond that. We have the obligation to give a lawyer access to any client in custody."

Patrick didn't respond immediately. The sudden stillness made it clear that their voices had been raised. With one hand, he combed back the russet-gray mixture of thick hair on his head. After a moment he spoke, quieter this time. "You also have an obligation to avoid any conflict of interest. Under the circumstances, I understand why you arranged for the lawyer. I wouldn't call it a strict breach of ethics. But the reality is that you *cannot* go visit her in the pens. Not now."

Again, he was right. Last night, Dana had convinced herself that it was perfectly okay for her to visit Anneke. The police and the prosecutor had already taken her statements, and Dana could do nothing to change them. But today, something new was thrown into the mix—Seth had given the DA's office notice of Anneke's intention to testify in the grand jury. A visit to her now would look bad for Patrick. If word of it got out, he would be open to further criticism. Speculation could abound that the self-interested prosecutor was breaching the Chinese wall, giving the accused information from the other side, feeding her ideas for her testimony.

Dana rose from the chair, indicating her surrender to reason. "Okay. I'll go home." She was still wearing her overcoat, which she hadn't removed since her arrival in Patrick's office. She was ready to go.

"You're clear on this?"

"I'm clear on it. And I guess..." She hesitated before continuing. "I guess I knew it all along."

"I usually don't say anything you don't already know."

Again, his show of respect and warmth was heartening. "I hope you don't mind when I do this to you."

"I never do. You can come and test yourself anytime."

"Thank you, Patrick. I'll remember that when you're navigating all that square footage in the new office across the street." Her reference to his imminent departure, on top of everything else, overwhelmed her. As she turned her back to him and stepped toward the door, she felt the tears start to well in her eyes. Before placing her hand on the doorknob, she pushed up the collar of her overcoat and said, without turning around, "I'm ready for them."

"I can lend you a hat if you'd like."

"No, thanks. If they get me, I'll smile for the camera."

On the other side of the door, she wiped away a tear.

20 »   OPERA

AURELINA VARGAS WAS glad to be back on days. After another swing shift, she and Forrester had come up with nothing. Now they had the chance to stop by the brownstone on 73rd Street during daylight hours, when a different set of people would be coming and going, people who might have seen Van Leeuwen and the child. Delivery people, dog walkers, postal workers, next door neighbors. Maybe the tenant directly under number 7 would return today. The man in number 5.

The name on the mailbox was "Adam Scordato." Adam was reported to be a single man in his late twenties. He was rarely seen, and no one in the building knew where he worked. The tenants in number 3 occasionally heard his footsteps or music, but they had nothing to report about the night in question—they hadn't been home. Gerald Bishop seemed to remember hearing music coming from that apartment on his way downstairs, when he made his trip to the deli. He didn't remember hearing anything when he returned.

Detective Greeley made some inquiries that led nowhere. The only information on file with the landlord was Scordato's 1987 lease application, listing his job as an aide in a nursing home. He no longer worked there. The entire staff had turned over in the past seven years, and no one at the nursing home knew where to find him.

In addition to Vargas and Forrester, other officers from the precinct had been covering the building around the clock. So they said. Vargas was skeptical about the extent of their dedication. She had seen the dead child. They had not. Any other team might have gone out for coffee just when the father decided to creep back into the building. She didn't doubt that possibility. The father's emotional attachment to the victim might trigger an irresistible impulse to return to the scene of the crime.

After Officer Tiriac arrested the mother, Vargas found out the details of her statement. Arrestees who talked usually denied the charges. But this was different. This was the nanny for ADA Hargrove, the prosecutor on homicide chart. This was a mother who hadn't seen her own child since birth. The father, on the other hand, was a statutory rapist, child kidnapper, and stalker. That's how it looked to Officer Vargas. Between the two suspects, who was the baby killer? No contest.

Vargas would have preferred to stick to the investigation all day, but Lieutenant Amundsen put up a roadblock. Only a day and a half since the crime, and already the case was old news to the Lieutenant. A child murder was rare in the 20th, something to investigate carefully and completely, but he wanted Vargas and Forrester on regular street patrol.

"Sir, request permission to work the murder scene on 73rd."

"Denied. We've stopped full-time surveillance. All leads have been followed up, except the one tenant. Greeley's on it."

"There could be other witnesses who saw the couple. Delivery people and next-door neighbors. And the father might come back."

The Lieutenant scoffed at the idea. "In broad daylight? A waste of time. He's not coming back, and no one saw what went on in that apartment."

Still, she persisted. "Sir, we have to find the tenant in number 5..."

"Okay, all right." He flung a hand into the air impatiently. "Nothing's stopping you from taking a drive by when it gets slow today."

She planned on taking a drive by, or two or three or more. Things would be very slow today. She was the driver. She had the power of the wheel. She also knew her partner well and was sure of his support, one hundred percent.

After getting into the patrol car, she turned to Forrester and said without fanfare, "We'll just take a look on 73rd." Within a few minutes, they were double-parked in front of the building.

"I guess this means we're going in," Forrester deadpanned.

"Just a ring on the bell. Maybe a quick canvass."

"Why not?" He looked at his watch. "Eight seventeen, and things are slow."

"I'll be right back," she said, opening the door. "Wait here if you want." She was suggesting that he cover for her, in case of a call.

He understood. "I'll listen for dispatch. Tell me if you need backup."

She took the ten stairs two at a time and tried the front door. It was locked, as it should be, no longer the gateway for an endless stream of police officers. If she wanted to get into the building, she knew that the Bishops would be home and would let her inside for the asking. But first, she pressed the button to number 5 and waited.

She was about to abandon the attempt when a male voice came over the intercom. "Hello."

"Mr. Scordato?"

"Yes."

She couldn't believe her luck! Her voice remained neutral and full of authority. "Police Officer Vargas, NYPD. I need to talk to you."

"Police?"

"Yes. Open up please."

The buzzer sounded, and she pushed the door open, holding it with one foot as she turned to look down the stairs at her partner in the radio car. He stared back in amazement. "He's home!" she yelled, cupping her mouth with a hand. "Call it in and get up here!" She waited while Forrester made the call and bounded up the stairs.

"Greeley isn't in yet, but they'll get the word out to him," Forrester said.

Good, thought Vargas. The witness was all theirs, for now.

Adam Scordato was just finishing his "dinner" of scrambled eggs and bacon when the buzzer rang. "Police," said the woman's voice. What could the police want? Adam hadn't done anything wrong that he could think of, but it was unnerving to have a police officer at the door first thing in the morning, just when he was trying to unwind from another harrowing night in the ER.

Maybe this was about one of the patients from last night. There'd been a stabbing, a pedestrian hit-and-run, and a rape victim, all worthy of police attention. Besides those cases, there'd been a stroke, an alcohol poisoning, and a dozen relatively minor ailments of uninsured patients who used the ER as their drop-in clinic for earaches, bronchitis, and hypochondria. Eight hours straight on his feet without a break, one crisis after another. Added to everything else, the night had started off very badly — an argument with Josie before he left for work. "I don't think I can do this anymore," she'd said. The words cycled endlessly in his mind.

If it was really a police officer at the front door, why was she taking so long to get upstairs? Already there'd been enough time to put his dishes in the sink, and then some.

Finally, the knock came. To make sure it wasn't a scam, he

looked through the peephole. A female police officer in uniform. He opened the door and found two of them. The male officer was standing off to the side, out of peephole range.

"I'm Officer Vargas from the 20th Precinct, and this is Officer Forrester. May we come in and ask you a few questions?"

"Sure, come in. What's this about?" He opened the door wider and they barreled in, filling his apartment with the immediacy of governmental authority. Uniforms. Badges. Guns. Static from a two-way radio, clanging and clattering items on their utility belts. It struck him as almost comical, the extremes in appearance, his and theirs. He was still wearing his light blue scrubs.

He backed away from them through the foyer and over to the threshold of the living room. He didn't invite them to sit, and they didn't ask.

"We're investigating an incident that happened in this building on Wednesday night, about ten thirty. Were you home at that time?"

He thought back to Wednesday night as he looked down into the eyes of Officer Vargas. She was short, not much more than five feet, plucky as hell, with lively brown eyes and a thick, black ponytail. She was the kind of person to zero in and grab hold of you with her eyes. Her charisma was not so much in her looks. More like a jazzy intensity that told him she was on a supreme mission. Whatever that mission might be, Adam was immediately on board.

"I was home that night, but I left for work at about that time." With effort, he pulled his eyes away from her and glanced up at Forrester. The second officer towered over them both and was more than a foot taller than the petite Vargas. Prompted by Adam's glance in his direction, Forrester jumped into the conversation. "Where do you work?" he asked, looping his thumbs into his belt.

"Roosevelt Hospital. I'm a nurse in the ER on the night shift, eleven to seven."

"How long were you home on Wednesday before you left for work?"

"Most of the day. I slept from about noon until seven thirty or so. Then I got up and had my breakfast, and—"

"We're talking seven thirty in the evening?"

"Right. I've been on nights for so long that dinner is breakfast to me."

Vargas took over. "So, you were here in the apartment the entire evening before going to work? Seven thirty to ten thirty?" Her voice was insistent.

"Yes."

"Is that your usual pattern?"

"Pretty much…"

"We didn't find you home last night. Officers came by."

"I was at my girlfriend's all day and evening. Yesterday morning I went to Josie's after work and stayed there until my next shift. I stay there a lot." Up until yesterday, he could have added. Josie made it clear last night that she didn't want him to come back. Something had happened to change her toward him. Tuesday night, everything seemed normal. Wednesday night, she had plans that didn't include him, an arrangement she'd made last week. Thursday night, they were back together again, but everything fell apart.

It took him by surprise. He'd always regarded their relationship with pride and tenderness. In their two years together, they'd overcome the difficulties of their incompatible schedules, her day job, his night job. The effort had been well worth it, he thought. Before he met Josie, he used to sleep from about three in the afternoon until ten, rolling out of bed and going right to the hospital. But he'd changed all that, getting to bed earlier so he could wake up earlier and spend his evenings with her, when she came home from work.

Now, it looked like he hadn't done enough. The warning signs had gone over his head. Small complaints he hadn't taken seriously. "The bed is cold at night," and "It's *impossible* for us to go out! You turn into a pumpkin at ten thirty." Her grievances were, at first, no more than gentle, sweet moans. She assured him that she was a homebody and relished the pleasure of cooking dinner in the apartment, and afterward, listening to classical music—and doing other things—on the couch. When he left for work, she got into bed alone with her lovely dreams of him to keep her company. This is what she told him.

He'd felt from the start that they were made for each other, an ideal couple with similar backgrounds and interests. They were both second generation Italians, bilingual, lovers of good food and wine and classical music, especially opera. They shared childhood stories of large family gatherings, households of siblings and cousins, a Pavarotti album playing in the background or an amateur tenor in the family bursting into song. They talked about their desire to keep some family traditions and discard others. They spent many romantic evenings on the couch listening to the great works of Rossini, Donizetti, Verdi, and Puccini in Italian, without the need of translation.

In the end, maybe it was the opera that did them in.

He realized now that her complaints had become edgier of late. In response, he would point out that the word "impossible" simply wasn't accurate. It was not impossible for them to have a night out. She forgot that they'd had many of them. He worked only five nights a week, a rotating schedule of different days of the week, which left many Fridays and Saturdays free. Still, she never avoided the chance to tell him whenever his work interfered with an event she wished to attend.

The latest example was the concert on Wednesday. If she'd given him enough notice, he might have found someone to cover for him. But she raised the topic only a week beforehand. "A friend of mine has two tickets she can't use. I'm not going to pass this up, just because you're working!" Tickets to *Madama Butterfly* at the Met, Catherine Malfitano singing the lead. Adam suggested that he come with her and leave at intermission. Josie balked. That would ruin it for her, she said. She would find someone else.

These were details that Adam kept to himself. Officer Vargas didn't need to know them. It was enough to say that he was at Josie's yesterday, and that he stayed with his girlfriend often. Her apartment was closer to Roosevelt Hospital.

"So that's why we missed you. Josie is her name?"

"Josephine Marinelli."

"You're a hard person to catch. Officers were here all day and night yesterday."

"All day? Why? What's going on?"

"There was an incident in the apartment above yours, number 7. We'd like to know if you saw or heard anything on Wednesday night."

Adam paused and thought. Yes. It made sense now. The argument. They wanted to know about the argument.

"Did someone get hurt?" he asked.

The officers exchanged a look that indicated he'd hit on something. But they didn't seem willing to reveal what they knew. "Why don't you tell us what you heard," said Officer Vargas.

Again, he didn't need to embellish. The details of his sorry personal life would be of no interest to these police officers. But this is what he remembered about that evening.

After waking up, as he prepared his evening meal, he was overcome by melancholy thoughts of all that he was missing. He imagined his girlfriend arriving at Lincoln Center, opening the door of a taxicab, extending a nylon-sheathed leg, and stepping out on a silvery high heel. He imagined her special way of moving when she wore heels and expensive clothing. The color was high in her cheeks as she clicked past the fountain in the plaza and approached the immense, light-filled, arched windows of the Metropolitan Opera. Inside the grand lobby, she ascended the right side of the diamond-shaped staircase, entered a door to the orchestra section, and showed her ticket to the usher, who handed her a program and directed her to the plush red seat that would be hers for the evening. In the multi-storied space above her head, twenty-one constellations sparkled in the cosmos, the crystal chandeliers that resembled starbursts.

She wasn't Josie that night. She was Josephine, escorted by a gallant lover. As the images in his head progressed, Adam inserted himself into the scene. That other person, whether man or woman, didn't exist. "A friend" is all she'd said, an unidentified being. Adam was the rightful holder of the second ticket, and he was at Josephine's side.

They settled into their seats, surrounded by connoisseurs of the arts in their finest apparel. Jewels and cuff links glinted. Josephine's alluring scent wafted and lent pleasure. She'd dabbed a drop at the nape of her neck with the stopper of a bottle she kept hidden behind all the others on her dressing table, the perfume she saved for special occasions.

The performance was about to start. The concertmaster bowed an "A," and a medley of instruments swelled and receded in variations on that single note. A few patrons clapped, and the tentative applause fanned outward and grew. Was that...? The conductor had entered the pit, snaking his way through the musicians. He dipped his head to the audience, turned, and took up the baton. The audience quieted amid coughs and rustling programs. The chandeliers dimmed and rose slowly upward, into the ceiling.

In his head, Adam heard the first notes. And then the idea struck that he didn't need to imagine the opera. He could listen to it now, just as she was listening, only a few blocks away in this bustling city.

He searched for and found his favorite recording of *Madama Butterfly*. Tomorrow, when they met at her apartment and she was Josie again, he would be fully reminded of the score, the libretto, the passion, the drama. They would have all of this to discuss, to sing, to enjoy together as they made love.

It was almost 8:00 p.m. when he put the first cassette into his player and turned the volume to a high resonance, just short of a level that would aggravate the neighbors. Without intermissions, he had about enough time to hear the whole opera before he had to leave his apartment.

"I was listening to music that evening," he told Officer Vargas, "almost that entire time before I left for work. I was pretty much absorbed in it."

"What were you listening to?"

"An opera. *Madama Butterfly* by Puccini."

The dark eyes of the petite official brightened in a way that suggested she was familiar with the work. *Do you know it?* The question was on the tip of his tongue, but he held back. It seemed impertinent to attempt casual colloquialisms with an officer of the law, especially at a time like this, in the middle of an investigation, her supreme mission.

"You were absorbed in it," said Officer Forrester. "I guess it was turned up loud."

"Fairly loud, maybe. I don't know what you'd consider loud."

Officer Vargas looked at her partner and said, "You can't play opera softly, Ted." She seemed fairly certain of this.

"I like a little volume to it," said Adam. "But I try to be respectful of the neighbors."

"Even with the volume up, were you able to hear anything in the apartment above yours?"

"If there were any normal kinds of noises up there, I missed them. I only remember something unusual at about ten twenty-five or ten thirty, right before I had to leave for work. I remember it because the noise interfered with my enjoyment of the opera, right near the end of it. I was annoyed. There were several minutes to go, right at the climax near the end. I wanted to finish it, but I was cutting it close if I wasn't going to be late for work."

"What did you hear upstairs?" asked Vargas.

"Loud voices, a man and a woman. They were arguing like maniacs. A baby or a young child was crying at the same time, just wailing, on and on. Screaming, really. All of this was happening in the middle of Butterfly's death scene. You know the one, where she has the knife in her hand, but the child runs in and she tries to hide it from him. She sings to the little boy, 'I'm dying for you, little one, so that you can go across the sea, and when you're grown, you'll never feel the pain of knowing your mother abandoned you.' That's the translation, more or less."

"My God," exclaimed Officer Vargas. "She's abandoning her child and killing herself?"

Maybe Adam had misread her? Officer Vargas didn't seem to know the opera after all. "She's giving the boy to Pinkerton and his wife. You know, Pinkerton, the man who... Anyway, I didn't get through it all. There were noises that sounded like wood furniture scraping the floor and banging around. Then there was a huge thud on the floor, like one of them fell down."

"Had you ever seen these people in number 7 before that night?"

"No, never. I really don't know who lives up there. I thought it was a single man. I've seen him now and then in the building. But I never saw a woman or any kids."

"What did you hear after that huge thud?"

"More arguing. The child was still crying, and then the door slammed. The whole thing lasted only a minute or two. Tell me, did that woman get hurt? I thought she was okay."

"Why's that?"

"Because I saw her running down the stairs. The door slammed really loud and I heard someone racing down the stairs. When she got to my floor, her running was so heavy that she almost shook the landing. I mean, I could feel it in my apartment. I opened my door after she passed by and saw her running down. Just saw the top of her head really. She was wearing a hat, but I could see a bit of hair coming out the edges. It was curly, light orange hair. She was running very fast and she seemed very fit and fine to me, not injured in any way. I was glad she got away from him. I thought he was going to hurt her. Is she all right?"

The officers didn't answer his question. Vargas simply posed another. "When did the baby stop crying?"

"When? I'm not sure, to tell you the truth."

"Do you remember, at least, whether the crying stopped before or after the door slammed?"

"Oh, sometime after the door slammed, definitely."

"You're sure about that?"

"Yes, positive."

"What makes you so sure?"

"Because when I opened my door and saw the woman running down the stairs, the baby was still crying. It sounded louder to me with my front door open. I don't know why, but it was louder. I was relieved to see that the woman was okay, so I started thinking of getting ready for work. The opera was playing the final measures. I missed half of the death aria. Actually, I was pissed. The finale was spoiled somewhat."

That would ruin it for me. In his mind's eye, he saw Josie responding to his ridiculous suggestion. Of course he couldn't go with her and leave at intermission. It would ruin the whole opera for her.

"I came back inside to turn off the stereo and get my coat.

Sometime in the middle of this, I noticed that the baby wasn't crying. Maybe it was the minute my stereo was turned off. All of a sudden it was very quiet upstairs."

"All of a sudden. Do you mean like that?" Officer Vargas snapped her fingers. "Did the crying stop like that?"

Adam was puzzled by the question. What was she getting at? "I really couldn't tell you. I was concerned about getting my things and leaving for work. All I can say for sure is that the baby was still crying when the woman ran down the stairs, and the crying stopped sometime after I came back inside."

The two officers exchanged a look. Officer Vargas took in a deep breath and sighed. Her mouth was twisted halfway between a painful grimace and a revealing grin, an odd mixture of resignation and accomplishment. Looking at her, Adam felt a sick heat spreading upward from the pit of his stomach, making him dizzy with belated realization.

"It's the baby, isn't it? Something happened to the baby?"

Vargas regarded him with compassionate eyes and nodded almost imperceptibly, enough to acknowledge the truth in this.

The room constricted into a black tunnel, haloed by intense brightness. In this impaired state, Adam unknowingly searched his daily existence for reference. With his own eyes he'd seen injury, illness and death in every form, had sopped up bodily fluids and stanched effusive bleeding, had pummeled chests to get hearts pumping, had delivered the ultimate news to loved ones in the waiting room, had caught fainting bodies, overcome with grief. Never had he felt like this.

The tunnel widened, framing two uniformed officers, propped up before him like mannequins. He vaguely remembered being deceived into climbing on board a mission, her mission.

With inexplicable fierceness, he wanted them gone. He wanted only to be with Josie, to talk to her, to feel her arms around him, to hear her say that everything was all right, that she'd forgotten her brief dalliance. It was because of her that they'd been apart that night. It was because of her that he was now feeling sick and desperate. He would make her see this, and she would understand.

Get out, get out! He didn't speak, they didn't hear. Faintly in the distance, from the mouth of the tunnel, came the stranger's voice: "There's nothing you could have done Mr. Scordato. Nothing you could have done…"

21 »   RUN

FRIDAY MORNING, ANNEKE opened her eyes and saw a flat surface of gray cement. She lay curled up in a fetal position on a bed. Somewhere behind her, a door slammed shut. She was immediately conscious of physical pain.

The details of her surroundings were the first memories to surface. Last night, the lumpy mattress and sagging bed frame only heightened her despair, preventing sleep. For many long hours she faced the wall, intermittently crying, with only the cuff of her long-sleeved shirt to soak up the tears and mucus.

It was a mystery how she'd managed to sleep at all. She couldn't know how long it had been. She was not conscious of having fallen asleep or having dreamed. A foggy, inaccessible thought told of some horrible mistake.

She remembered now that, for the first part of the night, she'd had the cell to herself and spent an hour or more pacing the tiny area between the two beds. The lights had been switched off and were out of her control. It was dark but not completely black. Light emanated from the hallway through the square window in the door. She kept moving as a way to tamp down the surging waves of panic that rose in her chest. *Out. Now. Out.*

The waves did not abate. She was suffocating. She tried a different remedy, absolute stillness on the bed. Lying on her left side, she faced outward into the room, staring at the empty bed on the other wall. It helped to make her body as small as possible. She was nobody. She was a piece of matter, a tiny speck. She squeezed in tighter and smaller, containing that beating heart, protecting it. This was somewhat better, but the crying wouldn't stop. The sinuses on the left side of her face were swollen shut.

About halfway into the night, a correction officer delivered her cellmate, an emaciated, foul-smelling woman of the street. Fortunately, the woman was not talkative. She collapsed on her cot and fell immediately into a noisy sleep. Anneke turned onto her right side and faced the wall.

Now, as she adjusted her cramped legs and stretched sore muscles, Anneke remembered the woman on the other side of the room. Perhaps she was no longer there. The snoring was gone. The noise and light had changed from last night. There was more activity out in the hallway. Doors opened and closed, shoes scuffled, footsteps and voices echoed in the distance. Abruptly loud, as if right next to her ear, a snorting intake of air startled her. Bedsprings squeaked. The woman was still there. Anneke did not turn around to face her. It was time, again, to face what was inside of herself.

The gray wall provided a backdrop for the image of her little girl. Kaatje. The smiling, delicate face, curls and pale skin, love and playfulness. Niels was right. Their baby was a miniature version of herself. She'd given life to the child, and now, so soon, that life had been taken. Kaatje's image was in her mind, but the person Anneke had to face today was herself.

She couldn't blame her mistakes on the naïveté of a seventeen-year-old. She was not the same person as the girl who first attended Mijnheer Van Leeuwen's art history class three years ago. She knew more than that. She knew herself and other people better than that. The moment Niels arrived in New York, all the signs had been there, begging for action while she vacil-lated and manufactured excuses. Do nothing and the problem will go away. Or maybe, carry out a crazy plan to solve the problem. Convince him to return to Renske. She could save her own skin at the same time, conceal her secrets. No one would know, not Dana, Evan, the police, or her family back home.

These had been her choices: avoidance or delusional madness. A fear of honesty.

She was stunned by the consequences of her deception. The trust of her employers—ruined. Any hope of caring for the little boy she'd grown to love—shattered. The moral obligation to alert Renske—arrogantly rejected. She had deprived Renske of the opportunity to confront Niels or to involve the law. She had failed to appreciate the reaction she would provoke by visiting him, kissing him, stirring up his passion for her, the raw emotion and volatility, triggering…allowing him to…what? Kill his own little girl?

She should have foreseen a bad ending, even a tragedy of some kind—but this one? Whatever might be said about Niels, whatever she understood about him now, she could not accuse him of heartlessness, cruelty or violence toward his little girl. He loved his daughter with all his heart. At this moment, wherever he was, she could be sure that he was hurting very badly inside for what he'd done. She didn't know what to call it. Not an accident. Not an intentional killing. Not volitional. Not excusable. An act of blinding emotion. A crime.

At 11:00 a.m., Anneke would be taken to a courtroom for her arraignment. Yesterday, that very nice man, Seth Kaplan, told her what to expect. The clerk would read the charge against her, and she would have to state her plea, guilty or not guilty. The felony complaint accused her of manslaughter in the second degree, recklessly causing the death of another person. If she stated a plea of not guilty, then, sometime next week, the case would go to a grand jury of twenty-three people. The grand jury would hear the evidence, including her own testimony, and decide whether it was enough to indict her for manslaughter or some other crime. Several months later, she would have a trial. The petit jury of twelve people would decide whether she was guilty of the crime. She might be kept in jail until the end of the trial if the court didn't order bail in an amount she could pay. Basically, she couldn't afford to pay anything.

At trial, the jury could find her guilty if they thought she aided Niels in recklessly causing the death of Kaatje. According to Mr. Kaplan, based on the statement she made to the police, she was not guilty of this crime. She was not even in the apartment when Niels shook Kaatje to death, and she certainly didn't anticipate that he would do such a thing. After Mr. Kaplan's explanation, she understood how, in the eyes of the law, she shouldn't be convicted of manslaughter. But she still felt guilty. She felt responsible for Kaatje's death.

She had no idea how much time remained before the hour of her arraignment. There was no clock in her cell, and they'd taken her watch and the mobile phone that Dana had given her. At least they hadn't taken her clothes or forced her to wear prison garb. She still wore the jeans and long-sleeved flannel shirt she put on yesterday morning, right before she'd foolishly returned to the brownstone on 73rd Street. *I'll show you, Travis. Kaatje is gone. Her daddy took her home.*

Maybe the Goodhues would be sitting in the courtroom today, witnessing her downfall and pain. Mr. Kaplan told her that Dana was originally assigned to prosecute this case. She'd gone to the apartment Wednesday night and saw her little girl dead on the couch. But Dana was taken off the case because she was an "interested" person. She wasn't even allowed to visit Anneke in jail, but she'd asked Mr. Kaplan to take the case for the defense. Dana had done this because she believed in Anneke's innocence. Mr. Kaplan had said so. Dana believed in her.

Dana believed, Dana believed. Anneke only wished that she

believed in herself. She curled up into a ball and started to sob. My little one, she thought. Where are you, and what have I done? All is dark where you once were. Slumber softly in heaven, *liefje*.

The deafening noise of the subway came closest to obliterating the noise in his head. In the underground cavern, a powerful reverberation rumbled just before the clattering tons of metal hurtled into the station, overcoming everything else. He always stood at the end of the platform where the train emerged from the tunnel, still traveling at near full speed. The weight and force of it thrilled him with the promise of annihilation.

Hundreds of chances, yet he hadn't taken a single one. He dared himself, over and over again. Steel the nerves. Jump into oblivion.

The underground system had dozens of routes. He'd taken every line, or maybe he'd missed a few. He was a survivor of two late nights in dangerous areas of town where the subway cars were nearly empty except for a few street punks and tough guys. He toyed with the fantasy of a slower kind of death. He picked out a vicious face or two and tried to incite a murderous reaction, staring into strange eyes provocatively. Take me. Beat me to a pulp. Stab and shoot me. Tell me what a coward I am, punishing a helpless baby and leaving her to die.

They ignored him, a pathetic character, not worthy of even a glare in return. He reverted to anonymity, a state that momentarily erased his memory under snatches of a thunderous din.

When the trains weren't loud enough, he heard her voice. He still felt the slight weight of her in his arms. From the day they landed in New York until her last night on earth, he carried her everywhere. Those slender, fragile arms would be looped around his neck, that tiny, bony chest would be pressed into his. The warmth of it, the whisper of a fast beating heart, her cheek against his, her complaints about his scratchy beard, their laughing about it, her soft breath in his ear, a velvet curl tickling his nose, the scent of baby shampoo. He carried her everywhere. He still carried her.

If he could go back, go back, go back. If he could go back. If he could.

Had he really done this? Had he? The events played incessantly in his mind. First, there was that music, a distant operatic voice, wafting up from downstairs. Then Anneke came. She was telling him to get lost, to go home and return the child to Renske. He should lead his own life, admit his sins and see how wrong it was for a married man to pursue a teenage girl half his age. Their "love" was not love at all but a distorted fantasy, a sick power play, a sugarcoated fairytale. After everything he put her through, she'd made the supreme sacrifice and relinquished Kaatje to him. Hadn't she given him enough? She asked him, wasn't it enough? Little Kaatje was his, and Renske was the rightful mother. Take her home. Take her home.

While Anneke screamed at him, the baby was crying and the sound pricked at his nerves, riled him, made him crazy. How could Anneke turn away from this child? Couldn't she see that they both needed her? He had to have Anneke—but so did Kaatje! Their child kept crying and wouldn't stop. He asked Kaatje to stop, he told her to stop, and Anneke was about to leave, making him frantic and the noise unbearable, intolerable, a sound of helplessness and weakness compared to Anneke's strength and clarity, a fierce anger shining from her eyes. She was unyielding. She slammed the door in his face. The baby wailed. Kaatje! Stop it!

He'd done this before with the child, hadn't he? He often scolded her, and this was no different. But why this? A wall behind her. And now look. She was vomiting and her eyes rolled back into her head. And then nothing. Not a cry. Not another breath.

The minutes afterward were long and frightening. She was limp and lifeless. Her lips turned blue. Her little chest didn't move. He pressed his mouth to hers and blew into her lungs. Her eyes didn't open, her breath didn't return. A putrid, wet puddle stained the front of her pajamas. In his hand, the back of her head was bloody, the hair matted. He couldn't stand it. She had to be clean and warm. He was a good father. He grabbed some paper towels, some wet, some dry. He cleaned her up and bundled her in a familiar pink blanket. She looked warm. She was sleeping.

After that, there was nothing left for him to do. Nothing at all. He kissed her forehead and stepped away from the couch.

Boldly, he ran down the stairs at a sure clip, a father in search of help for his child. He was on his way to get help. That was it. He would find help.

But as the blocks stretched on, as he thought of that lifeless body, he knew there wasn't a soul who could help. No help for his baby. No help for himself.

He walked and walked in the cold night, keeping his head low. Somehow, his pockets were full. Passport, money, checkbook. Had he done all this before leaving the apartment? The thought of it sent a dagger into his heart. He was rotten to the core. A rotten, rotten father, seizing the means of escape, leaving his baby to die.

He spied a subway entrance, and that's where his odyssey began. All the way to Van Cortlandt Park in the Bronx, down to Coney Island in Brooklyn, north again, then east to JFK airport, arriving at three in the morning. The airport was quiet, only a few stragglers, the luckless passengers who'd missed the last standby. The KLM counter was unmanned. The monitor showed the next scheduled departure at 7:00 a.m. He would wait. He had his passport, a credit card, and a wad of U.S. dollars. He could board a flight to Amsterdam, leaving everything behind. He could be back in the classroom next week, the trip to New York a forgotten dream. He didn't have to see Renske. He wouldn't go back to her. She didn't have to know.

And when she found him? There would be no explanation for the disappearance of a two-year-old.

He could board a plane to anywhere else in the world. Anywhere. A warm country. An easy country. A place to melt into the masses, where he'd do penance as an impecunious laborer. An eccentric vagabond speaking a foreign tongue. A dirt-poor artist with tragedy and misery for inspiration.

The fluorescent lighting in the terminal made him dizzy and claustrophobic. He picked out a seat in a row of empty seats at the edge of the wide concourse opposite the KLM counter. He sat down and stared at the familiar blue logo. The block letters comforted him. *Koninklijke Luchtvaart Maatschappij.* He was a Netherlander. This was the Royal Dutch Airlines, a reputable, respected business from his country. He would go back and find a place for himself there.

But by now, the New York City police would be looking for him. Anneke must have given him up. He was wanted. He would be sought. And the logical place to search would be at the airport.

The terminal was nearly empty. A listless janitor pushed a dust mop along the linoleum floor. On the next row of seats, a young man was stretched out awkwardly with his head resting on a bulky duffel bag. Niels carried no luggage, but he had plenty of identification in his pockets, enough to let a police officer know exactly who he was.

He got up and headed for the subway again.

Sometimes he slept without knowing it, a beautiful aria filling his head as the rhythmic motion rocked him into the void. A jarring stop would awaken him, and the conductor's loud voice, full of static, would make a final announcement: "This is the last stop.

Everyone get off the train."

He didn't eat. He had no appetite. There was no reason to eat. Soon he wouldn't exist. He would no longer walk this earth. Several times he hung his toes over the edge of the platform as the rumble grew louder, approaching from the tunnel. Each time, he pulled back with only a second to spare. *It will be quick. One jump, and nothing more.*

But there was something he had to do first. Just what it was, he didn't know. In his mind, he saw his attic studio, the afternoon light streaming through the small window, illuminating his portrait of Anneke on the easel. He may have boxed up that portrait and stored it in the crawlspace. He thought so. He didn't remember. There was something he had to do before he left this world. Something else.

His thirst overcame him. He bought a bottle of water at a newsstand and drank it in one continuous series of gulps. Still he didn't eat. The little one was cold and alone. He saw her face, the blue lips, the pale skin, the vomit, all of it making him nauseous. If he could only go back.

There were moderately busy times and lulls and periods of dense crowds, people caught up in their daily routines, angry or bored or impatient, dressed for work, going to work, coming home from work, going to work again the next day. They read their paperback novels and newspapers. It wouldn't matter if any of them knew he was wanted by the police because no one looked at him. Eyes were always averted.

In a moving train, he hung on the overhead metal bar and looked down at a man sitting on the bench. The man wore a gray business suit and was engrossed in the newspaper he was reading. He folded it neatly into long rectangular quadrants and flipped them expertly, managing to read the whole newspaper while confined in his small sliver of space on the bench, without trespassing on his neighbor. Niels stared over the top of the paper, but the man refused to look up. Finally, he finished the paper, refolded it, and placed it in his lap. In the middle of the front page were the black words: "Prosecutor's Nanny Murders Toddler."

Niels stared and blinked.

The man got off at the next stop and abandoned his newspaper to the seat. Niels grabbed it hungrily, drawing wary looks from the passengers around him. He remained standing, hanging by one hand on the metal bar and holding the newspaper in the other hand, his eyes devouring the words.

At Grand Central he dropped the paper and got out of the train. He pushed through the dense crowd on the platform and zigzagged around the sluggish bodies on the wide stairway up to the terminal. Tripping, bumping, and elbowing his way up, he ignored angry voices cursing him on all sides. He was unaware of the time or how long he'd been riding the subway, but the clues were everywhere. He was caught up in the height of the morning rush hour. This was the second morning after Kaatje had died in his arms.

Past the information booth with the clock, past the ticket windows, he found a bank of pay telephones. In his wallet he carried the number of those people, Anneke's employers. It was the only number he had for her. He'd called it just that one time, the first time he spoke to her after arriving in this country. He remembered the terror in her voice and the way she pleaded with him not to call this number again. Never again!

But this was different. This was the one thing he had to do before ending his life. He hadn't realized it until now.

As he punched in the numbers, all the surrounding noises receded into the distance. Every nerve of his body was concentrated on the round plastic disk pressed to his ear. He heard the interminable ringing, three, four, five times, a slow-motion click, and a male voice delivering the outgoing message from an answering machine. "Goodhue." That was the name.

"Hello," Niels told the recording device. "This is Niels Van Leeuwen. I know that Anneke was arrested. But she didn't kill anyone. It was me. I killed my own child!" He swallowed a sob and forced himself to continue. "Tell them to release her. And please, give this message to her."

The rest of it he spoke in Dutch, a long message, the last words he would ever say to her. He kept talking until the machine cut him off in mid-sentence with a final click.

Exhausted and spent, he dropped the receiver. A mix of hundreds of voices and shuffling feet gradually swelled, entering his consciousness.

A single voice came to the fore. "That's him! That's the man!"

He turned to see a middle-aged woman coming toward him with an irregular step. Her face was wet with tears, and she cradled her forearm and wrist protectively. A uniformed police-man and another man were on either side of her. She let go of her arm and pointed with the good hand, wincing in apparent pain. "Over by the pay phone. That one!"

The policeman walked right up. Niels didn't flinch. In that instant, everything seemed very fine. The air was infused with a golden and magical light, bathing him in warmth. A gentle smile lifted the corners of his mouth. He inhaled deeply and exhaled in sweet release.

22 »   *RELEASE*

OUTSIDE PATRICK'S DOOR, Dana quickly wiped away the tears, determined not to show her despair to the world. She had no desire to stop and talk to anyone on her way out. Wearing blinders, she made her way down the hallway, past the cubicles of paralegals and secretaries, past the offices of her colleagues, many of their doors wide open. *Just get out of here and go home.*

No such luck. "Dana!" Jared's unmistakable, rich voice called out to her from his office. She backtracked a few steps and entered through the open door.

He eyed her overcoat. "You're leaving?"

"Going home. Patrick just ordered a long vacation for me."

"Get in here and close the door. You're not going anywhere."

She pointedly stared at him, lifted her eyebrows, and complied with his demand. After closing the door, she settled into a seat opposite him at the desk.

"I just got a very interesting phone call from Officer Vargas. You remember her?"

"I certainly do. She's working the case."

"Well, she worked it good. She found another witness. Things are looking better for your nanny." The phone rang, and he held up a finger. "I'll tell you in a minute."

He turned away from her and picked up the receiver. "ADA Browne," he said, looking down at his desk, but quickly turned back again and met Dana's eyes. "Evan," he said into the receiver. He listened, keeping his eyes on hers. "She's sitting right here in my office... No... Wait a minute. *I'm* assigned to this case. Tell me exactly what's on the recording, and *then* I'll let you talk to her."

Dana fidgeted impatiently in her seat, watching Jared as he received the information she sorely wanted to hear. What was this all about?

Jared turned his full attention to the voice in his ear. Finally, he said to Evan, "Okay. Here's what you have to do. Don't unplug the machine. If it has a tape, don't take it out. We can't lose this. When I hang up, I'm calling our tech guys. They'll send someone to your apartment to make a copy before they take the machine itself." He listened to Evan again and responded, "Sorry, I changed my mind. You can't talk to her. Don't worry, I'll tell her you love her." Jared flashed mocking eyes at Dana, letting her know he was teasing. "She'll call you later. Gotta go." He ended the call and immediately punched in another number.

Dana lived through another painful three minutes of ignorance while Jared made the arrangements for the tech crew to visit the Goodhue apartment. Finally, with that out of the way, he told her what had happened. When Evan returned home after his breakfast out with Travis, he found a couple of messages on the telephone answering machine, one of them from their suspect, Niels Van Leeuwan. "He confessed to killing the girl," said Jared, "and he pleaded for Anneke's release. It's all recorded on your answering machine."

Dana's jaw dropped. "This is monumental."

"It certainly is."

She shook her head in disbelief, but her eyes were smiling. "I didn't know Evan's Dutch was so good."

Jared laughed at Dana's tongue-in-cheek. He rallied. "After confessing in perfect *English*, Van Leeuwen left a long message in Dutch for your nanny. According to Evan, it was all X-rated stuff, but we'll check his translation later with an official court interpreter."

Could they really be cracking jokes at a time like this? Had things turned so quickly for the better? Dana became serious again. "You have to drop the charges, Jared. You have nothing on her. The killer confessed, and Officer Vargas found a new witness. Is it the tenant they were looking for?"

"Yes, it is."

"Did he hear what happened? What did he see?"

"Listen, Dana. I should cut this short because you're not on the case anymore. I'm going in to see Patrick now, and we'll decide the best course of action." He stood up.

Dana also stood. "You can't possibly hold her after this." Her voice pitched up with the need to make him understand. "There's nothing left to charge her with, not even facilitation or leaving the scene. She couldn't have seen him do it. She never would have left that child."

"I can't discuss charging decisions with you."

"But the neighbor must have heard something. What did he say?"

Jared looked heavenward, lifted his hands in the air, and dropped them with a sigh, as if giving up. "He said she was already out the door before the baby was killed. He still heard the crying when he saw her running down the stairs."

"You see? She's completely innocent. You have to let her go. If you're afraid you'll never see her again, you can impose conditions on her release. Get her to sign a cooperation agreement. She'll testify…"

"We don't have a defendant for her to testify *about*…"

They were interrupted by a knock at the door. The visitor didn't see fit to wait. The door flew open, and in walked the Don.

He was out of breath. "Just heard," he rasped. "We got him!" The detective's face was red from neck to hairline.

"Van Leeuwen?" asked Jared.

Paul nodded and wheezed, "Yup."

"Brought in on the warrant?"

Paul shook his head. "You're gonna love this. He was collared for misdemeanor assault. The dirtbag knocked down a lady in the subway and broke her wrist. Transit cops put his name in the system and the warrant came up." He started to cough.

Dana smiled, pretending not to hear the coughing. "Well. Looks like good things came in threes today. You guys have a lot to tell Patrick." She stepped toward the door, coming closer to Paul. "Go have your meeting with the boss. I'll be in my office."

She paused, waiting for Paul to quiet down completely. When he stopped coughing, she touched his arm and their eyes met. He affected nonchalance, but his face couldn't conceal the significance of the moment and the pride he felt. It was enough—everything he'd done for her on this case and the hundreds of others over the past six years. For all they knew, this could be his last assignment. Neither one of them wanted to face that possibility or recognize it out loud.

Before leaving the room, she swiveled around to Jared and winked. "I guess you know what I'm going to do now."

"What would that be, Ms. Hargrove?"

"I'm going to call my big hunk of a husband so he can tell me how much he loves me."

Jared replied with one of his big, dazzling, movie-star smiles.

"Get outta here," Paul told her, swiping at the air with his hand.

The Honorable Morris Chomsky was on the bench when Dana took a seat in the front row of the audience of AR-3, the arraignment part. It was the largest courtroom on the ground floor of the Criminal Court building, the first one to be seen by every criminal defendant in Manhattan within twenty-four hours after arrest. Today, it was packed to the rafters.

The spectators included reporters and sketch artists who were required to sit in the side section. Dana wasn't hiding her face from them, but they weren't allowed to approach her in the courtroom. Chomsky enforced strict rules of decorum. Still, there would be no way to avoid the reporters outside the courthouse when the time came.

Dana was not acquainted with the rookie ADA handling arraignments today. It wasn't surprising, since the DA's office employed four hundred fifty attorneys. AR-3 never slept. Each of three eight-hour shifts was covered by an ADA who handled the arraignments for all the new arrests as they came in, except for any special cases in which a senior ADA wished to appear personally. *People versus Anneke Zonneveld* was one of those special cases, and ADA Jared Browne would be arriving shortly.

Currently in the dock was a man accused of a gunpoint robbery. The clerk read the charges, and the defense attorney whispered in his client's ear, prompting the defendant to look up at the judge and say, "not guilty." The attorney launched into a bail application.

As Dana looked on, memories came flooding in. Judge Chomsky was showing his age, the sparse hair on top of his head now almost gone. She'd been in this courtroom many times, but never like this, as a spectator wearing casual clothes, banned from her usual post at the prosecutor's table behind the bar. There'd been many appearances before Chomsky, including stints in night court during her rookie days. She'd spent many late nights handling arraignments seriatim in an atmosphere imbued with the surreal haze of sleep deprivation. At times, she was pitted against Seth Kaplan from Legal Aid.

But today, Seth was her friend. Today, he was representing Anneke Zonneveld in the case of her life. Dana waited for the moment when Seth and Anneke and Jared would appear. When all of this would be over.

It was ten minutes before eleven o'clock. A lot had happened since she stepped into Jared's office two hours ago.

Based on the new developments in the case, Patrick authorized dismissal of all charges against Anneke if she agreed to give truthful testimony in the prosecution against Van Leeuwen, and to refrain from suing the DA or the police department for wrongful arrest. The discussion in Patrick's office centered on whether the DA had the legal authority to compel her to sign a cooperation agreement. If she was innocent of all charges, what right had they to impose conditions on her release? There was always legal process—the power of the subpoena—to draw her into court to testify against her former lover. But they concluded that circumstantial evidence pointed to Anneke's knowledge that Van Leeuwen had taken the child to New York without his wife's permission. Her failure to report him to the police facilitated the crime of kidnapping. This slender case against her was enough to preclude any challenge to the validity of the agreement.

When Jared and Paul emerged from the meeting, they found Dana in her office and gave her the news. Jared returned to his office to call Seth about the proposal and to draft the cooperation agreement, while Paul stayed behind and gave Dana more details about the arrest of their suspected killer.

Van Leeuwen reportedly elbowed a woman on a crowded stairway in the subway at Grand Central, knocking her violently to the cement floor. The woman caught her fall with her hands and broke a wrist. A stranger helped her up to her feet, and they followed the culprit, losing sight of him as he wormed through the bodies on a packed escalator. Continuing their pursuit, the complainant and the helpful stranger enlisted the aid of a police officer along the way and searched the great room of the immense terminal. They didn't need to look for very long. Van Leeuwen gave himself away, standing in plain view at a pay phone. He was making the call to the Goodhue residence, leaving a message on the answering machine.

Paul left her office, and Dana called Evan. It was close to 10:00 a.m., and the DA's tech person had already come and gone, taking the backup recording and the answering machine along with him to place in safekeeping as evidence. Dana told Evan she was staying downtown to attend the proceedings at eleven o'clock. Jared planned to dismiss the charges in open court, to make a public record of Anneke's innocence for the sake of her reputation and to appease any media hounds.

After the hearing, of course, Dana would be bringing Anneke home. She had nowhere else to go, and her cooperation agreement required her to testify in the grand jury next week. After that, she was permitted to return to her family in Holland but would have to honor her pledge to return if Van Leeuwen's case ever came to trial. She was obligated to testify in front of the petit jury too.

"I'm coming downtown," insisted Evan. "We still have time, and I want to be with you."

"What about Travis? I don't want him to see this. What would he think, seeing his beloved Anneke facing a judge in a criminal courtroom, surrounded by court officers and attorneys?"

"Well…he *is* a very smart boy, but I don't think…"

"…that he'll know what's going on? Maybe not, but it's the impression it makes. You remember what he said last night?"

"Right." Evan said no more because Travis was in the room with him.

On her end of the line, Dana could hear their son babbling in the background, making conversation with an imaginary friend. She reminded Evan of their son's words. "He said 'police' and 'Anneke' in the same sentence. The shock of seeing her arrested was bad enough. Let's try to help him forget it."

"Okay. Don't worry. I won't bring him into the courtroom.

Maybe I can get Cheryl to watch him. I'll give her a call now."

After they hung up, Dana didn't hear back from Evan whether he succeeded in making arrangements with Cheryl. Now, as she waited for the fated hour, she glanced back at the courtroom door, hoping to see him walk in.

Behind the bar, the attorney for the alleged armed robber was requesting a bail of $25,000 for his client. The ADA gave an impassioned plea for a bail of at least $250,000, citing the defendant's extensive criminal record. The short speech was articulate and well-reasoned, yet the ADA lacked an air of authority or the power of persuasion. He was a creamy-skinned youth who looked like somebody's little boy dressed up in his Sunday best. *Did I look that young and inexperienced six years ago?*

"I'll go one better," replied Judge Chomsky when the ADA was through. "Remand without bail." The judge caught the defendant's eye and maintained a glaring look as he spoke. "Six collars in ten years. Did three of those on parole from the last one. State time for armed robbery. Didn't learn your lesson, did you? Caught red-handed, and the DA has an airtight case. You're not very good at what you do, and not very good at getting away with it. It's time for a career change! How about pressing license plates in state prison? Bail application denied. November 25th for grand jury action. Remand the defendant."

The judge cracked the gavel and twitched two fingers at the senior court officer. The hapless offender was escorted out to the pens.

While Chomsky was venting, things were taking shape behind the bar. Seth entered the courtroom through the door from the pens, and Jared entered through a door on the other side. Jared leaned into the court clerk and spoke in a low voice. Dana was watching him, keeping one ear open to the judge's speech, when Evan slid onto the bench next to her, where she'd been saving him a seat. "Oh," she exclaimed under her breath, mildly startled.

He whispered into her ear. "Hello, my love." His lips were so close that they touched the curled edges around her auditory canal. She pulled back and looked at him. His eyes sparkled with self-congratulation.

They conversed back and forth in warm, tactile whispers to the ear.

"Cheryl got there so fast?"

"She's out in the hall with Travis."

"She came with you?"

"I left her a message to meet us here and came on down with Travis."

"You didn't!"

"I wasn't going to come inside if she didn't show up."

Dana pulled back and regarded the innocent expression on his face. He squeezed her knee. She couldn't be angry at him. Ever.

The next words from the court got their attention. "It's eleven. Everyone here?" Judge Chomsky's impatience and punctuality had not changed over the years. He directed the court clerk to "call that case" and turned squarely to the audience. His eyes met Dana's. He knew what was going on.

The nameless rookie ADA stepped out of the way as Jared and Seth took their positions behind their respective counsel tables. The clerk read the docket number and announced, "People of the State of New York against Anneke Zonneveld. Counsel, state your appearances." Jared and Seth complied.

A hush descended like a veil from the high ceiling as everyone waited for the defendant. The only sound to be heard was an odd, low-level scratching—the swift strokes of artists energetically moving their graphite pencils on paper. The scratching became more frenetic when the door from the pens opened and Anneke entered, escorted by a court officer. Her clothing and hair were slightly disheveled, and her eyes showed signs of sleeplessness and grief.

She was led to the defense table. At her height of five foot two, she was dwarfed by Seth, who was nearly six feet tall. He lowered his head and spoke to her in a subdued tone.

The judge turned to Jared. "Well, Mister Prosecutor, are we arraigning this one, or do you have an application?"

"I do have an application, Your Honor. The People move to dismiss the felony complaint. The defendant was arrested almost twenty-four hours ago on the charge of manslaughter in the second degree in connection with the death of a two-year-old child."

Dana held her breath. How many details was Jared going to reveal? She hadn't thought of this until now. The newspapers had reported Anneke's relationship to Kaatje Van Leeuwen and her employment by the Goodhue family, but there was no reason to repeat and emphasize these facts in this proceeding.

Dana's trepidation vanished as Jared continued: "In the past few hours, developments in the investigation have led the People to conclude that the evidence does not support the charge against Miss Zonneveld. Just two hours ago, the police arrested a man who has been charged with this crime. His name is Niels Van Leeuwen. Although the evidence indicates that Miss Zonneveld was with Mr. Van Leeuwen and the child shortly before the crime, we have learned from a reliable source that she left their company before the child was killed. The People now move to dismiss the felony complaint against Anneke Zonneveld, if she agrees to provide her truthful testimony in the grand jury and at any trial in the prosecution against Niels Van Leeuwen. The cooperation agreement has been provided to Mr. Kaplan to discuss with his client."

Dana eyed Judge Chomsky warily. At this point, if he wanted to, he could make a big deal of this, asking for the details of the agreement on the record, even threatening not to approve it. Chomsky had always been a prosecutor's judge, sometimes even more prosecutorial than Dana. In a case as serious as this one, he might be inclined to question the DA's decision to drop the charges. But Chomsky had also shown himself to be an independent thinker, surprising her with an unexpected agenda. In this moment, Dana had no illusions that his agenda would include a desire to help her or her nanny.

The judge's eyes rested briefly on Dana before he turned to Seth and asked, "Well? What is it? She signed?" Dana exhaled in relief. This would go through without a hitch.

"Yes, Your Honor," responded Seth. "Miss Zonneveld has read the agreement. I've explained it to her, answered all her questions, and she has signed it. If I may approach?" The judge made a scooping motion with his hand, beckoning the defense attorney forward. Seth handed up a copy of the agreement, and the judge looked it over.

He raised his eyes over the document and asked Anneke, "Is this your signature?"

"Yes."

"Did your attorney explain this? Do you understand this?"

"Yes, I do."

"All right. The court is satisfied. Application granted. Felony complaint is dismissed." The judge banged the gavel.

Immediately, voices rose in the audience. The judge cracked the gavel even louder. "Quiet! The court stands in recess. Five minutes. I want all of this out of here." He eyed the press corps with distaste and made a sweeping gesture, eliminating them. "You know my rules! The court officers will enforce them. Five minutes." He stood and descended the bench, his black robe billowing behind him.

The court officers made good on the judge's threat, sternly directing the exodus of the press corps. Dana and Evan and Anneke were safe—for now. Reporters were not allowed to approach them inside the courtroom. Undoubtedly, they would jockey for position outside, hoping to get at the Goodhues and the newly-released arrestee on the courthouse steps the moment they walked out the door.

Dana and Evan stood. Instinctively, he took her hand. She accepted it, welcoming this reminder of his strength and support. The litigants behind the bar were concluding their business. "I'm planning on Monday at two o'clock for the grand jury," Jared said. "I'll call if that changes."

Seth turned to Anneke and explained what was expected of her before he responded to Jared. "Okay. We'll see you then. Monday at two."

The attorneys each regarded Dana and Evan, who were standing very close to the bar in the first row of the audience. In the shadow of her attorney, Anneke was stooped over in reluctance, submission, and shame. She had difficulty meeting the eyes of her employers.

Dana was having the same difficulty. Hoping to be rescued, she turned to Evan and whispered, "Would you...?" Subtly, he acknowledged his wife's plea by lifting his eyes to Anneke, who was still avoiding them, examining her shoes. Dana nodded a "yes" to his tacit question. They stepped toward the opening in the bar and split up, Evan walking right, approaching Anneke and her attorney, and Dana walking left, over to Jared.

"Hey, Denz."

"Hey, Dorothy."

As she faced Jared, Dana heard what was going on behind her. Evan thanked Seth in a respectful tone, without any hint of unease in the company of her so-called former "boyfriend."

"Thanks for everything," Dana told Jared. "It was a big help to us, putting Anneke's innocence on the record."

"I only wish we'd known more about this case sooner."

"Everyone did what they could."

"Speaking of which, the Don said he'd be waiting for you outside."

"Oh?"

"Says he has to go uptown to visit Greeley at the 20th anyway, so he might as well drop all of you off at home."

"Might as well." For the tenth time that morning, Dana felt a crushing tenderness for Paul and his transparent excuses to help her.

"He'll be parked at the curb in that beat-up ride of his. Says he'll have his service weapon ready in case you're accosted by rabid reporters. Gilbert is out there too. He'll help you down the steps."

"I feel protected."

"I'm avoiding the whole show and going back up to my office."

"I figured as much." Under the DA's internal policy, any contacts between an ADA and the media were strictly supervised and limited. She smiled and touched his arm. "You're allowed to abandon us. See you in a few weeks or so. When I come back, I expect to hear about your promotion." *If* I come back, Dana might have said. Her soul-searching was not over.

"I'm stealing the spot from the prime candidate. You're sure you don't want it?"

"Now is *not* the right time for me, and you're perfect for the job. I'll just have to get used to that other thing."

"What other thing?"

"Bowing low and calling you 'Mr. Browne' whenever I see you."

He laughed. "Absolutely forbidden."

She lifted a hand in goodbye and turned around to face Seth. Evan and Anneke had already retreated and were slowly walking through the audience section, headed for the main exit. They paused in the aisle to wait for her.

Taking another few steps toward Seth, she came close enough to see the worn lapel of his suit jacket and the twisted material of his cheap tie. The well-regarded defense attorney had the haggard look of a man who spent every waking moment working or thinking about his work. Did he have a personal life? Dana knew he was unmarried, and she hadn't heard any rumors about a girlfriend. "I don't know how to thank you, Seth." The feeling behind the words was sincere.

He averted his eyes bashfully, a look that was uncharacteristic for him. "I'll think of something."

"I can't return the favor exactly, since I can't take on any clients. My only client is the State of New York."

"True. And I'm not going to ask you to prosecute anyone as a favor to me."

She smiled. "I guess we'll just have to keep doing what we do best."

"That's good enough for me."

They parted, and she went to meet Evan and Anneke, midway down the aisle. On either side of her, the several rows of benches held only a handful of family members and friends of arrestees who were still locked up in the courthouse pens, awaiting their arraignments. The remainder of this day in AR-3 would be no different from any other. Despair, uncertainty, and tension laced the air.

Dana took a deep, calming breath and came up alongside her au pair. "How are you, Anneke?" she managed to ask, looking directly into her eyes.

For the first time, Anneke dared to return the gaze. Her eyes were moist and bruised looking. "Sorry," she said quietly. "I'm only sorry."

Dana placed a hand on her shoulder and said, "We'll talk later. Let's just go home." She caught Evan's eye over the top of Anneke's head. "Ready for this?"

"Ready if you are."

"Come on then. Let's get Cheryl and Travis. Paul is waiting to take us home."

With Anneke between them, they started for the courtroom door. In the last bench of the audience, a woman sat alone in the seat nearest the aisle. She was staring at Anneke. When they got very close, she stood up and moved into the aisle in front of them. She was a tall woman of about forty and gave an appearance of physical strength. Her face had a severe cast, and her eyes were jittery with nerves or lack of sleep. There was something ominous and final in her bearing.

Everyone froze. Dana's heart began to pound. At her side, she heard Anneke's sudden intake of breath, a small gasp.

The woman kept her eyes on Anneke and started to speak in Dutch. Her tone was not as harsh as Dana imagined it would be. The sound was mature and sonorous, heavy with regret, longing, grief, and resignation.

When she finished, Anneke said nothing. The woman didn't wait for a response but turned away from them and walked out the door.

In a daze, Anneke remained still, her face showing a subtle transformation from within. The despair that twisted her features softened, and her eyes filled with tears. In sudden release, the tears spilled down her cheeks, flowing freely. Only then did it seem appropriate to speak.

"Was that…?" Dana asked.

"Kaatje's mother, Renske. She thanked me. She said she never would have known the love of a child if I hadn't given her Kaatje." Anneke's voice cracked and her lips quivered. "There was something else too." She wiped at her cheeks, fought the emotion, and told them the rest. "She said she didn't blame me for anything that happened. Not for anything at all."

WALK

ON THE WAY HOME, Evan rode in the front seat with Detective Donegan. The three ladies were slotted cozily in the back, Dana between Anneke and Cheryl. Travis sat on Dana's lap, fastened under her seat belt. She gave Paul a lot of grief about this arrangement.

He looked at her in the rearview mirror. "So now you want baby car seats in every detective ride?"

"This is unsafe, Paul."

"Talk to your husband."

Evan turned around and lifted his brow apologetically, accepting responsibility for their situation. Travis was oblivious, happily doing the hand jive with Cheryl.

"You got a seat belt," said Paul. "I know you take the kid on the subway all the time without any seat belts or car seats..."

"But that's different..."

"...diseases and perverts up in the kid's face."

"Just go slow."

"You think I've got a choice? Look at this." He gestured and started coughing. They were caught in typical Manhattan traffic, alternating between a dead standstill and a cruising speed of, at most, twenty-five miles an hour.

When they arrived home, Dana and Evan thanked the Don

and wished him well before they tumbled out of the cramped car. Cheryl came upstairs with them. Anneke said she needed to write a letter to her family and retreated to her room, closing the door behind her. Travis was cranky, in need of lunch. Without a thought for the rest of them, Dana found a yogurt in the fridge and a brownish banana in the fruit bowl for her son.

"Give that to me," said Cheryl. "I'll feed him. You two go out."

"Out?" The thought stunned her, but Dana handed the items to her sister anyway.

"You should see yourself. You need a break." Cheryl placed Travis's lunch on the table and picked him up.

"I look that bad?"

"She exaggerates, my love," Evan consoled her.

"Get out of here. Take her to lunch, Evan. I don't have to be at the theater until six." Cheryl put the boy in his booster seat and sat down next to him at the table.

"I forgot the spoon." Dana ran back into the kitchen and retrieved one. "Here you go…"

"Okay. Enough already. Out!"

"We accept your gracious offer," said Evan.

"We'll be back in an hour," said Dana.

"Take at least three hours," said Cheryl. She peeled back the aluminum top of the yogurt container while Travis reached for it impatiently. "Hold on, Tug. It's coming." She fed him a spoonful. "He's going to need a nap after this. He's exhausted. Don't worry." Her eyes flitted toward Anneke's door. "I'll watch him."

"Thank you, sis. You're my savior."

An overcoat and a jacket, recently discarded on the sofa, were picked up and put on again.

In the elevator, Evan and Dana were the only passengers for the nine floors down to the lobby. They stood zombie-like, without saying a word. The trance held them through the ding of the elevator bell, the parting of the doors, the click of their heels on the marble floor, and the automatic exchange of greetings with Bashkim as he held the glass door open for them.

It was just after one o'clock on a gray, November afternoon. Hard to believe that little more than twenty-four hours had passed since Judge DuBois called Dana up to the bench to deliver the shocking news. After days of little sleep, Dana was in a state of nervous exhaustion, still wired, unable to empty her mind of the images spinning recklessly, dreamlike and unreal.

There'd been that look in Jack's eyes, the horrible meeting in the Dungeon, the call for Seth's help, the sight of Travis playing in the sex crimes unit, and the harrowing night of conflicting feelings: betrayal, anger, compassion, and helplessness. This morning there'd been her need for Patrick's wisdom and support, Jared's news of hopeful developments in the case, and Judge Chomsky's gruff dispensation of justice in the packed courtroom. So many faces, they floated like ghosts in Dana's consciousness. Overlaying it all was the vision of that delicate, pale face of a dead little girl and the grief written in the expressions of her two mothers. Those three faces would be the hardest to forget.

Finally, there'd been the daunting task of meeting that throng of reporters waiting for them outside. Dana knew the rules, and she had no desire to find an exception. She was allowed to say, at most, "No comment" or "The record speaks for itself."

They emerged from the courthouse and were brought to a halt at the top of the steps. Gilbert and two others from the DA's squad were there to help them. The reporters fired questions but were kept at bay. Evan was holding Travis, who smiled and waved gleefully for the cameras. Anneke stood next to Dana, and Cheryl was behind them.

Five seconds passed, maybe ten, an eternity. Dana fought to keep her cool, determined to carry out what she'd planned. As the reporters scrambled and yelled, she turned away from them, gave

Anneke a warm, genuine smile, and put her arm around the young woman's shoulder, holding her close to her side, protectively. Photographers clicked and cameras rolled. Later, the evening news would broadcast this visual message of their solidarity, along with the few words that Dana was permitted to speak.

That image of the day was her favorite, and she held onto it now, walking with her husband on city streets. They meandered aimlessly, caught up in their individual thoughts, not speaking or touching for several blocks. Then everything changed.

The air was cold and brisk, and the feel of it on Dana's cheek was delicious. She linked her arm through her husband's and said, "It's so good to get out of the apartment!"

"Isn't it though? Where to, Madam?"

"I don't know. Anywhere."

He glanced to the side. "How about here? We never seem to get a table at dinnertime, and they also serve lunch." He gestured to a popular French bistro, known for a long wait list after 7:00 p.m.

"But it's so expensive."

"Mere paper money. I wouldn't let it concern you." He ignored her mild protest, took the lead, and gently coaxed her inside.

The restaurant was wood-paneled and dim, with a sprinkling of patrons enjoying a leisurely meal on a Friday afternoon. These were the comfortably-situated gentry, who didn't have to worry about running back to an office after lunch.

The maître d' gave them their pick of several empty tables, all candlelit with white linen tablecloths. They chose a little round table tucked into a corner, away from the window on the street. Privacy was desired, even as they took this plunge into the outside world.

Scanning the menu, Evan asked, "Wine?"

"In the middle of the afternoon?"

"I insist."

"Okay. If you insist." A pattern was revealing itself. She was too stunned and overwhelmed to be making any executive decisions today.

They placed their order for wine and an appetizer, and soon, they were swirling, sniffing, and tasting the red liquid. Fuzzy and warm, Dana was momentarily sent to heaven, but she quickly came back to reality.

Her brow furled, and she jumped into the subject that was on her mind. "How did we miss this, Evan? I keep coming back to that. I felt I knew Anneke. The essential things, anyway. Her loving nature. Her steadiness and reliability. And I *did* pick up the clues that something was troubling her. I just didn't do enough to find out what it was."

"I don't know if she would have told you, even if you pushed for answers. This was obviously her big secret, something she thought she'd left behind a long time ago."

"I want to know so much more about that big secret, everything that just happened to her and to all of us. I won't be able to let go of this unless I do."

"If you're worried about Travis, he'll forget. He's only two years old. He won't know a thing. When he's grown up, if we have to, we can tell him what we need to tell him."

"But *I* want to know. Is that so selfish?"

"No. Not at all. She's grieving right now, and it's a tragedy what happened to the child. But she put us through a lot. I don't think it's too much to ask for an explanation. You two should have a heart-to-heart. It might even be therapeutic."

"For her or for me?"

"For both of you. She isn't leaving for a few days. You have time to talk."

"But not today. I couldn't do it today."

"No. Not today. Everything is still so raw."

They fell silent again and sipped their wine. The waiter wasn't in a hurry to return to take their lunch order. A few tables over, a gray-haired couple sat with their eyes intently on one another and their heads bent in whispered conversation. The man finished a long sentence, sat back with a gleam in his eye, and the woman reacted with subdued laughter.

Whether it was the alcohol or Evan's inimitable, buoyant character, he gave his wife a devilish grin, the kind that always foreshadowed lighter fare. "Here's some good news," he bragged. "The murderer wasn't the only one who left a message on our answering machine this morning."

"Oh? Who else called?"

"A potential applicant for the job of nanny."

"My goodness. I guess some people thought that the headline on the front page was a help wanted ad."

"Well, this applicant has been hoping for the job well before she saw that article. You might recognize the name. Brenda Goodhue."

Dana smiled to herself. She'd been hoping for this. Evan's mother was the perfect candidate. She was still spending her afternoons caring for Evan's nephew and niece, Ian and Kelly, in their Westchester County suburb. But now that the children were older, their beloved Grandma Goodhue was gradually beginning to feel "unnecessary" in the pleasant way that comes with inevitable change. Perhaps she was ready to consider switching jobs?

This was a sign. Brenda's message on the answering machine was her second call that morning. She'd also called very early, before Dana left for her meeting with Patrick.

"Let's see." Dana looked into the distance and drummed her fingers on the table. "Brenda Goodhue. The name *does* sound familiar."

"She indicated a willingness to wrap things up in her current job a little sooner than expected so she could come help us. Weekday mornings, she could take the commuter railroad down to the city and then the subway. Of course, she'd have to get up very early to do this. Door to door, the commute takes an hour and a half. Or, I was thinking…"

"You were thinking…"

"It would be most convenient if she stayed with us Monday through Friday and went home on weekends. Maybe we can move to an apartment with a bigger room for her. What do you think? A great plan, right?"

"Living with my mother-in-law?" Dana paused, pretending to think about it. She swirled the remnant of her Bordeaux and lifted the glass to her lips, draining it. "I suppose it's marginally better than living with a nanny who was arrested for child murder."

"I knew you'd approve."

She smiled and gazed lovingly at her husband. How could she be so lucky?

"I love you, Evan."

"No. I love *you*."

"But I *adore* your mother."

"She's a pain and a riot."

"She's your mother. And she made *you*, a perfect human specimen."

"Really now. Perfect?"

"Come here."

Dana placed her hand on top of his, leaned forward, and met him across the little table. Their kiss was long and deep, with the warmth of the candle under their chins.

Let them look. She didn't care.

———————

OPUS NINE BOOKS

All works published by Opus Nine Books are dedicated to the
nine members of the family headed by John and Kate
Swackhamer at 3 South Trail, Orinda, California — a large world
under one small roof.

DEAR READER,

As I write the afterword for this updated edition, the sixth (and last) Dana Hargrove novel is on the horizon, to be published in January 2022. For more than a decade, Dana, her family, friends, and colleagues have been a big part of my life. I hope you'll get to know them well!

Each novel is a standalone, finding Dana at a different stage of her personal life and career. Here they are, with the years in which each story takes place:

Thursday's List (1988)

Homicide Chart (1994)

Forsaken Oath (2001)

Deep Zero (2009)

Seven Shadows (2015)

Power Blind (2022)

Let me know what you think! Now's the time to return to your online bookseller and post a reader review of any length on the webpage for *Homicide Chart*. Or, send me a message through the contact page on my website, vskemanis.com. While you're there, subscribe to my blog and take advantage of the free e-book offer for one of my story collections.

To keep up with the latest news about my books and life, look for V.S. Kemanis on Goodreads, BookBub, Facebook, Instagram, Twitter, and YouTube.

Thanks for reading!

V.S.K.

www.ingramcontent.com/pod-product-compliance
Lightning Source LLC
Chambersburg PA
CBHW031935110726
47902CB00001B/191